PRAISE FOR KAREN ROBARDS

'You won't put down this riveting read, even to reapply sunscreen' *Cosmopolitan, USA*

'Karen Robards is one of the most popular voices in women's fiction' *Newsweek*

'Her [Robards] pacing is excellent, and regular infusions of humour keep the story bouncing along between trysts and attacks. This one is sure to please fans' *Publishers Weekly*

'Tough, sensual romantic mystery from the prolific and popular Robards' *Kirkus Reviews*

'A top-notch thriller filled with humourous characters and diverting subplots that leave the reader engrossed until the very end, this is yet another coup for Robards, and a fun summer read' *Booklist*

'Robards is one terrific storyteller' *Chicago Tribune*

Karen Robards is the author of over twenty novels. Her contemporary suspense novels have appeared on the *New York Times*, *Wall Street Journal* and *USA Today* bestseller lists. Ms Robards lives with her family in Louisville, Kentucky.

BAIT

KAREN
ROBARDS

HODDER

Copyright © 2004 by Karen Robards

First published in Great Britain in 2005 by Hodder and Stoughton
A division of Hodder Headline
This edition published in 2005

The right of Karen Robards to be identified as the Author
of the Work has been asserted by her in accordance with the
Copyright, Designs and Patents Act 1988.

1

A CIP catalogue record for this title is available from the British Library

ISBN 0 340 89573 X

Typeset by Hewer Text Ltd, Edinburgh
Printed and bound by in Great Britain by Mackays of Chatham, Kent

Hodder Headline's policy is to use papers that are natural, renewable
and recyclable products and made from wood grown in sustainable
forests. The logging and manufacturing processes are expected
to conform to the environmental regulations of the country of origin.

Hodder and Stoughton
A division of Hodder Headline PLC
338 Euston Road
London NW1 3BH

PETER, THIS ONE'S FOR YOU.

HAPPY 21ST, DARLING.

ACKNOWLEDGMENTS

I'd like to thank my husband, Doug, my sons Peter, Christopher and Jack, and Peggy Kennedy, all of whom helped with research, contributed ideas, insights, and comments, and generally told me when I was writing myself into a corner.

I'd also like to thank the people who made this book possible: my brilliant agent, Robert Gottlieb, my wonderful editor, Christine Pepe, and her noble assistant, Lily Chin; and Carole Baron, who is awesome as always.

ONE

Thursday, August 7

I t was a professional job, Sam McCabe saw at a glance. The bare mini-mum of fuss and muss. A couple sprawled on the floor of their cathedral-ceilinged great room, hands bound behind their backs, blood from the bullet wounds in their heads soaking into the already deep red of their Oriental carpet.

"I see dead people," E. P. Wynne muttered behind him. The words were slightly slurred by the enormous wad of bubble gum the big guy was chewing in an effort to quit smoking. Sam shot him a quelling glance. Granted, they were so tired they were more or less punch-drunk, but humor in the face of multiple homicides was never a good idea.

"Who the hell are you?" A brown-uniformed local yokel separated him-self from the pack at the corner of the room and came toward them, bris-tling. Considering that Sam was wearing jeans and a T-shirt and sporting a three-day growth of beard, while Wynne's two-hundred-fifty-pound girth was decked out in baggy shorts and a stained Hawaiian shirt, the man's attitude was understandable. But this was the culmination of another in a series of really lousy weeks. Sam was not in the mood for attitude, especially from a skinny kid who might or might not be just out of his teens.

"FBI," Sam growled, not even slowing down. Wynne, ever obliging, flashed his ID as they brushed past the kid like he wasn't even there.

"Nobody called the feds," the yokel protested to their backs, then, less certain, called over his shoulder, "Did anybody call the feds?"

"Hell, no." Another brown-uniformed local, a burly, surly-looking fifty-something with a bald head as shiny as a Christmas ornament, entered through an arched opening at the opposite end of the room in time to hear the plaintive question and headed toward them. "I'm Sheriff Burt Eigel. And sure as shit, nobody around here called anybody, feds or otherwise."

"Sam McCabe. E. P. Wynne," Sam said, jerking a thumb at Wynne as he introduced him.

"FBI," Wynne added helpfully, doing his badge-waving thing again.

Sam stopped beside the female victim and looked down at the bodies. Multiple strips of duct tape covered each victim's mouth. Thin, white cord secured their wrists. The fingers had purpled, indicating that the cords had been tied tightly enough to impede circulation—and to hurt. "Wendell Perkins and his wife, Tammy Sue, right?"

Eigel frowned. "How the hell did y'all know that?"

"Let's just say a little bird told me." Sam squatted and pressed his fingers to the carpet. It was made of fine wool, expensive, just like the furniture in the enormous great room was expensive, the newly built McMansion was expensive, and the gated Mobile, Alabama, retirement community was expensive. The blood soaking the soft, smooth fibers still retained a degree of warmth. This time he'd been close—so damned close. Twenty minutes earlier and Perkins and the missus would have been offering him a cup of coffee—or trying to sneak out their back door, depending on why they'd been hit.

Damn it to hell and back anyway.

"Who called this in?" Sam asked, still studying the bodies as he stood up and wiped his fingers on his already ripe jeans. It was not quite eleven-thirty p.m. Blonde, bird-boned Tammy Sue was dressed for bed in a pair of navy cotton pajamas and had a single white terry slipper on her left foot. Perkins, who appeared to be at least two decades her senior, was a beefy, big-bellied guy with a furry back and chicken legs. He was wearing nothing but boxers, which he had pissed. The pungent ammonia smell all but overrode the meat-locker aroma of fresh blood.

As Sam had noted on multiple previous occasions, there was no dignity in death.

"There's an alarm. Somebody here hit the panic button. We had a man on the scene nine minutes after the call came in. They were dead when we got here." Eigel paused and glared at Sam, who was glancing around without any real hope for shell casings. There were none immediately visible, and he'd be willing to bet dollars to doughnuts that none would be found. "Why the fuck should I be telling you this?"

There was that attitude thing again. Sam still wasn't in the mood. " 'Cause you like me?"

Eigel's florid face turned apoplectic. Ignoring him, Sam moved around the bodies, studying them from different angles. From the look of it, Perkins had died first. His wife's death had come moments later, most likely a by-product of the hit on her husband. A glance around the room revealed several possible points of entry for the killer: the front door, which opened into the slate-floored hall that Sam and Wynne had just crossed, and which provided access to the great room through a wide, arched opening; the smaller arched door leading into the kitchen through which the sheriff had entered; or the sliding patio door on the south wall. He calculated the steps from each to the black leather couch where, from the evidence—remote control and a bowl of melted ice cream on the coffee table in front of it; the mate to Tammy Sue's white terry slipper on the carpet between the couch and table; several sections of the newspaper scattered about—Tammy Sue had been sitting when the killer surprised her.

The most likely point of egress was through the kitchen.

Wynne pulled a tiny digital camera out of his pocket and started taking pictures of the crime scene. Sam, meanwhile, headed for the kitchen.

"What the *hell* do you think you're doing?" From the corner of his eye,

Sam saw that Eigel was looking from one to the other of them. By now his face was as red as the blood-soaked carpet, and his eyes were starting to bulge out of his head like a pug dog's.

"Our jobs, man. Just like you," Wynne said soothingly. As usual, he was playing good cop to Sam's bad cop. The roles suited both of them to a tee.

"You got no jurisdiction here. This is our case."

Eigel had elected to follow him, Sam registered absently as he glanced around the kitchen. It was gleaming white, wall-to-wall cabinets, an island, the latest appliances. State-of-the-art, fit to grace one of those women's magazines. An ice-cream scoop had been left in one of the pair of stainless-steel sinks. Other than that, it was immaculate.

Sam headed toward the patio door at the far end. Its bright floral curtain wasn't shut all the way. An approximately eight-inch-wide, floor-to-ceiling slice of glass was visible, black with the darkness of the night beyond. The door was closed and locked. Careful not to touch it, he studied the handle. It had a self-locking mechanism, so the killer could have exited this way as well. Turning slowly, he stared at the pale oak floor.

A thin sliver of grass nestled near the foot of the island.

Bingo.

"He entered and exited here," Sam said. "You can dust for fingerprints, but you won't find any. Footprints are a better bet, especially if the ground's soft outside. He would have had to walk around the house. Maybe he got careless."

Eigel bristled. "Listen, smart guy, I'm right now officially askin' you and your pardner in there to leave. Nobody here called you, nobody here wants you, and you got no call bustin' in and tryin' to take over."

Sam ignored the comment as he turned and headed back toward the great room, retracing the killer's path. Twenty steps to the great-room door, where he paused to try to visualize the scene through the killer's eyes. The couch faced away from the door. If Tammy Sue had been sitting on the couch, eating ice cream and watching TV, she probably wouldn't have seen him coming.

At least, not until it was too late.

Feeling his stomach tighten, Sam glanced at Eigel, who was behind him again. "You got roadblocks up? Say, five miles out in all directions, access to expressways blocked, vehicles being checked as they attempt to exit the area, that kind of thing?"

"Don't tell me how to do my job."

"I take that as a 'no.'"

As Sam spoke, more people rushed into the great room from the front hall: paramedics making an unholy racket as they rolled in a pair of stretchers, a grumpy-looking man in a rumpled suit and tie, and a mid-thirties brunette in white jeans and a black T-shirt, crying, "Daddy! Oh my God, where's my daddy?"

"Janelle!" Eigel abandoned him to rush to the brunette's side, reaching her just as she stopped, clapped her hands to her cheeks, and, eyes riveted on the corpses, let out a shriek that could have cracked windows as far away as Atlanta.

Holy Christ, Sam thought, wincing as his head gave another excruciating pang. *Somebody pass the Excedrin.*

"Da-a-a-ddy! Da-a-a-ddy!"

"Get somebody on the door!" Clumsily patting the screeching Janelle on the back, Eigel turned to bark the order at the skinny officer in the corner, who was looking appalled. "Nobody else gets in here unless I personally clear it, understand?"

"Yes, sir!" The kid hurried toward the door. Eigel glared at Sam, muttered something that looked like "Goddamn fucking zoo," and turned back to deal as best he could with Janelle's hysterics.

Following the kid with his gaze, Sam saw that the elaborate front door, which had been just slightly ajar when he and Wynne had pushed through it moments earlier, was now standing wide open. Beyond it, he could see the ambulance that had joined the pair of police cars that already had been parked in the driveway when he and Wynne had pulled up—their first concrete indication that they were too late. The ambulance's siren was off, but its flashing blue lights lit up the night. At the bottom of the small, manicured front yard, more cars were parking hurriedly, haphazardly. A TV truck was arriving; people were charging up the yard.

Wynne joined him, pocketing his camera. "Hey, at least this time we were right behind him."

"Yeah." Sam watched as deputies started to stick tape to the carpet to mark the positions of the bodies. The guy in the suit—from an overheard snatch of conversation, Sam gathered that he was the coroner—knelt beside Tammy Sue, carefully lifting a section of long, bleached hair, now wet with blood, away from her face. Even in death, she was a pretty woman, fine-featured, carefully groomed. As he had expected, a pair of black, oozing holes the size of dimes adorned her right temple.

Like all the others, she'd been shot twice in the head. From the look of the dark stippling surrounding the wounds, it had been at point-blank range.

He was hit by a wave of weariness so strong it almost made him stagger. Seventy-two hours without sleep, seventy-two hours spent frantically racing the clock—and it ended like this.

Again.

"Hell, let's go," he said dispiritedly to Wynne. "We can get everything else we need tomorrow."

"Yeah."

Sam headed for the door. Raising a hand in farewell to the sheriff, who had managed to get the now-sobbing Janelle into a chair, Wynne followed. Without saying so much as a word, they passed by the kid and another deputy who were holding down the doorway and slid, unnoticed, around the knot of people standing on the stoop, arguing heatedly for their right to be admitted into the house. The unaccustomed buzz of activity along with the stroboscopic lights from the ambulance had drawn the neighbors from nearby houses. Groups were congregating on nearby lawns, talking among themselves while they craned their necks to see what was going on. The TV camera crew raced toward the house. Even at that time of night, it was as steamy hot as a sauna. Stars winked lazily overhead above a canopy of feathery charcoal clouds. The moon was a distant, pale ghost of itself. A slight breeze, humid and unrefreshing, blew in from the lake across the street, rippling its moonlit surface. Walking down the golf-course-caliber lawn toward their rented Sentra, Sam took a deep breath and wished he hadn't. Flowers were everywhere, massive banks of them bordering the streets, the driveways, the walks. Their colors were muted by the darkness, but their perfume was not, lending a nauseating sweetness to the heavy air that didn't mix well with the death-scene smells that still lingered in his nostrils.

"He's watching us," he said suddenly, stopping dead and glancing at Wynne. "You know that, don't you? That son of a bitch is out here somewhere watching us. I can feel him."

"Sam . . ." Wynne began, and Sam knew from his tone that he was about to get lecture number 257—the one on not taking cases so personally—again.

Yeah, but this one *is* personal, Sam started to remind him, but before he could get the words out, his cell phone rang.

His heart jumped. Adrenaline shot through his blood like an injection of speed. Fumbling to get the phone out of his pocket, he suddenly wasn't tired anymore.

Error, the ID window on his phone read. He stiffened even as he flipped the thing open.

"McCabe," he growled.

"Close but no cigar." It was him: the sick fuck who had just whacked Wendell and Tammy Sue, who had killed at least three times previously that Sam knew for sure about, who was leading him and his team on a murderous wild-goose chase that had started with the killing of a retired federal judge in Richmond three weeks before and was proceeding south and westward, around the skirt of the country. The voice was distorted, digitally masked as usual, but by now Sam knew it better than his own.

"Where are you, you bastard?" Sam's fingers tightened on the phone as if they were gripping the caller's neck. He scanned his surroundings—the artfully placed groves of trees, the nearby houses, the shining black lake—without success. *"Where are you?"*

A chuckle was his only answer. "Ready for your next clue?"

"Just help me understand," Sam said, desperate to keep him talking. "Why? What do you want? What's the point of . . . ?"

"Here goes," the voice said. "Where in the world is—Madeline?"

"Look—" Sam began, but it was no use: The phone went dead. Whatever else he was, the guy wasn't stupid; he would know they were trying to trace his calls, just like he would know they were recording them. Cursing under his breath, Sam pressed a button.

"You called, master?" Gardner answered. The technical expert of Sam's team, she was back at the Comfort Inn just off I-264 that was serving as their temporary local headquarters.

"You get that?"

"Yeah."

"Anything?"

"Working on it. But I doubt it. He's probably using a prepaid phone card just like before."

"Sick bastard beat us again. We got two more dead." Sam's voice was glum. He could hear the flat tone of it himself. "Call the locals, would you, see if they can set up a roadblock around the perimeter, say, five miles out, check IDs, look out for suspicious characters, that type of thing. I'd handle it, but the guy in charge here doesn't seem to like me too much."

Gardner chuckled. "Big surprise."

"Love you, too," Sam said sourly, and hung up. Wynne was looking at him, tense, frowning, his eyes narrowed.

"Madeline." Sam was suddenly bone-tired again. "This time he's going after some woman named Madeline."

Wynne expelled his breath in a whistling sigh. "Shit."

"Yeah."

They headed for the car and got in without another word. After all, what was there to say? They were back on the clock again and they both knew it. If the pattern held, they had exactly seven days to find out who this Madeline was and get to her before the killer did.

If they lost this race like they'd lost the last three, Madeline, whoever the hell she was, was dead.

TWO

Thursday, August 14

Okay, so she was afraid of the dark.

It was stupid, Maddie Fitzgerald knew, but she just couldn't help it: Lying there in her hotel room bed, staring up into nothingness, her hand still in the process of withdrawing from the lamp she had just turned off, she felt as shivery as if she'd just plunged headfirst into a pool of icy water.

"Pretty pathetic," she said aloud, hoping that hearing her own voice might provide an antidote to the cold sweat she could feel popping out along her hairline. It didn't. Instead of being reassuring, the sound made her cringe as she immediately wondered who or what might be lurking there in the darkness with her to hear—and pounce.

"You're on the twentieth floor, for God's sake. Nobody's coming in through the window. The door is locked. You're safer here than you are at home," she told herself firmly.

That didn't help, either. Bravado was useless; logic clearly was, too. She was simply going to have to sweat it out. This time she was *not* going to give in. Taking a deep breath, she closed her eyes. The relentless drone of the air-conditioning unit under the window suddenly seemed as loud as an 18-

wheeler barreling along beside her bed. The bed itself—a king-size—was huge. Huddled on the side nearest the unreachable-from-the-outside window, she felt increasingly small and vulnerable. Which was ridiculous. She was five feet, seven inches tall; one hundred twenty-five well-toned pounds; a smart, competent, twenty-nine-year-old, soon-to-be-wildly-successful businesswoman, for God's sake—and yet here she was, heart boogeying like a whole dance floor full of hyperactive teenagers because she'd just turned off the bedside lamp. Maddie silently acknowledged that humiliating fact even as she fought the urge to grab for the switch, click the lamp back on, and put herself out of her misery.

If she turned on the light, she'd be able to sleep.

Her eyes popped open before she managed to put a brake on runaway temptation.

No.

Turning over so that she was facing the door, Maddie gritted her teeth and mentally groped for pleasant thoughts. She lay on her side, knees tucked almost under her chin, head propped on a pair of too-soft pillows, clutching the blankets tightly around her shoulders as she stared sightlessly into stygian darkness—darkness into which she had deliberately plunged herself. Closing her eyes a second time required real physical effort. Squinching up her face, she squeezed them shut. Moments later, when none materialized, she gave up on pleasant thoughts and instead began counting toward a hundred in her head. At the same time, she worked to control the physical symptoms brought on by the absence of light: ragged breathing, racing pulse, pounding heart, cold sweat.

By the time she reached fifty, her heart was thundering like an elephant stampede and she was breathing so fast she was practically panting. Even as she kept her eyes clenched tightly, despair filled her. Would she never be free of the specter that had haunted her for the last seven years? Every single time she tried to go to sleep alone in the dark, was she going to suffer a replay of that night? Would her dreams always be haunted by the sound of . . . ?

Shrill as a siren, a shriek split the darkness close beside her head.

Several seconds passed before Maddie realized that what she was hearing was the phone ringing. Peeling herself off the ceiling, taking a deep, steadying breath, she reached for the lamp, fumbled with the switch—oh light, blessed light!—and picked up the receiver.

"Hello?" If she'd just suffered a complete and utter nervous breakdown, her voice at least gave no hint of it. Never let them see you sweat: the mantra had been drummed into her at a hard school. Nice to know that it was still automatically operational.

"Did I wake you?"

Jon. He'd nearly sent her into cardiac arrest.

"Actually, I wasn't asleep." Maddie hitched herself up against the pillows. As she did so, she wiped her sweaty palms one at a time on the tastefully earth-toned comforter in which she was swaddled.

"Me neither. Hey, maybe we could keep each other company."

Maddie could almost see his smile through the phone. Jon Carter was a good-looking guy, blond, blue-eyed, tall and trim, oozing charm through his pores. It was one of the reasons she continued to employ him.

"Not a chance." Her voice was tart. Of course, the fact that he was still regularly hitting on her despite the change in circumstances that had turned her into his employer could not be considered a point in his favor.

He sighed. "You're a hard woman, Maddie Fitzgerald, you know that?"

"Believe me, the knowledge keeps me awake nights." Her heart rate was almost back to normal. "You want something?"

"I just had a thought—maybe we should try to work Mrs. Brehmer into the spot. You know, have her be the face of Brehmer's Pet Chow, or something."

"She's ninety years old and she looks like she died about ten years back."

Again, she could hear his smile. "So what's your point?"

Mrs. Brehmer was also worth about ninety billion, and her account, currently held by J. Walter Thompson, an advertising agency so huge that it was tantamount to sacrilege to mention Maddie's own fledgling agency in the same breath with it, was worth upward of ten million a year. The thought practically made Maddie salivate. She'd sunk her life savings into buying Creative Partners when the firm for which she and Jon were working had gone belly-up eighteen months before. Unfortunately, so far the company's finances hadn't exactly turned around on her watch. If something good didn't happen soon, this time when Creative Partners went down the tubes she was going down with it. *Not a happy thought.*

"I suppose we could coat the lens with Vaseline," Maddie said with a sigh. "Or put pantyhose over it. Something to soften the visual."

Jon chuckled. "See, I have good ideas."

"Sometimes." Maddie was thinking. "Maybe we could put her in a rocking chair in a long black dress, get her to look sort of like Whistler's mother. Just get a long shot of her. She wouldn't have to actually say anything. She could be like the company logo."

"There you go. Put a whole bunch of animals around her. Cats draped across the back of the chair, dogs at her feet. That kind of thing."

"Wouldn't hurt to pitch it." Cradling the receiver between her shoulder and ear, Maddie reached for the hotel-issue notepad and pencil by the phone. With a few economical strokes, she made a quick sketch of Mrs. Brehmer as logo, complete with slight smile, shoulder-perching cat, and oval frame, then examined it critically.

"Could work," she admitted.

"Want me to come up so we can put something together?"

"No." Maddie glanced at the bedside clock. It was not quite midnight. "Our appointment's not until ten. How about if we meet for breakfast at seven-thirty? That should give us plenty of time to go over everything. Remember, right now we're just floating this logo idea as sort of a trial balloon. If she likes it, we can go from there."

"Whatever you say, Boss."

"Get some sleep." Because being called *Boss* was still fresh enough to give her a thrilled little tingle, Maddie's voice was gruff. Then she bethought herself of something and pulled the receiver back. "Jon—good thinking, by the way."

"I try. Hey, if you change your mind, I'm only two floors down."

"Good-night, Jon." Maddie hung up. For a moment, she simply stared at the sketch she had made as various ways to work Joan Brehmer into the ad campaign they were proposing revolved through her head. The elderly widow was still sufficiently involved in the company her husband had founded in St. Louis fifty years before that Creative Partners had had to fly to New Orleans, where Mrs. Brehmer now spent most of the year, to pitch their ideas to her personally. Given that the old lady felt that strongly about the company, maybe including her in the spot was the way to go. Maybe it would even be the deciding factor.

Okay, so Jon's perpetual come-ons were annoying. The man still had some decent ideas. If Creative Partners landed this account . . .

The phone rang again. This time Maddie didn't jump. With the light on, she was as cool as a cucumber.

"What?" she said into the receiver.

"If this works, I want a Christmas bonus." Jon again, as she'd known it would be.

"We'll talk."

"Damn right we'll talk. I . . ."

"Good-*night*, Jon." But Maddie was smiling as she hung up. The idea of being in a position to give Christmas bonuses to her five employees was irresistible. If they got this account . . .

But getting the account would require a dazzling presentation, and a dazzling presentation would be greatly facilitated by a decent amount of sleep. Which at the moment she wasn't even close to getting. If she got up an hour earlier than she'd planned, there'd be plenty of time to work on the Mrs.-Brehmer-as-logo idea before she met Jon for breakfast. Right now, she needed rest.

Maddie returned the pad and pencil to the bedside table, then frowned at the lamp. It bathed all four corners of the standard-issue room in a warm glow. She could see her reflection, tinted gold and only faintly distorted, in its shiny brass base. Chin-length coffee-brown hair tousled from the amount of tossing and turning she had already done. Slender shoulders, bare except for the spaghetti straps of the silky pink shorty nightgown she was wearing, tan against white sheets. High-cheekboned, square-jawed face, complete with wide mouth, delicate nose, and dark-lashed hazel eyes, staring back at her.

She looked worried. And tired.

Maddie almost snorted. Big surprise. By now, worried and tired were practically her middle names.

But if Creative Partners managed to wow Mrs. Brehmer . . .

Phobia-busting was going to have to wait. The reality was that, for her, sleep required light. But the bedside lamp was almost too bright. Feeling a little like Goldilocks—*this porridge is too cold; this porridge is too hot*—she slid out of bed and padded barefoot to the bathroom. Flipping the bathroom light on, she closed the door until it was just barely ajar. Then, shivering as she inadvertently stepped right into the arctic slipstream that blasted from the air conditioner, she succumbed to the final temptation and stopped at the closet to pull Fudgie, the ancient, floppy-eared stuffed dog that was the sole surviving reminder of her misspent youth, from the suitcase on the floor. Clutching him, she bounded back into bed, pulled the covers up around her neck, and, with Fudgie tucked beneath her chin, turned off the lamp.

Ahh. The sheets were still faintly warm, warm enough to soothe the shivers away. Fudgie's familiar aroma and well-worn softness provided the illusion that she was no longer alone. The slice of light provided just enough illumination to induce sleep. A glance around verified that everything from the armoire at the foot of the bed to the small armchair in the corner was dimly visible, despite the fact that the room was now shrouded in a kind of grayish twilight. Not too much, not too little, just right.

'Night, Goldilocks, she told herself, and snuggled her head deep into the pillows. Her lids drooped. The bed was suddenly surprisingly comfortable. Even the growl of the air conditioner seemed companionable rather than obnoxious now. Fear shuffled off deep into the furthest reaches of her subconscious as images of Mrs. Brehmer in various increasingly ridiculous

poses flitted through her head: the old lady standing with a pitchfork and a Great Dane in a takeoff of *American Gothic;* in close-up (with the help of much lens-softening Vaseline), sporting an eyepatch and a Mona Lisa smile while a parrot perched pirate-style on her shoulder; sitting with a black cat on her lap and a yellow canary in a cage by her side, rocking away like Granny in a Sylvester and Tweety cartoon . . .

The pounding of her own heart woke her. At least, that's what Maddie thought at first as she surfaced what could have been minutes or hours later. Even as she blinked groggily, trying to get her bearings, she could feel the gun-shy organ knocking against her rib cage, feel the racing of her pulse, the dryness of her mouth, the knot in the pit of her stomach that told her she'd had a bad dream.

Another bad dream.

The good news, she thought as she wet her dry lips, was that she hadn't had one for a long time now. More than a year. Actually, not since she'd taken over Creative Partners and given herself a whole rash of new worries to keep her awake at night. Which, believe it or not, was actually a positive development in her life. Better to worry about being jobless, homeless, and broke than being dead.

The room was pitch-dark. The bathroom light was off.

Realization hit Maddie like a jolt from a cattle prod.

The bathroom light is off. Unless there was a power outage—no, that was out, the air conditioner was still doing its window-rattling roar—someone had turned off the light.

Someone had turned off the light.

Wait, her rational side cautioned, even as panic seized her by the throat. Stiff as a concrete slab now, she strained futilely to hear or see as she deliberately ticked off various *un*terrifying possibilities: The bulb could have burned out; there could have been a short in a wire; it . . .

There was someone in her room. He was stepping out of the narrow corridor between the bathroom on the left and the rows of closets on the right and moving toward the bed. Maddie didn't see him; the room was pitch-black. She didn't hear him—the air conditioner was making too much noise to allow her to hear anything so stealthy as a creeping footfall on carpet.

But she sensed him. Felt him. Knew with unshakable certainty that he was there.

Her heart leaped. Goose bumps raced along her skin like a rush of falling dominoes. The hair at the back of her neck shot straight up.

A scream ripped into her throat; instinct made her swallow it just in time. If she screamed he would be on her like a duck on a june bug. If she screamed, who, in this cheap, impersonal hotel with its noisy, sound-blocking air conditioners, would be likely to hear—except him?

Making a split-second decision, she moved, sliding as quietly as possible off the side of the bed, suddenly grateful for the air conditioner's racket to cover her movements. Flat on her stomach on the musty-smelling carpet, she discovered that there was nowhere to go: The window wall was maybe a foot away on her left, and, to her right, a quick, questing hand encountered the carpeted platform that supported the bed.

A couple of heartbeats passed before the true horror of her situation sank in: She was trapped. Her throat closed up and her stomach knotted as she faced the fact that she had nowhere to go. The only way out was the door—and the intruder was doing whatever he was doing between her and it.

Maybe he was nothing more than a garden-variety burglar. She'd left her purse on the floor beside the armoire. Maybe he would just take it and melt away into the darkness from which he'd sprung.

Yeah, and maybe she'd win the lottery too, but the way her luck had been running for the last few years, she wasn't going to hold her breath in anticipation.

Where was he? Her every sense was on quivering alert, but the darkness was impenetrable: She literally couldn't see the hands splayed flat on the carpet in front of her face. Hearing anything was equally impossible over the air conditioner. Her heart threatened to pound its way out of her chest. Fear quickened her breathing until, afraid he might somehow hear the fast, shallow pants even over the rattling air conditioner, she deliberately deepened and slowed it. Her fingers, still hopelessly probing the scratchy carpet barrier that prevented her from going with her first instinct, which was to hide under the bed, encountered a smooth wooden stick: the pencil she'd been sketching with earlier. They closed around it convulsively. It wasn't much, but it was the closest thing to a weapon she had.

The darkness lightened fractionally. Glancing up, her gaze widened on a pinpoint shimmer of light that was reflected in the lamp's base. He had switched on a flashlight, one of those small ones with the tiny beams. It was moving over the bed.

Her stomach clenched like a fist.

Move, she told herself fiercely. Scrambling into a low crouch, shivering with cold and fear, Maddie scuttled as soundlessly as possible toward the foot of the bed.

The light went out. That could not be good.

Thunk. Thunk.

The bed shuddered twice in quick succession. Her shoulder was just touching the mattress, using it as a guide to get where she needed to go, and she felt the twin jolts. Maddie almost yelped with surprise as she jerked away. Pulse pounding so hard that she could barely hear the air conditioner over the panicked beat assaulting her eardrums, she backpedaled until she came up against the wall. Sucking in air, she gaped toward the bed without, of course, being able to see a thing. The sounds made her think of a fist slamming hard into the mattress. Once. Twice.

Then, with sudden icy certainty, she realized that those sounds hadn't been made by any fist. The acrid smell drifting beneath her nostrils told its own tale: a gun. A gun with a silencer. Someone possessing a gun with a silencer had just fired two shots into her bed.

Into, as the shooter thought, *her.*

Oh, God, oh, God . . .

Pure unadulterated terror threatened to reduce her muscles to jelly. It froze her in place, left her unable to move.

The flashlight beam once again sliced through the darkness, playing over the bed. Maddie found herself staring in horror at the jumble of blankets and sheets. The light focused on the pillow where moments before her head had rested. A chocolate brown tuft that she recognized as Fudgie's ear was just visible above the tangled covers. In a flash Maddie realized that the gunman, whoever he was, had mistaken that tuft for the top of her head. And he'd fired at it.

All rational thought was swept from her mind as a hand in a black glove reached out to flip the covers down.

Move!

This time it was an internal shriek. Her body automatically obeyed. She catapulted away from the wall, panic giving wings to her feet as she bolted toward the narrow thread of light from the hall that just showed beneath the door.

She already knew she had almost no chance.

"Hey!"

It was a man's surprised exclamation. With all need for concealment past, Maddie shrieked for all she was worth as the flashlight beam swung around to follow her flight. There was a rush of movement behind her; horror turned her blood to ice water in her veins. He was going to catch her—but no, she was at the door. Her frantic fingers found smooth, cold metal: the knob. They closed on it . . .

Oh, God, it was slippery. Her hands were sweaty. *She couldn't turn the knob.*

A strong hand grabbed her shoulder, yanked her back. Maddie screamed like an air horn, twisting, kicking, fighting for all she was worth. He must have dodged, because her fists connected with nothing but air. Her bare toes did worse: They smashed painfully into his shin.

"Help! *Help!*"

Her screams still hung in the air as he slammed her against the wall. The back of her head hit the trim around the bathroom door so hard that an explosion of tiny white lights seemed to burst in front of her eyes. A gloved hand around her throat silenced her brutally even as it pinned her in place.

Clawing instinctively at that choking hand, she only remembered the pencil—her weapon—when she felt it drop.

Oh, God.

Her nails raked harmlessly down the leather, then hit pay dirt as they ripped at the vulnerable flesh of his wrist.

His gloved knuckles slammed into her right cheekbone so hard that she saw stars again.

"Scratch me again, bitch, and I'll rip your throat out."

Her eyes watered. Pain radiated from where he'd hit her. She couldn't breathe. His grip tightened cruelly as he leaned close, pressing himself against her so that she could feel buttons and smooth cotton and the terrifying strength of the body beneath imprinting themselves on her flesh. She hung motionless in his grip now, stunned, terrified, as vulnerable as a rabbit in the jaws of a wolf. His hand spanned her throat, fingers digging into the tender hollows below her ears. It hurt. Her cheek hurt. The back of her head hurt. But the pain was nothing compared to the surging tide of her fear. His breath, warm and stinking of onions, was hot on her cheek. His mouth was just inches from hers. She shuddered reflexively—then remembered the gun and went absolutely still.

Where was it? He'd had it—he must still have it—somewhere. In a holster or . . .

He changed position, and she felt his free hand fumble at his waist. The hand he'd hit her with—his right hand—

Is he going for his gun?

The thought that he might be getting ready to shoot her, that at any second now she might feel the impact of a bullet ripping through her flesh and muscle and bone, made Maddie go weak at the knees.

"There's m-m-money in my purse," she tried desperately. Her voice was a hoarse, halting whisper that hurt her bruised throat. A quick sideways glance told her that the door was close, so tantalizingly close. The glimmering line of light from the hall was maybe three feet away.

"I don't want your money."

His hand came up toward her head—*oh, God*—and then flattened on her mouth. A rubbery smell, a sticky strip molding her lips—duct tape. Shaking with horror, she realized that he was duct-taping her mouth shut. His touch almost tender, he smoothed the strip out, then applied a second one.

It was then that Maddie knew, without a single remaining flicker of doubt, that he meant to kill her.

Without warning a bright beam shone full in her face: the flashlight. It blinded her as thoroughly as the darkness had moments earlier. Flinching, shaking, light-headed with fear, she squinched her eyes shut and prayed like she had never prayed in her life.

For the space of a couple of heartbeats, he did nothing while the light played over her face. He seemed to be . . . *looking* at her.

Terror popped her eyes open again just as the light went out.

Maddie heard herself make a sound: a moan. No, a whimper, barely audible beneath the tape.

"Scared?" There was the faintest hint of enjoyment in his whisper. "You should be." His voice roughened. "Get down on your knees."

Fear surged like bile into her throat. She tasted the sharp, vinegary tang of it. His hand tightened around her throat, then shifted to the back of her neck, squeezing and forcing her down. It didn't require much effort. Her knees buckled; she was dizzy, disoriented, literally sick with dread. The carpet felt stiff and prickly beneath her knees. Her hands splayed out over it, supporting her weight as cold sweat drenched her. The wintry blast of the air conditioner hit her damp skin, worsening her shivers, turning her as icy cold on the outside as she already was on the inside.

Her single coherent thought was, *Any second now, I'm going to die.*

From out in the hall, just faintly, Maddie thought she heard voices. He must have heard them too, or felt her tense in response, because his hand tightened painfully on the back of her neck.

"Don't make a sound."

He was behind her now, leaning over her, his hand hard and controlling on the back of her bent neck, pushing her face toward the carpet. Even as the voices died away, even as her hands shifted automatically to compensate for the forced redistribution of her weight, the horrible vision of rape flashed into her mind.

Please, God, please, God, please . . .

Her fingers touched the pencil just as her cheek grazed the fuzzy nylon of the carpet. Instinct took over, and her fist closed around the pencil in a death grip.

"Stay still," he whispered, leaning closer. There was the faintest of metallic sounds, and tremors of horror raced over her skin as she felt his right hand move. Instantly she visualized what he was doing: positioning the gun.

To shoot her . . .

Galvanized, she gave it her last, best shot. Ramming the pencil up and back, she felt it thrust into something substantial, something firm but yielding, something that made her think of a fork sinking into meat . . .

He screamed.

"Fucking bitch!" he howled, falling back.

Just as quick as that, she was free. Rocketing to her feet, she hurled herself at the door, latching on to the knob with both hands and yanking for all she was worth.

It opened. Light so bright that it was blinding spilled over her. With every last bit of strength she possessed, she leaped into the light. A single terrified glance over her shoulder as she fled told her that he was already coming after her, hauling the closing door open again, a huge dark menacing shadow lurching in horrifyingly swift pursuit.

She ripped the duct tape from her mouth and screamed to wake the dead.

THREE

Friday, August 15

What in hell does she have in common with the others?" Sam muttered, mostly to himself. Hands thrust into the front pockets of his jeans, seething with barely contained frustration, he was standing in an inner hall of the New Orleans medical examiner's office, watching through a Plexiglas window as the county coroner, Dr. Lurlene Deland, made the initial Y-shaped incision in the body of Madeline Fitzgerald. His badge had been enough to grant him access to the autopsy. His grim-faced demeanor kept the flunkies who walked past from hassling him about the whys and wherefores of his right to watch. This time, he and Wynne hadn't even been close, arriving at the crime scene—a Holiday Inn Express—just as the body was being loaded into the coroner's van to be taken away.

"Could be anything. Or nothing. You ever thought about that? Maybe he's just picking victims at random. Playing with us."

Wynne was beside him, leaning heavily against the dull beige concrete wall, electing not to look through the window. Having just stuffed his face with half a dozen Krispy Kremes in a desperate bid to counter exhaustion with a blood-sugar rush, Wynne had turned green around the gills as soon as they had walked through the swinging doors that separated the office from the working area and the formaldehyde-based smell of the place hit him in the face. Sam had passed on the Krispy Kremes and was now heartily glad. Wynne was looking sick enough for the pair of them.

"There's something."

Sam watched as a thin line of blood marked the progress of Deland's scalpel. Naked, waxy-skinned, the victim lay on a sloped metal table, the upper half of which was textured to keep the body from sliding; running water flowed along the table into a shallow tub beneath a grate at the lower end.

To catch the effluvia, as another coroner had once told him.

"Nothing's turned up so far," Wynne said.

Sam grimaced. Wynne was right. Despite ongoing searches into each victim's background, they'd uncovered no links between them. Nothing to connect them at all. Not even the serial killer's special of age, sex, or race.

"Something will. There's a link, and we'll find it and we'll catch him. Sooner or later, he'll make a mistake."

"I hope he hurries the hell up. This case is losing its charm real fast."

Sam grunted agreement. Christ, he felt bad. The bright fluorescent lights on the other side of the glass were giving him a killer headache. Or maybe it was the chronic lack of sleep. Or the gnawing emptiness in his stomach. Or maybe even the sheer damned futility of the effort. They'd spent the last week searching the country for the dead woman, desperately dissecting every clue as the asshole had called it in. The second one, Peyton, had turned out to be part of the name of the street on which the hotel stood. The third clue, Fitzgerald, proved to be the woman's last name. The fourth was the link to the hotel: holiday. The fifth, called in just hours before the victim was killed, was *no*. As in New Orleans.

Figuring that out had been enough to allow them to finally put the puzzle pieces together and find the woman. But it had not been enough to allow them to find her while she was still alive.

Sam gritted his teeth against the curse words that crowded onto his tongue, and likewise battled an urge to rest his forehead against the sure-to-be-cool Plexiglas. A muffled version of "Satisfaction," courtesy of a local golden-oldies station, played on the sound system. Pity he wasn't getting any, in any shape, form, or fashion, he reflected. At the very least, he needed about six hours of uninterrupted sleep and a decent meal to feel halfway normal again. Sex would be good, too, but the way things were going that probably wasn't going to happen anytime soon. A real, honest-to-God lead—now what he wouldn't give for that.

A lead would be the best pick-me-up of all.

"Her ex-husband check out?" Wynne asked, clearly without much hope.

"So far." Working off background information on the victim given in the police report, Gardner had done the preliminary work, and Sam had gone over her report in the car on the way over. "At least, as far as anybody can tell at this point, he was where he said he was last night. Anyway, he's a shift worker at GE. He might or might not have had reason to murder his ex-wife, but for the life of me I can't see him roaming around the country, knocking random people off."

Wynne made a sound signifying disgust under his breath. "So what we got, basically, is nothing."

"Pretty much."

Beyond the transparent barrier, Deland was folding back the skin surrounding the incision. Turning the facts of the case over in his head for what must have been the millionth time, Sam watched without seeing as her hands in their thin, white surgical gloves wielded a pair of gardening shears to snip through the ribs. Below them, the internal organs glistened, still pristine.

The only real damage had been to the victim's head. Sam had watched as the coroner's first, careful inspection of the victim's scalp, skin, and body surfaces had all but confirmed this. Like the others, she'd been dispatched with two neat gunshots to the temple. A jar holding a single, deformed shard of lead that had failed to penetrate the skull waited on the wheeled metal cart at the coroner's elbow. Later, as more fragments were recovered from the brain, they would be added to the jar.

The pieced-together bullets would tell them nothing, Sam already knew. Every killing so far had been done using a different weapon. The killer was smart enough to prefer his guns, like his phones, disposable.

Who the hell was this guy?

Deland made a delicate movement with her scalpel, then lifted a bloody organ from the body with her two gloved hands and deposited it on a scale on the cart.

"I need some air," Wynne said.

Sam glanced over at him to find that Wynne was now watching the autopsy in progress. His eyes were squinched half shut, his face had blanched at least two shades, and his lips were tightly compressed. Before Sam could reply, the big guy turned on his heel and strode back down the corridor. His sandals went *slap-slap-slap* on the slick tile floor.

He was moving like he feared not making it to the john in time.

Sam glanced back at the body on the tilted metal table, followed the proceedings for a few more minutes, and gave it up. There was no absolution to be gained by watching, and no new knowledge, either.

The truth was, he was almost too tired to stand up, let alone think. And he was bugged, big-time, by the fact that the killer had not made contact since calling with the last clue. Up until now, there had been a clear pattern: a partial name first, called in not long after their arrival at the scene of the previous murder. Then two or three random clues that only made sense in retrospect. Finally, a hint to the city was always last, called in just a few hours before the next killing occurred. This time, they'd had to scramble to hop a plane from Houston, where they'd been en route to interview a Madeline Peyton who worked for Fitzgerald Securities, one of at least a hundred Madelines on their list who met the parameters of the information they'd been given so far, when the last clue had come in and they'd pinpointed New Orleans. It was as if the killer wanted to make a game of it—to see if he could pull off the crime while Sam's team raced to make sense of the clues, raced to locate the victim, raced to stop him. So far, the killer was winning. The stats were grim: FBI 0, Insane Bastard 5—no, 6 if you counted Tammy Sue Perkins, which, since she was dead and he had killed her, you had to do. With this last victim, they'd been a good two hours behind the killer. Sam had barely gotten a glimpse of the victim as she was taken away, just enough to know that she was a woman, dark-haired, attractive, and dead. The crime scene was her hotel room. Apparently, the attack had occurred as she slept.

But why? Why? Why?

Sam hated to admit even to himself that he had no clue.

His last contact with the killer had come—he glanced at his watch; it was 9:17 a.m.—at five minutes until seven p.m. the previous day. That was more than fourteen hours ago. Before, the bastard had always called him within no more than an hour of Sam's arrival at the death scene to gloat—and to provide the first lead to the next victim.

This time there'd been no contact.

Maybe, this time, there was no next victim? Maybe the bastard had gotten it all out of his system? Maybe the game was over?

Yeah, and maybe he was going to get a raise in his next paycheck, too, but he didn't think so, Sam concluded gloomily.

Still, he had to ask himself: What was different about this one? Why hadn't the killer made contact afterward? There was a reason—there was always a reason. He just didn't know what it was. *Yet.*

The questions that crowded into his mind in the wake of that were so urgent and the answers so elusive that Sam banged his fist against the Plexiglas in frustration. Deland and her assistant glanced his way, their eyes frowning at him above their surgical masks.

The message was clear: He was disturbing their work.

Sam didn't even bother mouthing an apology. He turned on his heel and went in search of Wynne.

He found him outside, to the left of the frosted-glass front door, leaning against the four-story building's grimy stucco wall. Located just off Canal Street, the coroner's office was in a seedy area heavy on small shops and ethnic restaurants that swarmed with activity even this early in the day. Pedestrians clogged the sidewalks. Vehicles of all descriptions crawled bumper-to-bumper in both directions, creating a continuous background buzz that sounded like a swarm of angry wasps. The heat wrapped around Sam's face like a hot, wet towel the moment he left the air-conditioning behind. Inhaling was like breathing in soup. The smells—car emissions, decaying plants, various kinds of spicy food cooking—would have been nauseating if he'd let himself pay attention to them, which he didn't. Two tortured-looking palmetto trees struggled to survive in wrought-iron cages set into the sidewalk. Wynne—or at least as much of Wynne as could fit, which was about a fourth—stood in the spindly shadow of one of these. His arms were crossed over his massive chest, his head was bent, his eyes were closed. His mouth worked as he chewed something very slowly and deliberately. Bubble gum, Sam assumed, because of the faint grape smell and the fact that Wynne had bought a six-pack of grape Dubble Bubble along with the doughnuts he'd scarfed down earlier. Since quitting smoking six weeks ago, Wynne rarely went longer than fifteen minutes without putting something in his mouth. As a result, he was gaining weight like a turkey in October, enough so that his baggy shorts were growing less baggy by the day and his shirts—today's model was vintage Hawaiian, featuring a big-bosomed girl doing the hula on the front—strained at their buttons.

"Okay?" Sam asked, surveying him.

Wynne gave a single slow nod.

Despite the nod, Sam continued to eye him skeptically. Sweat beaded Wynne's forehead, his face was flushed red, and his curly, fair hair had frizzed in the heat until it looked like a brass-colored Brillo pad. To put it mildly, Wynne was not, at the moment, a poster boy for FBI spit and polish. *But then, that's what four weeks on the road chasing a murderous nutjob did to a man*, Sam thought. He himself was a case in point. He was sporting a couple of days'—he'd forgotten exactly how many—worth of stubble, faded jeans, and a T-shirt that had once been black but had been washed so often and so haphazardly over the past month that it was now a kind of tie-dyed-looking gray. The jackets and ties that Bureau protocol called for had been left back in their hotel rooms. This particular August, New Orleans was a hundred degrees in the shade with a sticky humidity that never seemed to let up.

In other words, it was just too damned hot.

Wynne opened one bleary eye. "I need a cigarette. Bad."

"Chew your gum."

"Ain't helping."

In front of them, a black Firebird pulled over to the curb and stopped. Both doors opened at almost exactly the same moment, and two men got out. Tensing automatically, doing a quick mental check to make sure his Sig Sauer still nestled in the small of his back where he could get to it in a matter of seconds if need be, Sam squinted at them through the shimmer of heat that rose from the sidewalk, watching, narrow-eyed, as the pair headed purposefully toward him and Wynne. Their initially brisk pace slowed as they drew closer.

"You guys learn anything in there?"

Sam relaxed as he recognized the speaker as Phil Lewis, an FBI agent from the local field office whom he had first met some six years previously, when Sam had come to town to spearhead an investigation into a hashish-smuggling ring that was using the port of New Orleans as an entry point to the U.S. drug market. Despite the camouflage provided by the inches-high blond pompadour the guy tended like a girlfriend, Lewis was short, maybe five-nine or so beneath the hair, stocky and cocky in the way small men often are. Today he was decked out in a pale yellow sport coat, a gleaming white T-shirt, pressed jeans, and Ray-Bans. The African-American guy with him was taller, thinner, and a little more conservative in a crew cut, navy sport coat, and khakis. And Ray-Bans.

"Nah," Sam replied, leaning a shoulder back against the building and folding his arms over his chest. "Long time no see, Lewis. I see you're still a fan of *Miami Vice*."

"What?" Lewis looked bewildered and suspicious at the same time. Beside Sam, Wynne snickered.

"Forget it." Sam jerked a thumb at Wynne. "This is E. P. Wynne. Phil Lewis. And . . . ?"

"Greg Simon," Lewis's partner said. Perfunctory handshakes were exchanged all around, and then Sam looked at Lewis.

"You got anything?" Sam meant anything he needed to know, which Lewis perfectly understood.

"Nothing but a call from Dr. Deland's office about two suspicious-looking characters claiming to be FBI agents forcing their way into the Fitzgerald autopsy."

"That would be us," Sam said. Wynne nodded.

"Yeah." Lewis frowned. "You want to tell me why we're interested in this case?"

Ordinarily, murder investigations were left up to local police forces in the jurisdictions in which they occurred. The FBI was called in only on certain extraordinary cases.

"Possible link to multiple homicides with the UNSUB crossing state lines," Sam said. Bureau policy was to share information on developing cases with local field agents, but in this case Sam interpreted that to mean on a strictly need-to-know basis. At this point, in Sam's estimation, what he'd just said was about all Lewis needed to know. He remembered all too vividly how the details of the last investigation they'd worked on together had gotten leaked to the *Times-Picayune* within hours of the investigative team uncovering them. For all its population, New Orleans was a small town that way, and unless something had changed, Lewis had a way-too-cozy relationship with local reporters.

Having this thing turn into a media circus was something they did not need. Especially when they were no closer to making an apprehension today than they had been when Sam had gotten the first call at the first murder scene four weeks ago.

"Hot damn," Lewis said, rubbing his hands together in transparent glee. "You mean we got ourselves a serial killer?"

"Nah. Looks like a series of professional hits." Sam slouched against the wall again. " 'Course, it's too early to say for sure."

Lewis gave a nod toward the building. "What was she into to get herself whacked?"

"Could be a lot of things. At this point, we don't really know."

"But you've got an idea," Lewis said, watching Sam.

"Actually, I've got no fucking clue," Sam said, which had the double virtue of being the absolute truth while at the same time visibly annoying Lewis. Beside him, Wynne was working on blowing a big purple bubble. The sickly sweet grape smell wafted beneath Sam's nose.

"Bullshit," Lewis said.

Sam shrugged. "Think what you want."

"You're operating in my neck of the woods now." Lewis's voice was sharp. "Whatever you've got on this case, I have a right to know it."

"You're absolutely correct. You do."

"So?"

"When I find something out, I'll send you a memo."

"You . . ." Lewis went red with anger but swallowed the rest of what he'd been going to say. Sam gave him the faintest of smiles. Wynne's bubble popped with a loud *smack*.

"You got a problem with memos?" Sam asked innocently. "I can do e-mails."

"You suck, you know that?" Lewis said through his teeth, and started walking. "Come on, Greg, we need to head on in and tell Dr. Deland's staff that, hard as it may be to believe, the creeps they were complaining about really are FBI agents." As Simon started to move, Lewis glanced back over his shoulder at Sam. "You gonna hang around for a few minutes? When we come back out, maybe we can give you a lift over to Goodwill, help you pick out a couple of sport coats."

"Sounds good."

"Dickhead." If that was meant to be a mutter, Lewis blew it big-time. Sam heard and gave him a jaunty little farewell wave.

"So when are you planning to start writing your book on winning friends and influencing people?" Wynne inquired with a sideways glance when Lewis and company had disappeared inside the building.

Sam grinned. "Anytime now. I'm just working on building up the fan base first."

"You know he's probably gonna call Smolski"—Leonard Smolski was the head of the Violent Crimes division and their boss—"and complain that we're holding out on him. And Smolski's gonna go ape-shit."

"Last time I shared details of an investigation with Lewis . . ." Sam began, meaning to fill Wynne in on the ins and outs of the media blitz that nearly derailed the drug-smuggling case. But he was interrupted by the sudden strident peal of his cell phone.

Sam became instantly alert at the sound, and he straightened away from the wall. Wynne watched him like a dog with a squirrel in view as Sam thrust a hand in his jeans pocket, yanked the phone out, and glanced down at it. A number flashed on the ID screen. It made him frown.

"Yo," he answered, already knowing that the voice on the other end was not going to be the one he both wanted and dreaded to hear.

"Something weird," Gardner said in his ear. "We've turned up another Madeline Fitzgerald. Attacked last night at the same hotel."

"*What?*"

"Yeah. Only this one lived."

"You're shitting me, right?"

"Nope. She signed into the emergency room at Norton Hospital at 3:12 a.m. with unspecified injuries, was treated and released."

"What? What?" Wynne demanded, balancing on the balls of his feet now as he stared at Sam and tried to make sense of the conversation. Sam waved him off.

"And we're just now finding this out?" Sam felt like slapping his palm to his forehead *duh*-style. They were the FBI, after all. Consistently being a day late and a dollar short was not how they were supposed to operate.

"Hey, not my fault. Apparently a friend drove her to the hospital. Hotel security notified the police, who called us. Ten minutes ago."

Sam took a deep breath. Lack of timely cooperation from the local police was nothing new, of course. But it was still maddening as hell. "Where is she now?"

"I knew you were going to ask me that." Gardner sounded smugly self-satisfied. "She caught a cab in front of the hotel fifteen minutes ago. The driver took her to the Hepburn Building. One-thirty-six Broadway."

"Gardner, you da man," Sam said, and hung up with Gardner's pert "not in this life, lover," echoing in his ears.

FOUR

So her throat hurt. So she was bruised and sore and scared. So she was operating on about two hours sleep. *Get over it,* Maddie told herself fiercely as she washed her hands in the Hepburn Building's first-floor ladies' room. She could think about what had happened later, after the presentation was over. If she and Jon did a good job now, if Creative Partners got the account, her struggling business would suddenly, for the first time ever, be on solid ground. Even better than solid ground. They'd be making money—lots of money. Enough money to buy the kind of settled, secure life she'd always dreamed about. Now was clearly not the moment to fall apart. Just because some psycho maniac had broken into her hotel room and tried to kill her was no reason to lose focus.

You gotta have priorities, she thought wryly. A nervous breakdown would just have to wait. What she needed to do was just stay in the moment. After all, what was the alternative? Turn tail and head back to St. Louis with a whimper while waving a fond farewell to the Brehmer account?

Not happening.

So get a grip. Maddie took a deep breath and worked on taking her own advice. While she'd been in the hospital basically having her tonsils examined, Jon had already tried to have the appointment postponed, without success. Mrs. Brehmer's people had made it clear that either the meeting went down at ten a.m. today as scheduled or it didn't go down at all. Reliability was Mrs. Brehmer's watchword, as Susan Allen, her personal assistant, had apologetically informed him. If Brehmer's Pet Foods couldn't even rely on Creative Partners to be at such an important meeting on time, well, then . . .

Right. Reliable R Us, Maddie thought, turning off the taps and drying her hands on a paper towel. The show must go on and all that. She had always been good at compartmentalizing, and she would compartmentalize this, tucking it away to be examined in depth later. Popping in another pain-deadening throat lozenge, she grimaced at the Listerine-like taste even as she gave herself one last critical once-over in the mirror. Her hair was brushed into a sleeker-than-usual business-friendly bob. The slight bruise on her cheek had been camouflaged into near invisibility by a crafty combination of coverstick and blush, and the rest of her makeup was flattering but minimal. Her cream linen suit with its slim, knee-length skirt was resolutely conservative. The white silk shell beneath was the epitome of tastefulness. The beige pumps and shoulder bag continued the ladylike theme. The only jarring note in her understated ensemble was the bright blue-and-yellow silk scarf, grabbed on the fly from the hotel gift shop, that she had twined around her neck to conceal the ugly purple bruise that marred the front of her throat.

Last night someone tried to kill me.

A shiver raced down her spine as Maddie did her best to thrust the wayward thought back into the "I'll worry about that later" compartment. Jon had reported that Susan Allen's dominant emotion on being informed of what had befallen Creative Partners's owner and CEO during the night had been dismay.

"You know, Mrs. B. is not real big on getting involved in her associates' personal dramas," the assistant had said doubtfully.

A personal drama. That was certainly a unique way to look at just managing to escape a would-be ruthless killer by the skin of her teeth, Maddie thought with some asperity. But the bottom line was, Mrs. Brehmer just didn't want to know, which was fine with Maddie. *She* didn't want to know, either. Unfortunately, though, she had no choice: At some point she was going to have to face the reality of what had happened and deal with it.

But not now. She was not going to think about it now. The unavoidable residuals of the attack—terror, panic, questions, decisions—all were going to have to be put on hold until later. Just for this morning, she was going to think about nothing except how much the Brehmer account mattered to her, to her employees, to Creative Partners as a whole, and go out there and do her best to wow the old witch. Or, um, make that wow the demanding-but-rich business owner who could put Creative Partners on the map with one stroke of her pen.

As she held on to that view of the situation with dogged determination, Maddie shook off the shivers, picked up her briefcase, and exited the bathroom.

Jon was standing where she had left him, among a milling group of people in business dress waiting over by the bank of gleaming brass-doored elevators, looking his usual handsome self in a navy suit, white shirt, and red power tie. He smiled at her, and she headed toward him, her sensible two-inch heels clicking on the terrazzo floor. The Hepburn Building was a fifty-story skyscraper located in the middle of one of New Orleans's busiest commercial blocks. It was sleekly modern, an anachronistic new addition to a city that owed its fame to a decaying antebellum charm. Today the brown marble lobby was crowded, and the line at the security desk, where visitors were required to sign in, was growing longer by the minute. Two men, somewhat scruffy for such an elegant environment, were leaning over the counter, apparently holding up the proceedings as they carried on an intense conversation with the uniformed guard behind the desk.

Even as she noticed them, the guard looked around. For an instant his gaze combed the shifting ranks of people waiting for the elevators, walking to and from the restrooms, visiting the small flower kiosk opposite the elevators. Then she must have made some attention-attracting move—perhaps the sunlight filtering in through the oversized windows had glinted off her gold earrings or something—because all of a sudden he seemed to focus on her.

"Over there," Maddie heard him say, and then to her surprise he pointed right at her.

Me? she thought. Her eyes widened, her step faltered, and her hand rose in a gesture of disbelief to press against the cool silk between her breasts.

The men who'd been talking to the guard followed the path of his pointing finger with their eyes and looked at her. Finding herself suddenly pinned by the gazes of two unsavory-looking strangers could not be considered a positive development at any time. But after what had happened the night before, her heart could be forgiven, Maddie thought, for the insane attempt it made to leap out of her body through her throat.

Surely there must be some mistake—but if there was, it was a mistake that kept on keeping on. The men straightened and, without taking their eyes off her, began walking purposefully toward her. They made an unlikely pair, as if a street bum had hooked up with a slovenly tourist. Together, they looked so ratty and out of place in these upscale surroundings that Maddie couldn't believe that the guard had even let them pass. But they had gotten through, and they were coming in her direction. As she registered the unescapable reality of the situation, her feet seemed to sprout roots that sank deep into the floor. Her eyes stayed glued to them; she could not look away. Her heart pounded. Her pulse raced. Her fight-or-flight response kicked in, veering strongly toward flight. Unfortunately, even if she could move, which she didn't seem to be able to do, she was out of luck. Barring a retreat to the ladies' room, which was the biggest trap in the world if they decided to follow her in or even wait outside, or the timely arrival of one of the cursedly slow elevators, there was no place in this starkly designed lobby to go.

Could one of them have been the man in my hotel room?

At the thought, Maddie suddenly went light-headed. Still, she couldn't move. She could do nothing but watch with growing horror as they strode toward her through the bars of light that the tall windows on either side of the lobby threw down across the highly polished floor. They were both good-sized men, but the fair-haired one in the garish Hawaiian shirt and rumpled shorts was taller by several inches, and fat. Too fat to be her attacker? *Yes,* she thought, *yes. Please, God, yes.* Her gaze shifted. Though the bigger man was moving fast, he was still a few steps behind the black-haired guy in jeans whose eyes were fastened on her like she was a refrigerator and they were magnets. He looked like someone on the morning after the night before, with a couple days' worth of stubble darkening his jaw and short but untidy hair that probably hadn't seen a comb since before he had last shaved. This man was definitely not fat. What he was was powerfully built and mean-looking, the kind of guy that she wouldn't want to run into in a dark parking lot or on a deserted street.

Or in a dark hotel room.

At the thought, all the air left her lungs. Was it him? Was she about to be attacked again? Here and now, in this crowded lobby?

Her eyes widened, and her heart went all fluttery.

But then something about the way they moved, about their quick strides and erect posture, struck her.

They're cops, she thought. *Some kind of cops.*

With that, her feet released their death grip on the floor, and she was able to take a quick, defensive step back. To her left, one of the elevators announced its arrival with a *ding.* The population of the lobby shifted noticeably as a herd of people surged toward it. Pivoting, she turned toward the elevator as every instinct she possessed shrieked at her to flee.

With the single exception of the guy who had attacked her, cops were the very last people she wanted to see.

"Perfect timing," Jon said, glancing around at her over his shoulder. A few quick steps had put her right behind him, so close that her nose was in danger of flattening itself on his slender, tropical wool—clad back. He was clearly unaware of the drama that was playing out behind him, of the oncoming men, of her urgent wish to escape. Caught up in the throng crowd-ing into the elevator, he paused courteously to allow a pair of elderly women to precede him. Ordinarily, Maddie would have awarded him brownie points for the gentlemanly gesture. Today, stuck behind him, she had to fight the urge to place the flat of both hands in the center of his back and shove. Hard.

Hurry, hurry, hurry. The refrain beat urgently through her brain.

Jon moved at last, clearly one of the final few who were going to make it into the crowded car, then turned to face her, edging back just enough to create a place for her at the very front. In her haste to join him, Maddie got the corner of her full-to-bursting briefcase hung up on the door.

"Piece of crap," she muttered furiously. Forced to pause long enough to jerk the thrice-damned thing free, she was just about to step into the eleva-tor when a hand caught her arm from behind. Maddie let loose with a sound that was more squeak than scream and practically jumped out of her skin. The strong fingers that gripped her firmly just above her elbow hung on. Her stomach sank as she realized that she'd just been effectively stopped in her tracks.

"Madeline Fitzgerald?" A deep, southern-tinged voice asked.

"Hey!" Jon said sharply, starting forward as he realized what was hap-pening at last. Maddie whipped around, inadvertently clearing a circle in the crowd around her with her ungainly briefcase. From the corner of her eye she caught just a glimpse of Jon's startled expression as the elevator doors slid closed in his face. Then just like that he was gone, and she was on her own. With the elevator no longer available, everyone around her seemed to simply disperse. Everyone, that is, except the guy holding on to her arm.

"Let go of me."

It was all she could do to keep the panic out of her voice. Instinctively, she jerked her arm free and moved back until she could feel the smooth, slick coolness of the marble wall against her shoulder blades. Left with no place to go, she pressed her briefcase up against her legs like a shield. Her gaze collided with narrowed eyes the color of black coffee.

"Madeline Fitzgerald?" he asked for the second time. From the dispassionate but assessing way his eyes were moving over her, she was all but certain that her original estimate was correct: This guy had law enforcement written all over him.

Her heart threatened to pound its way out of her chest.

"Who wants to know?" she parried, knowing that her response was a throwback to her younger days, knowing that it was all wrong for who she was now, for who she aspired to be. But she couldn't help it, she'd been caught by surprise, she was rattled and still recovering from last night and definitely *not* in control. He frowned at her, his eyes narrowing still more as they held her gaze. He was—no surprise—the black-haired half of the pair who'd come chasing after her across the lobby. The mean-looking one.

"FBI," said the other, fair-haired half of the pair as he came panting up in time to hear her question.

FBI. Maddie's stomach dropped all the way to her toes. This was far worse even than she had expected, worse than she would have dreamed. Suddenly unable to draw a breath, she glanced his way. He opened the wallet that was already in his hand to flash something—Maddie presumed it was his ID—at her. Panic swamped her, leaving her too unnerved to focus, much less to try to ascertain whether or not whatever he was waving in her face was the real thing. This guy was huge, maybe six-four, six-five, overweight, with a big beer belly that was not flattered by the scarlet hula girl dancing across his middle. Flushed and sweaty, he looked like he'd just run a marathon in the swampy heat outside. A forest of tiny dark gold ringlets sprang up around his head, giving him the appearance of a giant cherub on summer vacation. Anyone who looked less like an FBI agent would be hard to find.

Except maybe the frowning street bum directly in front of her.

Still, she didn't doubt for so much as an instant that they were what he claimed. There was something about him, about the pair of them, that practically screamed *feds.* She should have realized it from the first. Maybe, somewhere deep inside, she *had* realized it from the first. Maybe that's why her eyes had been drawn to them to begin with. Maybe that's why she had felt such alarm on realizing that they were heading her way.

"What do you want?" she asked, her mouth so dry that her voice sounded croaky. Like she had no idea. Like she hadn't been dreading this day for years. Like she hadn't expected that sooner or later they would show up . . .

"To talk to you." The black-haired man took a step toward her so that he was once again close enough to make her feel crowded. She could see the tiny lines around his eyes, the deeper ones bracketing his mouth. Too close. Oh, God, she couldn't deal with this. She wasn't ready. *She wasn't ready.* Her stomach did its best imitation of a pretzel. Her heart was already pounding so hard that she was surprised he couldn't see its panicked beating beneath her thin silk shell.

Things had been going so well, she mourned. *At least, they had been going so well until someone had tried to kill her . . .*

"I'm Special Agent Sam McCabe. This"—McCabe threw a quick glance over his shoulder at the larger man—"is Special Agent E. P. Wynne. You *are* Madeline Fitzgerald, right?"

What are my choices here? Maddie asked herself wildly in the split second before she replied. With escape no longer even remotely possible, they were basically down to two: tell the truth—or lie.

"Yes," she said, and to her own surprise her voice sounded perfectly calm. Or maybe it wasn't so surprising after all. The first hot rush of panic had receded; she was cold now, icy cold, so cold that her lips felt bloodless, her fingers and toes numb. Her pulse raced; her palms were damp; goose-bumps prickled her arms. But she looked steadily back at him, meeting his gaze without, she hoped, giving any of her inner turmoil away.

Play the hand out. She could almost hear her father saying it. *It's not over till it's over.*

She had to force herself to breathe.

"We want to ask you a few questions about what happened last night," McCabe continued. "Do you have a minute?"

About what happened last night. It was so unexpected that it was disorienting. Maddie blinked once as the words sank in. Her lungs deflated like a punctured balloon as all the air suddenly whooshed out. They wanted to talk to her about *last night*. Waves of relief washed over her. Of *course* they wanted to talk to her about last night, she scolded herself. What else could they possibly want to talk to her about?

What else indeed, she thought, still feeling faintly dizzy. Still, the sooner she got away from them the better. She needed a little time to recover her composure, at the very least.

As shaken as she was, it would be way too easy to let something slip.

She got a grip and shook her head.

"Actually, I'm late as it is. I have an important meeting in just a few minutes. And you made me miss my elevator." The faintly accusing note in her voice as she said that last was, she thought, pitch-perfect for the occasion.

"Sorry about that," the big one—Wynne—said with an apologetic grimace.

"Could you come with us, please?" McCabe reached for her arm again. This guy obviously wasn't used to hearing the word *no*. His fingers slid around her elbow, making her glad for the long sleeve of her jacket, which kept him from touching her skin. As his grip tightened, she felt as if the marble walls of the lobby were closing in on her. Suddenly, she felt like she was suffocating.

Déjà vu all over again, she thought with a stab of near hysteria. Here was one more FBI agent doing his level best to intimidate her. Only this time, it wasn't happening. This time, she was all grown-up.

The thought put some steel back in her spine.

"Sorry, Mr. Special Agent, I really am in a hurry." Her voice was cool as she pulled her arm free for a second time. "What is it, exactly, that you want to know?"

McCabe's lips compressed with obvious displeasure. His eyes darkened, seemed to weigh her. Whatever he saw in her face must have convinced him that the only way he was dragging her off somewhere was if she went kicking and screaming, because he didn't try to grab her again.

Which was a good thing. Making a scene was the last thing she wanted to do. Although, if she had to, she would.

He glanced around as if to assure himself that no one except his oversized friend was near enough to overhear, took a step forward, and lowered his voice. "You were a guest at the Holiday Inn Express on Peyton Place Boulevard last night, right?"

"Yes."

He was crowding her. Maybe deliberately, maybe not. Either way, his nearness made it an effort to breathe. Stepping out of his path was not an option. With the wall at her back, she had no place to go.

"Can you tell me what happened?"

Between shattered nerves and no sleep, she wasn't quite operating on all cylinders, and she knew it. Still, his interest made no sense. She knew the kinds of things the FBI investigated, and an attack on an anonymous woman that hadn't even resulted in significant injury was way beneath their notice. Was there something here that she was missing? Or were they playing with her?

The thought was galvanizing. It made her palms grow damp.

Don't panic, she warned herself even as she looked at him warily.

"Since when does the FBI care about stuff like that?"

"Since now," he said. "Could you just answer the question, please?"

For a moment their eyes clashed, and the issue hung in the balance. But answering his questions was probably the quickest way to make him go away, Maddie realized, and what she wanted more than anything else in the whole wide world right at that moment was for him and his partner to do just that.

Just keep it short and sweet.

"A man attacked me in my room." She swallowed before she remembered that swallowing hurt. Quite above and beyond her reluctance to have anything whatsoever to do with the FBI, recalling the previous night's near-death experience was not something she wanted to do. If luck, God, whatever had not been on her side, she wouldn't be here now. She would be in the city morgue, with a tag reading *Madeline Fitzgerald* tied to her toe. "Look, I've already gone over this with the police. It should all be in their report."

Never mind that the only reason she had talked to the police was because they had shown up at the hospital and she had been left with no choice. And the only reason she had gone to the hospital in the first place was that Jon had taken advantage of her shocked state to take her there. Mr. Special Agent here didn't know that. All he would see was that in the aftermath of the attack, she had done just exactly what any other upstanding citizen would be expected to do: go to the hospital, talk to the police.

McCabe ignored her attempt to dismiss him. "What time did the attack occur, exactly?"

Maddie made an impatient gesture. "I don't know. I realize it was short-sighted of me, but when I woke up and found a man in my room, it didn't occur to me to check the clock. Sometime between midnight and three is the best I can do. I fell asleep just after midnight, and I was at the hospital by a quarter after three."

Her sarcasm seemed to roll off him like oil off waxed paper. If anything, his expression grew more intent. "Did you get a look at him?"

Maddie repressed a shiver as she remembered the terrifying bulk of the man.

"No."

"Nothing? Not even a glimpse? Come on, you must have seen something."

"I didn't see anything, okay? It was dark. No."

Their eyes clashed. A beat passed.

"So walk me through what happened, step-by-step."

Maddie took a deep breath.

"It upsets me to talk about it, you know? If you want details, read the po-lice report." Her stomach was doing its twisty thing again. The urge to es-cape was so strong that she could practically feel the muscles twitching beneath her skin. But escape was impossible for the moment. With the elevator gone, there was, once again, no place to go. That being the case, she needed to not lose it with him, she reminded herself. She needed to stay cool, calm, and in control. All the things that at the moment she definitely was not feeling.

His eyes slid over her face. He rocked back on his heels, folded his arms over his chest, and appeared to consider her.

"Is it my imagination, or am I sensing some hostility here?"

Oh, God. Careful.

She had to fight the urge to swallow. He was watching her too closely for such a telltale action to pass unnoticed.

"I just don't see the value in going over this umpteen times. Like I said, it upsets me." Her voice turned tart. "Anyway, aren't you the FBI? Don't you always get your man? So why don't you go get him, and stop harassing me?"

"That's the Mounties," McCabe said dryly, as, unable to help herself, Maddie cast a longing glance to her left.

Where, oh where, was that fricking elevator?

"Miz Fitzgerald . . ."

As if on cue, the elevator closest to them arrived with a *ding*. The doors opened, and a gush of people spilled out into the lobby.

Thank God.

She met his gaze, summoning the best she could manage in the way of an "it's been nice" smile.

"Look, I really have to go. Like I said, I already went over the whole thing with the police. You should be able to get whatever you need from them."

With that and a dismissive nod, Maddie stepped away from the wall and turned to battle her way through the once again surging crowd. Using her briefcase as a makeshift battering ram, she managed to wedge her way through the stream of riders disembarking and make it onto the emptying elevator ahead of the hordes still more or less politely waiting their turn.

It did her absolutely no good.

"Miz Fitzgerald . . ."

McCabe was right behind her, damn him, his Southern drawl unmistakable, persistent as a dog after a pork chop as he followed her toward the back of the car. Finding herself nose to nose with the gleaming brass wall as a jostling crowd filled the elevator, Maddie tensed as she realized that, once again, she had nowhere to go. Seconds later she experienced a sudden sinking feeling in the pit of her stomach. Glancing up, she discovered that, sure enough, he still loomed like the big bad wolf behind her and was, in fact, watching her reflection. For a moment their gazes met and held. They stared at each other, a pair of faintly blurred golden images apparently equally surprised to find their gazes colliding in a too-shiny wall.

Her stomach clenched.

Then, *be cool*, Maddie ordered herself fiercely, and pulled her gaze from his. Grabbing hold of her vacillating courage with both hands, she turned around, deliberately bumping his legs with her briefcase and forcing him to step back a pace.

"Sorry," she said in a voice as bland as milk. Then, to the group at large, "Could someone hit fifty for me, please?"

"Fifty. Got it," a man replied from the front.

With a slight lurch the elevator headed up. A glance around the packed car told her that McCabe was alone. His supersized friend hadn't made it on board.

Like the proverbial elephant in the room, he was impossible to ignore. But she tried, staring ahead at the elevator doors. Unfortunately, they too were made of brass.

Their eyes collided in the reflective wall. He was, she realized, once again watching her reflection. Since ignoring him was proving impossible, she decided to take the war into the enemy's camp.

She turned her head. Their gazes met, but this time without the softening buffer of the brass.

"Are you *following* me?" That the question was muttered almost under her breath in no way detracted from the force with which she said it.

"Looks like it, doesn't it?" He gave her the smallest of mocking smiles.

Maddie scowled. She fumed. She thought. Then, after an ostentatious glance down at her watch, she met his gaze again.

"Look, I have a really important business meeting in exactly seventeen minutes," she said, low-voiced. "What, exactly, does it take to make you disappear?"

FIVE

alk to me," McCabe said, his voice equally low. "Five minutes of your time. That's all I need."

"Then you swear you'll go away?"

"Cross my heart."

"Fine." Maddie glared at him. Whatever happened, she couldn't let him follow her up to the fiftieth floor, where Brehmer's Pet Food reigned supreme. Not unless she was prepared to kiss the account good-bye. She would give him five minutes. She would be super-careful. And then, if she was lucky, he would be satisfied and go away, and leave her to get on with her life.

Except that someone had tried to kill her last night.

The elevator slid to a stop and the door opened.

"Is this the third floor? Could you let me out, please?" A woman on the other side of the car was edging toward the front. Maddie found herself wedged even more tightly against the back wall as the population of the elevator shifted. It was so crowded that several people were forced to step out into the corridor to let the woman exit.

"Come on, then," Maddie muttered with a resentful glance up at McCabe, and used her briefcase to clear a path. When both she and McCabe had been disgorged, the elevator doors closed behind them. The woman who'd gotten off just before them was already walking away. A gold-framed mirror hung above a walnut console table on the wall directly in front of the elevators. *Funny,* Maddie thought, catching a glimpse of her reflection, except for the big bad wolf beside her—who, incidentally, was once again wrapping his hand around her arm—she looked unchanged. No one seeing her would guess that icy shivers chased one another up and down her spine or that her legs felt like rubber bands. A quick look around told her that to the left was a solid wall, covered like the others in blue-patterned wallpaper. To the right, the hall opened up into what looked like a mezzanine level. Groupings of beige leather couches and chairs stood in front of a polished metal rail that gave promise of a large open area below. At the far side of the open space, a towering wall of windows provided a panoramic view of cerulean sky peeking out between the surrounding skyscrapers.

"This way." McCabe took charge again, pulling her along beside him as he headed toward the mezzanine.

Maddie jerked her arm free and kept walking. His eyes cut sideways at her, but he didn't say anything.

By this time she had absorbed a great deal of visual information about him, starting with the fact that he was at least six feet tall, or maybe even a little taller. Even in heels, she had to look up to meet his gaze. He was swarthy-skinned, muscular, with a wrestler's powerful build. His hair was short, black, untidy. He had thick, straight, black eyebrows above heavy-lidded eyes that were, at the moment, bloodshot, with puffy bags beneath. His cheekbones were flat, almost Slavic, his nose was blunt with a bump on the bridge, his mouth was well shaped but thin, with, at the moment, a sardonic twist. He had a long, square jaw that angled sharply into a strong chin. He badly needed a shave, a change of clothes, and, from the looks of it, a shower, too. She pegged his age at somewhere in the mid-thirties, though it was hard to tell past the smirk and the bristles, which had left the five-o'clock–shadow stage behind about three days back. Despite all the muscles, though, he wasn't a hottie by any stretch of the imagination; he was way too scruffy and way too thuggish-looking for that.

Besides, as far as she was concerned, the terms *FBI agent* and *hottie* were mutually exclusive.

He walked all the way to the rail before turning to look at her. His eyes flickered as they moved over her, registering something, but she couldn't tell what it was. Didn't care what it was. Unless it was recognition, but now that she was growing calmer, she didn't see how it could possibly be that.

If he knew the truth about her, she was all but certain that she would already be well aware of it.

"The clock's ticking." Her voice was frosty as she stopped perhaps two feet away from him. As she had guessed, the area beyond him, beyond the rail, was open space with a view of the restaurant below. The restaurant wasn't busy; only a few tables were occupied. A pair of escalators ran up and down, with about half a dozen people traveling in each direction. Farther along the mezzanine, long tables had been set up. A small crowd was gathered in front of the tables, intent on whatever business had brought them there. Waiters carrying loaded trays flitted in and out of the conference room beyond. A buzz of muted conversation provided background noise. The smell of coffee hung in the air.

Maddie inhaled the fumes longingly. She'd already drunk so much coffee that morning in an effort to keep herself awake and functional that she was pretty sure that if she cut herself she would bleed java, but the energizing effects of even that much caffeine were beginning to wear off.

"You want coffee?" he asked.

Her lips thinned. "No," she lied.

"Are you always this friendly, or am I just getting lucky here?" McCabe leaned back against the rail, gripping it with a hand on either side of surprisingly lean hips. He looked a whole heck of a lot more at ease than she felt. Which wasn't surprising. *He* hadn't been nearly murdered during the night. *He* wasn't being interviewed by the FBI. And *he*, presumably, didn't have anything to hide.

"I told you, I have a meeting." Her tone was abrupt. With light from the windows pouring over him, he looked more like a street tough than ever. Then she realized that his back was to the windows. Hers was not. With a little frisson of unease, she became aware that the light was spilling onto her face, revealing every nuance of her every expression to him.

Careful, she warned herself again, and broke eye contact to glance down at her fingers, which she had just realized were cramping from clutching the handle of her briefcase so hard. Shifting it to the other hand, she made a little production of stretching her fingers out to ease the stiffness.

"What do you have in that thing, anyway?" He was looking at the battered brown briefcase now instead of her face. It was the old-fashioned kind, soft-sided, satchel shaped, with a strap securing the top. It was also clearly full to the point of bursting.

"My laptop. Some files. Sketches. Things I need for the presentation I have to make in"—she consulted her watch—"fifteen minutes." She frowned at him. "Look, if all you want to do is make small talk, I don't have time."

"Presentation for what? What do you do?" Folding his arms across his chest, he looked prepared to stay where he was all day. Feeling as if she was about to jump out of her skin with the urgency of her desire to get this over with and get away from him, Maddie registered his posture and stewed.

"I own an advertising agency. We're small, we're struggling. The account I'm about to make a pitch to is huge. Landing it would change everything for us."

"I see." His gaze met hers, and suddenly his manner became all business. "What's the name of your agency? For the record."

"Creative Partners."

"And you're the owner?"

"Yes."

"Sole owner?"

"Yes."

His gaze swept her. "Kind of young to own an advertising agency, aren't you?"

Maddie bristled. "As far as I know, there's no minimum age for owning a business."

"All right." His gaze swept her again, as though trying to guess the age she had deliberately not told him. He did not, however, ask her outright. Not that he needed to: Her date of birth was in the police report, which she had little doubt he would obtain in due course. "Your advertising agency is headquartered where?"

"Saint Louis." That was in the police report, too. Damn Jon anyway for making her go to the hospital! She should have guessed that the hospital would call the police. Not that she could blame the whole sorry debacle on Jon. Shocked or not, she was the one who knew the score, and she should have had more sense than to go.

"And that's where you live?"

"Yes."

"You're here in New Orleans because . . . ?"

She shifted impatiently. "I told you, to pitch this account. We—my associate and I—flew in from Saint Louis yesterday."

"What's your associate's name?"

"Jon Carter."

"Were you meeting anyone at the hotel? A relative, maybe, who was staying there, too? Someone with a name similar to yours?"

Maddie frowned. "No."

"Okay. What time did your flight get in?"

"About four-fifteen."

"What did you do after the plane landed? Did you go directly to the hotel?"

"Yes. Jon and I checked in, walked over to the French Quarter, grabbed some dinner, came back, worked on our presentation, and went to bed."

"Separate rooms?"

"Yes. Look, is this actually leading somewhere?" Maddie glanced ostentatiously at her watch again. A faint *ding* behind her heralded the arrival of another elevator. She wanted to turn tail and board it in the worst way. Footsteps and the faint rustle of clothing announced the sudden influx of more people, most of whom seemed to be making for the tables in front of the conference rooms.

Play the hand out.

"You never know." McCabe made a gesture at someone behind her. Maddie glanced around to see a waiter headed their way. He was carrying a tray laden with a coffeepot, cups and saucers, and dessert plates holding tiny pastries in fluted white paper doilies. "I need coffee. Sure you don't want any?"

Before she could answer, the waiter reached them. He was young and African-American with close-cropped hair and a thin build, dressed in the traditional tux.

"Yes, sir?" The waiter was looking past her at McCabe.

"Could I get some coffee, please?" McCabe asked. The fact that the coffee was obviously intended for the attendees at the conference didn't seem to bother him.

"Cream or sugar?" The waiter, having set the tray down on the round glass table beside the nearest couch, poured out a cup and handed it to McCabe, who had shaken his head in answer to the query. McCabe took the cup, and the waiter looked at Maddie.

"Would you like some coffee, Miss?"

"Be a devil," McCabe said, his cup already at his mouth.

The waiter grinned. Maddie shot McCabe a look, but now that an actual caffeine fix was so close at hand the prospect was too tempting to turn down.

"Thank you," she said to the waiter, setting her briefcase down and accepting a cup, complete with the packet of sugar she'd requested stirred in. She would have asked for more than one—a sugar rush was second only to a jolt of caffeine on her list of preferred stimulants—but considering her present company, she decided against it.

"Danish?" the waiter asked, proffering the tray.

McCabe took one. Maddie shook her head and downed a swallow of coffee. It wasn't particularly hot and it wasn't particularly good, but she badly needed the lift she hoped it would give her.

In about twelve minutes, she had to make the sales pitch of a lifetime. On almost no sleep. After being terrorized and nearly murdered just a few hours before. With the FBI sniffing at her heels. And maybe, if her life had really gone down the toilet, the killer still somewhere around. Looking for her.

Life just didn't get much better than that.

"I'll leave some in case you change your mind," the waiter said with a quick smile, and deposited a dessert plate crammed with goodies on the table before leaving. Taking another swallow of coffee, Maddie averted her gaze—her stomach was in such a state that just looking at the gooey confections made her feel unwell—then frowned as McCabe, having disposed of his first small pastry in two quick bites, reached for another one.

"Just so you know, your five minutes are up," Maddie said as the second pastry went the way of the first. She set her still-half-full coffee cup down on the table. "I'm out of here. Enjoy your breakfast."

"Hang on one more minute." He drained his cup and set it down.

"What?" She was already picking up her briefcase.

He wiped his fingers on a napkin. "I want you to tell me everything that happened in your hotel room last night. A blow-by-blow account."

As if his words had conjured it up, the memory of the attack flashed at warp speed through her mind. It was all she could do to repress a shudder.

"Sorry, no can do," she said, straightening with her briefcase once again in hand. "I have to go."

He smiled at her, a slow and distinctly un-charming smile that succeeded in raising her hackles before he ever said a word.

"I could take you into custody." His tone was almost idle. "If that's what it takes to get you to answer my questions."

Her brows snapped together. "Don't mess with me. You have to charge somebody with something to take them into custody. What are you planning to charge me with, being a victim?"

"How about obstructing an investigation?"

Maddie's stomach clenched. She pressed her lips together as her heart skipped a beat, then managed to get hold of herself enough to meet his gaze. His expression was bland. Was he bluffing? Maybe, but she didn't want to find out.

"Okay," she said, hating him. "I'll go over what happened in my hotel room *again*. Then that's *it*, understand? I have to go." She clasped her suddenly cold hands in front of her and glared at him. At least the surge of antipathy she was experiencing toward him was a strong enough emotion to override the shivery terror she felt when she recalled the attack. "I was in bed. Something woke me up. I realized someone was in my room. I slipped out of bed. Two shots—I think it was two, and I think they were shots— were fired into the bed, which thankfully I was no longer in. I ran for the door. He—it was a man—caught me. He . . . he slammed me up against the wall, held me there with his hand around my throat, hit me, and threatened to kill me if I made a sound. Then he—" Despite her determination to make her recitation coldly clinical, Maddie couldn't help the wobble her voice had suddenly developed. She had to pause to take a deep breath before she could continue. "He put duct tape over my mouth and forced me to my knees. I th-thought he was going to shoot me. Kill me."

Despite her best efforts to reveal no hint of weakness, she had to clench her teeth then to keep her voice from shaking. She stopped there, hoping he wouldn't realize that it was because she simply could not continue. Instead of looking at McCabe, she looked past him out the wall of windows. The soft summer sky was such a brilliant blue, complete with fluffy clouds like sleeping lambs—hard to believe that the horror she'd feared for so long could have come home to roost on such a gorgeous day.

But then, maybe it had not—maybe there was some mistake. Maybe she shouldn't be so quick to write off everything she'd worked so hard for. There was always a chance . . .

She could feel McCabe's gaze on her face as she fought to regain her composure.

"But you got away," he said softly after a moment. "How?"

Knowing that he was watching her was, finally, enough to enable her to pull herself together one more time.

She met his gaze head-on. "I had a pencil in my hand. I stabbed him with it. In the leg, I think." Her voice was steady now.

His eyes widened. "You stabbed him in the leg with a pencil?"

Maddie nodded. Remembering how it had felt made her go all woozy. *Breathe,* she told herself. *Just breathe.*

He pursed his lips in a silent whistle. His eyes were now sharp with interest and fixed on her face. "Then what?"

It took her a second. "What do you mean, then what? What do you think? I got out of there."

His lips quirked fractionally. "Could you possibly be a little more specific?"

Maddie took a deep breath and fought for calm. "He let go of me, and I managed to get the door open and get out. The duct tape—I must have pulled it off because I was screaming. A man down the hall heard me and opened his door. I ran into his room. I stayed in there with him and his wife until security got there."

She stopped again. McCabe said nothing for a moment, which was a good thing because with the best will in the world, Maddie didn't think she could have replied. Her heart was thudding, her stomach had twisted itself into a knot, and she was cold all over—so cold that it was all she could do not to shiver visibly.

Finally he asked, "What were their names? The couple in the room?"

She shook her head. "I don't know." It was something of a relief to discover that her voice still worked.

"How long were you in their room?"

"I don't know that, either. Maybe five, ten minutes."

"Where did the guy who attacked you go? Did he follow you? Try to get in?"

"He was chasing me, at first, but . . . I didn't see him again after I ran into that other room. I don't know where he went. He didn't try to get in."

"Did you happen to see him in the lighted hallway?" He was looking at her with an intent expression that reminded her of a cat at a mouse hole. "Maybe you glanced over your shoulder while he was chasing you? Caught a look at his face? Something?"

"I didn't see anything. I just ran." Maddie couldn't help it; she shuddered so hard that he had to see it. Then, catching herself before she could weaken any further, she took a deep breath, then another.

It's over, she told herself. It happened, but she survived. Soon this would be over, too. All she had to do was keep it together. For just a little longer.

He was watching her closely.

"You okay?"

"Fine."

No way was she falling apart in front of him. Quite aside from the fact that he was an *FBI agent,* and an arrogant jerk to boot, there was too much at stake. In fact, nothing less than her entire life.

"You said you stabbed him in the leg with a pencil," McCabe said. Maddie nodded. He continued. "So what happened to the pencil? Did you take it with you when you ran?"

Maddie frowned, trying to remember. Concentrating took a surprising amount of effort. Reliving the events of the previous night—to say nothing of enduring this more recent trauma—had left her feeling drained and disoriented.

"No, I . . . after I stabbed him I let go. Maybe it was still in his leg. Maybe it fell. I don't know."

He nodded. "Okay. What about a description? Even if you didn't see him, you must have gotten some impressions about what he looked like. Was he taller than you, for example?"

Maddie wet her lips. "He was taller than me. I was barefoot so he was— maybe six feet or a little less. And . . . and he seemed husky—broad, you know? Not fat but strong." Memory washed over her and she shuddered again. "Very, very strong."

"Anything else? Had he been drinking, for example? Could you smell liquor on his breath?"

"I smelled . . . onions."

"Onions. There you go, there's something we can work with. There are a couple of fast-food places near the hotel. Maybe one of the workers will remember a guy who ordered extra onions." He was studying her. "You married?"

She met his gaze, surprised at the question. "No."

"What about exes? Any disgruntled exes?"

Now she saw where he was going. "No."

"Do you have any enemies that you know of? Anybody who really doesn't like you or who might want to do you harm?"

Maddie could almost feel the color leeching from her face. "No. *No.* There's nobody like that. Nobody."

He was probing too close to the bone—and she was too shaken. He could threaten all he liked, but she'd had enough.

"Okay, that's it. You got way more than your five minutes. And now I've really got to go." She glanced at her watch. "It's almost five till ten."

"Fair enough." McCabe straightened away from the rail. "I'll walk you to the elevator."

No. But she didn't say it aloud. She didn't want to make it more obvious than she already had how very eager she was to get away from him. If she could just keep her cool for another couple minutes, he would be history— just one more unpleasant chapter in her life. And a very small unpleasant chapter, at that. She turned, but she was still so rattled that she was clumsy. The corner of her briefcase hit the table and knocked it over. Table, crockery, coffee, and pastries went flying.

"Oh, dear!" Thanks to the sound-deadening properties of the carpet, it was more of a rattle than a crash, but as Maddie stared down in dismay at the mess she was suddenly conscious of being the cynosure of dozens of pairs of eyes. Even as she watched, the mud-colored puddle that was her leftover coffee was being soaked up by thirsty dark-blue carpet fibers. Her cup—identifiable because it rested at the apex of the puddle—lay on its side beside the overturned table. His had rolled closer to the rail. The plate that had held the pastries was right side up, but the pastries themselves were scattered everywhere.

Instinctively, Maddie crouched to clean up the mess. She righted her cup, then reached for the pastries. Scooping one up, she returned it to its plate, then picked up another. This one had sticky yellow custard oozing out the sides that got all over her fingers.

"I'll do that, ma'am." The same waiter who had brought the coffee squatted beside her, dropping a handful of gold cloth napkins beside the shrinking puddle. Grabbing one, murmuring an apology for her clumsiness, Maddie stood and wiped her fingers while the waiter blotted the mess. A quick glance at her watch made her heart lurch. In three minutes she would be late. She dropped the napkin on the table the waiter had just flipped upright again, added a couple dollars for his trouble, and grabbed her briefcase.

"It's been fun," she said to McCabe, and without waiting for any response, she headed for the elevator.

To her annoyance, he fell into step beside her.

"Any other details come to mind about the guy who attacked you? Length of hair? Beard?"

"I . . . don't think he had a beard." Terrifying memories of being slammed against a wall replayed themselves in her head. She seemed to remember her hand brushing a smooth jaw. "I don't know about his hair."

"What was he wearing? Long sleeves? Short sleeves? Shorts? Tennis shoes? Sandals? Try to remember as much as you can." McCabe spoke from behind her now as she punched the elevator button with considerably more force than the action called for.

"Long sleeves, long pants—" She was going all shivery again, and, especially at such a critical moment, this she did not need. Stepping back into the center of the hall, she rounded on him. "You said if I answered your questions you'd go away."

"The thing is, I'm not done asking questions yet."

"Well, Mr. Special Agent, here's a newsflash: I'm done answering them."

His eyes moved over her face, turned thoughtful. "You know, most people can't wait to tell us their story. Where we usually run into problems is getting them to shut up."

An icy finger of warning slid down her spine.

"It's two minutes until ten," she snapped, taking desperate refuge in the truth. "At ten, I'm scheduled to be at a meeting that means the world to me. I can't be late, and I can't screw this up. The account's worth a lot of money, and my company needs it. *Really* needs it. Without it, Creative Partners might not survive the year."

Their gazes met and held. The elevator *ding*-ed.

"I'll be in touch," he said, stepping back.

Though he almost certainly hadn't intended it as such, to Maddie that was as dire a threat as any she'd ever heard.

The elevator was packed. Under normal circumstances, she would have waited for the next one. But she was out of time, so she wedged herself in at the front of the car without looking at McCabe again.

"Fifty, please," she said to the woman nearest the buttons. She could feel McCabe's eyes on her. Unable to help herself, she glanced at him as the elevator doors started to slide shut. He was frowning, watching her—and then the elevator doors closed and cut off her view.

But she could still see him in her mind's eye, arms crossed over his chest, feet planted apart, his eyes narrowed, his expression—thoughtful. Or—oh, God—had it been suspicious?

Of course not, she scolded herself. She was imagining things, a victim of her own guilty knowledge. He had no reason, none whatsoever, to suspect that she was anything other than what she appeared to be: an innocent crime victim.

But telling herself that didn't help. As the elevator carried her upward, her knees were about as solid as Jell-O. Her pulse raced. Her stomach tanked.

Imagination or not, she could practically hear the hounds baying at her heels.

SIX

"W here've you been?" Jon greeted her with a frantic whisper as she
stepped off the elevator. He was there right in front of the elevator banks in the hall on the fiftieth floor, and he looked vastly relieved to
see her. "Susan already came out to take us into the meeting. I told her you
were in the ladies' room. She'll be back any second."

Just like that, she was thrown into deep water again. Like the survivor she
was, she swam. Clamping down on emotions that threatened to swamp her,
lifting her chin and straightening her spine, Maddie concentrated on drawing back inside the cool shell that kept others from seeing more of her than
she cared for them to see. The elevator had stopped—and stopped, and
stopped—until at last she, the only person left, had made it all the way to
the top.

When the doors opened, it was three minutes past ten.

"The FBI wanted to ask me some questions about last night," she said,
also whispering. "The guy at the elevator downstairs—he was FBI."

"I know." His reply was impatient. "God, do you think I wouldn't have turned this place upside down if I'd thought some stranger had grabbed you? I got off as quickly as I could and called security. They checked with the guard at the front desk, who told them about those guys being from the FBI." Jon paused for an instant, then added, as an obvious afterthought, "How did the FBI get into this, anyway?"

"I have no idea."

Time for a subject change. Maddie was almost relieved when a bright voice behind them asked, "All ready now?"

"Susan," Jon said, cranking the charm up to full wattage as he turned from Maddie to beam at Susan Allen. "This is Madeline Fitzgerald, Creative Partners's owner and CEO. And my boss."

"So nice to finally meet you, Ms. Allen." Shaking hands, Maddie likewise turned on as much charm as she could muster. A quick look told Maddie that Mrs. Brehmer's assistant, whom she had spoken to on the phone numerous times but had never before met, was a tall, thin, flat-chested woman with a long face and narrow, not particularly attractive, features. She wore her mouse-brown hair straight and earlobe-length, with a too-short fringe of bangs, and if she had on any makeup other than a touch of pale pink lipstick, Maddie couldn't tell. Her skirted suit was a severe black that did nothing for either her figure or her sallow complexion. Her pale blue eyes, seen through rimless glasses, looked Maddie over anxiously.

"Susan, please. I'm so glad you wore a skirt," Susan said under her breath as she gestured at them to follow her. "I meant to warn you and I forgot. Mrs. B *hates* to see a woman wearing pants. She probably would have canceled the meeting as soon as she saw you."

On that reassuring note, they reached a sleek metal door, which Susan opened.

"Here they are," she announced to the people within, and stepped aside for Maddie, with Jon behind her, to enter.

Five people were seated around the long table in the center of the conference room. As Maddie walked in, five pairs of eyes immediately focused on her. Glancing around nervously, Maddie realized with a sinking feeling that nobody was smiling. Plastering a big smile on her own face, she had one coherent thought as she extended her hand and headed for the grim-faced woman at the head of the table: She now knew just exactly how Daniel must have felt when he got thrown into the lion's den.

SAM GOT off the elevator in the lobby to find Wynne, still chewing his gum, sprawled in a chair waiting for him.

"She give you any trouble?" Wynne asked, standing up as Sam joined him.

"Nah."

"I didn't think she would. She seemed kind of antsy, though."

"Yeah."

" 'Course, I might be, too, if somebody had just attacked me in my hotel room a few hours before."

"Maybe." Sam gave Wynne the abridged version of what Madeline Fitzgerald had told him. As he spoke, the two of them headed toward the wall of tinted glass that marked the entrance to the building. The line at the security desk was nearly as long as it had been when they'd rushed inside earlier, but its length was no longer a problem. At least, not for them. Not that it had been before, either. They'd felt no compunction whatsoever about bypassing it.

"So what d'you think?" Wynne asked finally.

"I think he made a mistake. I think she just might be the break we've been looking for." Sam pushed through the revolving door, walking into swampy heat that felt as though it had increased tenfold during the brief period he had been inside. The sun was now a big, hazy yellow fireball hanging just above the jagged city skyline. It seemed to pulsate with energy, broiling the pavement, glaring off the roofs of passing cars, turning the windows fronting the street into shiny, black walls of one-way glass.

"You don't think she was the intended target?" Wynne caught up to him again, and they headed toward the parked Saturn, paying scant attention to the mix of tourist- and business-types that crowded the sidewalk around them. The shuffle of dozens of moving bodies was almost drowned out by

the cacophony of traffic sounds. Whiffs of something sweet and doughy—
a quick glance identified a mobile beignet stand on the nearest corner; the
sizzle of dough being dropped into hot grease added to the ambient noise—
overlay the combination of coffee, sugar, and humidity that made up The
Big Easy's distinctive smell.

"One thing's for sure: They both weren't."

Reaching the car, Sam saw the Day-Glo orange slip of paper tucked beneath his windshield wiper and groaned. The Bureau was tightening up on
expenses as part of its big push to make itself leaner and meaner in this era
of the extremely expensive war on terrorism, and Smolski had interpreted
that to mean that miscellaneous expenses like parking tickets were basically
the problem of the agent who incurred them. A quick glance at the parking
meter showed the red flag up.

Shit.

"Didn't you feed the meter?" he asked Wynne in a tone of purest disgust,
plucking the ticket from its berth as he walked around the front of the car.

"Didn't you?" Wynne countered. They exchanged measuring looks over
the Saturn's roof, then opened the doors and got in. The car was white with
black vinyl upholstery, which meant that the interior was hot as an oven.
Sam immediately pulled his 9mm free of his waistband and placed it on top
of the console between the seats. Without a jacket, a shoulder holster was
no good; without a shoulder holster, the most convenient place to carry a
weapon was nestled into the small of his back. Wynne followed suit, then
flipped a section of newspaper that was in the car for just that purpose over
their mini-arsenal while Sam turned the ignition on. As hot, stale air blasted
from the air-conditioning vents, he and Wynne both choked and hit the
buttons that lowered their windows.

"So, you planning to turn that in on expenses?" Wynne asked. The strong
scent of grape Dubble Bubble was slowly weakening as the suffocating air
inside the car was displaced by the sweltering air outside.

Sam glanced down at the ticket in his hand and snorted expressively.
Then he crumpled it up and tossed it out the window.

"Never saw it."

"Good call," Wynne said. The air coming out of the vents was actually cooler than the air outside now, so they both rolled up their windows.

Sam dug around in his pocket for his cell phone. "Keep your eye open for the Fitzgerald woman. I don't think she'll be out this soon, but you never know."

Wynne nodded and settled back in his seat, his eyes on the building they'd just left, as Sam punched buttons.

"Hey, handsome," Gardner said.

"Way to answer the phone," Sam groused. "Real professional. Listen, I need a quick background check on this other Madeline Fitzgerald. She owns an advertising agency in St. Louis. Name's Creative Partners."

"Creative Partners." Gardner sounded like she was writing it down. "Okay, I'll check her out."

"And I want to make sure that somebody took an evidence kit over to the hotel room she was attacked in, did a test for blood on the rug, fingerprints, hairs, that kind of thing. Also, check on the whereabouts of a pencil. Possibly bloody."

"A possibly bloody pencil?"

"She claims she stabbed the UNSUB in the leg with it. For all I know, New Orleans PD has it. Or maybe it's still just lying around in the room. Wherever it is, I want it found, and if there's blood on it, I want the DNA test results back quick."

"Yes, oh, master."

Sam ignored that. "What about the security cameras in the hotel? They get anything?"

"Unfortunately, they're the kind that tape over themselves every thirty minutes. Apparently nobody got to them in time."

"Way to run an investigation." Sam puffed out air. "You turn up anything on the dead one?"

"Just what I told you before: longtime resident of Natchitoches, forty-six years old, grown daughter, saleswoman for Davidson-Wells, a pharmaceutical firm, been with the company for four years, in New Orleans for just the one night on business, messy divorce finalized three months ago. Liked to gamble. Regular at the horse tracks, casinos. Oh, yeah, there is one more thing: Her husband's served time for aggravated assault."

"So how's his alibi for last night holding up?"

"So far it's holding."

"We got a time of death?"

"Same as before: between ten p.m., when she was last seen, and three a.m., when the body was found."

"Is that the best they can do?" On TV, forensic specialists managed to nail the time of death almost to the minute. In real life, at least in his real life, nothing was ever that simple. Or that exact.

" 'Fraid so."

"Let me know when you get something on the other one."

"You got it," Gardner said. Then, as Sam pulled the phone from his ear, about to break the connection, he was almost sure he heard her add, "Sweet cheeks."

Wynne, clearly having heard the same thing, grinned at him as Sam stared at the phone for a beat before recollecting himself and clicking it closed.

"Woman wants it bad," Wynne said. "When you planning to put her out of her misery?"

Sam shook his head. "Not anytime soon."

"Hey, you haven't had a girlfriend since Lauren dumped you last year. Why not give Gardner a whirl?"

"Lauren didn't dump me"—actually, she had, after six months of increasingly acrimonious complaints about the amount of time Sam spent on the Job—"and anyway, I got a rule about sleeping with women I work with. Why start something when you know going in that it's gonna end up being nothing but bad news?"

"Because Gardner's built like a brick shithouse."

"Yeah, and she's got the personality of a pit bull."

Wynne's grin widened. "Who cares?"

"So you give her a whirl."

"It's not me she wants to hook up with. It's you." Wynne gave him an exaggerated leer. "Sweet cheeks."

"All right, give it a rest, would you?" Sam wasn't in the mood for Wynne's teasing. He was so tired that his eyes felt grainy, and his stomach was leaving him in no doubt that it didn't appreciate the breakfast he'd commandeered on the fly. "Can we get back to work here?"

"Sure." Wynne was still grinning.

Sam refused to notice. "Okay, here's what I think we've got going on: Obviously, one of our Madeline Fitzgeralds was attacked by mistake. How could the killer have guessed there would be two women with the same name staying at the same hotel on the same night? I don't think he realized. I think he went to one of their rooms, killed or tried to kill whichever one was inside, somehow found out that he had made a mistake, and went after the other. The question is, which one did he mean to kill?"

"Good question." Wynne, pondering, smacked his Duble Bubble thoughtfully. "At a guess, I'd say the one who's dead. Gambling's a red flag. Maybe she owed somebody money. Hell, maybe they all owed somebody money. Maybe that's the link."

"We got no evidence that Judge Lawrence"—the esteemed judge had been the first victim, found with two bullet holes in his temple in his family's mansion in Richmond, Virgina; the fact that he was a longtime acquaintance of Smolski's was what had brought Sam into the case—"ever gambled, much less owed anybody money. Or Dante Jones, either, for that matter."

Dante Jones, a used-car dealer from Atlanta, had been the second victim. Allison Pope, a retiree in Jacksonville, Florida, had been the third.

"If Dante Jones didn't gamble, it's the only vice he didn't have."

"True," Sam said.

"Anyway, that girl in there—Madeline Fitzgerald—she doesn't seem like the type that would merit a professional hit. Too young, for one thing."

"What you mean is, too attractive." He and Wynne had been together for going on five years now, and Sam knew how his partner's mind worked.

Wynne grinned. "Actually, *hot* is more the word I was thinking of."

"Yeah, well, being hot doesn't mean you can't get yourself whacked, you know."

Wynne hooted. "There you go, I knew it. You think she's hot, too. So don't go bustin' my balls, pard."

"Whether she's hot or not isn't the point. The point is, she's alive."

"Yeah, baby."

Sam slid down a little in his seat, resting his head back against the headrest and folding his arms over his chest, and considered his options. Getting comfortable was probably a mistake, but to hell with it. He was so tired he felt practically boneless. So tired he felt practically brainless. It took real effort just to stay awake.

"Which is another reason I think she wasn't the intended target," Sam said. "But whether she was or wasn't—and we just don't know at this point—the fact remains that she was attacked and is still around to tell the tale. And our guy won't like that."

Wynne's eyes widened. "Good point. So what are we going to do?"

"For now, keep our distance and watch our survivor. And pray that the bastard doesn't like to leave loose ends."

". . . AND GIVE FIDO something to bark about," Maddie concluded on an upbeat note that belied the throbbing in her head. Standing in front of the room, she looked at the video of the pink tutu–attired Jack Russell terrier balancing on its hind legs while it barked at a bag of Brehmer's Dog Chow that was being lifted away by an elephant's trunk, and thought, *This is good. They've got to like this.*

The thought was revivifying.

Then she turned away from the screen to glance around the table and got a horrible sinking feeling in the pit of her stomach.

Or not, she concluded. Forget the chuckles she'd been hoping for. Not one of the six people present besides herself and Jon had so much as cracked a smile since the two of them had entered the room.

Time to face the truth: The presentation wasn't going well. Maddie could sense the flatness in the air as Jon turned off the projector and clicked the lights back on. Someone hit a button and the blinds that covered the windows slid up with a motorized *whirr,* flooding the room with bright sunlight. Beyond the windows, New Orleans baked. The sun glared off the steel sheathing of the skyscrapers that crowded the skyline like unevenly spaced teeth. In the distance, she caught the merest glimpse of the deep marine blue of the Gulf of Mexico, where it met the azure sky. *Blue sky, blue water, blue steel—all that blue was a good match for her mood,* Maddie thought glumly. Glancing around the conference table again, waiting with bated breath for a comment, any comment, that might give her a little badly needed encouragement, she realized that no one was meeting her gaze.

Uh-oh. Bad sign.

The quartet of suits, which was how she'd quickly come to think of the four sixtyish, buttoned-down businessmen who actually ran the company, appeared underwhelmed. Howard Bellamy, Brehmer's Pet Food's tall, distinguished, silver-haired president and chief operating officer, was fiddling with his pencil. Emil White, the bald, hook-nosed executive vice president in charge of marketing, who was sitting beside him, had turned sideways in his seat and was staring past his beach ball–sized belly at the shiny tip of his cordovan wing tips. Lawrence Thibault, executive vice president in charge of product development, who was seated across the table from White, was already typing something into the laptop that rested on the table in front of him and appeared completely oblivious to what was going on in the rest of the room. *Forget trying to decipher his expression,* Maddie thought despairingly. He was slouched so far down in his chair that all she could see of him over the laptop's monitor was the top of his head, which was covered by an expensive-looking jet-black rug. Seated beside Thibault, stocky, grizzled James Oliver, executive vice president in charge of finance, pushed his wire-rimmed glasses down his nose, steepled his fingers under his chin, and looked at Bellamy. From the beginning, he'd made Maddie think of a basset hound with his worried frown and small, sad brown eyes, and he was looking sadder than ever now, which could not be considered promising. Standing not far from Maddie, Susan Allen absently chewed a fingernail and frowned as she watched Mrs. Brehmer, who was, of course, sitting at the head of the table. Following Susan's gaze, Maddie decided that the old lady looked a lot more formidable on her own turf than Maddie remembered her. Of course, they'd met only once previously, three months before at an awards banquet sponsored by the St. Louis Chamber of Commerce, where Mrs. Brehmer, herself a former winner, had presented Maddie with the Saint Louis Young Woman Business Owner of the Year Award. It was at that dinner that Maddie had suggested to Mrs. Brehmer that hiring Creative Partners might be the solution to the growth problems the old lady was complaining that her company was experiencing. Today's meeting was the result of that conversation.

But if Maddie had been expecting that, because of their mutual ties to St. Louis—all Brehmer's manufacturing was still done there, at the plant that had served the company for half a century, and Mrs. Brehmer retained the original family home there—Mrs. Brehmer would be inclined to look on Creative Partners favorably, she was discovering that she'd been sadly mistaken.

Mrs. Brehmer alone met Maddie's gaze. Her eyes were a soft, faded blue—and as sharp as twin knives.

"Is that circus thing it?" she barked in her hoarse smoker's voice. A tiny, stooped woman, she was dwarfed by her oversized black leather chair—the largest at the table. A triple strand of pearls circled her neck, and she was dressed in a powder-blue suit that Maddie wasn't sure, but suspected, was a genuine Chanel. Her hair was white, short, and perfectly coiffed. Her skin was almost as white as her hair, with the overly taut look that came with too many plastic surgeries. In fact, it had been pulled so tightly that it seemed molded to the bones beneath. Heavily made-up, with lashings of mascara and blush and a bright scarlet mouth, she reminded Maddie irresistibly of the Joker in the Batman movies. Only, Maddie thought, right about now the Joker seemed positively warm and fuzzy in comparison.

"We have other ideas, of course," Maddie said, improvising hastily, because as of the end of that video they were pretty much fresh out. "Take, for example, your packaging."

"What's wrong with our packaging?" Mrs. Brehmer asked, bristling.

"Nothing's wrong with it. Only . . ." Fighting the urge to wet her lips, Maddie turned to gesture at the blowup of the sack of Brehmer's Dog Chow that was standing on an easel in the corner. It was an uninspiring brown with a dark green stripe across one corner, absolutely ripe for a makeover, whether the suggestion had been planned or not. "In today's marketplace, the name of the game is attracting attention. You might want to think about going with brighter colors, perhaps even something as bold as fuchsia or lime green. Research has shown that the primary buyer of pet food is a middle-aged woman with a family, and bright colors have been found to hold the most appeal for her as well as having the added bonus of jumping off the shelf visually."

"*Hmmph,*" Mrs. Brehmer said. "My husband designed that bag himself. Brehmer's Dog Chow has always come in a brown bag." Her gaze slid from Maddie to Susan. Her voice sharpened even as its volume dropped. "You. I need a glass of water."

Susan started.

"Yes, Mrs. B. of course. I'll get it right away," she murmured, and moved toward the door. Since the door was located behind Maddie, Maddie got a good look at Susan's expression as she went by. Instead of rolling her eyes or seeming angry, as Maddie would have expected (actually, one or both of which she probably would have been guilty of herself), Susan merely looked more anxious than ever. Perhaps, Maddie thought, terminal anxiety was her natural expression.

White nodded at Mrs. Brehmer. "That's a good point, Joan. If we change our bag, our customers won't know what to look for. That brown bag is a Brehmer tradition."

The other men nodded agreement.

"We're pretty big on tradition around here, young lady. Somebody should have warned you," Bellamy said to Maddie, wagging his pencil at her. "Fuchsia and lime-green packaging may attract some customers' attention, but it won't tell them that it's *us.*"

"That's where the national advertising campaign comes in, Mr. Bellamy. After they see spots featuring the redesigned bags on TV, your customers *will* know it's Brehmer's, and they will buy, because it's the same quality product they love at the same fair price they're used to paying. And you'll pick up new customers, *younger* customers who will stay with your products for years, because of the new, hip packaging, and fun ads that make them laugh."

Bellamy tapped the eraser end of his pencil on the table and gave a skeptical grunt. Still smiling gamely, Maddie felt almost sick as she read the handwriting on the wall: They weren't going to get the account. After all the expense of coming, the worry and hard work, and the nightmare of last night and today, they were going to come up empty.

It was as clear as the expression on the prospective clients' faces.

Maddie swallowed. If Creative Partners didn't start landing some big accounts soon, the money was going to run out. Their current clients provided more or less steady work, but the billing from them barely covered all the monthly expenses. And, sometimes, it didn't even do that.

Of course, given what had happened last night, she might not have to worry about such mundane matters as company finances much longer . . .

"We're a big believer in tradition ourselves." Jon jumped boldly into the breach when, Maddie realized, she had remained silent too long. All eyes, including Maddie's, turned to him as he joined her in front of the pull-down screen on which the proposed ads had been projected. Maddie was thankful to no longer be the focus of attention. She needed a moment to thrust the memory of last night and the spurt of burgeoning panic that had accompanied it back into the "I'll think about it later" compartment.

An instant later, she caught herself nervously fingering the scarf around her neck, and dropped her hand.

"And, of course, tradition is one of Brehmer's strong points." Jon was in full flow now. "Actually, we think you should emphasize the fact that your business has been family owned and operated for fifty-seven years." Jon moved toward the blowup of the bag. "Besides the fresh new packaging"—he tapped the company's B-in-a-gold-circle logo dramatically—"we suggest giving Brehmer's Pet Food a more human face: yours, in fact, Mrs. Brehmer. Right here, in a gold frame, on every bag of pet food your company produces."

For a moment there was dead silence. Maddie held her breath. She and Jon between them had decided to table that idea, but since nothing else was working she agreed with his reasoning: There was no reason not to try one more shot in the dark. Mrs. Brehmer's eyes widened, and her brows twitched ever so slightly.

What did that mean? Did she like the idea?

Vacillating wildly between despair and hope, Maddie did a quick visual sweep of the table. The men's eyes were now fastened on their boss. Their expressions were frozen, as if they weren't sure how they were supposed to react. They would, Maddie realized, take their cue from Mrs. Brehmer.

"Brown-nosing is not a quality I admire, young man," Mrs. Brehmer snapped. It was all Maddie could do not to sag. Frowning, placing her bony hands with their plethora of rings flat on the table, Mrs. Brehmer seemed prepared to end the meeting. The men shifted in their seats in response, and Maddie feared they were all about to rise.

"Now, hear me out. I'm serious." Exhibiting the kind of never-say-die valor that in Maddie's opinion merited a raise if only she'd had the funds to fund one, which she didn't, Jon held up a hand in protest and somehow kept them in their seats. "Putting his face on his product worked for Dave Thomas with Wendy's. It worked for Harlan Sanders with Kentucky Fried Chicken. You are the soul and spirit of Brehmer's Pet Food, Mrs. Brehmer. Why shouldn't you be the face of it, too?"

Momentarily speechless in the face of such heroic eloquence, Maddie barely managed to stop herself from applauding as she waited with clasped hands and a thudding heart for Mrs. Brehmer's reply.

"Because nobody wants to look at an ugly old woman," Mrs. Brehmer said tartly. "Don't waste your time bullshitting a bullshitter. I may be old, but I'm not stupid." She looked around the table. "Well, gentlemen . . ."

The door opened, and Susan appeared with a glass of water.

"Linda's brought . . ." she began as everyone glanced around, and then chaos erupted behind her. Shrill barks and the scrabble of clawed feet on slick floors were drowned out by a woman's shriek.

"*Ouch!* No! Stop! You come back here! *Zelda!*" The yell came from somewhere down the hall.

"Zelda!" Mrs. Brehmer called, coming to her feet as a foot-tall mop of golden brown hair shot past Susan, who flattened herself against the open door with a gasp and dropped the glass of water. The resulting crash and sound of glass shattering was as loud as an explosion. Maddie jumped. The suits leaped up.

"What the—"

"Look out!"

"There she blows!"

"It's that damned mu—uh, darned dog!"

"You idiot! She'll cut her feet!" bellowed Mrs. Brehmer at Susan, her voice a full-throated roar that all but drowned out the exclamations of her employees as the mop—Maddie realized it was a small, long-haired dog trailing a lavender leash at just about the time it dashed past her feet—ran through the spreading puddle and made a flying leap for the window.

Maddie's mouth dropped open as it crashed headfirst into solid glass. With a single truncated yelp, it then dropped like a stone to lie motionless on the floor.

SEVEN

The dull thud of impact still reverberated in the air as the room erupted.

"Zelda!" Mrs. Brehmer and Susan cried at the same time. Chairs skittered backward as everyone rushed toward the scene of the accident. Because she was closest, Maddie reached the fallen one first. The dog was lying, sprawled on its stomach, looking for all the world like a small fur rug, eyes closed, chin resting on the floor, all four limbs and fluffy tail splayed out flat around it like spokes in a wheel. A small, incongruously perky pink satin bow adorned its head, pulling the long hair between its ears up into a floppy topknot. Except for the flat monkeyish face and the tips of four black-clawed paws, it was all hair. For a moment, as she tentatively placed a hand on the silky coat, Maddie feared the dog was dead. It was motionless, inert, and didn't seem to be breathing. Touching its face, she was not reassured. She didn't know a whole heck of a lot about dogs—she'd never had the chance to own one—but were their noses supposed to be cold?

Having their sales pitch end with the sudden, shocking death of Mrs. Brehmer's pet would plunge this already-nightmarish trip to New Orleans to a whole new low.

"Watch out, she might bite," Susan warned under her breath as Maddie held her fingers in front of the animal's smashed-in-looking nose to see if she could feel air moving. Both Susan and Jon were looming over her, Maddie realized, and the suits were gathering around, too. The rapid clack of Mrs. Brehmer's high heels told Maddie that the old lady was coming on fast from the far end of the table. Not that Maddie glanced around to check. All her attention was focused on the dog.

Nothing. Nada. Not breathing. Or at least, if it was, Maddie couldn't detect it.

"Never saw anything like that in my life. Dog tried to jump right out the window," Mr. Bellamy said.

"Guess she didn't realize we were on the fiftieth floor," Mr. White replied in a hushed voice.

"What do you think it is, a rocket scientist? It's a dog," Mr. Oliver said impatiently. "What does it know about fiftieth floors?"

"Hadn't somebody ought to go call a vet?" Mr. Thibault was the only one of the men who sounded at all concerned for the animal. "Or something?"

"Is she hurt?" Mrs. Brehmer asked. There was a quaver of real fear in her voice.

Maddie hesitated, pressing her fingers right up against the animal's muzzle in a desperate quest to feel it breathing. The prospect of telling Mrs. Brehmer that the pet might be dead appalled her. Not knowing what to say, she rolled an eye up at Susan, who was looking even more appalled than Maddie felt.

No help to be had there.

"I, uh . . ." Maddie began, preparing to stand up and move aside as soon as she broke the bad news in case someone else felt more qualified than she did to attempt doggie CPR. Just then she felt something warm and wet on her fingers. Her gaze shot back to the animal.

"She's licking my hand," she said with relief.

"Give her to me." Mrs. Brehmer strong-armed her way to the front of the group and held out her arms. Instinctively complying, Maddie gathered up the dog and stood. For all its seeming stockiness, it was surprisingly lightweight, she discovered, not much heavier than a good-sized cat. The abundant hair gave visual bulk to a tiny body.

"She's moving," Maddie was pleased to report as the dog stirred in her arms. Clearly, she thought, looking down at it, this was a pampered pooch. Its coat was shiny and well-brushed, its collar was lavender patent leather studded with what looked like real amethysts, and it smelled—maybe too strongly—of some floral perfume.

It was also very sweet. Its eyes had blinked open now—they were slightly protuberant and shiny-black as olives—but it was still licking her fingers. Avidly. The eager swipe of the rough, warm tongue continued even as Maddie handed the animal to Mrs. Brehmer, who clasped it to her bosom like a baby. Mrs. B. must have been holding it too tightly, because it immediately began to squirm to get free. *Or perhaps,* Maddie thought, *it had not yet quite recovered its wits.*

"She likes you." Susan regarded Maddie with what looked like surprise. For her part, Maddie was just barely managing to resist the urge to wipe her licked fingers on her jacket. They felt surprisingly sticky, stickier than she would have imagined that a small dog's tongue could make them. Then, remembering the pastry that had been shedding cream filling when she picked it up earlier, Maddie realized that she'd found the answer to the animal's apparent affection. But if Susan and the others chose to think that the dog had been licking her because it liked her, well, who was she to correct them?

At this point, Creative Partners needed any advantage it could get.

"She's cute," Maddie said, putting her sticky hand in her pocket.

"Cute?" Mrs. Brehmer, glancing at her, sounded affronted. "I don't think I'd call her *cute.* This is Zelda von Zoetrope. She's a Grand Champion Pekingese who's taken best of breed at Westminster. Twice."

"Oh, my." As responses went, this probably ranged right up there with "cute" in the inadequate department, but at the moment it was the best Maddie could come up with. Ready and willing to acknowledge herself as a philistine as far as the world of championship-winning dogs went, Maddie struggled for a more fulsome reply even as she looked at Zelda with fresh eyes. With the dog wrapped in Mrs. Brehmer's arms, though, there wasn't much to see but a still-squirming tangle of brown fur.

"You must be very proud," she achieved.

Too late. Mrs. Brehmer was no longer looking at her. She was once again focused exclusively on the dog.

"Oh, we are," Susan said.

"Zelda, Zelda," Mrs. Brehmer crooned as she hugged her wriggling pet. "My dear, darling girl, whatever were you thinking? You might have been killed!"

Zelda growled, the sound low but unmistakable. Mrs. Brehmer stiffened. Then, lips tightening, she set the dog on its feet. Zelda seemed momentarily unsteady. Then she shook herself vigorously and started to trot away, only to be brought up short as she reached the end of the leash Mrs. Brehmer held. Zelda tugged. Mrs. Brehmer reeled her back in, and at the same time looked daggers at Susan. "Where is that fool Linda? I pay her good money to look after this dog."

"Now, Mrs. B.," Susan began in a conciliatory tone, taking the leash from Mrs. Brehmer. "You know Linda is doing her best. She . . ."

Susan was interrupted by the arrival of a heavyset woman in a light blue maid's uniform who stopped in the doorway to glare at the assembled company.

"Oh, Linda, there you are," Susan said with obvious relief.

"She bit me again." Linda's chin quivered with indignation as she pointed at her ankle, where an extra-large Band-Aid had been stuck on top of a torn stocking. It was spotted with blood. "Just as soon as I let her out of her carrier. It was like I no sooner set her on the ground than she went *chomp*. Hurt like a mother."

"You see?" Mrs. Brehmer said to Susan. "You see? I want you to call that groomer right now and ask what happened during that last session. That was five days ago, and my poor darling has been cross as a bear ever since! Why, she's bitten Linda twice, and she growls at everybody all the time and now she's tried to jump out the window."

"I'll check into it," Susan said. "Shall I take her and . . ."

"I need you here," Mrs. Brehmer interrupted decisively, and looked at the new arrival. "Linda, you take her on downstairs to the car. Mind you don't let her get away from you this time. She could have been killed."

Linda flung both hands in the air as if in surrender and took a step backward. "No, ma'am. I ain't gettin' paid enough to take care of that dog no more."

"Now, Linda . . ." Susan began.

Linda shook her head. *"Uh-uh.* I mean it. I quit."

"With that attitude, you're fired," Mrs. Brehmer shot back.

With an indignant *hmmph,* Linda turned on her heel and limped away. Susan looked alarmed.

"Oh, let her go," Mrs. Brehmer said when Susan would have hurried after her. "She's only been with us for two weeks and now she's been fired for cause, so we don't owe her any severance. And Zelda obviously doesn't like her."

"I hope she doesn't sue us," Mr. Bellamy muttered.

Mr. Oliver pursed his lips. "This is an excellent example of why we have an umbrella policy."

"Mrs. Brehmer," Jon said, in the tone of one who had just had an epiphany. "If you don't want to be the face of Brehmer's Pet Food, why not let Zelda do it?"

A heartbeat passed in which everyone stared at Jon. Then Maddie took one look at Mrs. Brehmer's expression, grabbed the idea, and ran with it.

"Zelda would be perfect," Maddie said with enthusiasm, beaming down at the dog who was now sniffing around her ankles. She could clearly feel its warm doggie breath through her hose. Given Linda's recent experience, Maddie had a horrible suspicion that she just might be about to experience the power of Zelda's chomp for herself. Having Mrs. Brehmer's prized pet sink its teeth into her ankle would be a bad thing in more ways than one. Certainly, it would not enhance Creative Partners' chances of turning this thing around. In the spirit of heading trouble off at the pass, Maddie went down on her haunches and held her hand out to the animal. Zelda, who'd jumped back, looked at her extended fingers suspiciously while Maddie, trying not to cringe, held her breath.

Zelda's nose quivered, and she seemed to inhale. Then she trotted forward and started licking Maddie's fingers as sweetly as could be.

It was only when Maddie heard a funny *whooshing* sound overhead that she realized that the rest of the group had been holding their collective breath.

Never underestimate the power of a cream-filled pastry, Maddie thought, and patted Zelda's perfumed head.

"Susan's right, she likes you," Mrs. Brehmer said abruptly. "I've always said that the very best judges of character are dogs. Very well. Your company has our account, Miss Fitzgerald. Don't screw it up."

For the space of a couple of heartbeats, Maddie couldn't believe her ears.

"Oh, no, Mrs. Brehmer, I mean, yes, Mrs. Brehmer," Maddie gasped when it finally sank in, and stood up so fast she was momentarily lightheaded. Thrusting her hand out at Mrs. Brehmer before she remembered her telltale sticky fingers, Maddie could only hope that the old lady wouldn't notice as they shook hands. "Thank you, Mrs. Brehmer."

"We'll do a good job for you, Mrs. Brehmer," Jon said, also shaking their new client's hand. A glance at him told Maddie that he was having as much trouble keeping his excitement in check as she was. His cheeks were pink, his eyes were bright, and he was grinning from ear to ear. Now shaking hands with the suits, Maddie only hoped she didn't look quite as much like a kid on Christmas morning.

"You will indeed, young man, or I'll jerk this account away from you so fast it will make your head spin," Mrs. Brehmer said. Maddie, for one, had no doubt whatsoever that she meant it. "Susan will be in touch with you next week about the details." Mrs. Brehmer looked at Susan, and her mouth tightened impatiently. "Oh, give the leash to me and I'll take Zelda down myself. It's almost time for lunch anyway."

"I'll be glad to take her . . ." Susan said, sounding slightly alarmed.

Mrs. Brehmer practically snatched the leash away from her assistant. "I said I'll take her. I'm going home now anyway. She can ride in the car with me. We haven't spent much time together lately. Maybe she's upset because she's been missing me." With a curt nod at the suits and an unsmiling good-bye for Maddie and Jon, she started to walk away. "Come, Zelda."

Zelda, who was looking longingly toward the window again, didn't move. Mrs. Brehmer was forced to stop as she reached the end of the leash. Having already decided that it probably would be best to get out of Mrs. Brehmer's orbit before something happened to make her change her mind, Maddie had moved away to start packing up their gear and was thankfully a couple yards away from the center of the action by that time. From the corner of her eye, she watched Mrs. Brehmer glower at her dog.

"Zelda!" Mrs. Brehmer said. *"Zelda!"*

Zelda didn't move. She didn't even glance around until Susan, who was standing near Mrs. Brehmer, clapped her hands.

"What did that groomer *do* to her?" Mrs. Brehmer demanded of her assistant. "She hasn't been the same since she got back from her weekly shampoo and blowout." While Susan shook her head in apparent mystification, Mrs. Brehmer looked despairingly at Zelda, who was standing stock-still at the very end of the leash, with all four feet planted like she never intended to move again. "Maybe she cut her toenails too short. Darling girl, is that it? Do your little feetsies hurt?"

Zelda didn't reply. Mrs. Brehmer, muttering something that Maddie was too far away to hear, turned away.

"Come, Zelda," she said again, giving the leash a yank. As Susan held the door open for her, Mrs. Brehmer exited, hauling a still clearly reluctant Zelda in her wake.

"Oh my God, we got the account," Maddie said to Jon a few minutes later, after the elevator doors closed behind them and they were headed down. She was dazed with excitement, jittery with it, still not quite able to take it in. "I don't believe it. We got the account!"

"Yeah," Jon said. "We did."

They looked at each other. Then they whooped, high-fived, and did a little dance that ended with Jon picking Maddie up off her feet and swinging her around in a bear hug. Their celebration stopped abruptly when the elevator paused on seventeen and three other people got on.

For the rest of the ride down they were circumspect. Then, as they stepped out into the lobby, Jon looked at her and grinned.

"Now, how about that raise?"

"We'll talk," Maddie said, "when the money starts coming in."

"Admit it. I was brilliant."

With Jon behind her, Maddie pushed through the revolving door and stepped out into the scorching heat.

"You were pretty good," Maddie admitted, twinkling at him as he joined her and they headed toward the corner where, with luck, they might be able to flag down a cab. The street was noisy, crowded. The sidewalk was packed with people, and they had to weave in and out to keep from running into anyone. Vehicular traffic was heavy in both directions. "*I* was brilliant. Oh my God, we got the account!"

This time they low-fived right in the middle of the sidewalk.

Jon said, "Does this call for a celebration or what? How about if we take ourselves to lunch at some really swanky restaurant? Be a shame to leave New Orleans without trying, say, *Chez Paul*." He looked hopefully at Maddie.

"I don't know what planet you're living on, but down here in the real world, Creative Partners still has bills to pay." The sugary-sweet smell of frying dough from a stand on the corner they'd nearly reached reminded Maddie that she really was hungry. When had she eaten last? That cup of coffee with Mr. Special Agent didn't count . . .

Just as quick as that, the euphoric bubble that she'd been floating along in burst. The good news was that they had the account. The bad news was that someone had tried to kill her, and the FBI was sniffing around, and the whole can of worms that was her life felt like it was getting ready to explode at any minute.

Any way she looked at it, the bad news won.

"We'll grab something at the airport," she said, suddenly almost desperately eager to get out of New Orleans. One unpleasant but necessary stop by the hotel to pick up the luggage that the concierge had promised to hold for them, and they could go to the airport and get on a plane and fly away. Not that getting back to St. Louis would necessarily solve her problem . . .

The hair on the back of her neck stood up as her sixth sense suddenly went on red alert. Jon was looking at her with a frown and saying something, but Maddie didn't hear whatever it was. She could feel eyes boring into her back. There was someone watching her, someone coming up behind her . . .

Whirling, she beheld a wild-eyed stranger rushing purposefully toward her, extended right hand wrapped around something black and metallic that was aimed right at her. Her heart leaped. Her stomach did a nosedive.

Hefting her way-too-heavy briefcase in front of her for what little protection it might afford, she gasped and stumbled back.

She should have expected it. She had expected it. She just hadn't wanted to face the awful truth.

She should have run when she had the chance. Now she was going to die.

"HOLY CHRIST, there he comes!" Sitting bolt-upright in his seat, Sam grabbed for his gun and the door handle at the same time. Beside him, Wynne cursed and did the same thing. They'd been sitting there in the car, idly watching Madeline Fitzgerald as she practically waltzed down the sidewalk with the same tall, blond, good-looking guy she'd been with in the lobby. Sam personally had been admiring her legs while Wynne speculated with good-natured vulgarity about her prowess in bed and whether Blondie, as Wynne had dubbed the guy, was getting any.

That all changed in the space of a heartbeat as she whipped around and they spotted the man racing toward her. Terror was written all over her face, and Sam didn't blame her. If the creep had a gun—he had something in his hand, something he was pointing at her . . . Jesus, if it was a weapon, she was as good as dead. Sam was right there but not close enough. Instead of saving her life, he was going to witness the ending of it.

Shit.

With 9mm in hand, Sam rolled out of the car and sprinted for the sidewalk, barreling past startled onlookers, knocking a portly businessman on his ass. Meanwhile, the lady screamed, the crowd scattered, the boyfriend took a couple steps back and looked surprised, and the creep kept coming on.

"Federal agents! Freeze!" Sam roared, leaping between the onrushing man and the woman at what, in his estimation, was probably the last possible second before a shot was fired. He braced himself, half expecting to get slammed by the bullet that was meant for her if the creep was even a little slow on the uptake, which in his experience creeps universally tended to be. But no: The creep saw the gun leveled at him and let out a shriek, stopping dead and dropping the object in his hand. Shiny black, it hit the sidewalk with an unmistakably metallic sound. The crowd had already started breaking up; now those still nearby doubled over, scrambling for safety. Screams filled the air. Cars braked and honked. Sam heard at least one crash.

Wynne, beside him now, bellowed, "Get your hands in the air!"

"WGMB! WGMB!" the creep cried, thrusting both hands high in the air. "I'm a reporter! We're a TV crew, you idiots! Don't shoot!"

TV reporters. Sam's jaw went slack as he saw his life pass before his eyes. They'd drawn on a television camera crew and, yep, here it came . . .

"Gene, Gene, I got it all! Oh, man, if we hurry, we can make the noon news!" Another man came running up behind the first, a black, boxlike camera perched on his shoulder. He was tall, thin, and freckled, with long, dark red hair drawn back into a ponytail. "This is great!"

"Great my ass! I almost got shot!" Gene snapped.

Feeling like every kind of fool, Sam thrust his gun into his waistband, out of sight. Beside him, Wynne performed a similar sleight of hand with his weapon. The guy with the camera was turning, filming the ducking, staring, exclaiming crowd. The reporter—Gene—was a black-haired Geraldo Rivera–type, complete with Frito Bandido mustache and white dress shirt rolled to just past his elbows. He bent, scooping up the round black thing he'd dropped and holding it in front of his face.

A microphone. Great. Just fucking great. If this got out—and there was no way it wasn't going to get out—he and Wynne were never going to live it down.

Looking at the camera, Gene spoke into the microphone. "As you just witnessed, talking to the survivor of last night's attacks on two different women with the same name got a little hairy there, but we survived and we are, as always, doing our best to get the story for *you*. After what appears to be the contract killing of Madeline Fitzgerald of Natchitoches last night, federal agents are on the job, protecting *another* Madeline Fitzgerald from Saint Louis, Missouri, who was apparently attacked by the same killer by mistake and survived. Ms. Fitzgerald"—Gene moved past Sam, thrusting the microphone out toward the surviving Madeline Fitzgerald, who was looking unnerved and horrified in equal measure as she stared into the camera—"what can you tell us about what happened last night?"

"I-I," she stuttered, backing away and holding her briefcase up in front of her face to block the camera's view. "I have no comment."

"Is it true that you were attacked in your room at the Holiday Inn Express on Peyton Place Boulevard last night?" Gene persisted, following her. The cameraman was right behind him. They brushed past Sam as if he wasn't even there.

"Get away from her," Blondie said, attempting to push the microphone away.

"You ever hear of the Fourth Amendment, bud?" Gene snarled at Blondie, and focused on the woman again. "Did you see a weapon?"

"No, I—no comment." Still backing up, almost tripping over her own feet in their beige high heels, she sounded scared to death. Her knuckles went white as both hands seemed to tighten around the edges of the heavy-looking leather case.

Hell, she *was* scared to death, Sam realized with disgust, and felt an unexpected surge of protectiveness toward her. Getting up close and personal with the subject of a surveillance operation was not ordinarily something he tended to do, but unlike most, this one seemed to be an innocent caught up in events not of her making. And she looked so damned vulnerable.

"Did he have a weapon?" Gene persisted.

"Look, what part of 'no comment' do you not understand?" Blondie protested angrily. Gene went right by him, intent on his quarry. He and the cameraman were so close to Madeline Fitzgerald now that if it hadn't been for the briefcase she was using to block them out they would have been right in her face.

"Please . . ." she said from behind it. "Leave me alone."

Sam had had enough. Under the circumstances, antagonizing this particular camera crew further was probably not the smartest thing he had ever done, he knew. He did it anyway. Shoving past Gene and company, he caught the woman by her arm. The briefcase slipped as she looked up at him with eyes as big as a startled fawn's. They were the warm gold of honey beneath a lush sweep of feathery lashes; he'd noted their beauty the first time she had looked at him. Beneath her thin linen sleeve, he could feel her arm shake. It was a slender arm, firm but unmistakably feminine.

He didn't much like the fact that he was noticing.

"Come on. Let's get you out of here," he said. Her eyes flickered, and she seemed to hesitate. Then she nodded jerkily, and her arm relaxed in his grip.

"Did you know your attacker? Recognize him?" Gene persisted, thrusting the microphone at Madeline again.

"Maddie . . ." Blondie was looking at Sam's hand on her arm.

"It's okay," she said to him, already moving at Sam's side.

"Back off," Sam growled at Gene. Something in his face must have told the reporter that he meant it, because Gene took a step back. "Get that camera out of here."

He was moving as he spoke, taking Maddie with him. She stayed close to his side as he pulled her toward the car, clearly trusting him to get her out of there.

"Hey," Blondie said, following. "Wait just a minute . . ."

"Are you getting this, Dave?" Gene looked around at the cameraman behind him.

"Oh, yeah," Dave replied with relish.

"You're interfering with federal agents," Wynne said, bringing up the rear.

"You're interfering with the public's right to know," Gene retorted. Behind him, the camera followed Maddie's every move.

"To hell with the public's right to know," Sam said as he opened the car door for Maddie and Gene darted forward. He blocked the reporter's access with his body. "I said *back off*."

"Are you taking Miss Fitzgerald into custody?" The microphone was thrust into Sam's face instead.

"*Back off*." Sam took her briefcase from her, thrust it down in the footwell, and bundled Maddie into the front passenger seat. Wynne and Blondie caught up just as he was slamming the door.

"What . . ." Blondie began.

"Get in," Sam said, opening the rear door. Blondie looked at Maddie in the front seat and got in. Sam was already rounding the front of the car as Wynne slid into the backseat, too, and slammed the door.

"Are they under arrest?" Never-say-die Gene yelled from the sidewalk as Sam opened his door. With a grim smile, Sam flipped him the bird, then got into the car, started it up, and pulled away from the curb.

EIGHT

O ut of *the frying pan, into the fire*. That was what kept running through
Maddie's head as the car pulled into traffic, muscled its way into the
far lane, and then turned a sharp left, leaving the TV crew and all the other
witnesses to the debacle thankfully far behind. The problem was, she wasn't
exactly sure which was frying pan and which was fire. The reporter and his
camera had been a threat to her. But then, so was the FBI.

"Smooth move," Wynne said dryly to McCabe.

"Tell me about it," McCabe replied. "Think we're going to make the
noon news?"

"Oh, yeah."

"What the hell *is* this?" Jon demanded. His raised voice filled the car.
"What's going on?"

"Chill, man," Wynne sounded tired. "Everything's copacetic."

"Good word," McCabe said.

"The hell it is. Maddie, are you all right?" That was Jon again. He was
starting to sound belligerent, which, in her experience, wasn't like Jon.

"Could somebody please tell me why there was a TV crew chasing you back there?"

Maddie had been staring almost unseeingly out through the windshield, with her arms wrapped around herself to combat the bone-deep chill that, she hoped, could be laid at the door of the car's cranked-up air-conditioning rather than shock. The euphoria that had accompanied winning the Brehmer account was long gone. It was as though it had happened to someone else. All she wanted to do now was escape—but at the moment, escape wasn't possible.

Suck it up, girl. I didn't raise my daughter to be some little pussy.

She could almost hear her father saying it. *Words to live by,* Maddie thought wryly, and did her best to make him proud. She sucked it up, got a grip, and shifted positions, turning in the slick vinyl seat so that she could see the others. Besides Jon, who still looked as natty as he had while making his pitch to Brehmer's, with nary a crease in his navy suit, his red tie still knotted perfectly, his white shirt spotless, and not so much as a single golden hair out of place, there was Wynne, red-faced, sweaty, his hairy, bare calves visible beneath the legs of rumpled khaki shorts, arms crossed over the hula girl on his chest, jaw working as he chewed on something that smelled like a grape Popsicle, and McCabe, still unsmiling, still unshaven, and about as natty as an unmade bed.

Shining examples of the federal government's finest. God, she was in a car with a pair of FBI agents. *This just keeps getting better and better.*

"I'm fine," she said to Jon, which was a lie. She was freezing, so cold she feared she might never get warm; her head ached; her throat hurt; and she was so scared, so worried, so appalled by what was happening that just pretending everything was relatively okay in her world was an acting job worthy of an Academy Award. But until she figured out what to do, she had no choice but to continue to act, so she added, with an assumption of ease, "You remember these guys. FBI. From the building."

"Sam McCabe," McCabe said to Jon with a quick flick of his eyes to the rearview mirror. He turned left again, onto St. Charles Street, and as he moved the wheel, Maddie could not help but notice the muscular flexing of his arm.

The combination of tanned skin and bulging biceps would have piqued her interest had they belonged to anyone else.

"E. P. Wynne," Wynne said between chews.

"Jon Carter," Jon said. Then his voice sharpened. "Is this about what happened to Maddie last night? Because it was terrible, and it scared the be-jesus out of her, but she wasn't even badly hurt. What is this, New Orleans's slowest news day ever?"

"Something like that." Then McCabe, with a quick glance Maddie's way, asked, "Where to, folks?"

"The hotel, I guess," Maddie said. She was looking at McCabe, who was negotiating the heavy traffic with careful competence. As they changed lanes, sunlight played over his profile, and she noted absently that his features were well proportioned, handsome even, if one ignored the general scruffiness. He blinked, and she focused for an instant on his lashes, which were black, thick, and stubby. Then he glanced her way and she realized that she'd been staring and looked away quickly. She realized, too, that she wasn't quite herself, to put it mildly. The one-two punch of terror and re-lief she'd just experienced had left her in something of a daze. Now it was starting to lift, and her brain was starting to fire on more cylinders.

"What were you doing out there on that street anyway?" Her eyes cut toward McCabe again. Her tone turned accusing. "Were you *following* me?"

There was the briefest of pauses.

"It just so happened we were still in the neighborhood," McCabe said, and Maddie thought she caught a spark of what might have been humor in his eyes. Outside the window, one of the streetcars that was a prime New Orleans tourist attraction clanged its bell. Maddie jumped and looked around to ascertain where the noise had come from. Her nerves were still too jan-gled to permit her to calmly absorb unanticipated sounds.

"You *were* following me," she said when she had recovered. "Admit it, you were."

"If we were, and if that had been a man with a gun, we would have saved your life back there."

Good point.

"But it wasn't a man with a gun. It was a TV reporter with a camera, and now, thanks to you, I'm going to be all over the noon news."

"Miz Fitzgerald, believe me, you would have been all over the noon news without me."

A beat passed as Maddie thought that over.

"The man back there—the TV reporter—said there was another Madeline Fitzgerald attacked last night. He said it was a contract k-killing," Maddie said slowly. With the best will in the world, she couldn't help it: Her voice shook on the last word.

McCabe stopped at a red light and looked over at her. His expression was grim.

"We don't know that it was a contract killing," he said. "But right at this moment it looks like it might have been. Did you know her?"

"Know her?" Maddie took a deep breath and tried to keep her voice steady. "No. No, I didn't. Why didn't you tell me about this earlier?"

His lips thinned. "Because you didn't need to know."

"Well," Maddie said with a hint of bite, "now I do. So how about you fill me in?"

The light changed and the car started moving again. They turned onto Canal Street, one of the widest avenues that was open to traffic in the world, and the crush of vehicles increased. Outside the window, picturesque nineteenth-century commercial buildings with wrought-iron balconies and slatted shutters slid past on either side. Gold lettering on glass windows advertised such businesses as "Madame Le Moyne, Psychic, Open 24 Hours," "Tarot Reading—Learn Your Future," "Patisserie," and "Le Masque Shoppe," among others. Planters bursting with purple wave petunias, baby's breath, and trailing ivy hung from the lampposts. The crowd here was more casually dressed, touristy-looking, with lots of Starbucks cups being carted around. It was Friday in New Orleans, and just about everybody in the city who wasn't driving around seemed to be out there on the sidewalks, enjoying it.

McCabe glanced at her again and seemed to hesitate. Then he returned his attention to the road and said, "Okay. Here's the story: There were two women named Madeline Fitzgerald staying at your hotel last night. Both were attacked in their rooms. One died. One—that would be you—lived."

Maddie sucked in her breath.

"You wanted to know," McCabe said.

"You're kidding." That was Jon from the backseat.

"Nope," Wynne said. "I don't think you realize how lucky you are, Ms. Fitzgerald. The other woman took two bullets to the head."

"Oh my God." Maddie felt dizzy. She remembered the sound of the bullets hitting the mattress, remembered what it was like to think she was going to be shot at any moment, remembered what terror felt like, how it tasted . . .

The other Madeline Fitzgerald had died. Because of her? The thought made her go all light-headed.

"You okay?" McCabe asked.

Maddie supposed her face must have paled. Remembering who he was—what he was—was enough to snap her back to her senses, and she managed to push everything except her immediate situation out of her head. Only then did more ramifications of what he had told her begin to occur.

"You mean there's a possibility that I was attacked by mistake?"

A beat passed in which no one said anything.

"You think there's a possibility that it *wasn't* a mistake?" McCabe asked. His tone was neutral—too neutral. He was probing for answers—and Maddie, catching herself up, wasn't about to give any. Not by the hair of her chinny-chin-chin.

"Of course it was a mistake," she said. "How could it not have been a mistake?"

McCabe's eyes cut her way. "You tell me."

"I thought it was just a random attack, kind of a sex thing gone wrong," Jon said, frowning.

"I don't think so." McCabe glanced in the rearview mirror. "But the possibility is not completely off the table yet. What are the chances, though, two separate perps attack two different women named Madeline Fitzgerald on the same night at the same hotel? Completely unrelated?"

Nobody said anything. The answer, clearly, was *not good*.

"So what do you think happened?" Maddie asked.

"We think it may have been a paid hit," Wynne said.

Maddie felt hope, that small eternal flame, spring to life in her breast.

"A paid hit on the other woman?" She took a deep breath and ran with the ball. "And the killer got the names mixed up and came to my room by mistake. When I got away, he somehow discovered his mistake and went after her. *She* was the target."

The relief was so intense that she was almost limp with it. *Please, God, please, God, please let that be the answer. Let it all have been a terrible mistake. Let it not have been about me at all.*

What she wanted most in the world at that moment was for that to be true. If it was, she could put the whole terrible experience safely behind her and just go on with her life.

"Or maybe it was the other way around." They stopped at an intersection, and McCabe looked at her as he spoke. "Maybe the killer went to her room first, killed her, figured out his mistake and came after you. Maybe it was you he wanted dead. Maybe *you* were the target."

Doing her best to keep her face expressionless, Maddie met his gaze.

"Why?" she asked simply.

"Yeah, why?" Jon asked. "Why on earth would a hit man want to murder Maddie?"

"I have no idea," McCabe said, and glanced at Maddie again. "That's why I'm asking you one more time, and I want you to rack your brain before you answer: Do you know anyone, anyone at all, who might want you dead or have something to gain from your death?"

His gaze reverted to the road as the light changed and they started moving again. Maddie had no idea whether she had imagined the glimmer of doubt in his eyes or not.

What she did know was that her palms were damp. "No," she said.

He didn't reply to that. For a moment there was no sound in the car except the hum of the air-conditioning.

"Here we are." McCabe swung into the semicircular drive that fronted the hotel. A waist-high hedge of hot-pink azaleas lined the drive. Beneath the white-columned portico, a uniformed bellman loaded luggage onto a cart. A black Honda with a parking valet at the wheel pulled away from the entrance as the couple who owned the car disappeared inside. The only sign of the previous night's tragedy was the police car parked just past the entrance. "So, you two—you got plans for the rest of the day?"

"We grab our luggage and head for the airport," Jon said as McCabe stopped the car. "That pretty much sums it up."

"Want a ride?" McCabe's question was directed at Maddie.

"No." Maddie was already opening her door. "We'll catch a cab. Thanks."

"Hang on a minute." McCabe leaned over and caught her by the wrist as Jon opened the back door. "I have something I need to say to you."

His hand was warm and dry, big, long-fingered. She'd always liked men with big hands, she thought in that first fleeting instant of surprise at being grabbed. Then she frowned. FBI agents with big hands, however, were in a whole separate category. One she didn't want anything to do with.

She tried to tug her hand free without result. If anything, he tightened his grip. Her eyes met his, narrowed.

"It'll just take a minute," he promised.

"Look, I've got to go. What with security and everything, getting through the airport takes forever now."

He didn't let go. Jon, who had gotten out, was leaning down to look in at her through her partially opened door.

"She'll be just a minute," McCabe said to Jon. Then, as Jon frowned and looked like he was about to protest, Wynne walked up beside him and said something. Jon straightened to talk to Wynne.

"Close the door," McCabe said. He was looking at her steadily, his expression serious, even slightly grim.

Maddie's heart skipped a beat. Then she rallied, lifting her chin. "You're good at giving orders, aren't you?"

"Please." His voice was very quiet.

What could she do? Maddie, keenly aware of a whole summer's worth of butterflies taking wing in her stomach, closed the door.

"So what do you want?" she asked, just barely managing to keep the truculence out of her voice. She felt trapped, panicky, and the unbreakable hold he was keeping on her wrist was not making her feel any more relaxed. It reminded her of a handcuff. . . . The image was unnerving, and she instantly banished it. The trick was not to let him realize just how very apprehensive she was. *Did* he realize? He was watching her, the faintest of frown lines between his brows, his expression unreadable.

"If you've got anything you want to tell me, anything at all, this is the moment. I thought you might feel more comfortable doing it if the boyfriend wasn't here."

It was all Maddie could do not to suck in telltale air.

"I don't have anything to tell you." She forced a little laugh. Her only hope was that it didn't sound as fake to him as it did to her. "What could I possibly have to tell you? And, just for the record, Jon's not my boyfriend. He's my employee. We work together, and we're friends. We don't sleep together."

McCabe smiled. If he hadn't been an FBI agent, Maddie realized with some surprise, she might actually be feeling kind of attracted to him about now.

"Duly noted."

His smile deepened. Oh, God, he had dimples. Deep ones on either side of his mouth. Maddie looked, blinked, then realized that she really, really didn't want to go there. Brows twitching together, she glanced pointedly down at his hand wrapped around her wrist. "Would you mind letting me go now?"

"What?" He looked down at their linked hands, too, and then let go. "Oh, sure."

"Is there anything else?" Maddie was already reaching for the door handle. "Because I have a plane to catch."

"Just one more thing." He was leaning back in his seat, his hands resting casually on the bottom of the steering wheel, his head turned slightly toward her. Her whole side was pressed against the door now. Her hand curled around the handle, and it was all she could do not to simply release it, open the door, and bolt. "Even if the attack on you was a mistake, even if you were not the intended victim, that doesn't let you off the hook, you realize. This guy, whoever he is, attacked you, and you escaped. You lived. You're a witness. He may believe that you can identify him. It's very possible that he might be coming after you to finish the job."

Maddie's eyes widened. That aspect of the situation hadn't occurred to her. In other words, even if she hadn't been the intended victim originally, now she was? What was this, 101 reasons for someone to want to kill her?

"I can offer you protection. Someone to stay with you twenty-four hours a day until we get this creep."

Maddie's breath caught. Like she was going to accept protection from the *FBI?* On any other day, in any other mood, she would have laughed.

"No," she said. "No, no, no. I just want to forget all about this. I just want to go home."

And with that she opened the door and stepped out into the enervating heat. Something—rising too swiftly, the lack of sleep and food, the multiple traumas she'd suffered over the course of the last twenty-four hours, who knew?—made her suddenly light-headed. The world seemed to tilt, and she had to steady herself with a hand on the car roof. The metal was hot and faintly gritty from dust. The sun bouncing off the pavement was blinding. The smell of melting asphalt was strong.

"Forgot your briefcase," McCabe called after her, and Maddie stiffened. Then she sucked it up one more time, turned, and dragged her briefcase out of the footwell. The last words he said to her as she slammed the door shut were, "You take care of yourself, Miz Fitzgerald."

NINE

"What the *hell* were you thinking?" Smolski swiveled in his chair, his eyes almost bugging out of his head as they fixed on Sam. His scream was loud enough to make Gardner jump, and it wasn't even directed at her. Sam, at whom it *was* directed, grimaced. Wynne, who was only a secondary target, took a step back. "That thing made us look like the fucking Keystone Cops!"

It was just before six p.m., and they were standing like a trio of schoolkids who had been called before the principal in the uber-luxurious cabin of a private jet that had touched down on the tarmac at New Orleans some twenty minutes earlier. Smolski was seated in a bone leather chair that seconds before had been facing a wide-screen plasma TV. A video clip of the morning incident with Gene Markham of WGMB had just ended with a close-up of Sam's middle finger riding high.

"It was a quick-response kind of situation. We just happened to have read it wrong," Sam said by way of an explanation. It was lame, and he knew it. The whole situation had been farcical, and he'd made it ten times worse by flipping the news guy the bird. It was juvenile, and he should have known better.

"We thought he was coming after her with a weapon," Wynne added. *Big mistake.* It sounded like an excuse, and if there was anything Smolski hated more than screwups, it was excuses.

"You thought he was coming after her with a weapon," Smolski mimicked in a savage falsetto. "It was a fucking *microphone,* you morons. You drew on a TV reporter in the middle of a crowded city street. And they got it all on TV."

There wasn't much to say to that except "Sorry, my bad," and Sam refrained. One thing he'd learned in the six years he'd spent working under Smolski in the Violent Crimes division was that being an FBI agent meant never venturing to say you were sorry—because if you did, Smolski would wipe the floor with you. Smolski put no more stock in apologies than he did in excuses. He wanted it done right the first time, and he wanted it done yesterday. The head of Violent Crimes was a former Marine who'd once been muscular but had now gone to flabby seed, and despite the thousand-dollar suit he wore, there was no hiding the roll of pudge that hung over his belt. He had a Mediterranean complexion and thinning black hair. His nose was big; his eyes and mouth were small. His temper was legendary.

Fortunately, at least as far as Sam was concerned, Smolski's bark was worse than his bite.

"I thought we agreed to keep this thing on the down-low? All we need is the media on our asses, telling the whole world how people are being knocked off like ducks in a shooting gallery while you guys make like the Three Stooges. To say nothing of the fact that if the public finds out that the UNSUB's calling you on your cell phone, we might as well throw the damned thing out the window because everybody and his mother will start calling that number and the killer will never be able to get through." Smolski was still yelling loud enough to cause Melody, his longtime administrative assistant, to make a sympathetic face at Sam behind her boss's back. A plumpish, blue-eyed brunette in a navy pantsuit, she was a nice girl—well, a nice woman now, thirty-three years old, married with a couple of kids. She'd once been a babe, and when she'd first come to work at headquarters, Sam had taken her out a few times. The fling had fizzled when it had become obvious that Melody wanted forever while Sam was allergic to same. But she still retained a soft spot for him, which Sam from time to time took shameless advantage of.

Now, while Smolski spread the love by glaring at Wynne again, Sam seized the moment to nod significantly at the white telephone on the console behind Smolski.

She looked shocked, and then the corners of her lips quivered. Good girl, Melody.

Melody disappeared from view, and Smolski redirected his vitriol toward Sam. "You got anything? Huh? You got anything? Hell, no, you don't got anything, because if you did, I'd already know about it. You've been chasing around the country after this guy for a month now. You've been spending money like you think you're the fucking Sultan of Brunei. And you got what to show for it? A TV clip that's an embarrassment to the Bureau, and that's it. The *vice president* got a call from his sister, who lives here in New Orleans, complaining about my guys pulling weapons on a streetful of innocent civilians. 'Deal with it,' he says to me, so I have to interrupt my trip to L.A., make a big detour to stop here, and for what? I'll tell you for what: to kick your guys' asses from here to Sunday. What were you *thinking*? You . . ."

The telephone rang, cutting Smolski off in full spiel. Melody reappeared to answer the phone, and Smolski turned his head to listen while Melody had a brief conversation with whomever was on the other end. Melody then held the phone out to her boss.

"Your wife," she said to Smolski, who took the receiver with obvious reluctance.

"Cripes," he said, one hand covering the mouthpiece. "Why didn't you tell her I'm in a meeting? She's been badgering me to go to some damned fund-raiser for PETA or something. I've had my cell phone turned off all day. How the hell did she know where to reach me?"

Smolski spent much of his life doing his best to avoid his wife, who spent much of hers tracking him down. Sam was willing to bet that Melody, a kindhearted sort, had just alerted Mrs. Smolski to her errant hubby's availability to take a call.

Smolski uncovered the mouthpiece, said, "Hang on a minute, honey, I'm dealing with a situation here," listened, winced, said, "Of course I'm not trying to avoid you. I promise, just one minute," and covered the mouthpiece again.

"You guys get the hell out of here." He dismissed them with an angry wave of his hand. "I see any more dumb moves like you pulled today, and I'll bust you down to file clerks. You understand me?"

"Yes, sir."

Acting on the dismissal with alacrity, Gardner was already on the steps that led down to the tarmac, Wynne was in the doorway right behind her, and Sam was bringing up the rear by the time Smolski had the phone to his ear again.

"Thanks, Mel," Sam whispered to Melody, who had followed them to the door.

"Anytime." She smiled at him, and for a moment he had a bad pang of the might-have-beens. But there were a lot of might-have-beens littering his life, and so he shrugged this particular one off, clasped the metal handrail, and headed down the steps. It was overcast and drizzling now—no more than a light mist, really—but enough to make steam come up off the pavement, so it looked as though they were stepping down into a cloud. Sam wasn't bothered by the fine drops that beaded on his face and dampened his clothes, but the moisture caused Wynne's hair to frizz even more than usual and wilted Gardner's short-and-spiky look, which, by way of a change, this week she had dyed fire-engine red.

"And, by the way, you guys look like shit!" Smolski's voice followed them. The bellow was muffled, but neither Sam nor Wynne nor Gardner nor the half-dozen mechanics and luggage handlers in the vicinity had any trouble hearing it. "Shave! Put on some decent clothes! Do something about your hair! Quit embarrassing me!"

"The sad thing is, that's the most excitement I've had today," Gardner said pensively as they dodged an orange luggage cart and headed toward the terminal. A commercial jet raced toward takeoff in the background, the roar of its engines blunted by distance. "Do you think he'll really be named head of the Bureau?"

"I heard it's a done deal," Wynne said.

"They're waiting to announce it until after Mosley"—Ed Mosley was the current FBI director—"announces his retirement. That won't be till after the election." As he spoke, Sam absentmindedly watched the jet that had just taken off do a graceful U-turn and head north, rising until it disappeared within the lowering bank of iron-gray clouds that covered the sky.

"So, who's going to replace Smolski?" Gardner wondered aloud.

Sam shrugged. They had reached the terminal by this time. Wynne pulled open the glass door that led to the escalator that would take them up to the main level, then stood back to let Gardner precede him. She walked in, swinging her butt provocatively. It was a J.Lo butt, big and curvy in a clingy black skirt, and Wynne could hardly tear his eyes from it. Her equally generous breasts jiggled like water balloons beneath a pink silk blouse. Her waist was cinched by a wide black belt pulled so tight that Sam wondered how she could breathe. He also wondered, just in passing, where she was carrying her gun. Did they have bra holsters now? Deciding he really didn't want to go there, Sam followed them inside, only half listening to their conversation. Wynne's face was turning shades of puce as Gardner continued to do her high-heeled strut in front of him all the way to the escalator. As the three of them rode it up, Sam, still bringing up the rear, shook his head. Poor guy had it bad for Gardner, and the sad thing was that, knowing Wynne, he was never going to do anything about it. As far as he himself was concerned, Gardner had all the right equipment even if it was a little abundant for his taste, and she was attractive enough with her bright blue eyes and big, bold features that matched her five-foot-ten, big-boned frame, but he was not going there. No way, no how.

As his grandma told him nearly every time he saw her, it don't mean a thing if it ain't got that zing.

"You drive," Sam said to Wynne, tossing him the keys as they reached the Saturn, which they'd left in short-term parking. He'd already punched the button to unlock the car, and Gardner was already sliding into the front passenger seat. Sam had no doubt that she would spend the drive back to the hotel, where they'd set up shop, crossing and uncrossing her legs at him, just like she'd done on the drive out to the airport. She was going to so much trouble to be provocative, Sam thought, that the least he could do was provide her with an appreciative audience.

Namely, Wynne.

"Don't wreck us," Sam added as an afterthought, only then considering the possible consequences of Gardner's come-hither act on Wynne, but it was too late. Wynne was already making himself at home behind the wheel, and, anyway, Sam personally was just too damned tired to drive. The headlights coming at them as they pulled around the spiral exit ramp were blurry, and his head pounded like the bass on a teenager's stereo. Plus, the interior of the car smelled of cheap vinyl, stale cigarettes, and Wynne's everlasting gum. The combination didn't do a thing for his stomach, which was quivering on the verge of nausea.

God, just how long had it been now since he'd had any sleep? He didn't even want to think about it.

In the front seat, Gardner crossed and uncrossed her legs at Wynne for at least the third time, with a predictably deleterious effect on his driving. It was rush hour, and traffic on the interstate heading back into the city was heavy. The rain was coming down more steadily now, and the roads were slick. The windshield wipers swished back and forth with the mind-numbing rhythm of a metronome.

Wynne, distracted, was one scary-ass driver. There was only one thing to do, Sam decided, if he wished to preserve life and limb, and that was distract Gardner from distracting Wynne.

"So tell us about Madeline Fitzgerald. The live one," Sam said to her.

"Anybody ever tell you you're a slave driver, McCabe?" Gardner protested good-naturedly, despite tugging her briefcase onto her lap and rooting some papers out of one of the pockets. Glancing down at them, she turned in the seat to look at him. "What do you want to know?"

"Why don't you start all over again?"

Gardner had been in the process of filling them in on their survivor when Smolski's call had come in, ordering them to meet him at the airport. A fresh start without worrying about how hard Smolski was getting ready to come down on them would probably be a good thing. Especially since all three of them were so tired that their brains were sputtering along like a car getting down to its last few drops of gas.

Gardner looked down at the papers again. "Madeline Elaine Fitzgerald, twenty-nine years old, owner of Creative Partners advertising agency, which she purchased nineteen months ago from the previous owner, who sold because of poor health. Previous to that she was an employee of said advertising agency for two years. Previous to that she was an independent contractor for an outfit selling advertising space in various local publications. A BA in business administration from Western Illinois University. Parents, John and Elaine Fitzgerald, deceased. He was a dentist, she was a homemaker. No siblings. Never married. Pays her bills on time. No arrest record."

"Any history of gambling?" Wynne asked, easing into the slow lane as an eighteen-wheeler shot past on the left with a tooth-rattling roar.

"Nothing showed up."

A vision of Maddie as he had last seen her rose in Sam's mind's eye. Big brown eyes, lush mouth, luxuriant hair, slender, alluring body, legs that went on forever. Tons of sex appeal, as he personally could testify, and a lot of class besides. Business owner. College degree. Should ooze self-confidence. But there'd been insecurity there. And hostility, too. In fact, he'd almost gotten the impression that she was afraid of something. Afraid of him.

"What about boyfriends? How's her romantic history?" he asked.

"We don't have anything on that yet. This is just a preliminary report. I haven't had time to really dig down deep."

"Keep working on it."

"You have Gomez picking her up on the other end?" Wynne cut back into the middle lane again. Sam couldn't help glancing around warily. There was a minivan to the left, a compact car to the right. . . .

"Yeah," Sam said. Pete Gomez was an agent in the St. Louis field office. "He'll be with her from the time she steps off the plane."

Wynne chuckled. "She won't like that."

"She won't know about it. Unless she needs to." Sam's meaning was clear: Maddie would only find out about Gomez if he had to step in and save her ass.

"Still think our UNSUB's going to go after her?" Gardner asked.

Sam was so sure of it that, barring an act of God, he planned to have them all in St. Louis within the next twenty-four hours. "Wouldn't you?"

"I don't know," Gardner said, frowning. "It depends on a couple of things. Number one, if she was the intended target—and the other Madeline Fitzgerald has a lot more red flags in her background, so it seems unlikely at this point—then he will definitely go after her. Number two, if he thinks she can identify him, then he will go after her. But barring either of those circumstances, I . . ."

Sam's cell phone rang.

He jumped. Gardner's eyes widened. Wynne almost drove off the damned road.

"Watch where the hell you're going," Sam growled at Wynne, digging in his pocket for his phone, which continued to ring. As Wynne straightened the car out with a muttered "sorry," Sam dragged the phone free and squinted to read the number in the ID box. Because of the rain, the streetlights were on, and the bright beams of cars going in the opposite direction slashed through the Saturn's interior. If it hadn't been for that, Sam wasn't sure he would have been able to make out what was written in the little box.

Error, it said.

"Jesus. I think it might be him." His pulse shot into instant overdrive as he flipped open the phone and spoke into it. "McCabe."

"You're screwing up, McCabe. That time you weren't even close."

It *was* him. At the sound of the digitally altered voice, Sam felt every muscle in his body tense. He nodded to let Gardner and Wynne, who was looking at him through the rearview mirror, know.

Another semi, dangerously close, rattled past on the right.

"Where you been? I thought you forgot about me," Sam said, concentrating hard on anything he might be able to hear in the background. The sound of traffic, for example—the interstate was noisy, and if the bastard was in one of the vehicles around them he might be able to hear it. His eyes cut left and right, trying to see into nearby cars.

"Don't you worry, I wouldn't do that." Sam couldn't hear any kind of background sound at all. His own surroundings were too noisy. "Ready for your next clue?"

"How's your leg?" Sam asked, hoping to throw him off. "I imagine a pencil wound's a nasty thing. Lead poisoning and all that."

If the bastard got rattled, Sam hoped against hope, he might just keep talking long enough for them to get a fix on him. It didn't take long. . . .

"You're dreaming, asshole. Now here's your clue. Better shut up or you'll miss it. Where in the world is—Walter?"

There was a click as the bastard hung up, followed by nothing but dead air. The silence in the car was equally thick and heavy.

"Shit," said Sam. His eyes met Wynne's through the mirror. "Looks like we're back on the clock again."

THE FIRST thing Maddie saw when she cleared the last of the airport security barriers in St. Louis was the sign: *Way to go, Maddie and Jon.* It was printed in big block letters on a white piece of posterboard, and it was being waved above the head of Louise Rea, Creative Partners' pleasantly plump, pleasantly wrinkled—just plain pleasant, period—sixty-two-year-old administrative assistant. Beside her, Ana Choi, a slender twenty-one-year-old college student whom Maddie had hired six months before on a part-time basis to handle graphic design, stood on her tiptoes, scanning the stream of disembarking passengers as they emerged into the visitor-friendly part of the airport. Judy Petronio, a forty-seven-year-old mother of four who was in charge of retail accounts, was wedged in next to Ana; behind Judy, fifty-two-year-old Herb Mankowitz, who handled the direct-mailing part of the business, looked faintly impatient. But he was there. They were all there, the entire staff of Creative Partners. It was just after six p.m., they'd worked a full day, and it was clear from their dress that they'd come straight to the airport from work.

On a Friday, when presumably they all had way better things to do.

Their presence was as touching as it was unexpected.

Surveying the motley crew, Maddie thought, *This is my family,* and felt her throat tighten.

"I called Louise from the airport," Jon said. He was striding along beside her, and his face broke into a broad grin as he spied the welcoming committee among the crowd greeting the deplaning passengers with little cries of excitement and pleasure. In fact, he looked buoyant, just the way Maddie knew she should be feeling. The way she *would* be feeling if it hadn't been for the little matter of her life having just been blown all to hell.

Ana spotted them first. Her eyes fixed on Maddie and widened. Her long, black hair was tied up in a ponytail, and she was wearing lowrider black slacks with a shrunken-looking white tank that bared enough skin so that the tattoo of a dragonfly above her left hip was clearly visible. Maddie presumed—hoped—that there was a jacket, cardigan, something that made the ensemble work-friendly, lying around somewhere that Ana had doffed after five p.m. She would graduate in December, and she'd already made it clear that she was dying to be offered a full-time job at Creative Partners. It hit Maddie that now that they had the Brehmer account, she was suddenly in a position to do just that. A financial position, anyway.

Ana grabbed Louise's arm and pointed. "There they are!"

Four pairs of eyes fastened on Maddie and Jon. Four mouths opened wide. Then the Creative Partners staff shouted, cheered, clapped, and broke ranks with the rest of the waiting crowd to storm the new arrivals, sur-rounding them on all sides, dealing out handshakes and hugs and exclamations indiscriminately.

"We got the account! I can't believe we got the account!" Louise enveloped Maddie in a suffocating hug. "Maddie, you did it! Oh, my dear, I think I'm going to cry!"

Louise, of all of them, had known how precarious the company's position was. She handled the bookkeeping. Feeling her own eyes unexpectedly stinging, Maddie hugged her back warmly. Louise was wearing her usual polyester pants and a matching striped blouse, and she smelled of lotion, soap, and just faintly of the hairspray she used to keep her short, unruly silver curls under control. She smelled just the way Louise always smelled, and Maddie found it unexpectedly heartbreaking.

Ana was next, flinging her arms around Maddie as soon as Louise released her.

"This is so cool!" As exuberant as a puppy, Ana squeezed Maddie so hard she could almost hear her ribs cracking. "Does this mean you can keep me? Say yes. Please say yes!"

Wincing slightly, Maddie hugged her back anyway. Ana the Ever-enthusiastic would be a great permanent addition to the team. If only . . .

"We'll talk on Monday," Maddie promised, and managed a smile.

Judy's hug was more brisk. She and Herb had worked for Creative Partners since long before Maddie had come on the scene, and Maddie knew that they had worried a lot about the agency's future over the last few months.

"I've already contacted Maury Pope with *BusinessMonthly*. There'll be an article about this in the next issue. Maury was all excited when I called him. He said us landing the Brehmer account is just huge." A rare grin transformed Judy's rather severe face. "And the timing couldn't be better. Matthew"—Matthew, entering his senior year of high school, was her second son; her oldest, Justin, was a rising sophomore at the University of Missouri—"just told me he wants to go to Vanderbilt."

She made a comical face, and Maddie rolled her eyes sympathetically even as her stomach twisted. *Judy needed her job. . . .*

"Rising tides lift all ships," Herb said, giving Maddie a hearty slap on the shoulder. "Way to go, Boss."

Boss. There it was again. Despite everything, Maddie felt that warm little glow, followed by a pain, sharp and swift as the stab of a knife, right in the region of her heart.

"You guys. You're the best," she said, and to her horror felt herself tearing up as she looked at them.

"Oh, don't cry," Ana protested. Louise promptly burst into noisy tears, which made everyone laugh and hug her and enabled Maddie to get her emotions more or less under control. By this time, the rest of the crowd greeting arriving passengers had pretty much dispersed, so at least they were spared an audience for the love-fest that followed.

TEN MINUTES LATER, the group was standing en masse in front of one of the silver carousels in baggage claim, waiting for Jon and Maddie's luggage to be disgorged. Multiple flights had apparently landed at approximately the same time, so the warehouse-like space was crowded. The sounds of excited conversation and squeaking cart wheels and the thud of suitcases being dumped on the conveyor belts overlay the rumble of the moving carousels, making conversation difficult. "You feel like going to dinner to celebrate?" Jon asked Maddie in a louder than normal voice as they watched the various bags tumbling out through the chute.

The lump in her throat got bigger. Maddie shook her head. "Not tonight. I'm too tired."

"Yeah, well, you've had a rough twenty-four hours," Herb, overhearing, observed sympathetically. Jon had filled the group in on everything, apparently, and as soon as they'd stopped exclaiming over the Brehmer account, they'd started exclaiming over what Ana called "Maddie's mugging."

"Of course you want to go on home and relax," Louise said. "You enjoy your weekend, and then we can celebrate on Monday."

"Yeah, you can take us all to lunch." Jon grinned at Maddie. "Somewhere expensive."

"With a wine list," Ana added, and the group made enthusiastic noises. Drawing on some deep reservoir of strength she hadn't even known she possessed, Maddie pinned a smile to her face and did her best to pretend to be cheerful.

"Sounds like a plan," she said. Then her familiar small black suitcase appeared, bumping into view in a sea of others. Rescuing it and securing her briefcase to the top of it gave her a chance to steel herself for what was to come.

"Herb's going to drop me off." Jon had retrieved his suitcase, too, and it trundled along behind him as they all headed for the exit together. "You need a ride home?"

Maddie shook her head. "I drove. My car's in the lot."

"You want some of us to come home with you?" Ana asked, frowning at her. "In case you're scared or something?"

"I'm not scared." Now there was a lie if she'd ever told one, Maddie thought, but the kind of scared she was wasn't anything that the presence of Ana or any of the others could fix. "The way I look at it is, what happened last night was just one of those things that happens sometimes in big cities. Now that I'm back home, I'll be fine."

"You sure?" Louise asked, surveying her a little anxiously. Afraid of what Louise might be able to read in her face, Maddie concentrated on looking serene. "You can sleep over at my house if you want."

"You can sleep over at *mine*." Jon gave her an exaggeratedly lascivious grin.

That did make her laugh, and she was grateful to him because of it.

"Thank you both, but I'll be fine."

They reached the pair of sliding glass doors marked "Short-Term Parking."

"We're here," Herb said, and everyone stopped near the door. "Maddie, can we at least walk you to your car?"

"Well, I guess you could—except I'm taking a shuttle to the long-term lot. Think I'm going to pay forty dollars to leave my car in short-term parking overnight? No way." Heart aching, she smiled at the assembled group, all of whom were looking at her with varying degrees of concern. "Would everyone please stop worrying about me? This is *St. Louis*. I'll be fine."

They all seemed to feel the force of that, because their faces relaxed.

"All right, then."

"Have a good weekend."

"See ya."

"Don't think we're not going to talk about that raise on Monday."

Jon, bless him, struck just the right note with that last comment, and the cheery smile with which she bade good-bye to them wasn't quite as much effort as it could have been. Maddie lifted a hand in farewell and watched them turn away, with the lump in her throat now so big it felt like an egg, then turned away herself and headed off toward the exit marked "Long-Term Parking," where she knew from experience that a shuttle made periodic trips back and forth to the distant lot.

She walked through the sliding glass doors. It was necessary to go through one more set to actually get outside, but she stopped in the twenty feet or so of dead space between the doors and waited. Five minutes later, she turned and walked back inside the terminal.

As she had expected, Jon and the others were gone. Maddie felt her shoulders sag as she realized that in all probability she would never see them again.

Friends. Family. A place to belong. She had worked so hard to acquire them all. That she had to give them up just when she was finally on the verge of getting everything she had always wanted didn't seem fair. It *wasn't* fair. But such, as she had already learned way too many times before, was life.

So cry me a river, she thought sardonically as her throat started to tighten up again. *It won't change a thing.*

She sucked it up one more time.

With her suitcase rolling along after her like the faithful dog she'd always wanted and never permitted herself to acquire, Maddie hurried toward the taxi stand.

She'd had plenty of time to think on the plane ride from New Orleans. And the conclusion she'd reached, had been inevitable from the first second she'd awakened to find the man in her hotel room.

What had happened wasn't an accident, and it wasn't a mistake. She would be a fool to believe either.

Deep in her gut, she'd known the truth all along: They'd finally found her.

If she wanted to survive, she was going to have to cut and run.

TEN

She had been preparing for this day for seven years, but that didn't make it any easier now that it had finally come. Hopping into a taxi, Maddie directed the driver to take her to the Galleria, one of the area's busiest malls. It was Friday night. There would be lots of action at the mall. Lots of action made it easier to lose a tail, which she hoped she didn't have. But it was possible. It could be. It might be.

It would be foolish to assume that no one was following her. Worse, it might even be fatal.

The Galleria was swarming with shoppers, just as she'd expected. On autopilot now, following a script she'd composed in her head long since, Maddie made her way into Dillard's, bought some clothes, basic gear like jeans and T-shirts and sneakers and underwear, things she hadn't brought with her on what was to have been an overnight trip. She bought a suitcase, too, a nondescript-looking tapestry bag that was larger than the little black one that had served her so well. Since she was still able to use her credit cards, paying was not a problem. Maddie signed the charge slip, looked down at the signature, and felt her throat constrict.

Ya gotta do what you gotta do.

Her father's words again. She could almost hear him saying them, could almost see him just the way he'd looked the night it had all started to go so badly wrong, when she had tried to stop him from going on what he'd called "an errand" for Big Ollie Bonano. He'd been—what? Maybe fifty? Beefy and balding, with deep horizontal worry lines cut into his forehead, he'd looked a decade older. She'd been in bed in the cheap little apartment they had rented by the week, but she had heard him go out and had run down to the car in the oversized T-shirt and panties she had worn back then to sleep in, not caring that it was a tough neighborhood, that someone might see. He had rolled down his window to talk to her. But even as she begged, she had known he was already in too deep. There was no way he could have said no to Big Ollie, he owed him—them—too much money. Gamblers who can't pay make good fish food, as Big Ollie's lieutenant Charlie Pancakes had put it. Or good errand-runners.

Though he'd never meant for it to happen, her father had gotten her caught up in the mob's sticky web, too. In the end, he hadn't been able to get out. But she had. With both hands, she had grabbed an opportunity that had presented itself and had run for her life.

Just like she was going to run for her life now. Because that hit man in New Orleans had come for her. She knew it as well as she knew her own name. She'd been hiding for seven years, and now they'd found her. The terrible thing about it was that an innocent woman had died in her place.

Thinking of that other Madeline Fitzgerald, Maddie felt sick to her stomach. Guilt over her death would be something she would carry with her for the rest of her life. But there was nothing she could do to change what had happened now. It was over. It was a done deal. The only thing she could do in the aftermath was try to save herself. And to do that, she needed to disappear.

At least, this time, she knew the drill: Lugging her purchases, she went into the nearest ladies' room and changed into jeans, a T-shirt, and sneakers, stuffing the clothes she'd been wearing along with the remainder of the new things she'd bought into the old suitcase, which went inside the new suitcase so that, when they started looking for her, they wouldn't find the old one abandoned at the mall. She crammed in her briefcase, then tucked Fudgie in a little more carefully. Thank God she'd brought him with her.

If she wanted to stay safe, she was never going to be able to go back to her apartment—her *home*—again.

At the thought, she found her eyes stinging once more.

Get over it, she told herself fiercely, and splashed her face with cold water until the incipient tears went away. Then she set about changing her appearance as much as possible, brushing her hair flat with water, tucking it behind her ears, slicking a dark maroon lipstick she'd just bought at Dillard's on her lips, clipping big gold hoops from the same source to her ears. She tied a bandanna around her throat to hide the bruise there, and was done. Finally she left the ladies' room and headed for the part of the mall opposite where she'd come in. Taxis cruised there, as she knew from experience. She was dressed differently, her hair was different, she looked different. More like a college student than a businesswoman. Unless a tail had dogged her every step—and no one had, she was as sure as it was possible to be of that—he wasn't going to recognize her unless he got up real close and personal. Not in the mass exodus of shoppers streaming out of the mall now that it was closing time. Not in the brief period of time it would take her to step out into the open and grab a taxi.

"Where to?" the driver asked as she pulled open the back door of the cab.

Sliding inside, Maddie ignored the tightness in her chest and told him.

"WHAT DO YOU MEAN, you lost her?" Sam's voice rose to a near shout as the bad news registered. "How the hell could you lose her?"

It was not quite nine p.m. Sam was standing in front of a map of the United States that he'd tacked to the wall in the New Orleans hotel room that was serving as their temporary headquarters. Red pushpins marked the sites of the killings: Judge Lawrence in Richmond. Dante Jones in Atlanta. Allison Pope in Jacksonville. Wendell and Tammy Sue Perkins in Mobile. Madeline Fitzgerald in New Orleans. The *other* Madeline Fitzgerald, that is. Not the young, pretty—all right, *hot*—one that he was annoyed to realize he was beginning to take way too personal an interest in. He had been trying to discern a pattern to them that was more precise than just a general southwesterly direction along the country's interstate system, the miles apart, a common denominator between the cities, something, when his cell phone rang. The sound had made him stiffen and had startled Wynne, who was sprawled on his back on the bed, and Gardner, who was hunched, bleary-eyed, over her computer screen, into semialertness. Now, at Sam's words, Wynne rose up on his elbows and Gardner hitched her chair around. Both of them watched him with wide-eyed attention.

"She never came out of the airport." Gomez's voice on the other end of the phone was full of apology.

"What?" Sam felt his gut clench.

"She got off the plane, because I checked with the airline. But she never came out of the airport. I've even had them search—restrooms, bars, the lot. She's not there."

"Holy Christ." Sam breathed in deeply, starting a silent count to ten in an attempt to keep himself from losing it before abandoning the effort at number three in favor of immediately addressing the situation. Gomez was a new guy, a *fucking* new guy in Bureau parlance, and new guys were expected to fuck up (hence the nickname), but to have it happen now, on his case, on *this* case, threatened to drive Sam around the bend. He'd wanted Mark Sidow, a veteran agent, to handle the assignment, but he'd been informed that Sidow was on his annual August vacation and Gomez was the only one available. And now, sure enough, the fucking new guy had fucked up.

Sam exhaled. "You were supposed to pick her up off the plane."

"Her car was in the lot. I waited by it. She never came."

You fucking moron. The words were never said. Sam swallowed them, reaching deep inside himself for a semi-patient tone. Hell, he'd been the fucking new guy once. They all had. Anyway, chewing out Gomez would not help find Maddie.

"Did you check her place?"

"Yep. She hasn't been there."

Sam ran a hand through his hair.

"Maybe she went home with that guy she was with—uh, Jon Carter."

"No. I checked that, too. He's alone."

This time Sam didn't bother to try to swallow the curse words that fell from his lips.

"Did you try her office?"

"She's not there."

Okay. The possibilities were endless. The key was not to overreact. But the thought of Maddie alone out there somewhere while the sick bastard who had attacked her once before was God-knew-where made it difficult to keep a lid on what he recognized as a bad case of incipient panic.

"What you're saying to me is that she never showed up at her car. You never even set eyes on her, right?"

"Right."

"If she's not in the airport, then she had to leave it somehow."

What if the UNSUB had been waiting for her in the airport? What if he'd somehow managed to grab her right out from under Gomez's nose? In that case, she was probably already dead.

Cold fear filled Sam at the possibility. It took a real physical effort to keep his voice even. "Find out how. Check the security cameras to see if you can see her hooking up with anyone. Check the cab stand, the buses, the car-rental agencies. Call Needleman." Ron Needleman was the agent in charge of the St. Louis office. "Tell him you need some help."

"Uh, he's on vacation," Gomez said in a small voice.

"Then call whoever's in charge. I don't care what it takes. *Just find the woman.*"

"Yes, sir."

From the chastened tone of Gomez's voice, Sam got the feeling that at last the urgency of the situation was starting to filter through.

"Now."

"Yessir." It was the equivalent of a verbal salute.

Sam hung up, ran a hand around the back of his neck, and looked at his team. "Pack up. We're heading for St. Louis."

THE SECOND cab dropped her off at the Greyhound Bus station.

Maddie went into the terminal, glanced around. The place was, appropriately enough, all gray: gray walls, gray-speckled linoleum floor, rows of gray plastic chairs, about a quarter of which were occupied. People of all descriptions—a pair of soldiers in uniform, an elderly black woman with two cornrowed little girls, a heavyset white couple sharing a pizza—waited in the seats. None of them paid the least bit of attention to her. Along the far wall, tall windows looked out on a loading zone where a line of buses waited under a canopy, motors running, silver skins gleaming beneath bright halogen lights.

A short line had formed in front of the window where tickets were sold. She joined it, bought a ticket on the bus leaving at 10:15 for Las Vegas, then headed along the hall marked *Restrooms*. There was an exit at the end of the hall. Pushing through it, she stepped outside. The heat wrapped around her like a blanket. It did nothing to ease the bone-deep chill that made her feel as though she would never be warm again.

The time was ten minutes after ten p.m. It was full night, with stars scattered across the velvety black sky and the moon a giant orange globe riding low on the horizon. Moths and other assorted insects swooped around the tall lights that lit the parking lot. Maddie crossed the pavement quickly, heading for the alley that ran between two rows of rundown commercial buildings. Stepping into the darkness of the alley, she couldn't resist a quick glance over her shoulder.

No one, nothing. Gritting her teeth, she hurried on.

This was the most dangerous part of her journey. She was alone outside in the dark, hideously vulnerable to the hired thug who was on her trail. But she was almost certain that he wasn't behind her at that moment, that she wasn't being followed. She was almost certain that she was alone.

Almost.

So far she thought that she was doing a good job of keeping a step ahead of him. When he picked up her trail—and she knew that he would, probably soon and probably at the airport—he would eventually be able to trace her to the mall. He would probably even track her down to the bus station. But by the time he figured out that she hadn't gotten on the express to Las Vegas, she meant to be long gone.

In a manner no one would be able to trace.

She walked two blocks, then turned left down another alley. The buildings were a mix of residential and commercial now. It was a poor section, a bad section. The faint smell of decomposing garbage hung in the air. Broken pavement made pulling her suitcase difficult, so she slowed down, choosing her route carefully, lest the rattle of the wheels should attract too much attention. A homeless man slept on a flattened cardboard box. A man and a woman rooted around in a Dumpster behind a small Korean restaurant. A car pulled up some distance in front of her, dousing its lights. Her breath caught, and she stopped walking. Her heart thudded. Her stomach knotted. But it was nothing, a false alarm. After a moment that seemed to stretch into hours, a man got out, glanced around, and disappeared inside a rickety privacy fence. She remembered to breathe then, and started walking again. Straining her ears for the sounds of pursuit, she heard instead the whirr of insects; an occasional crash, as though a dog was investigating a garbage can; muffled yelling from a fight inside one of the houses; and the wail of a siren in the distance.

By the time she reached her destination, she was bathed in cold sweat.

The detached garage was dark and deserted. Unlocking the door, she slid inside, pulling the suitcase in after her. When she closed the door behind her, it was so dark that she literally couldn't see her hand in front of her face. The air was stifling, and the place smelled musty, dirty. She stood motionless for a moment, listening, getting her bearings. Her heart raced. Her breathing came fast and shallow. Icy prickles chased one another over her skin.

But she heard nothing out of the ordinary. Sensed nothing out of the ordinary.

Finally she moved, finding the ten-year-old Ford Escort by touch, unlocking it, opening the door. By its interior light, she saw that the car was covered in a thick layer of dust and the garage was festooned with cobwebs. Everything looked exactly as it should—as if no one had been there in the three months since she had last visited. Opening the trunk, she heaved her suitcase in beside the emergency kit she had prepared long ago. She had cash in the emergency kit, papers, things she would need to survive until she could start anew.

No one in the world knew about her emergency kit, or that she owned this car or rented this garage. She'd always considered this place her safety net, her Plan B.

If she had the sense of a gnat, she told herself, she would be busy about now, thanking God that she'd had the foresight to prepare it.

Instead, as she drove away, she felt sick inside. For seven years she had been prepared to run—but she realized now that as more and more time had passed, she had grown increasingly confident that she would never have to.

She had hoped and prayed she would never have to.

The last thing in the world she wanted now was to abandon the life she had so painstakingly built for herself—but what choice did she have?

Basically, it came down to this: Leave or die.

Some choice.

Hating what she was being forced to do, she pulled onto I-64 and headed east. Traffic was moderately heavy, and as she approached downtown she could see the brightly lit arch that was the symbol of the city curving silver against the night sky. It dwarfed the surrounding skyscrapers. Beyond it, the Mississippi River rolled south toward New Orleans, its slow-moving waters reflecting the glowing lights of the city. Since it was Friday night, the riverfront would be busy. Tourists would be thick in the park beneath the arch, visiting the gift shop, strolling the paths, lining up to ride the little train that took them up inside the arch to the monument's pinnacle. As she reached the bridge, she saw the steamboats that had been converted into floating gambling casinos plying the river, lights twinkling festively. On the other side of the river, East St. Louis stretched out, deceptively dark and quiet. It was a dangerous place, East St. Louis, and except for those who lived there, the cops who patrolled it, and a few unwary tourists, people tended to stay away from it at night. A handful of long-established factories still existed there, Brehmer's among them. Maddie was just coming off the bridge when she saw its neon sign glowing orange against the worn brick wall of the manufacturing plant.

We won the account.

On any other day, under any other circumstances, she would have been hugging the victory to her like a beloved child, giddy with happiness, overwhelmed with possibility. Now the knowledge was like a lead weight inside her, making it hard to breathe.

Impulsively she took the exit that led past the plant. She needed gas anyway. Might as well get it there as anywhere, and spend her last few minutes in St. Louis mourning what might have been.

We won the account.

At least the others—Jon, Louise, Ana, Judy, Herb—would have this weekend to celebrate before everything turned to ashes.

When she was reported missing, what would happen to Creative Partners? She didn't know. Didn't even want to speculate.

They'd all be out of work. The clients would go elsewhere. The Brehmer account—forget the Brehmer account. It would vanish like smoke in the wind.

She drove past the tall chain-link fence that surrounded the plant, then slowed as she came even with the manufacturing facility itself. It operated twenty-four hours, producing food for nearly every kind of domestic animal, and tall, frosty lights illuminated the scattering of cars in the parking lot. Smoke poured from a smokestack on top of one of the buildings, and a uniformed security guard manned a white hut beside the gate.

Landing this account was the culmination of every dream she'd had since she'd arrived in St. Louis. She had been terrified, broke, friendless, with no one in the world to depend on besides herself. Gravitating to the area's colleges because she had felt she would blend in with all the kids her own age, she'd slept on couches in the libraries and dormitories in those first hard weeks, until she'd scraped together the money to rent a room in a ramshackle old house that catered to students. Unable to find a job, she had made her own work, using campus kitchens to bake cookies and brownies from mixes and peddling them to tourists on the waterfront along with "souvenirs" she made herself from rocks on which she painted things like the arch above the name of the city. Impressed with her entrepreneurial skills, a man whose business was selling advertising over the phone offered her work on a commission-only basis. She'd made seven hundred fifty dollars her first week.

After that, she had never looked back. She had worked hard, saved, dreamed, all the while doing her best to put her past behind her. When the chance to buy Creative Partners had arisen, she'd jumped at it. She knew, knew, *knew* she could make the agency a success.

And after an admittedly slow start, she was now well on her way. Out of all the advertising agencies who'd pitched them, Creative Partners had won the Brehmer account.

Then the clock had struck midnight. Like Cinderella at the ball, she was left with no choice but to flee.

She'd come so far. Was she really going to just let it all go?

Slowing, she turned right into the parking lot of a QuikStop just beyond the plant. Through its windows she could see a couple of customers inside the store, and there was an old Chrysler at the gas pump. She pulled up to another of the pumps and stopped the car.

Then she just sat there, hands tight around the steering wheel, staring out through the windshield at the glowing Brehmer's sign.

"WELL?" SAM growled into the phone. He, Wynne, and Gardner were in the air now, about a third of the way into the three-hour flight to St. Louis. They had been experiencing varying degrees of turbulence since they'd taken off, and right at that moment the small chartered plane was bouncing all over the sky. Gardner, in the seat facing Sam, was wrapped in a blue blanket and slumped against the fuselage, fast asleep. Beside her, Wynne was sprawled in his seat as if he didn't have a bone left in his body. He was pale and slack-jawed, his parted lips faintly purple from his gum— hopefully discarded before he went to sleep—which Sam could still smell. Only a gleam from beneath nearly closed lids told Sam that the ringing phone had roused him—unlike Gardner—from oblivion.

"We think she took a taxi to the mall," Gomez said on the other end. "Looks like she went shopping."

"*Shopping?*" Sam repeated, momentarily dumbfounded. Then he frowned. How likely was that? "Directly from the airport? Without picking up her car?"

"This cab driver says he gave a woman matching her description a ride to the mall," Gomez repeated doggedly.

"So she's at the mall."

"Well . . ." There was something in Gomez's tone that told Sam that the other shoe was getting ready to drop. "The thing is, the mall's closed now and she doesn't seem to be there. Actually, uh, we can't seem to locate her anywhere. I'm thinking maybe she, uh, met some friends at the mall and went somewhere with them."

Breathe. "Find out."

"I'm trying. I've got Hendricks with me now, and we're doing everything we can to locate her."

Deep breath. Deep, calming breath. "Do more. Put out an APB if you have to. I want her found."

"Yes, sir."

"*Now.*"

"Yessir."

And on the heels of that verbal salute, Sam broke the connection.

"Fucking new guy still fucking up, huh?" Wynne asked. As far as Sam could tell, the only muscles he'd moved were connected to his eyelids. His eyes were open now, and he was looking at Sam.

"Yeah." The plane pitched. Sam's fingers curled instinctively around the arms of his seat. Outside the windows, the night was black. No stars, no moon. Just—nothing. A void. "You know, that guy isn't going to just let her walk away. He's going to kill her if he can."

He tried to keep the tension he was feeling out of his voice. He knew himself well enough to know that if it hadn't been for the turbulence, he would have been up, pacing the cabin.

"You think he's already going after her again? Or is he out there somewhere, planning a hit on this Walter?"

"I don't think he has to plan a hit on Walter. I think he knows exactly where Walter is, and can hit him any time he wants. The others, too. They were all planned in advance. This chase thing he has us doing is a game to him. He likes to drive us crazy trying to figure it out, then do the hit right before we close in. He's taunting us, letting us know he's smarter than us."

"Sick son of a bitch." But Wynne said it lazily. This case wasn't getting to Wynne the way it was to him, Sam realized. Of course, the phone calls weren't directed at Wynne. And now, there was Maddie Fitzgerald. "You think he's having fun with it?"

"Oh, yeah," Sam said. "But we'll get him. He's already made one mistake. And one mistake is all it takes."

"Leaving Maddie Fitzgerald alive."

"That's the one."

"So you think he's in St. Louis."

If the bastard was already in St. Louis, and Maddie Fitzgerald was missing, things weren't looking good. The idea that she was out there, unprotected and possibly in danger, while he was stuck in this tiny cabin, miles above the earth, made Sam nuts.

"Depends on how he's getting around. If he's driving, which I think he is, it's possible. But even if he isn't in St. Louis yet, he will be. Soon. I'm as sure of it as I am my own name. There's no way he can be sure she can't identify him."

Wynne looked at him. "Think it's fair to abandon Walter to his fate while we mount guard over her?"

The plane dropped a couple hundred feet, and Sam's grip on the seat arms tightened until his knuckles turned white. Wynne the Placid never even moved.

"You ever hear the saying about a bird in the hand being worth two in the bush? Maddie Fitzgerald is our bird in the hand. We don't know where Walter is, and chances are we're not going to figure it out in time to save him. We do know where she is. And we can assume the UNSUB's off-balance, because he hadn't figured on having to get to St. Louis to take care of a mistake. This is probably our best chance to catch him, and the best way to save Walter, whoever the hell he is, and anyone else who might have made the sick bastard's hit parade. What we do is put a tail on Maddie Fitzgerald, and wait. He'll show up. Always supposing he hasn't already gotten to her, that is."

Sam's insides twisted at the thought. Since this case had started, they'd been too late five times already. If it turned out to be six, and the next victim was Maddie Fitzgerald, he knew he'd be haunted by her honey-colored eyes for the rest of his life.

THE SMELL of gasoline was slow to dissipate in the muggy air. Topping off her tank, Maddie thought she could almost see the vapors as a diaphanous, glistening film, rising hazily beneath the harsh light. Returning the nozzle to its niche, she screwed her gas cap back on and headed for the cash register. She paid for the gas, walked back to her car, and got in.

The Brehmer's sign still glowed orange in the distance.

A sharp tap on the window made her jump so high that she almost banged her head on the roof. Her heart was hitting about a thousand beats per minute by the time she realized that the man on the other side of the glass was the same man she had paid for the gas.

Cautiously, she rolled the window down a few inches.

"Forgot your change," he said, handing over a couple of limp bills and some coins.

"Oh. Thanks." Rolling up the window, she dropped the change in the console, stuffed the bills in her pocket, and started the car. Her pulse was still racing as she pulled out of the QuikStop. Her hands shook and she was freezing cold again, jittery, basically one big nerve.

It had taken only that tap on the window to make her realize just how vulnerable she was. The hit could happen anytime, anywhere.

No matter how hard she ran.

If they'd found her once, they could find her again.

She drove past Brehmer's, heading for the expressway, but she didn't even notice the glowing sign because the truth of her situation, now that she had been awakened to it, pulsated through her brain in its own huge neon orange letters.

Now that they knew she was alive, they would never stop coming after her.

Sooner or later, they would find her. And she would die.

Boom. Just like that.

Blindly, she drove right past the expressway ramp.

Unless she beat them at their own game. Unless she got over the paralyzing terror that had haunted her for seven years. Unless she fought back.

She was not defenseless. She had a weapon. The only question was, did she have the guts—the smarts—to use it? And survive?

The bright warning of a red light stopped her. Glancing around, she realized that the expressway entrance was a good three blocks behind her, that she was waiting at an intersection with a gang of up-to-no-good toughs eyeing her from the corner, that the dark storefronts sported iron bars and the only other vehicle in sight was pulled over at the next corner with a miniskirted hooker leaning through the window.

Not that any of that scared her particularly. She knew this part of town, knew East St. Louis, knew all the East St. Louises out there. They were in her blood. She'd grown up in a succession of them, each rougher than the first.

But she had gotten out, made herself over, become *somebody*. She was a member of the Chamber of Commerce, for God's sake. How funny—how cool—was that?

She pulled into the parking lot just past where the hooker was now sliding into the car, turned around, and headed back toward the QuikStop. She would park there, make a couple of phone calls.

It was called taking back her life.

Then, maybe, if the gods were kind and the heavens smiled and her luck was just a little bit good, she would be going home.

Or maybe not.

ELEVEN

Saturday, August 16

By the time the taxi dropped her off at the airport, it was nearly five a.m. Pulling her little black suitcase behind her, Maddie headed for long-term parking, so tired that just putting one foot in front of the other required a serious effort. But she felt better. Not good, but better. *Safer.*

She thought she'd managed to call off the dogs.

The number was seared into her brain. She had called it often enough, years ago. The phone was still operational, still answered in the same way. "A-One Plastics."

The company didn't really exist, of course. Or, rather, it did, but only as a front for the real operation: a loan-sharking outfit with ties to the Mob. She'd asked for Bob Johnson, and had been answered by a couple of heartbeats' worth of dead silence.

Then the man on the other end of the phone had asked sharply, "Who's this?"

His voice had bristled with paranoia.

Identifying herself, Maddie had almost smiled. She was still scared to death of them, of what they could do; she knew her life hinged on how this phone call turned out; but still, it felt almost good to carry the war into the enemy's camp at last.

The man had denied any knowledge of Bob Johnson, but had asked her to leave a number where she could be reached.

Not very many minutes later, her cell phone had rung, just as she had known it would.

"This is Bob Johnson," the voice said. Maddie thought she recognized it, but she couldn't be sure. It had been a long time ago. And, after all, Bob Johnson was a code, not a man. For all she knew, maybe more than one person answered to it. Or maybe the person answering to it had changed. "Who is this again?"

Maddie identified herself for a second time, and the pause with which her name was greeted told her that he recognized it.

"Where are you, babe?" he asked finally.

That was so blatant that Maddie laughed.

"Like I'm going to tell you," she said, then glanced nervously around the lighted parking lot to make sure that they had not already managed to track her to this out-of-the-way QuikStop. The Chrysler had been replaced by a red Dodge Neon. Its owner, a black man in a blue mechanic's uniform, was busy pumping gas. She nestled the small silver phone closer to her face. "Remember all those 'errands' you guys had my father run? He kept things from them. Evidence. Enough to put quite a few people away for a long time. I'm just calling to tell you that if anything happens to me, if I die younger than eighty in any place other than my bed, letters are going to be mailed, giving certain locations where certain things are hidden, and that evidence is going to start popping up all over the place like a bad rash, and a lot of people are going to go down."

This time the silence wasn't as long.

"You know what happens to little girls who make big threats?" The voice had turned ugly. "Things that aren't so nice."

Maddie laughed again, the sound as brittle as she felt. "You mean, like somebody sending a hit man to knock me off? Oh, wait, somebody's already done that. But he messed up, and I'm still here. And I mean to stay that way. Look, I don't want any trouble. I just want to live my life in peace. So I'm trying to come up with something here that works out for all of us. Nobody bothers me, and I don't bother anybody. That evidence never sees the light of day."

"What kind of evidence are we talking about?"

Maddie thought fast. "You want an example? Okay. My father was there the night that Ted Cicero was whacked. The guy who did it threw the gun away afterwards. Later, my father went back and got the gun." She paused for effect. "I can't be sure, of course, but I'd be willing to bet that there are fingerprints all over it."

The sound of an indrawn breath told her that she'd scored. She remembered well the night her father had come back from witnessing the hit on Ted Cicero. He'd gotten drunk and cried, and told her everything, to her horror.

"Where is it?" he asked, rasping now.

"I want to be let alone," she said, keeping her voice steady with an effort. "If I even think there's a hit man in my vicinity, I'm going give the gun—and everything else my father kept—to the FBI. They've already been in touch with me, you know. Looking for your hit man. I don't want to, but if I have to choose between getting whacked and going to the feds, I pick the feds."

She could hear him breathing hard. "If I recall right, you got a history with the feds yourself."

"So don't make me choose."

Maddie could feel his tension emanating through the phone.

"What kind of other stuff are we talking about here?"

Her heart was racing, and her stomach had tied itself in so many knots by this time that Houdini himself couldn't have straightened it out. But she didn't let so much as a hint of that come out in her voice. She knew these guys: They were jackals who preyed on the weak. The key to surviving was to convince them that she was strong. Strong enough to carry out her threats.

"Tapes, for one thing. He used to carry a little mini tape recorder in his pocket sometimes. When he went out on jobs. And, let's see . . . oh, yeah, there was that stack of hundred-dollar bills Junior Rizzo gave him—I don't know what job it was from, but I'm sure the feds would find it interesting. And other things. Lots of other things. He liked keeping souvenirs."

There was more silence.

Then, "Babe, let me give you some advice. The smart thing for you to do is to come on back here where you belong, and bring all this stuff you're talking about with you. Hand it over, and quit threatening people. Nobody wants to have to hurt you."

Maddie snorted. "Don't give me that. Nobody gives a shit about hurting me. But I'm telling you: You hurt me, and you hurt yourselves. I have enough evidence here to put a lot of people away for a long time. And I've arranged it so that if anything happens to me, anything at all, if I have a heart attack or choke to death on a pretzel or whatever, you better believe the shit's going to hit the fan—for you and yours."

"Potty mouth," he said, sounding angry now. "In my book, there's nothing worse than a woman with a potty mouth. Just for the record, I don't know nothing about no hit man. Or no Fat Ted Cicero. Or Junior Rizzo."

"What, are you afraid somebody's listening in? They're not, at least not from my side. Like you said, I don't want anything to do with the feds. Not unless you make me choose."

"I don't know nothin' about anything you're talking about."

Maddie made a sound of disgust. "You go tell whoever's in charge what I said," she said. "And get back to me. Real soon. Like within the next couple of hours. Or I'm going to have to start making some moves to protect myself."

With that, she hung up. Then, not sure how technologically advanced the goons might have become since she'd last had occasion to cross paths with them, she peeled rubber out of the QuikStop and headed back toward the city, where she drove aimlessly around the interstates because she was afraid to stop anywhere.

Call her paranoid, but she had hideous visions of hit men with global-positioning devices zeroing in on her cell phone. Maybe they had some twisted version of an On-Star service of their own now, an automatic lo-cater, something like 1-800-Bang-Bang-You're-Dead.

By the time the phone rang again, she was a raw bundle of nerves, hav-ing scared herself to the point where she was on the verge of chucking the whole plan and hightailing it for as far away from St. Louis as she could get.

But then Bob had gotten back to her, telling her that while nobody had any knowledge concerning any of the stuff she'd been talking about ear-lier, they had a deal. Basically, live and let live.

Of course, when the Mob acts like you're their new best pal, the next thing you're liable to feel is their knife in your back.

Maddie knew that as well as anyone, although she thought she had suc-ceeded in making them think that they had more to lose than to gain by killing her.

On the plus side, she was telling the absolute truth about the stash of ev-idence. Her father had always been convinced that someday he could use the things he had secretly squirreled away to free himself from the Mob's grip. He had called his accumulation of stuff his "insurance policy," and had kept it in a locked strongbox, which he carefully hid. Unfortunately, the last time she had seen that strongbox had been about a week before she'd fled.

But since she was the only one who knew that, it didn't really matter. Having the evidence didn't help her at all. Having them *think* she had the evidence was what mattered.

And it just might be enough to keep her alive. It was a risk, a gamble. Up until this moment, she'd never thought she had a propensity for gambling. But it seemed that now that the chips were down, she was proving to be her father's daughter after all.

Everything she had ever wanted was suddenly within her grasp. During the last seven years, she had even managed to make herself over into the person she had always wanted to be. The wrong-side-of-the-tracks, lock-up-your-sons, her-father-is-a-criminal girl was respectable now. Looked up to, even. A pillar of the community. "An inspiration to others," as the president of the Chamber of Commerce had described her at the dinner where she'd gotten her award.

She was not going to just close the book on that, or on the life that went with it. It had been too hard-won. Having done everything that it was in her power to do to make sure she kept safe, she was going to take a chance. She was going to stay.

Which is how she came to be walking wearily past rows of cars in the St. Louis airport's long-term parking lot as the sun pushed its first tentative feelers of color over the horizon. It was still dark, but not as dark as it had been. It was, rather, the deep, hazy charcoal of a newborn dawn. Beyond the yellow glow of the tall halogen lamps that illuminated the area, the airport was still and somnolent, not yet alive with the day's bustle. In the distance she could hear the *swoosh* of an airplane as it raced along the runway. Closer at hand, the only sound was the steady hum of traffic from the nearby interstate. The faintest tinge of motor oil hung in the air. Even at such an early hour, it was still hot and humid outside—it was always hot and humid in St. Louis in August—but as she headed toward her blue Camry, Maddie was shivering.

But not with the cold.

She was scared, there was no getting around that. And she probably would be for a long time to come, until she had determined to her own satisfaction that her threats had worked to stuff the bogeyman back under the bed. But she should be safe enough at the moment, she calculated. To begin with, she was almost certain that she had not been followed on her aborted run. And if she had not been followed, then logic dictated that the hit man—whom she had last encountered in New Orleans—would not be lurking in this particular parking lot at this particular ungodly hour, just waiting to pick her off. Her flight had landed almost eleven hours before. Even if he had followed her to St. Louis, even if he had found her car in the lot, what were the chances that he was still around?

Slim, she judged. *But not quite none.*

Which left her as jittery as a caged bird in a roomful of cats. The nervous looks she could not help casting around were purely involuntary. So, too, was the quickening of her step as she neared the spot at the back of the lot where she had parked her car. When she had parked the car, on a bright, sunny Thursday afternoon, when the thought that her carefully constructed house of cards might be in imminent danger of collapse had never crossed her mind, it had seemed like as good a place as any, as well as a chance to work in a little aerobic exercise before she boarded her flight. Now, the closer she got to the space, the more isolated it seemed.

The misty pools of light thrown down by the overhead lamps were a fair distance apart, and her Camry, in the last row, was almost beyond the reach of all of them. The farther she got from the last streetlight, the darker it got. The darker it got, the antsier she got. Her eyes darted hither and yon like bees drunk on picnic beer. Behind the line of cars, a tall, grassy bank rose just high enough to block a view of the road that veered off from the central artery to the terminal to feed the long-term lot. To her right, across another vast, mostly empty expanse of asphalt, clustered a group of large metal buildings, probably airplane hangars. To her left, even farther away, was the blocky concrete box that was the terminal.

The good news was, there was not another human being in sight.

That was also the bad news.

What she wouldn't have given, just at that moment, for a patrolling cop.

She was close enough to her car now so that she could almost read the license plate. The weariness that had caused her steps to drag just moments before had been wiped out by a burst of fear-fueled adrenaline. Walking faster, probing shadows for possible danger, she cursed the rattle her suitcase wheels made because she could not hear anything much over them and because they gave her presence away. Maybe she was being paranoid, but they seemed about as loud as a marching band. So loud that no one within earshot could be ignorant of her approach.

But then, no one was within earshot—were they?

Her nerves were getting the better of her, she knew. But she couldn't help it. Her imagination went into overdrive, seeing danger in every swooping moth and hearing it with every random sound. She was alone. She was sure she was alone. But her body refused to be convinced. Independent of logic, her pulse raced and her stomach fluttered and her mouth went dry.

As she drew even with the Camry's back fender, her heart was pounding so hard that she could barely even hear the clatter the suitcase was making over the drumming in her ears. The sense of being isolated and vulnerable was so strong as she turned into the cramped space between her car and the Town Car beside it that she had to fight the urge to just abandon her suitcase on the spot and jump inside her car and zoom out of there as fast as she could go. But she couldn't leave Fudgie—or her other things, either. Stowing them in the backseat would take just a few seconds more.

Anyway, she was being totally paranoid. She couldn't see anyone. She couldn't hear anyone. And the reason for that was—*ta-dah!*—there was no one else in the parking lot.

Punching the button on her key ring that unlocked the car, she hurried to grab the door handle at the same time as the interior lit up.

Her breath stopped. Her eyes widened. She recoiled.

There was a man in her car. In the driver's seat. Bent over, as though he was hiding. Waiting.

For her.

In the split second it took her brain to register what her eyes saw, he moved, straightening, his head twisting as he looked around at her.

Maddie screamed, dropped the handle of her suitcase as if it had suddenly gone red-hot, and turned to run.

And smacked full-tilt into a warm, solid body that grabbed her arms and held on.

Reacting instinctively, screeching so loudly that she wouldn't have been surprised to learn that windows were shattering in Kansas City, she shoved him away as hard as she could and jammed a knee up into his groin.

"Oomph!" He let go and doubled over. She whirled to run.

"Hold on there."

Strong male arms clamped around her waist, dragging her back into a bear hug that imprisoned her elbows. Heart racing like a NASCAR engine, terror tying her stomach into a cold, hard knot, she screamed and fought like a wild thing as she was swung up off her feet. He staggered sideways with her, his grip all but crushing her rib cage, and her feet found the side of her car. Pushing off with all her might, she nearly succeeded in knocking both of them over. But he held on grimly, somehow managing to stay on his feet while he carted her backward over about a yard of concrete. In a single petrified glance around, she caught just a glimpse of a white panel van, the rear doors of which were being swung open to receive her. Another set of hands reached out to help subdue her. . . .

"Help!" she screeched, even as she was being bundled inside. "Somebody, help!"

The man doing most of the bundling said something, but she couldn't hear him over her screams, which were cut off abruptly as she was dropped on her stomach in the carpeted cargo area of the van and all the air *wooshed* out of her lungs.

"I don't fucking believe this," a man in the front passenger seat said. Invisible except as a shape because of the darkness, he had twisted around to watch as she was shoved inside the van. He was too far away to reach her, and so she forgot about him as, strengthened by panic, she rebounded onto her knees. Her blood pounded in her ears; her lungs expanded as she sucked in air. Having recovered her ability to scream, she shrieked like a banshee as she tried to dive past her captor to freedom. But he blocked her, shoving her down onto her stomach on the carpet a second time and then yanking her right arm behind her back. He was in the process of fastening something cold and metallic around her wrist as the other man bellowed, in the tone of someone who had said it more than once, "Gomez! *Let her go!*"

Something about the voice, about the shape of the head and shoulders silhouetted against the windshield, rang a bell of recognition in her head.

She stopped struggling, and her head snapped up so fast she nearly sprained her neck.

"But you saw her!" the man holding her protested. "She kneed Hendricks! She . . ."

"I said let her go." His voice was quieter now, probably because he no longer had to make himself heard over her screams. "This is Miz Fitzgerald."

That drawled *Miz* was what did it.

"*You,*" she gasped, staring at him in total disbelief. "What are you doing here?"

But if Mr. Special Agent from New Orleans heard, he didn't reply. Instead, he swung out of the van and came around toward the back, as the man holding her arm reluctantly released it. Maddie whipped around, rising to her knees. Then, as it became obvious that she was no longer in danger and, in fact, had not been since she'd spotted the man—almost certainly an FBI agent—in her car, all the adrenaline drained out of her like water out of an unplugged bathtub. Her body accordioned and she sat abruptly on her folded legs. Glaring at the wiry guy with the brown brush cut and navy sport coat who had thrown her into the van—he was backlit by a halogen glow that made it impossible for her to see enough of his face to form an impression of it—she transferred that glare to Mr. Special Agent as he joined the party.

"Nice to see you again, Miz Fitzgerald."

The dry drawl earned him a full-blown scowl, which he probably was unable to fully appreciate because of the darkness in the back of the van. Like his friend, he was backlit, which made him look tall and broad and formidable.

"Give me the key," he added in a resigned tone to the other man, holding out his hand. It was only then that Maddie realized that a pair of shiny silver handcuffs dangled from her wrist.

"You've got to be kidding me." She held up her cuffed wrist and looked down at the restraint hanging from it in disbelief. "Handcuffs?"

"I think what happened here was a slight case of mistaken identity."

McCabe took hold of her wrist, held it up, and leaned forward to squint at it.

"Mistaken . . ." Her voice trailed off.

She remembered the warmth of that hand. The size of that hand.

"Madeline Fitzgerald, meet Special Agent Pete Gomez."

Resisting her attempt to tug her hand free, McCabe lifted her wrist higher and turned it this way and that, apparently trying to catch enough light to enable him to fit the key into the cuffs.

"Hope I didn't scare you," Gomez said sheepishly.

"I think you can safely assume that grabbing her and throwing her into the back of a van scared her." McCabe was talking to Gomez, even as his thumb slid over Maddie's wrist. The tender skin there registered the heat of that hard, masculine thumb, instinctively recording how long and strong it felt, even as her mind rejected the inevitable association.

"Let go of my hand," she said through her teeth, and jerked her wrist from his hold. The handcuffs jingled as she pressed her hand to her chest.

He shrugged, focused on her now. "Your call. People might think you have odd taste in jewelry, though."

Maddie's lips compressed. She really couldn't go through life with a set of handcuffs attached to her wrist.

"Fine. Get it off." She held out her arm to him again.

His fingers slid around her wrist. "Just hold still a minute. . . ."

This time, Maddie refused to notice how his hand felt and was rewarded just a few seconds later when the key slid into the lock. A turn, a click, and the bracelet fell away from her wrist. McCabe caught it and released her hand.

"You said she was wearing a white skirt suit. How was I supposed to know? And then she kneed Hendricks," Gomez said, sounding aggrieved.

"You changed clothes," McCabe said to Maddie. "That would account for some of the confusion, I think." He handed the cuffs back to Gomez.

Maddie experienced another moment of panic as she realized that she was indeed still wearing the jeans, T-shirt, and sneakers that she'd bought at Dillard's to run in. But, of course, she reassured herself even as her heart gave a sudden lurch, he couldn't know why she'd bought them or that she'd meant to run. The Escort had been returned to its garage, the new tapestry suitcase had joined her emergency kit in the trunk, and she'd made her way back to the airport by a route every bit as circuitous as the one she'd used to leave it.

He couldn't know any of that. He . . .

"Wait a minute," she said, as the full implications of his presence burst upon her. "You were just in New Orleans. Are you *following* me?"

McCabe stuck his hands in the front pockets of his jeans and rocked back on his heels. If ever there'd been a stance that denoted guilt, Maddie thought, she was looking at it right there.

"It just so happened that we were in the neighborhood," he said.

"Oh, yeah. Right. St. Louis is definitely in the same neighborhood as New Orleans." Her brows furrowed. "You are, aren't you? You're following me!"

"I'd like to point out here that you found us. We didn't find you. So tell me how that's following you."

"That's just splitting hairs, and you know it."

As she spoke, she sat down and swung her legs around in front of her, scooting out of the van. McCabe grasped her arm as she slid to her feet, steadying her. That big, strong hand imprinted itself on her skin all over again. Maddie jerked her arm from his grasp with a little more emphasis than was strictly necessary, took a step away from him, and then stopped abruptly as she came face-to-face with the seemingly solid wall of people that had materialized behind him. They curved around the back of the van, making it impossible for her to reach her car without strong-arming her way through them—which she was not entirely certain they were prepared to let her do.

"What is this, a convention? Who are all these people?" she demanded, rounding on McCabe. But her peripheral vision had already picked out the giant at the back of the crowd. The frizzy golden nimbus that the weird light made of his hair was unmistakable. Seeing that her gaze rested on him—

Maddie realized then that the lights that backlit them must illuminate her face to a certain degree—he gave her a feeble wave.

"They're FBI agents, too!" she gasped before he could reply. "Aren't you?" she said to them. "Aren't they?" she said to McCabe.

He sighed. "Special Agent Mel Hendricks. Special Agent Cynthia Gardner. And you already know Wynne. And Gomez."

As he introduced them, McCabe gestured to each one in turn. Hendricks, whom Gomez had identified as the man she had kneed, seemed slightly stoop-shouldered. Maddie didn't know if that was his natural posture or the result of lingering pain. Gardner, the only woman in the group, was as tall as most of the men. She had opened the doors of the van for Gomez. And replaying the scene in her head again, she realized that Wynne had been the man in her front seat. That cherub-on-steroids look was hard to mistake.

"What were you doing in my car?" she asked him. Then her eyes swung back to McCabe. "What was he doing in my car?"

"Searching it?" Wynne's tone made it more of a question than an answer.

"Searching it," McCabe confirmed.

Outraged, Maddie drew herself up to her full height as the wheels in her head began to turn. So many agents in St. Louis for a murder in New Orleans—what was wrong with this picture? Did somebody say "overkill"? Her stomach clenched as the question occurred to her: Did they *know*? But if they did, wouldn't she already be under arrest? McCabe had made his fellow agent take the cuffs *off*. . . .

They didn't know. They were present strictly for reasons of their own. And it didn't take a genius to figure out what those reasons were. Unfortunately for their plans, however, FBI agents on her tail were the last thing she wanted. Except, of course, a hit man on her tail, but she was relatively certain she'd already taken care of *him*.

If, however, the Mob were to somehow get wind of their presence and think she was in bed with the FBI, she knew as well as she knew her own name that all bets would be off.

The thought of having her hard-won deal screwed by the meddling presence of the feds she despised maddened her. Her eyes narrowed at Mc-Cabe. "Where the hell do you get off searching my car?"

His tone was probably meant to be soothing. "Your plane landed eleven hours ago. You never picked up your car. We were worried about you."

"Hah!" Maddie glared at him, then let her eyes flash around the circle before her gaze once again fastened on McCabe. "That's the lamest thing I ever heard. You think I don't know what you're doing? You're following me because you think that guy in New Orleans is going to take another shot at me, and you want to use me to catch him!"

The silence with which that was greeted told her that she was right on.

"Well, you can forget it," she said, and stormed right through the group, which parted like the Red Sea to accommodate her.

"Miz Fitzgerald . . ." McCabe was right behind her. A sizzling glance over her shoulder told her that his fellow agents were following him like a tail follows a dog. "It's in your best interest to cooperate with us. It seems to me that you don't fully understand the danger you're in. I don't know how to put this any more plainly: *There's a killer out there, and I'm as sure as it's humanly possible to be that he's coming after you.*"

Maddie bent to snag the handle of her suitcase, which, thanks to the weight of the briefcase secured to the top of it, had fallen over on its side, and snatch up her keys, which had dropped to the pavement not far from the suitcase.

"So what's your plan? To follow me until he kills me, and then arrest him?" Opening the Camry's rear door, she wheeled the suitcase up to the threshold and wrestled it, briefcase and all, into the backseat. "Maybe that works for you, Mr. Special Agent, but it doesn't work for me."

Slamming the door, she shot poison darts at McCabe with her eyes.

"Actually, we were kind of counting on arresting him before he kills you."

"No." Maddie opened the driver's-side door.

He caught her arm, his long fingers gripping hard as he stepped close, so close that she had to look up to meet his gaze. His eyes were dark and intent. "You're not hearing me. You need us. You're in danger."

Maddie snorted. "The only dangerous people I see around here are you"—she hit McCabe with another venomous glance—"and you"—the next one was for Wynne, who was right behind him—"and the rest of you." As a finale, she shared the wealth.

"Miz Fitzgerald . . ."

"Let go," she said through her teeth, jerking her arm from his grasp. "And step back." She sketched an area around herself with her index finger. "This is my personal space. *Stay out of it.*"

She slid into the driver's seat and reached out to pull the door closed.

"Miz Fitzgerald . . ."

"No," she repeated, pausing to glare up at McCabe. "I don't want you following me. I want you to leave me alone. I refuse. So *go away.*"

She slammed the door and started the car. After a glance in the mirror to make sure that McCabe and the rest of them were out of the way, she backed out of the parking spot. McCabe, with his henchmen behind him, had regrouped behind the open-doored van, which, not coincidentally, was parked directly behind the spot her car had just vacated. Reversing past them, she shoved the transmission into drive and glanced their way again. The halogen glow coupled with the lightening sky permitted her to see them all more or less clearly now. Gomez looked young, Hendricks looked grumpy, Wynne looked tired, and Gardner had spiky, red hair. They were all watching her, and so was McCabe. His arms were folded over his chest and his feet were planted slightly apart as he tracked the Camry's progress. From what she could tell, he was still wearing the same grungy jeans and T-shirt that he'd had on the previous day, he needed a shave more than ever, and his eyes were so narrowed and hooded beneath the thick, black brows that were drawn together over them that if she hadn't known who and what he was, he would have won her choice for best candidate for hit man hands down.

He was also wearing that sardonic little smile of his again.

She didn't like that smile. She didn't trust that smile.

Pulling even with them, she braked and rolled down her window.

"I mean it," she said forcefully when he raised his eyebrows at her. "I refuse to have you following me. So back off."

"The thing is," he said, his drawl more pronounced than she could remember hearing it, "we don't really need your permission."

He smiled at her. She scowled at him. Then she rolled up her window and peeled rubber toward the exit.

TWELVE

Maddie wasn't really surprised to glance in her rearview mirror some few minutes later and discover the white van behind her. She was, however, furious. Her jaw clenched, her hands tightened around the steering wheel, and she muttered something not very nice under her breath. Then she came to her senses and jerked her eyes back to the road. The very last thing she needed was to have a wreck because she wasn't paying attention to her driving.

Having told McCabe to leave her alone, and having been ignored, she didn't see exactly what else she could do to rid herself of her escort.

Except fume. And ignore them.

This she set herself to do. Breathing in deeply, she relaxed her grip on the steering wheel and turned on the radio. The soaring vocals of Christina Aguilera's rendition of "Beautiful" filled the car. That was good. Easy to listen to. Humming along, she deliberately did not look in the rearview mirror again, instead concentrating on easing around the U-shaped entrance ramp that emptied out onto I-270. It was still not quite full dawn, and besides her Camry and the van several discreet car lengths behind it, only a few vehicles were on the road. Lights from cars going in the opposite direction flashed through her windows as she headed south.

She lived in Clayton, a moderately upscale older suburb that contained a mix of housing, from huge old single-family homes to square brick apartment buildings and commercial buildings. Convenient to shopping and other amenities, it was about fifteen minutes from the airport. Once she was safely inside her apartment, she planned to shower and fall into bed. She'd now been basically without sleep for almost forty-eight hours, and she was so tired that her eyes burned. It probably wasn't even safe for her to drive.

It then occurred to her that if the FBI was planning to stake out her apartment, which she assumed was the next step in their plan, one good thing might yet come of their meddling: She should at least be able to catch a few hours of decent sleep. With the feds providing multiple eyes to watch and ears to listen, at least she would feel safer inside her apartment in the short term. On her own, she certainly would have slept, because she was too exhausted not to. But she would have been afraid. She would have had nightmares. And every squeaking floorboard in a building with lots of them would have startled her awake.

Just in case.

As she turned off the expressway onto Big Bend Boulevard, she noticed that the sky was growing lighter. The entire eastern horizon was limned with fiery orange now, and she was able to see, with help from the dimming illumination of the streetlights that lined the road, dew shining on the grassy median. She turned left, into the residential section where she lived, and eased around a garbage truck parked by a curb. The trashman was in the process of dumping the contents of a can into the back of his truck as she passed. The clank of garbage being emptied into the big green crusher compartment rose above the rushing sound of the commuter train just blocks away as it headed into the city.

For a moment, as she pulled onto her street, Maddie thought that she'd lost the van. Or perhaps they had decided not to follow her after all. Because they weren't there in her rearview mirror when she glanced back.

But by the time she drove into the lot behind the house in which her apartment was located, she'd caught sight of it again. They were just turning onto her street, so far back that she wasn't even sure they could still see her car. Maybe she *had* lost them? Almost? Then it occurred to her that they didn't have to follow her all that closely. They were the FBI, after all. She was willing to bet dollars to doughnuts that they already knew precisely where she lived.

And with that, she remembered just exactly why she experienced fear and loathing every time she thought of the FBI.

Her apartment was on the third floor of a big old Arts and Crafts–style house that had been converted into multiple units years before. The third floor, with its dormer windows and odd angles, was the smallest, and she had it all to herself. The house itself was a homey-looking place, all deep brown siding and covered porches and gables. The front yard was the size of a postage stamp, and the backyard had been converted into a parking lot, but honeysuckle bushes grew riotously around the front entrance and had tangled themselves into a thick hedge behind the parking area, and tall old oaks and elms shaded the fresh new asphalt. Maddie knew she would be enfolded by the intoxicating scent of the honeysuckles as soon as she stepped out of the car. It was one of the reasons she loved living there. It was one of those little somethings that made a place feel like home.

It also didn't hurt that the rent was very reasonable.

Only June Matthews's green PT Cruiser was parked in the shadowy lot, Maddie saw as she cast a quick glance around. A divorced middle-school teacher, June rented one of the two apartments on the second floor. The other tenants, a young couple and a single woman lawyer in each of the two first-floor apartments and a pair of sixtyish sisters who shared the other second-floor apartment, didn't appear to be home. At least, their cars weren't home.

Maddie nosed the Camry into her designated spot beside the walkway to the back porch. Actually, her lease allotted her two—each apartment came with two parking spaces, for a total of ten—but she never used the other one, so it had been designated the guest spot by common consent. She braked, put the transmission into park, and slewed around to look for the van. By now she should be able to see its lights.

This was private property. She was a little hazy on the laws, but she didn't think that they had any right to follow her here.

Of course, in practical terms, the FBI was pretty much like the proverbial eight-hundred-pound gorilla. It could do anything it . . .

Something stung her left shoulder, and both the front and rear windshields shattered with a thunderclap-loud *boom,* all at approximately the same instant. BBs of glass blew inward, showering her with what felt like an explosion of hail. Reflexively closing her eyes, still registering the unexpected burning heat of the sting, she reopened them almost instantly and turned back around to gape in blank incomprehension at the open hole where the windshield had been. Then she felt something—a bee?—whiz past her left cheek.

Not a bee. *A bullet.*

Oh, God, someone was shooting at her. That sting—it was a bullet. She'd been shot.

Making the connection, Maddie threw herself across the seat. At a minimum, survival meant getting down below the level of the dashboard.

The sound of squealing brakes and slamming doors somewhere close at hand was followed almost instantly by the thud of running feet. Someone wrenched open the driver's-side door. The interior light blinked on. Maddie screamed—the sound was shrill and high, like an infant's wail—and recoiled from the man who crouched there, doing her best to scramble over the console in a frantic, instinct-fueled attempt to escape.

"Stay down!"

McCabe. She recognized him with a great rush of relief as he pushed her down again, then threw what felt like his entire body on top of her. As his weight crushed her against the hard plastic casing of the console between the seats, she cried out, instinctively shifting onto her stomach a little to ease the pressure, but she didn't even think about trying to push him off. He was putting himself between her and the next bullet, putting his life on the line to keep her alive.

Another shot could come at any second. It could penetrate the car's thin aluminum skin, hit him, tear through his flesh, then bury itself in hers.

Maddie realized that she was trembling. Her stomach roiled. Her heart raced like a runaway train. Terror swirled over her skin like an icy wind. Every tiny hair on her body sprang to prickling life.

Please, God, keep us safe. Both of us.

What could have been seconds or minutes or hours later, she felt him shift. He started to ease off her. Maddie's lips parted and she sucked in much-needed air as she clutched him, caught his shoulder, his arm, his hand, and held on.

"Don't leave me," she said. Her voice sounded like nothing she had ever heard emerge from her throat before. Their gazes met. He loomed above her, his eyes black and hard and alive with some emotion she couldn't quite name. His expression was grim.

"I'm not leaving you," he promised, but still her cold fingers twined with his warm ones and clung with every bit of strength they possessed to make sure he kept his word. He slid out of the car then, and when she tried to follow he freed his hand to catch her hipbones and pull her out after him. She ended up sitting flat on her bottom on the warm asphalt with her back against the rear door of her car and her knees bent. Little chunks of glass from her windshield littered the pavement all around her. McCabe crouched in front of her, his shoulders blocking most of her view of their surroundings, and she realized that he was once again placing himself between her and possible danger. Behind him, at a little distance, she thought she saw the bulk of the white van. To her right, the open door provided more protection. The dim glow of the car's interior light illuminated them both clearly but made everything beyond their small circle look hazy and dark.

The shooter could be anywhere.

At the thought, Maddie sucked in air, looking all around, desperately trying to see through the darkness. Van and door notwithstanding, the pool of light they were in made her feel as though they were easy targets.

They needed to run.

"It's all right. By now he'll be long gone," McCabe said in the calmest of voices, apparently correctly interpreting the abortive attempt she made to get her legs beneath her. It didn't work. She was still too shaken, and her muscles seemed to have a mind of their own.

So she sat and breathed, and kept her eyes fixed on him because he was the only thing within view that didn't scare her senseless. He looked big and tough and comfortingly capable of fending off all comers. Her eyes widened as she realized that he was holding a gun.

Probably a good thing, but, looking at it, she started to shake all over again.

He cast a quick, seemingly calculating look around, and then the gun disappeared behind his back as he thrust it somewhere out of sight. When his hand reappeared, he rested it gently on her arm. Her left arm. The one that, she saw as she glanced down at his hand, was covered with blood.

Oh, God, she'd been shot. She'd been shot, and the funny thing was, it didn't even really hurt.

"You're bleeding," he said.

Her lips parted, but no sound emerged. Everything—McCabe, the parking lot, the rustling bushes beyond it— began to dissolve.

"Don't faint on me," he said, and she guessed she must have been in the process of turning a whiter shade of pale because he slid a hand around the nape of her neck and pushed her head down between her raised knees.

"I've never fainted in my life." Her voice was faint, distant-sounding, but gritty. Clenching her teeth, Maddie fought the dizziness that threatened to whirl her away with it. She could feel the hard heat of his hand on her bloodied arm, feel his long fingers delving cautiously beneath the hem of her sleeve. It created an island of warmth in the sea of ice that seemed to be slowly swallowing her up.

"My shoulder." She remembered the sting. "I think it hit the back of my shoulder."

If she hadn't turned at that precise moment to look for his van, the bullet wouldn't have slammed into her shoulder. It would have—it was an effort to rerun the sequence of events in her mind to arrive at the exact position she'd been in just seconds before she'd been hit—*struck her in the approximate vicinity of her heart.*

She felt faint all over again.

McCabe withdrew his hand from her sleeve and touched her neck. The solid warmth of his hand sliding down the sensitive chord that ran from ear to shoulder was welcome, comforting, distracting even, and she was sorry when it was withdrawn. She only realized that he was cautiously lifting the back of her T-shirt away from her body when she felt the painful stab of cloth being pulled out of what she realized must be her wound.

"Ouch," she said.

He let go of her shirt. "Sorry. You got anything on you I can use to staunch the bleeding?"

"A couple of tissues—in my pocket." Maddie slowly and deliberately breathed in and out, trying to regain some measure of composure as he made a disgusted sound under his breath to indicate what he thought of her offering. "How bad is it?"

"Not bad, as bullet wounds go. About three inches long, looks like more of a graze than anything. But it's bleeding pretty good."

She could feel him moving, hear what sounded like the slither of cloth over flesh. Lifting her head, she was just in time to watch McCabe pull his T-shirt over his head. Having a very masculine-looking chest suddenly appear at eye level was a surprise, and she blinked. His shoulders were broad and heavy with muscle, his chest wide and adorned with a nice amount of black hair. As he stripped his shirt the rest of the way off, she watched the play of muscles under his skin with a kind of detached interest. His biceps flexed as he lowered his arms, holding his crumpled shirt in one hand. Her eyes slid lower, to discover that he had a nice six-pack disappearing into his jeans.

"What are you doing?" she asked, still processing assorted thoughts, feelings, and concerns in connection with that chest.

"It's called administering first aid." He wadded the shirt up into a ball and flattened a hand on the back of her head, pushing her head down between her knees again.

As he leaned over her to press his shirt firmly against the wound in her shoulder, Maddie winced. Some of the numbness—the shock—was starting to wear off, and the wound throbbed and burned. He was very close to her now; she could feel the sinewy strength of his forearm pressing against her upper arm. Her fingertips—her hands were resting on her knees— brushed his chest. She curled her hands into fists to escape the contact, but not before she registered the crispness of his chest hair, and the firm, smooth warmth of the flesh beneath. But what she could not avoid even with her eyes closed and her fists clenched was his body heat, which made her want to scoot closer, and the distinctively masculine scent of him. It was like aromatherapy for the traumatized, she thought; simply breathing it in made her feel safer. *He* made her feel safer, and aware of him in a way she didn't want to be. Which was not a good thing, she realized with dismay. With any other man, under any other circumstances, she would have labeled what she was experiencing here as serious attraction.

The sheer surprise of it caused her head to lift again.

"Hold still," McCabe said irritably, the pressure he was putting on her wound keeping her shoulder horizontal even as their gazes met. "You'll make it bleed worse."

"She okay?" The voice belonged to Wynne, and it came from behind McCabe. Wynne stood just outside the circle of light, and, although in her current position she couldn't see him, Maddie could feel his eyes on her. He seemed to be panting slightly. She couldn't be sure, but she had the hazy impression that he—and whoever else had been in the van—had gone running past her car, toward the honeysuckle hedge and beyond, while McCabe had stopped to tend to her.

"Flesh wound. Across the shoulder blade." McCabe's tone changed as he added, "Anything?"

"Nothing. Gardner and the others are still out there looking, though. Think he made us?"

"Maybe."

As they continued to talk above her, Maddie quit listening and rested her head on her knees. Taking a deep breath replete with *eau de man*, she pondered the situation. The first conclusion she reached was that she was going to live. That being the case, she had to decide what to do. If the deal she'd made with her friend Bob had been bogus, just a sop to keep her happy until they could try again to kill her, then she was faced with a choice: She could run again, with no turning back this time, or she could turn herself, along with everything she knew, over to the FBI. Which, as she knew from experience, would probably be a huge mistake, and one that she never before would have even contemplated. So why now? She grimaced and realized that the answer lay about six inches from the tip of her nose. Another sneaking glance at McCabe confirmed it: He was the only reason she was even considering such a thing. Almost against her will, she was beginning to think she might be able to trust him. And if nothing else, he—they— would keep her alive.

For a while, at least.

But then again, McCabe's hunkiness quotient—and she had to admit that crouched all shirtless and buff beside her, he was looking pretty good— might be clouding her judgment. And, like running, spilling all to the FBI would be the equivalent of dropping a nuclear bomb on her life: When the smoke cleared, nothing recognizable would be left.

Including Creative Partners. Including the Brehmer account.

Yes, she wanted to live. But she also wanted her *life*.

Anyway, the FBI couldn't keep her alive forever. Sooner or later, they would get everything they wanted out of her and she would cease being the flavor of the month. Then she would be left to manage on her own—and the Mob would be waiting.

The mob was like an elephant—it never forgot.

Before she did anything, anything at all, Maddie decided, she needed to get on the phone and call her good friend Bob and see what the hell was going on. Not that he would tell her if he had been lying, of course. But it was possible—maybe even likely—that the word to back off had not yet filtered down through the ranks to the hit man.

If that was the case, she meant to make sure it did. *Pronto.*

The wail of a siren made her lift her head again.

"Here comes the cavalry," McCabe said on a note of extreme irony, looking in the direction of the sound, which seemed to be growing louder by the second. Maddie realized that they were all gathered around her now: Wynne, Gomez, Gardner, and Hendricks. And, like her, they were all looking down the street, where flashing blue lights were just coming into view.

As suspected, the lights were headed their way.

Just what she needed, Maddie thought dismally: *more cops.*

BY THE TIME the local police had left, along with the ambulance whose crew had treated Maddie's wound when she had declined to be taken to the hospital, it was full morning. The heat was starting to get oppressive. A dog barked in the distance. A motorcycle roared past on the street. Maddie was safely tucked away in her apartment with Gardner playing guard dog. Now wearing a white T-shirt he had pulled out of his bag in the back of the van, and his jeans, McCabe watched the last police car drive away, then turned in time to catch the eye of the thin, fortyish, dried-up looking woman who had popped out of the house briefly earlier, wearing her robe, to say something to Maddie, then popped back in again, and was at that moment walking down the back steps, eyeing him with obvious reservations. A neighbor, McCabe assumed. She had short blond hair and a long nose, and was now dressed in floral capris, a white blouse, and sandals. McCabe endured the nervous glance she gave him as she passed stoically.

At one point, drawn by the police car and ambulance, quite a few neighbors had crowded around, but when nothing more of interest had happened, they'd dispersed by ones and twos to go to jobs or whatever until there was no one left. Except the woman who was now getting into her PT Cruiser, of course.

"No way that was random," Wynne said, coming up beside him. Wynne was chewing his gum again, and the smell of grape Dubble Bubble combined with the scent of honeysuckle from the hedges, which was particularly strong now that they'd been disturbed by being thoroughly searched, was an unfortunate mix in the ovenlike heat. Along with Gomez and Hendricks, Wynne had been scouring neighboring yards for evidence. So far nothing had turned up, not an indentation in the grass to show where the shooter had lain in wait, not a bullet lodged in a tree, nothing. Of course, the fact that they were all so tired by now that they were practically out on their feet might have something to do with it. The way he, personally, was feeling, he was pretty sure that he couldn't find a whale in a bathroom.

"Possible, of course, but I don't think so." A random gunshot—apparently such happenings weren't unknown in the area—had been the local yokels' preferred explanation. Sam understood, of course. As a solution, it involved a hell of a lot less paperwork. But he didn't believe it. If nothing else, it was too much of a coincidence, and he had stopped believing in coincidence a long time ago.

"You think he'll be back?" Wynne had a twig caught in his hair, Sam noticed, and his shorts and hula-girl shirt looked like he'd slept in them for a week. The whites of his eyes pretty much matched the red of his shirt, and for the first time since Sam had known him, he was able to see the beginnings of curly, gold fuzz on Wynne's chin. Since Wynne rarely had to shave, that was significant. It told him they'd been working flat-out for a hell of a long time.

"Oh, yeah." Sam had been thinking about that. "I don't think we could scare this guy off if we tried. If he made us—and he might or might not have, depending on how fast he got out of here and how far away he was—I don't think it's going to make any difference. I think he's going to keep coming after her until either we catch him or she's dead. Hell, he might even like the idea of trying to kill her right under our noses. He seems to get off on knowing we're right behind him."

The thought of just how close Maddie had come to being dead still had the power to weaken his knees. They'd been pulling into the lot when her windows shattered. One second she'd been sitting there behind the wheel of her car, and the next her windows had exploded and she'd fallen out of sight. Christ, he'd thought she was hit. Hit worse than a gash on her shoulder. Hit as in *dead*.

He didn't like remembering how that had made him feel. Way worse than it should have, considering Maddie Fitzgerald's role in his life.

Okay, reality check: She had no role in his life. Except as the object of a surveillance operation.

Never mind that she had silky soft skin and big take-me-to-bed eyes and smelled of—what was it?—strawberries?

His lip curled. Now there was a true romantic for you. Think of a girl, picture food.

"Think we ought to pull her out of here, take her into protective custody or something?" Wynne asked. "That was close. Too close."

Sam had been thinking about that, too.

"She can't stay in protective custody forever. Sooner or later, she'll get cut loose. And unless we've caught the bastard by then, he'll be waiting."

"Who the fuck *is* this guy?" Wynne's frustration showed in the kick he aimed at a rock on the asphalt. His exhaustion showed in the fact that he completely whiffed.

Sam had to smile at the stunned look on Wynne's face. But something was niggling at the back of his mind, something that if he wasn't so tired, he thought he might be able to shape into a point of significance. His smile faded.

"The thing is," he said slowly, "this guy's not trying to keep what he's doing a secret. He's been taking us right with him all along. He wants us to know where he is. Just as long as we stay a step behind."

Gomez and Hendricks came pushing through the bushes at the back of the parking lot just then, both looking slightly the worse for wear. Gomez had lost the jacket and tie, and his short-sleeved white shirt was untucked and bore several obvious smears of dirt. Hendricks's tan dress slacks had a rip in the knee, and, Sam saw as he drew closer, the tassels to one of his shiny brown loafers was missing.

"Damn big-ass dog in a backyard about half a block down," Hendricks said by way of an explanation, seeing where Sam's gaze focused. "I had to vault the fence."

"Thing got his pants leg, then his shoe." Gomez was grinning. "Hey, Hendricks, are you having a bad day or what? First you take a knee to the nuts, then Cujo tries to eat you alive."

"Shut up, Gomez."

"Find anything?" Sam asked, before the situation could deteriorate.

They both shook their heads.

"Keep looking."

Gomez grimaced. Then, at the expression on Sam's face, he burst into speech. "The thing is, Hendricks and I have been up all night. We need some sleep, bad. From the look of you guys, you do, too."

Hendricks nodded. "It's not like there's anyplace around here we haven't searched. Anyway, those shots could have come from anywhere. A couple of streets over, even. I can tell you already, we're not going to find crap."

Sam frowned. This case ate at him, and he hated to take a break from it, even for a few hours, because time was definitely not on their side. What it had turned into, basically, was a race. If the killer won—and so far he was winning big—somebody died. But Gomez had a point. In order to function at anything approaching maximum efficiency, they needed sleep. They had Maddie safe upstairs. The next clue to the identity of Walter could come at any time, but he didn't actually expect it before tomorrow at the earliest. That left open this brief window of opportunity where they could sleep, eat, do all the little things ordinarily deemed necessary to human existence.

Like shave.

"Yeah," he said. "Okay. Get out of here. I'll call you when I need you. I'll need the van back ASAP, though."

"No problem." Gomez looked at Hendricks. "I'll drive you to your car, then you can follow me back over here. Then you can take me to my car."

"I'll drive you to my car," Hendricks said. "It's closer."

"You could start banging on doors asking the neighbors if they saw anything," Sam suggested.

Gomez and Hendricks looked at each other.

"We did that," Hendricks said. "Nobody saw crap."

Gomez made a face.

"Okay, you drive," he said to Hendricks, and then they took themselves off with quick *see ya*'s, clearly afraid that Sam would find something else for them to do if they gave him time to think about it. Minutes later, the van pulled out of the lot.

"So, what's the plan?" Wynne asked, still beside him.

"You mean we've got a plan?" Sam's voice was dry. His eyes skimmed over the parking lot. Maddie's Camry, shattered windows and all, remained where she had parked it, not far from where they were standing. Other than that, the lot was empty.

"We were going to stay undercover and keep Ms. Hot Bod under surveillance," Wynne prompted him. Sam was getting used to the sound of gum smacking in his ear now. He was even starting to find it kind of soothing.

Not.

"Ye-a-ah." Sam drew it out. Gomez had started referring to Maddie as Ms. Hot Bod after the full-body wrestling match he had engaged in with her in the airport parking lot. Wynne and Hendricks had picked it up, much to Gardner's loudly expressed disgust. Sam didn't doubt that Maddie would have a problem with it, too, if she ever heard it, but, hey, the truth was, it was apt. "I'd have to say that under the circumstances, that's no longer operational."

"Since she made us," Wynne said.

"Exactly."

"So?"

"So we forget the undercover bit and just keep her under surveillance."

Wynne stopped chewing and looked at him. "How do we do that? She knows we're here."

"We enlist her cooperation," Sam said.

"Oh, boy. Yeah. Like she's going to go for that."

"So we persuade her," Sam said, and turned toward the house.

THIRTEEN

Gardner opened the door to Sam's knock. Having snatched a couple hours of sleep on the plane, she was looking marginally less bleary-eyed than either he or Wynne. That didn't mean that she was looking good, however. Her bottle-brush hairdo was flat on one side, and the only makeup she seemed to have left had morphed into black smudges under both eyes. She had traded her black skirt for snug, black pants before they had boarded the plane, and with them she was wearing a clingy black T-shirt. Tucked in. With what looked like the same wide black belt as before cinched around her waist. Combined with the double D's and the J.Lo butt, the outfit made her look hot. And hungry.

Like a woman on the hunt.

She smiled at him, which sent a warning chill racing down Sam's spine. He'd found himself in dangerous situations often enough to recognize them when they occurred. And this was definitely one.

"Yo," he said. "Everything okay?"

"Just peachy keen." Her smile widened as she pushed the door wide.

Finding himself caught squarely in the crosshairs, Sam's instinct for self-preservation kicked into high gear. To save himself, he offered up a sacrifice: He took a step back and pushed Wynne through the door ahead of him. Wynne looked at Gardner as she closed and locked the door. Sam looked around the apartment.

His initial impression was that it was cheerful. Homey, even. The walls of the room he was in, the living room, were a soft, bright yellow. The floors were hardwood. The huge couch that dominated one whole wall was—he didn't want to call it pink; call it, rather, the color of raspberries. Two armchairs, one green, one flowery, were drawn up on either side of the couch. There was a rug, a couple of tables and lamps, a coffee table. A TV. A trio of big windows directly opposite the door looked out into a vista of leafy tree branches. Sniper city? The branches he could see all looked like they might hold about ten pounds max, so not unless the sniper was a squirrel. Just to double-check, Sam crossed to the window and looked out, evaluating the risk. He could see down into about a dozen tiny backyards, all separated into grids by a myriad of fences. About four fences over, a big black dog snoozed on its side in the grass. Even from this distance it looked about the size of a small pony, and, remembering Hendricks, Sam grinned: He was pretty sure he was looking at Cujo. The upper stories of neighboring houses were obscured by the leafy foliage of big old oaks and maples, with the occasional elm and chestnut-trunked birch thrown in. Good. Nobody was going to be shooting through the windows from nearby roofs. Relaxing slightly, he turned to survey the rest of the apartment. To his right he could see part of a kitchen. To his left, a pair of closed doors.

"So where is she?" he asked Gardner when his visual sweep turned up no sign of Maddie.

"Taking a shower. We all should be so lucky." Gardner had dropped into a corner of the couch while Sam had been looking out the window. Her legs were crossed and she had twisted herself into a position that he suspected was calculated to show off her eye-popping figure. Now she nodded at the closed door on the left to indicate where Maddie could be found, then let her head drop back to rest on the high, rolled back of the couch. Sam immediately realized exactly how half of her hairdo had ended up flat. "Come sit down. I think this is where we do that thing called hurry up and wait."

Gardner made shameless eyes at him from beneath half-closed lids, and patted the couch beside her invitingly. Wynne frowned, while Sam caught himself leaning backward just a little, probably an instinctive result of his determination to stay well out of harm's way.

"You checked the bathroom out before she went in there, didn't you?" Sam asked, ignoring Gardner's gesture in favor of walking toward the closed door. Beyond it, very faintly, he could hear the sound of water running.

Gardner gave him a look that said yes, she definitely had. For his part, Wynne headed toward the couch, then veered off at the last minute and lowered himself into the green armchair. Lips thinning in exasperation, Sam had to fight the urge to walk over and smack him upside the head.

Faint heart never won fair lady, you big wimp. Sit on the couch.

"So, what's the plan?" Gardner asked, just as Wynne had minutes before.

"Same plan." Restless, Sam prowled toward the kitchen. "We keep watching Miz Fitzgerald until we catch our UNSUB."

The kitchen was old-fashioned, with white Formica countertops and tall wood cabinets and a gold-speckled linoleum floor. The refrigerator and stove were white, freestanding rather than built-in. There was a stainless-steel sink in front of another window. As he glanced out, he saw that the squirrel thing applied to this one, too. A rectangular oak table with four chairs occupied the center of the room. On the counter beside the sink, a draining board held a single white cereal bowl.

Looking at it, Sam wasn't all that surprised to feel his stomach rumble. Jesus, how long had it been since he'd eaten? He tried to remember. Not today. Yesterday. Fast food in the hotel room. If he was lucky, sometime today he might snag more of the same.

Yum.

The only area of concern was a rear door. Sam crossed to it, looked out the multipaned window in the upper half, then opened it and stepped out into the muggy morning. He found himself on a small wooden stoop, which was connected by three zigzagging flights of open wooden steps to the ground. Clearly a do-it-yourselfer's version of a fire escape, probably added when the house was converted to apartments. He checked the lock—it was a deadbolt, but flimsy—and made a mental note to do what he could to make the rear entrance more secure. *Pronto.*

Retracing his steps, he returned to the living room and found Wynne watching Gardner, who had cut her eyes toward him as soon as he had reentered the room. With an inward roll of his eyes, Sam gave up on the whole matchmaking thing and started pacing again.

What the hell was she doing in there?

"Okay. We need sleep, we need food. We also need to keep Miz Fitzgerald under a twenty-four-hour watch. Which means for the time being we'll be taking shifts." He glanced at Gardner. She smiled at him. *Christ.* "I assume you've got the computer working on locating possible targets?"

"Oh, yeah. By now we probably have a database of about a hundred thousand people with Walter for a first or last name in the cities the computer deems most likely to be the location for the next killing. Without anything more specific than a single name to go on, though, it's pretty useless. Take our girl in there, for example. She didn't even live in New Orleans, so her name didn't come up on any of the searches I ran. Neither did the dead one's, for that matter."

Get her focused on work and she turns totally professional. Go figure.

"Yeah." Sam was already well acquainted with the ways in which their attempts to locate the next victim could get screwed up before the sick bastard did his thing again. And just to complicate matters more, now that his plans had been thrown off by Maddie's survival, the parameters of the game might well have changed. They could no longer take anything for granted.

Except, Sam was almost certain, that he'd be coming after Maddie again.

"You're something with that computer," Wynne said admiringly to Gardner.

"Thanks." She smiled at him, and Sam watched with fascination as a flush the color of Maddie's couch started to creep over Wynne's face.

Jesus. The perils of being blond.

"Right," he said by way of a distraction. "First thing is, we need to establish a base here. There's bound to be a hotel somewhere nearby. Next . . ."

He outlined the way he expected the next few days to play out. By the time he finished, the atmosphere was strictly business all around. Also, he'd circled the room about ten times, and there was still no sign of Maddie.

Pausing outside the closed bathroom door, he frowned at it. What the hell was she doing in there?

"Why don't I take the first shift with her? At least I got a couple hours of sleep on the plane," Gardner suggested. "And I have trouble sleeping during the day anyway. You guys go on, get us a hotel, get some sleep."

Sam nodded absently. It was a good suggestion. He didn't expect another attack to come today; the UNSUB was as human as the rest of them, and if he was the shooter—and Sam was fairly positive that he was—he had to be suffering from lack of sleep, too. He seemed to like to work under cover of darkness, and by the time night fell again, Sam had every intention of being personally back on the job. But he didn't say any of that. Instead, he was concentrating on the sounds he could hear beyond the closed door.

Water still running? Yes, but something else, too.

His brows snapped together. Was she talking to someone?

He glanced sharply at Gardner.

"She have a pet or anything?"

"Not that I saw. Why?"

"She's talking to someone." Could the UNSUB somehow have gotten into the bathroom with her? Sam could feel his muscles tensing even as he rejected the thought as unlikely.

Unlikely, but not impossible.

He rapped sharply on the door.

Just like that, she shut up.

"Miz Fitzgerald?" He banged again. He didn't know why, exactly, but he was getting the feeling that something about the situation wasn't quite right. "Could you open the door, please?"

He could no longer hear water running. Just as he registered that, the door opened a few inches. Sam found himself looking down into narrowed honey-colored eyes. With straight black brows furrowed into a V above them.

Even frowning at him, she was pretty, he registered against his will. Tired-looking. Pale as paper. Face marred by a faint, blue-tinged bruise angling across her left cheekbone. But still very, very pretty.

The last time he'd looked down into those eyes, they'd been big and scared. Now she just looked annoyed.

"Did you want something?" she asked.

Sam had expected her to be all damp and dewy, maybe wrapped in a bath towel and showing more skin than it was probably good for him to see. And she was, indeed, wrapped in a bath towel, a fluffy blue one. And she was, indeed, showing some skin. The towel fit snugly up under her armpits and was tucked in between her breasts, he saw as his gaze swept her. He could see a nice amount of cleavage, her bare shoulders, and the neat white bandage on her back the paramedics had left her with. Below the towel, which ended at approximately mid-thigh, her legs were long and slender and shapely. They were, as he had noticed before, great legs.

The thing was, though, she wasn't all damp and dewy. In fact, she was dry as a bone. Her hair still hung in tangles around her face. There was a faint smear of blood on her jaw, and another down her arm where the paramedics hadn't quite gotten her all cleaned up. She'd traded her bloody clothes for the towel, but otherwise, as far as he could tell, nothing about her except her expression had changed a lick from when he had last set eyes on her.

In other words, she hadn't been taking a shower.

"What on earth have you been doing in there?" Surprise probably rendered him something less than diplomatic. She'd been in the bathroom a good twenty minutes that he knew of, with the water running the entire time. And she wasn't even wet.

Maybe she'd been answering nature's call? He toyed with the idea, rejected it. Not for that long.

She smiled way too sweetly at him. Oh, God, the attitude was back.

"Maybe you want to tell me how that's any of your business?"

He remembered then why he'd banged on the door in the first place. "Were you talking to someone?"

The too-sweet smile faded. "How to put this? Not your business."

She had let the door fall open a little wider as they'd talked, and he was able to see past her into most of the bathroom now. His gaze swept the room. It was a typical bathroom, smallish, with a tub/shower combo, toilet, and vanity sink. A big mirror covered the wall behind the sink. Lots of white tile, trimmed in a kind of sea green. Clean. Empty except for her.

There was a cell phone on the vanity. Light dawned.

"You were talking on the phone."

Her lips compressed as she followed his gaze.

"What, are you my keeper now? So I was talking on the phone. Big deal." Her eyes met his again. They were less than friendly. "Why are you still here, anyway? You've done your thing. Not wanting to be rude or anything, but it's probably time you toddled off on your way now."

His eyes narrowed. "What happened to *don't leave me*?"

"I got over the shock," she snapped.

He almost smiled. There was that hostility of hers again in spades. He wasn't sure if it was directed at him personally, if she just didn't like men in general, or if there was something else going on here that he hadn't quite tumbled to yet. Not that he minded it particularly. It was kind of cute, kind of different. The thing was, though, right at the moment it was damned inconvenient. Then another odd thing hit him. The mirror. It was clear as a summer's day. Not steamed up a bit. The water she'd been running since before he'd entered her apartment had not been hot.

Either she was into cold showers—and she didn't seem like the type—or a shower had not been on her agenda when she'd turned the water on. Which meant she'd been running the water for some other reason. To cover up a sound. Of using the toilet? Maybe, especially if she was shy. But the water had been running a long time. To cover up the sound of her voice as she talked on the cell phone?

Bingo.

"Mind telling me who you were talking to?"

"My boyfriend, okay?" Her eyes flashed at him. "What's it to you?"

Good question.

Maybe somewhere deep in his subconscious, he'd suspected she was talking to a boyfriend all along. Maybe that was what was bugging him.

Because something was. He was definitely getting one of those little niggles of his again. Hell, maybe it was just knowing that she was naked under that towel that was throwing his thought processes off. The thing was, he was so damned tired that he couldn't think straight enough to reason out the whys and wherefores of this feeling he had that something here was not quite right.

"If you really want to know, I was calling my insurance company about my car," Maddie said, her tone a little friendlier now. "And the reason I'm not in the shower yet was that I can't quite figure out how to do this without getting my shoulder wet, too."

O-kay. That made sense. Kind of.

"Plastic bag," Gardner said from her position on the couch, and Maddie looked past McCabe to where the other two were, clearly, taking in every word.

Since Maddie had appeared in the towel, Sam realized with some chagrin that he had completely forgotten that they were even in the room.

"You got trash bags?" Wynne asked her. When Maddie nodded, he heaved himself to his feet. "I'll get you one. Where are they?"

"In the kitchen under the sink." Maddie looked at Sam again. "Is there anything else you want to know?"

"Since I'm going to be leaving in a minute"—he watched her face brighten—"we need to talk about a few things."

"Such as?"

"What you can and can't do. The kinds of precautions you need to take. Wynne and I are going to be taking off for a few hours, but Gardner's going to be here with you. We probably won't have outside backup until tonight. That means you . . ."

Maddie's brows snapped together again. "Whoa. Hold on just a minute. *What?*"

Wynne came up behind them and held a white plastic trash bag out to Maddie. "Just poke a couple of holes in it for your arm and your head, then scootch it up everywhere you don't need protection. It should keep the water off that wound."

Momentarily distracted, she took it, giving Wynne a quick smile and a *thanks*. Then, as Wynne retreated, her eyes immediately refocused on Sam. And the frown returned.

"What are you talking about?"

"One of us is going to be with you twenty-four hours a day until this guy is caught. Gardner's on for the next few hours, and it would probably be best if you stayed inside your apartment. I don't really expect anything to . . ."

She was shaking her head. "Wait. Stop. *Uh-uh.* No way. I already told you, I don't want to be kept under surveillance. I appreciate the offer, but no. What part of 'I refuse my permission' did you not understand?"

Sam could feel another one of those killer headaches coming on, but he held on to his patience with some effort. "I was hoping that since we saved your life out there, you might have rethought that."

A beat passed.

"You did not save my life."

Sam's brows twitched together. "You're alive, aren't you?"

"Whoever fired that shot missed. *That's* what saved my life."

Sam took a deep breath. "The point is, you're alive. And we mean to keep you that way. It would help if you would cooperate. By that, I mean you want to stay inside as much as possible. You want to take care to keep your curtains closed at night. If you have to go out, you want to get into and out of buildings as fast as you can. One of us will be with you. . . ."

"No," Maddie said. "I'm not going to do this. I *refuse.*"

Sam's head throbbed. His patience, never his strong suit, wobbled dangerously. "You can't refuse."

"Oh, yes, I can."

"Mind telling me why you have a problem with this?"

"Because I have a company to run, and right now things are kicking into high gear for us. I have clients to see, advertising campaigns to work on, PR to do. Having an FBI agent dogging my every step is probably not going to make anybody real eager to do business with me, in case you haven't figured that out. In fact, just the opposite. Anyway, the police said the shooting was probably random, and I agree with the police. So I appreciate the offer, but no. Thank you. If it makes you feel better to know this, I'll be extra careful. But I don't *want you.*"

Sam looked at her for a moment without saying anything at all. Her eyes glinted militantly at him. Her jaw looked mulish.

He sighed. "Look, I'm not going to argue about this. I'm dead on my feet here. We all are, you probably included. So here's the deal: Either you cooperate, or I'll take you into protective custody and whisk you off to a safe house so fast you won't know what hit you, and let you try running your company from there. At least that's one way to keep you from getting killed while we try to figure this thing out."

Her eyes flashed. "Is that another threat, Mr. Special Agent? Well, guess what? This time I'm not buying it. You can't just take somebody into custody because you feel like it."

Sam's patience crashed and burned.

"Can't I?" He smiled, and from the way he was feeling, it was not a nice smile. "Try me."

Their eyes clashed, and Sam was reminded forcibly of the old saying about irresistible forces and immovable objects.

In this case, the immovable object—that would be him—won. Which, under the circumstances, wasn't surprising, since he'd meant every word he'd said, and she must have been able to read that in his eyes.

Because for a long moment all he got was a sizzling look. Then . . .

"Fine," she snapped, and slammed the door in his face. Seconds later, from the other side, he distinctly heard her mutter, "Jackass."

Glad his nose hadn't been any closer to the solid wood panel when it connected with the jamb, he turned away from the closed door to find Wynne and Gardner looking at him.

"Way to be persuasive," Wynne said, giving him a thumbs-up, and Gardner looked at Wynne and laughed.

UNBELIEVABLE, Maddie thought hours later.

There was an FBI agent making himself at home on her couch, and there didn't seem to be a thing in the world she could do about it. He had what was left of the pizza they'd had for dinner on the table by his side, his stockinged feet were on her coffee table, and her remote control was in his hand. The sounds emanating from the TV jumped spastically from cartoon voices to a feverish play-by-play for some ball game to eerie mood music to a talking head waxing eloquent about the falling economy as he, apparently, flipped channels indiscriminately.

From where she lay—flopped on her stomach in the middle of her queen-size bed in her shadowy bedroom—she couldn't see the TV. She couldn't even see him. But that was the position he'd been in when she'd last exited the bathroom at a little past midnight—it was now shortly before one a.m.—and if her ears were any judge, nothing had changed.

For the last hour she'd been trying to sleep, without success. It was possible that the exhausted nap she'd succumbed to in the middle of the afternoon had something to do with that. Or maybe sleep was elusive because her shoulder throbbed, or her thoughts raced, or she kept having flashbacks to the moment she'd gotten shot every time she closed her eyes.

Or maybe because there was an *FBI agent* in her living room.

McCabe, to be precise.

Or any combination of the above.

"I'm trying to sleep here," she finally yelled in frustration through the door he had insisted she keep partially open. "Think you could turn it down?"

If he replied, she missed it, but the volume lessened.

Maddie rolled onto her good side and pulled her knees up under her chin. Her movements were gingerly, because her shoulder ached like she'd been shot—oh, wait, she had been—and the pain pill she'd taken around nine didn't seem to be touching it. If she had been alone, she would have gotten up to watch TV, but her babysitter was already doing that and, since she had only the one set, that meant TV was pretty much out.

Unless she wanted to watch TV with him.

Definitely out.

Closing her eyes, snuggling under the smooth top sheet that was the only covering she could stand, given the sweaty realities of third-floor apartments, inefficient air-conditioning, and tropical heat, she breathed in the faint sea-breeze scent of the fabric softener sheets she habitually used in the dryer and tried to put herself to sleep by counting her blessings.

She was alive. She was home, with her life still intact. And they'd gotten the Brehmer account.

All good. All, unfortunately, also subject to change at any moment.

Before she could stop herself, her mind went over to the dark side.

Number one, *there was an FBI agent on her couch*.

Number two, she'd spent the entire day cooped up in her apartment with a woman who looked like Rambo Barbie. On a really bad hair day.

Number three, she hadn't gotten any of her usual Saturday errands done. Her dry cleaning was still at the cleaners, she was out of bread and cereal, the milk in her refrigerator expired two days ago, and she had three rented DVDs that were racking up late charges even as she lay there.

Number four, her car was pretty much undrivable until they came to replace the glass, which she'd been told would happen sometime Monday.

And number five—this was the biggie—someone was trying to kill her.

Although her friend Bob, whom she'd been talking to in the bathroom that morning when McCabe had come banging on the door, had sworn it wasn't true. If there had been a contract out on her—which he had no knowledge of whatsoever—it had been withdrawn after their previous conversation. If a shot had been fired at her that morning—which again he had no knowledge of whatsoever—it was an accident, and had nothing to do with them at all. Or—*ahem*—an easily rectified mistake.

They had no reason to kill her, he assured her, as long as she kept her end of the deal and stayed away from the feds.

As far as Maddie was concerned, however, there were two problems with Bob's assurances: First, *someone* had taken a shot at her; and, second, even as her buddy Bob had warned her to stay away from the feds, one had been banging on her bathroom door.

And he was still here.

Since getting rid of McCabe and Co. clearly wasn't going to happen anytime soon, all she could do was try her best to maneuver around him. The only thing her protests had done so far was make him start to wonder why she wasn't just jumping up and down with joy at the prospect of taking advantage of his offer of government-funded bodyguards; she'd seen it in his eyes. So she had given in—possibly with something less than good grace, but, hey, as far as she was concerned, losing well was overrated—and now she was stuck.

Performing the highwire act that her life had turned into.

As long as Bob and his friends kept their word and didn't find out about her new babysitters, she was good. And as long as McCabe and Co. didn't know about her past, she was equally good. But if any of them found out about the rest of them, the situation was going to go to hell in a handbasket.

Worrying about just such a mischance was probably the primary reason she couldn't fall asleep. That, and the fear that one of her patented nightmares hovered waiting in the wings. Tonight of all nights, when the scary truth that she had to once more be afraid for her life was really starting to sink in, being transported back seven years in her sleep would be more than she thought she could bear.

And, oh, yeah, there was the little fact that someone had tried to kill her. Twice now. Wasn't there some saying about third time being the charm?

Even the thought made her shiver.

After another fifteen minutes or so of wriggling—she couldn't toss and turn because of her injured shoulder—Maddie was still wide awake, and forced to admit that she had a new problem: She had to go to the bathroom.

And given the fact that her apartment was just old-fashioned and inexpensive enough so that it only had *one* bathroom, which wasn't connected to her bedroom but opened off the living room, that meant that she was going to have to walk past McCabe.

She felt funny about the whole thing. She felt funny about walking past him knowing that she had on her little shortie nightgown, even if she was going to pull her big terry-cloth bathrobe on over it. She felt funny about him knowing she had to wee. She felt funny about having him in her apartment, period.

But whether she felt funny or not, she decided a few minutes later, she had no choice: She really, really had to go.

Sliding out of bed, pulling her robe on—carefully, because of her shoulder—and tying it around her waist, she hesitated, looking at the partly open door that glowed blue from the TV, then took a deep breath, headed toward it, and paused in the opening to glare his way.

Just as she had suspected, McCabe was still parked on her couch. As far as she could tell, he hadn't switched positions in a couple hours. Except, maybe, to change the channel and stuff his mouth. The TV provided the only illumination in the apartment, and by its flickering light he was little more than a big, solid, dark presence that dominated the small room. Much as she hated to face it, though, she didn't need light to know just exactly what he looked like. His black hair and coffee-brown eyes and mobile mouth and chiseled chin—to say nothing of his muscular bod—seemed to have implanted themselves in her consciousness, whether she liked it or not. When he had arrived at about eleven p.m. to take over from Wynne, who had taken over from Rambo Barbie at four, McCabe had been looking good. In fact, in a clean navy polo shirt and jeans, freshly shaven and with his hair combed, he had been looking handsome. Actually, *way* handsome.

And way sexy.

To her chagrin, she had realized that the serious attraction she'd felt toward him earlier was definitely not a figment of her imagination. FBI agent or not.

Not that this had in any way endeared him to her, then or now. In fact, just the opposite. A complication of that sort she absolutely did not need.

So quit looking at him, she told herself, and, taking her own advice, averted her gaze and marched toward the bathroom.

Caught in the act of taking a swig out of a can of Diet Coke, McCabe choked and swung his feet to the floor as her sudden appearance apparently caught him by surprise.

"Something the matter?" he asked when he had recovered from his coughing fit. She was already halfway across the living room by that time.

"Not a thing in the world," she said, glancing over her shoulder. Their eyes met, and she realized he'd been tracking her across the room.

If he was as flustered by her presence as she was by his, he did a darn good job of hiding it.

"Oh. Good." With that, his attention returned to the TV, and he relaxed into the couch again.

Having reached the bathroom by that time, Maddie turned on the light, shut the door and locked it with a decided click, then paused to eye her surroundings. A thought occurred, and she turned on the faucet in the sink. The idea that he might be able to hear her using the facilities even over the TV was embarrassing, of course. But the idea that she might be able to allay any suspicions she had aroused in him that morning when he had caught her running the shower to cover her phone conversation was a consideration, too. If she was lucky, he might just hear the shower and think that she always used running water to cover bathroom sounds.

Play the hand out.

That's what her father would have told her, and that's just what she was going to do.

Emerging from the bathroom a few minutes later, Maddie padded back across the smooth, cool hardwood floor toward her bedroom. Beyond casting a single glance her way when the door opened, McCabe ignored her, for which she was grateful. The easiest way to deal with having him in her apartment was to simply pretend he wasn't there.

But, even when she had crawled back into bed and pulled the sheet up around her neck and closed her eyes, she couldn't get the thought that he was approximately twenty feet away out of her head.

She wriggled some more and dug deep in her mind for pleasant thoughts and counted everything she could think of to count, then finally gave up all thought of sleep and lay, listening unwillingly to the TV. It was about then that she realized something: If she had been in her apartment alone, she would have been curled up in a little ball in the farthest corner of her closet by that time, gibbering with terror.

At least, with McCabe in the next room, she was not afraid.

FOURTEEN

Sunday, August 17

W hen Maddie awoke the next morning, her bedroom was dark. That might seem like a small thing, but it was enough to remind her of how radically her life had changed: Her bedroom was never dark in the mornings. She always opened the thick, oyster-colored silk curtains that covered the window just behind her bed right before she fell asleep so that the single halogen that illuminated the parking lot could cast its distant glow over her as she slept. That way she could turn off the lights, yet never have to sleep in the dark. Fudgie, too, was out of place. Instead of watching over her from his usual spot on her dresser, he'd been tucked away in a drawer.

Fudgie was like her that way: He and the feds were fundamentally incompatible.

As she swung her legs over the side of the bed, it occurred to her that she was going to have to walk past McCabe again to get to the bathroom. That made her frown. On the best of mornings she was something less than a rosy-faced, sleep-tousled beauty. This was not the best of mornings. Her shoulder throbbed, her head ached, and she needed caffeine like a vampire needs blood. When she got to her feet and opened the curtains, blinking in the sudden brightness, then glanced in the mirror over her dresser, her reflection confirmed it: Her hair was all over the place, there was a red crease across her cheek where she'd slept on her pillow wrong, and her eyes were all puffy and heavy-lidded.

She looked, in a word, scary.

She hated the thought of having McCabe see her that way. And she *really* hated the thought that she hated the thought of having him see her that way.

There was no help for it, though. Although her instinct was to spend the day skulking in her bedroom, out of sight, she couldn't: Once again, she had to go to the bathroom.

To hell with it. Looking good for Mr. Special Agent was not something she needed to be trying to do anyway.

Shrugging into her robe, running her fingers through her hair, determined to do her best to behave as though she were home alone, Maddie gathered up her clothes, marched to the bedroom door, opened it—and heard voices. Multiple voices. Coming from the kitchen. A peek into the living room confirmed it. The coast was clear. Her babysitters—all three of them from the sound of it—were nowhere in sight.

Huffing a quick sigh of relief, she scuttled for the bathroom.

When she emerged some twenty minutes later, she was looking—and feeling—much better, having showered and blown her hair dry and dressed in navy shorts and a loose sun-yellow camp shirt that put no pressure on her tender shoulder. She'd flicked on mascara, slicked on lipgloss—things she normally wouldn't have bothered to do on a lazy Sunday morning unless she was heading out to church—and patted concealer over the bruise on her cheek. The one on her throat was in the process of changing from purple to an even uglier yellowish green, and she didn't even bother to try to hide it. After examining it in the mirror, she had concluded that there was not enough concealer in the world.

The best thing about having a houseful of FBI agents, she reflected, was that it gave her a really good excuse not to go to church as compared to her usual lousy one of sleeping in. The worst thing about it was everything else.

Padding barefoot toward the kitchen, drawn by the smell of coffee, she frowned slightly as she realized that she heard nothing. Total silence was potentially not such a good thing, Maddie realized, and as the possible ramifications began to revolve through her brain, her step slowed, her heart speeded up, and her stomach went all fluttery. A sideways glance at the front door showed her that it was still in one piece, and the lock seemed to be intact. A quick visual sweep of the room found nothing out of place. But still—no voices, no TV, no sound at all except, from behind her, the steady drip of the shower, which always took a few minutes to shut off completely. Her mind raced. What if the hit man had broken in and murdered her minders while she was in the shower, blissfully unaware? What if he was waiting for her somewhere in the apartment? What if . . .

Someone walked out of the kitchen. Squeaking—she only barely managed to swallow the rest of what would have been a full-blown scream if it had gotten all the way out—Maddie reflexively jumped a good foot in the air even as she recognized Rambo Barbie, today dressed in black pants and an acid-green T-shirt, with the ubiquitous black belt circling her waist. She, too, was looking better today. Her Raggedy Ann–red hair was clean and actually more tousled than spiky, her makeup, while a little heavy on the black eyeliner, was at least where it was supposed to be, and her cornflower blue eyes were clear.

"Did I scare you? Sorry." Gardner didn't *sound* sorry as her eyes slid over Maddie. She sounded just the slightest bit contemptuous of a woman who would jump and squeal when surprised. She was carrying a cup of coffee in one hand and a newspaper—Maddie couldn't be sure, but she guessed it was probably *her* newspaper, retrieved from the rush mat in front of the apartment door—in the other.

"No, not at all," Maddie said, skirting the other woman to reach the kitchen. "I always jump and squeal first thing in the morning. Gets the blood circulating."

A green-and-white Krispy Kreme box took pride of place in the center of the table. Other than that, the kitchen looked just as it always did: clean and neat and empty, except for a few dishes in the sink that hadn't been there when she'd gone to bed. Pale morning sunlight streamed in through the window over the sink; the refrigerator hummed. She was just starting to feel disappointed because she had missed McCabe—and registering with alarm that she *was* feeling disappointed—when she spotted him through the window in the kitchen door. He had his back to her and was standing on the back stoop, talking to Wynne.

As her gaze slid over as much of him as she could see, over the back of his head, over his wide shoulders and strong arms and tapered back, her heart gave an odd little skip.

You're being really stupid here, Maddie thought, and wrenched her eyes away from him. It helped that she could smell coffee. Directing her gaze toward the coffeemaker instead was, therefore, not quite as difficult as it might have been, and was amply rewarded. A freshly brewed pot of coffee sat on the burner, keeping warm.

Maddie had just poured herself a cup when the back door opened and McCabe—and Wynne—walked into the kitchen.

"All clear outside?" she asked, as much to cover the sudden confusion she felt when her gaze encountered McCabe's as because she had any real doubt of the answer.

"A few birds, a couple of squirrels. Nothing potentially fatal." McCabe grinned at her. The sudden warming of his eyes as they met hers—to say nothing of the dimples that appeared on either side of his mouth—made her breath catch.

Stupid, her brain warned all on its own.

"Glad to hear it," she said, proud of how casually offhand she sounded. Lifting her cup, she took a swallow, hoping that the caffeine would jolt her to her senses. It was nothing short of idiocy to notice that his hair was all mussed and his chin sported a nice, studly amount of five-o'clock shadow and his eyes looked sleepy. Of course, unlike herself, he had stayed up all night. Knowing that he was keeping watch was what had enabled her, eventually, to fall asleep.

"How's your shoulder?" The grin had faded. His eyes darkened as they touched on her shoulder.

"Oh, I don't know—kind of feels like I got shot yesterday," she said wryly.

He laughed, and, lo and behold, there were those dimples again. Funny, Maddie thought, until she met him she never would have believed that she could be such a sucker for dimples.

"Want a doughnut? Help yourself," Wynne said, having crossed to the table and opened the box. He was talking to her and, glad to be distracted, Maddie tore her eyes away from McCabe and moved toward the table just in time to watch Wynne hook one out of the box.

"Thanks." Except for the fact that he was an FBI agent, she actually had no beef with Wynne, who was looking even more cherubic than usual this morning in a candy-pink polo shirt and khakis. She smiled at him as she set her coffee cup on the table, then fished out a chocolate-covered doughnut from the already half-empty box and took a bite.

"I thought you were watching your weight," Gardner said from the doorway. This was directed at Wynne, who swallowed the last bite of doughnut with a guilty air as he looked at her.

"I am. I'm watching it creep toward three hundred."

"You know, it's probably counterproductive to quit smoking and then eat yourself to death."

Wynne flushed.

"It's hard to quit smoking." To her own surprise, Maddie found herself leaping to Wynne's defense. Okay, he was a grown man, and an FBI agent to boot, but under his fellow agent's disapproving gaze he suddenly looked so—vulnerable. "I would think that anything somebody could do to make it through until the craving gets easier would be a good thing."

"You smoke?" Wynne asked her, clearly grateful for the distraction.

"No. My father did, though. He kept saying he was going to quit, but he never made it longer than maybe a day and a half." Then it occurred to her that talking about her father in such company was probably not wise. Although that particular memory was harmless, she didn't even want to start the conversation down that path.

"How long has it been now?" McCabe asked Wynne, joining them at the table. He stopped so close to Maddie that his arm brushed hers, warm skin against warm skin, and to her annoyance she felt that brief contact all the way down to her toes. Sidling sideways away from him even as she chomped down on her doughnut for cover—and if ever there was a waste of a good doughnut that had to be it, because she suddenly couldn't even taste it—she glanced around the kitchen for a distraction. Those dishes in the sink—three plates, three cups, a couple of spoons. Maddie realized that what she had heard earlier was the three of them chatting over coffee and doughnuts.

"Two months, four days, and"—Wynne glanced at the clock over the window; it was not quite nine a.m.—"nine hours."

"That's impressive," Maddie told him through her mouthful of tasteless fat and sugar.

"Okay, Elvis, I admit it: It *is* impressive," Gardner said, coming toward them. "I didn't think you had it in you. Now all you need to do is wean yourself off the food you used to wean yourself off the cigarettes."

"Elvis?" Maddie looked at Wynne.

"It's his name," McCabe said to Maddie. "Elvis Presley Wynne."

Maddie couldn't help it. She smiled.

"Gets that reaction every time," Wynne said glumly. "That's why I pretty much go by Wynne."

"All right, enough picking on Wynne," McCabe said, and held something out to Maddie. Taking it, she saw that it was a key.

"It's to your back door," he said in response to her questioning look. "We replaced the lock, just so you know. We're still getting things in place, so for today it would be best if you'd just stay inside your apartment. The hardest thing to guard against is a sniper shot, and we saw yesterday that he's willing to try to take you out long-distance. That's actually a good sign, it means he's desperate enough to get to you that he's willing to abandon his usual MO, but what we want him to have to do is to come after you physically. If he breaks into your apartment, we've got him. If he comes into your workplace after you, we've got him. What we want him to have to do is put himself where we can see him. That's all we need, and then it'll be over. Just to make sure we cover all the bases, I'm having your car windows replaced with bulletproof glass as we speak, so when they're done you should be able to drive without worrying about a repeat of yesterday morning. We'll be following your vehicle everyplace you go, so if he tries anything while you're en route somewhere, we'll be right there. Oh, yeah, and we'll be sweeping your car periodically for bombs."

"Bombs?" The thought of a bomb being placed in her car was so unnerving that Maddie momentarily quit breathing. She hadn't thought of that, and she realized she should have. Her blood ran cold as she wondered just what else she hadn't thought of yet.

Of course, she reminded herself quickly, the odds were good that she had managed to get the hit called off. If she had, McCabe and Co. could follow her until the cows came home and they would come up empty-handed. Eventually, they would get tired of following her and go away, and her life could get back to normal. That was poor justice for the dead woman who'd had the misfortune to share her name, she knew; but then, no amount of justice would help that other Madeline Fitzgerald now. What *she* had to do was concentrate on saving herself.

"You're scaring her," Wynne said to McCabe in a reproving tone, which made Maddie wonder exactly what he'd seen in her face. She wanted to be careful about that. McCabe seemed uncannily attuned to her emotions, and he was looking at her, too, with an inscrutable expression that made her faintly uneasy. Hunky or not, when all was said and done he was a fed, and it would behoove her not to forget it.

"I was just thinking." Maddie looked at Wynne. "If there'd been a bomb in my car yesterday morning at the airport, *you* would have been toast."

"We checked it before I got in," Wynne assured her, absentmindedly reaching for another doughnut.

"Oh, no you don't, Elvis." Gardner snatched the box out of reach.

"Listen, *Cynthia*, the last thing I need is for you to go around acting like the calorie police." For the first time since Maddie had set eyes on him, she saw Wynne frown. It was directed at Gardner, who scowled right back at him.

"You need somebody to," Gardner retorted, hugging the box to her.

"Put the damned doughnuts down."

"No."

"Okay, I'm out of here," McCabe said to the room in general. He glanced at Maddie. "I don't expect him to try anything while you're at home today. Too bright out, too many people around, and he'll think he'll get a better chance later. Still, I wouldn't want to be proved wrong, so consider yourself grounded for the day and stay inside." He headed toward the door, then glanced back over his shoulder. "Wynne?"

Wynne was still glowering at Gardner, who was glaring back with both arms wrapped around the box. "Yeah, I'm coming."

"Wait a minute." Hurrying, Maddie followed McCabe across the living room to the door. "I can't just stay inside. I have errands to run. I have to go to the grocery, for one thing. And I need to pick up my dry cleaning. And . . ."

He paused with one hand on the knob. She was only a couple feet behind him as he turned back toward her, barely arm's length away, close enough so that he had to look down to meet her eyes.

"Like I said, I want to make this hard for him." His voice was dry.

"Well, *I* want to go to the grocery."

"Maybe tomorrow," he said, as though it was entirely his decision to make.

Maddie's lips tightened, but before she could reply his hand came up to cup the side of her face. The gesture was so unexpected that anything that she might have been going to say was instantly forgotten. Her eyes widened as the warmth of his skin coupled with the feel of his big, capable hand against her cheek just blew her away. Her gaze locked with his.

"Your bruise is getting better," he said, and his thumb brushed her cheekbone.

Her insides turned to liquid. Just like that. All it took was the slide of his thumb over her skin.

"Exercise," she heard Gardner say behind her.

Thank God for small favors, Maddie thought as the interruption startled her enough to break the spell. McCabe's hand dropped away from her face. Taking a quick step back, she glanced around to find Wynne charging toward her with the Krispy Kreme box in his arms and Gardner right behind him. Wynne was looking over his shoulder at Gardner. Gardner, however, was suddenly looking at Maddie.

"I know, I *know*," Wynne said over his shoulder. "Sheez, we've been on the road for a month. I'm not smoking. I can eat doughnuts if I want. Give me a break."

McCabe opened the door for Wynne, who stomped through it while at the same time waving a dismissive hand behind him at Gardner.

"Keep her inside," McCabe said over Maddie's head to Gardner. Then, to Maddie, with the faintest hint of a smile in his eyes, "Be good."

He was gone before she could reply.

For a moment Maddie simply stared at the closed door. Then she got a grip and turned away to find Gardner watching her.

"So you've got a thing for McCabe, do you?" Gardner said, her eyes narrowed. Then she snorted. "Honey, might as well get in line."

Maddie was momentarily struck dumb.

"I do not have a thing for McCabe," she said with what dignity she could muster when she had regained her power of speech. Gardner dropped onto the couch and picked up the newspaper she had left on the coffee table along with her cup of coffee. Not that she was trying to end the conversation or anything, but Maddie headed toward the kitchen.

Somebody had to put those dishes in the dishwasher.

"Don't bullshit me." Gardner snapped the paper open. "I can spot a fellow sufferer a mile away."

Arrested, Maddie stopped just short of the kitchen doorway and turned to look at Gardner.

"*You've* got a thing for McCabe?"

Gardner looked at her over the top of the paper.

"Oh, yeah," she said wryly. "He knows it, too. I'd hop in the sack with him like *that*." She snapped her fingers. "Problem is, I'd have to knock him cold to get him there. I'm not really his type."

Maddie couldn't help it. She knew she should drop it, knew she should walk away, but the topic was just too fascinating. Folding her arms over her chest, she cocked her head inquiringly at Gardner.

"So what's his type?" she asked cautiously.

"Slim. Pretty. Brunette. Youngish—under thirty. Sweet little wholesome girls. Yeah, in case you're wondering, you fit the type."

Maddie blinked. "What?"

Gardner nodded. "You're his type. One hundred percent. On the plane up here from New Orleans, he was about to jump out of his skin from worrying that the UNSUB—the sick bastard we're chasing—would get to you before we did. As soon as I saw you, I had it figured out: He was so worried because you're his type."

"Do men even have a type?"

Gardner lowered the paper to her lap. "You mean you haven't noticed? Honey, where've you been? Of course they do. They all have a type. And if you don't fit his type, you have to work like the devil to get a particular guy to even look at you."

The faint undertone of bitterness underlying that comment made Maddie look at Gardner in a whole new light. She sounded genuinely pained.

"So you're really interested in him? McCabe, I mean?" Maddie approached the seating group and sank down into the squashy depths of her green corduroy armchair. Yesterday she and Gardner had barely exchanged half a dozen words. Today they were going to chat? This was new. Intriguing, though.

"If he gave me half a chance, I'd have his babies." Gardner gave a wry little grimace. "I'd take him home to Mama. I'd wrap him up in cellophane and . . . well, you get the idea. Maybe it's something to do with my age. I'm thirty-seven. All of a sudden, I keep hearing my biological clock ticking. And every time I hear it tick, McCabe's is the face I see."

"He's not married, then?" Maddie asked cautiously. It was bad enough to be asking the question. It was worse to be so interested in the answer.

"Single, just like me. Just like Wynne." Gardner made a face. "Hell, who would have us? Except Wynne. Somebody might take Wynne."

"Wynne seems nice."

"Wynne *is* nice. Just the nicest guy around. But you have to admit, he's no stud-muffin."

Maddie thought about that. "Maybe a stud-muffin isn't the best choice to give you what you want. Maybe for a long-term relationship—for babies—you should be thinking in terms of just a really nice guy."

"Like Wynne." Gardner sounded less than convinced. Then she sighed. "To tell you the truth, the thought's crossed my mind. The thing is, Wynne seems to be interested in me. So far, McCabe doesn't. And I know Wynne's probably a better long-term prospect. But I hate it that he smokes. . . ."

"He quit," Maddie interjected swiftly.

"And I hate it that he doesn't take better care of himself."

"The doughnuts," Maddie said, suddenly understanding.

"Yes. Exactly. You saw him with the doughnuts." Gardner sighed. "See? It's always something. That's the thing with men. None of them—not one I've ever met—is perfect."

"Unlike us," Maddie said.

Gardner looked at her sharply. Then she grinned. "All right. Point taken. But if I could somehow take Wynne's personality and stuff it inside McCabe's body . . ." She paused, her eyes gleaming. Then her face fell. "The new perfect hybrid would not be interested in me. How dismal is that? Oh, forget it. Hey, you want part of the paper?"

Maddie laughed, and accepted the Metro section.

By late afternoon, though, Maddie was going stir-crazy. Having been stuck inside her apartment—which, ordinarily, she loved—for almost two full days, she was ready to climb the walls. After finishing the paper, she'd worked on her laptop. She'd played back all the phone messages that had been left—it was amazing how fast the news had gotten around that her car windows had been shot out—and returned a judicious few. She and Cynthia—they were on a first-name basis by that time—shared soup and crackers for lunch, as Maddie's cupboard was practically bare. Over the meal, she'd learned just about everything there was left to know about the other woman. In a nutshell, Cynthia had been born and raised in New Jersey, her marriage had been right out of high school and had lasted two years before ending in divorce, and she'd joined the FBI twelve years earlier, as soon as she had finished college. Maddie had also learned a great deal about Wynne. Wynne was also thirty-seven, also divorced once, also childless. He'd grown up in Connecticut and had very WASPish elderly parents still living there, to whom he was devoted. He visited them all the time, whenever he got the chance, and Cynthia had met them once. They hadn't seemed overly impressed with her, which Cynthia professed to find amusing. As for McCabe—Maddie especially enjoyed the nuggets Cynthia let drop about McCabe, although she did her best not to ask any more leading questions about him than she could help. According to Cynthia, he had parents still living, too, although she had never met them, a gaggle of siblings she had likewise never met, and a string of ex-girlfriends—Maddie imagined all the aforementioned slim, pretty brunettes—a mile long. He was thirty-five years old, never wed, and basically married to his job.

And Cynthia wanted him bad.

It had been on that note, reiterated with a kind of wry smile, that Wynne had knocked on the door. Cynthia had immediately reverted to Rambo Barbie mode, motioning to Maddie to stay back while she looked through the peephole. Recognizing Wynne, she had relaxed and let him in. When Maddie saw that he was bearing bags of groceries, she was ready to fall on his neck.

Cynthia left, and Maddie fixed a light supper—spaghetti and salad, which had the dual advantage of being easy and nutritious—for herself and Wynne. They talked while they ate, and Maddie got the distinct impression that

Wynne was as taken with Cynthia as Cynthia was with McCabe. Not that Wynne said so in so many words. Unlike Cynthia, he seemed inclined to keep his secrets. After supper, Wynne helped her clean up and then watched TV while she settled down with her laptop at the kitchen table. She checked her e-mail, checked the next week's schedule, and gave some thought to a campaign Creative Partners was preparing to pitch to a local ice-cream chain, making a few sketches and writing a few lines of copy that she was unhappy with almost as soon as she finished them. Vowing to work on it more the next day, Maddie allowed herself a moment to bask in the remembered glow of Friday's success—*we got the Brehmer account*—then packed her laptop into her briefcase and left the kitchen. Given the fact that she hadn't been able to get to the cleaners, her choice of outfits for the morrow was somewhat limited, so she settled on her favorite basic black summer dress. Sleeveless and made of some kind of wrinkle-proof synthetic that looked like slubby raw linen, it was cool and comfortable. Add a loose white linen jacket to wear with clients and spectator pumps, and she was good to go.

By then it was after ten. McCabe would be coming at eleven. Maddie took a bath, applied ointment and a fresh bandage to her shoulder—which, she was glad to observe, was healing nicely—put on her nightclothes and, with a quick good-night to Wynne, retreated to her bedroom. There she meant to stay until the following morning.

She'd been careful to limit her liquid intake after supper, so there should be no need for her to see McCabe at all.

A thing for him.

Even if she had one, which, okay, she might, she was absolutely not stupid enough to encourage it. Given what he was—and what she was—she would stand a better chance of emerging whole from a game of Russian roulette.

She was already in bed with the lights off, trying desperately to go to sleep, when she heard McCabe arrive. He and Wynne talked for a few minutes. Although she couldn't quite hear what they were saying over the TV, the deep drawl of his voice was unmistakable. Wynne's tones were a little higher-pitched, a little more clipped, milk chocolate rather than dark. Listening, Maddie was ready to concede that Cynthia was exactly right— Wynne even *sounded* like the nicest guy in the world.

McCabe sounded like pure sex.

On that sleep-inducing thought, Maddie pulled the sheet up over her head and squeezed her eyes shut. It only helped marginally. She heard McCabe laugh, heard the door close, heard a *pop* as though he had opened a tab-top can. More Diet Coke? Probably. She lay there with the door ajar, listening to what sounded like ESPN, unable to keep from picturing McCabe sprawled out on her couch—and fell asleep.

THE DREAM CAME, as she had known that sooner or later it must. It was late at night, and she was in bed—another bed, a long-ago bed. In a house that wasn't hers. It was a narrow bed—a cot, really—and it was old and creaky and smelled faintly of mildew. She was alone in it, alone in the room. The dark room. So dark that even with her eyes open, she couldn't see the broken chest that she knew was pushed up against the opposite wall just a few feet away. There were people in the house—people who scared her. She could hear them talking. The voices got louder, and she could feel the pulse knocking below her ear. Her fingertips throbbed—her hands were tied behind her back. Something stabbed painfully into her palm—her nails. She was just absorbing this when, without warning, the door opened. A rectangle of light spilled over the bed. Her eyes closed instantly, and she lay very still. A shadow fell across the bed, across her. A terror unlike any she had ever known twisted her stomach, tightened her throat. Even as cold sweat drenched her, she took care to breathe—*in, out, in, out*—in the slow cadence of deep sleep. All the while she watched the shadow from the tiny slit between her upper and lower lids, watched the horrible elongated thing that spilled like pure evil from the dark figure silhouetted in the doorway. She watched it, and prayed that he wouldn't come any closer, wouldn't come into the room. *In, out, in, out.* Lying still as death, just breathing in that interminable rhythm, while her heart beat like a trapped wild thing in her chest, she started to shake. God, he would see. . . . *Don't let me die. Please, don't let me die.* Then the shadow rippled, moved—a scream crowded into her throat but she forced it back—*in, out, in, out . . .*

Maddie startled awake. For a moment, she lay blinking up into the darkness, her heart pounding, her breathing coming in shuddering gasps. The dream—of course it was the dream. Would she never be rid of it?

Then it hit her. Darkness . . . her room was dark. She wasn't dreaming, and her room was dark. The apartment was dark, too, and quiet. Too quiet. The TV . . . it was off, dark, soundless.

Her ears picked up a sound, a movement. Her breathing stopped as her eyes swung blindly in the direction from which it came.

This time it was for real.

There was someone in her room.

FIFTEEN

M addie." It was McCabe's voice, the merest thread of sound.

Maddie drew in a shuddering breath and sat up. Her thundering heart slowed, and the knot in her stomach seemed to loosen.

"McCabe?"

"*Shh.*" He was beside her, beside the bed. She could see him now, indistinctly, as a denser shadow in the darkness. It wasn't absolute, she saw. Not the pitch-blackness of her dream . . .

She shuddered at the memory.

"Get up." His tone was urgent. His hand touched her arm, slid around her back. Before she responded, he was all but lifting her off the bed.

"What?" Whispering, too, trying to get her still-foggy mind around what was happening, she slid to her feet, then stumbled against him. His chest was a solid wall that kept her from falling. His arm tightened around her, hard and supportive—and insistent.

"Someone's coming up the fire escape. I want you to get in the bathroom, lock the door."

He was already hustling her out of the bedroom. Still slightly dazed, not one hundred percent sure she wasn't dreaming this, too, she went with him, shivering slightly despite the warmth of his arm around her, weak and drained as she always was in the aftermath of the dream. As they moved into the living room, the darkness lightened a degree, and Maddie saw that the long curtains covering the windows did not quite meet in the middle. A sliver of moonlight slid between them to paint a pale gray line across the floor. There was just enough light to permit her to see that in his other hand, the hand that was not clamped around her waist, McCabe held a gun.

Her heart lurched. What was happening became suddenly, sharply real.

They reached the bathroom and he thrust her inside.

"Lock it," he said, voice low, and pulled the door closed behind him. "And stay put. I'll be back."

Maddie locked the door. Then she leaned against the thin panel, fingers wrapped around the knob, bare toes curling against the cold tile. The bathroom had no window, and she dared not turn on a light. The darkness was absolute, rendering her effectively blind. The faint scent of soap reached her nostrils. Shivering, pressing her cheek against the smooth painted wood, she listened with every fiber of her being. The toilet ran slightly; the air-conditioning hummed. Above those homely sounds, she could hear nothing—no footsteps, no rush of movement, nothing.

Except the drumming of her own heart in her ears.

A man is coming up my fire escape.

Cold panic curled deep inside her stomach at the thought. Her knees went weak.

Oh, God, would this never end?

Where was McCabe?

There was no way to tell. He might be right outside the door. He might be in the kitchen. He might have rushed down the fire escape to confront the intruder. He might be silently, horribly dead. . . .

All she knew for sure was that she was alone in the dark, the terrifying dark, waiting for something to happen, for someone to come. . . .

Swaying, she clutched the doorknob for support. She was shivering, breathing fast. Her heart knocked against her ribs.

The dream still had her in its thrall. Maddie recognized that she was reacting to the situation she saw over and over again in her nightmares rather than to what was happening right at that moment, in what was now her real life. It was an effort to remember that the girl who had shivered so helplessly on that bed was long gone. She had grown up, grown resourceful, grown strong.

Get a grip, Maddie said it to herself savagely. Taking a deep breath, straightening her spine, willing her rubbery knees to hold up, she turned away from the door. Feeling her way along the tile wall, she found the sink, then the cabinet above it. Opening it, flinching slightly at the tiny creak, she touched the shelves, reaching for the can of hair spray she knew was there.

As a weapon, it didn't even make the charts, she realized as she lifted the smooth metal cylinder from its accustomed spot. Mace or pepper spray it wasn't. But in a pinch, if aimed at an intruder's face, it might buy her time—maybe even enough time to get away. In any case, it was the closest thing to a weapon she could get her hands on.

Pressing the small of her back up against the unyielding contours of the sink so that she faced the door, her every sense trained on the deathly silence beyond the bathroom, Maddie clutched the can and waited.

Time spun out interminably.

A quick footstep just outside the door.

She caught her breath.

A brisk tap. "Maddie?"

Exhaling, Maddie rushed to the door and opened it. The apartment was still lit only by that sliver of moon. She could see no more of him than a powerful, dark shape. But even if the voice hadn't identified him, she would have known it was McCabe.

It was clear from his tone, his knock: The danger was past.

Her knees gave out, and she practically fell forward against him.

"Hey," he said on a surprised note, catching her by her elbows. "It's over. It's okay."

"Did you get him?" She was cold, so cold that she was shivering in her thin little ivory slip of a nightgown, and weak with reaction to the dream and the scare combined.

"No." McCabe must have felt the tremors that racked her, because he wrapped hard arms around her, pulling her comfortingly close even as he answered her question. He felt strong and solid, and he smelled of the outdoors and the faint but intoxicating *eau de man* that she had noticed before, and, best of all, he radiated heat like a stove. She absorbed the warmth greedily, snuggling closer yet, unable to resist the temptation to let her head droop forward like a too-heavy flower to rest against the firm, broad expanse of his chest.

Encouraging him to hold her like this was probably a mistake, she knew. But she couldn't seem to summon the willpower to push herself out of his arms. Always, she'd had to stand on her own two feet. Always, she'd had to take care of herself, to be strong. Where was the harm, for once in her life, in surrendering for just a few moments to the pure luxury of having somebody to lean on?

"Was it—him?" she asked in a faint voice.

"I don't know. He was about a third of the way up your back stairs when something apparently spooked him. He took off like a bat out of hell."

Maddie closed her eyes. What were the chances that this was a totally random thing? In the four years she had lived in her apartment, no one had ever been caught climbing her fire escape in the middle of the night—until now.

"I'm glad you were here." It was quite an admission, and she recognized its enormity even as the words came out of her mouth. Her eyes popped open in alarm and she glanced up at him. Of course, it was impossible to see anything more than shadows upon shadows in the gloom.

"Yeah. Me, too."

His tone told her that he had no clue just how huge her admission had been. She took a deep breath, knowing that she had to make a move and yet not able, just at that moment, to do so, and his arms tightened fractionally around her. His body was tense, and Maddie guessed that he was still wired, on edge, from the intruder. He exuded controlled power, and without any real surprise at all, she discovered that she had absolute faith in his ability to keep her safe.

From night-crawling hit men, at least.

The problem was, who was going to keep her safe from him?

With that thought, Maddie started to regain her sense of self-preservation.

What are you doing? she scolded herself. *He's an FBI agent, you numbskull.*

Willing herself to get back with the program while she still could, she lifted her head from his chest. At the same moment, he moved. Maddie only realized that he was reaching behind her for the switch when the bathroom light clicked on.

She blinked with surprise, glanced up to discover just how close his face was, and found herself a little unnerved. He was looking down at her, frowning slightly. Her eyes were on a level with the top of his shoulder, and in the space of a heartbeat she took in the wide expanse of those shoulders in the dark green T-shirt she had only felt until now, absorbed the sturdy bronze column of his neck and the flexing muscles of his arm that was in the process of dropping away from the light switch. She saw that his chin was once again dark with stubble, and his hair was mussed like he'd been running his hands through it, and his brows had twitched together so that there were faint lines corrugating the space between them. His mouth was only inches from hers. She fixated on that hard, masculine mouth and felt her own lips part. He seemed to be breathing harder now than his strictly stationary posture called for, she realized. She could feel his chest rising and falling against her breasts, and the warmth of his breath brushed her face where she hadn't been aware of it before. Their eyes met, and in the coffee-brown depths of his, she saw something—a hot little flicker. An awareness . . .

The air between them was suddenly charged. Maddie felt the electricity, and heat curled somewhere deep inside her. Her breathing quickened. Her body began to tighten, to throb.

Oh God, she thought, panicking. *I want him.*

His eyes slid to her mouth. Which promptly went dry.

Then his gaze dropped lower still and his frown deepened.

"What the hell?"

Confused, Maddie followed his gaze and discovered, to her own surprise, that she was still clutching the can of hair spray. It was sandwiched between them, its little black spray nozzle pointed directly at his chest.

"Oh," she said, feeling foolish. Apparently, while she'd been busy getting all hot and bothered, he'd been passing the time wondering about the hard, round thing that was poking him in the chest. Struggling to think of this amorous lapse on his part as a positive development, she looked up at him. "*Uh*—it's hair spray."

"I can see that." His lips twitched, and then he grinned, a lopsided, charming grin that warmed his eyes and brought those to-die-for dimples into roguish life. "Planning to style somebody's hair?"

"I was in the bathroom. It was the only thing I could think of to use as a weapon," she said with dignity.

He laughed out loud. "Pencils. Hair spray. Darlin', God help the bad guys if you ever get your hands on a gun."

Outraged, she pushed against his chest, aerosol can and all.

"Let go."

"You don't want me to," he said.

Then he kissed her.

Maddie was so surprised that, for the space of maybe a heartbeat, she didn't even move. She just stood there with her eyes wide open, clutching the aerosol can while he pulled her so close that the can's metal edge dug into the side of her breast, and slanted his lips across hers and licked into her mouth with a hungry urgency that sent fire shooting clear down to her toes.

How long had it been since someone had kissed her like this? Too long. Never.

The question, complete with its telling answer, ricocheted through her stunned brain even as her body reacted quite independently. Her eyes closed, her lips parted all on their own, and her free hand slid around his nape, her fingers curling into the short, crisp hair at the back of his head. He deepened the kiss, and the heat of it melted away the last rational thought left to her name. Head reeling, she kissed him back, feeling the hot, slick glide of his tongue against hers, tasting the faint tang of Diet Coke in his mouth. His hands splayed over her back, big and strong and hot through the thin nylon of her gown. Pulse racing, she surged against him, loving the silky slide of her gown against his clothes. Hot little ripples of pleasure slid down her thighs as she discovered the hard bulge beneath his jeans and moved sensuously against it.

He broke off the kiss, lifted his head, sucked in air.

"McCabe," she whispered, rocking against him then going up on tiptoe to seek his mouth again.

"Christ," he said and bent his head, kissing her harder, exploring her mouth with an expertise that made her dizzy. The hot, sweet throbbing in her loins that he'd awakened earlier was back, times ten. Her breasts swelled, and her nipples contracted until they were needy little nubs pressing urgently against his chest.

His lips left hers, found the soft, sensitive spot beneath her ear, then slid down her neck. His mouth was hot and wet and firm, and the feel of it crawling over her skin made her dizzy. Her heart lurched, her bones liquified, and if he hadn't been holding her so tightly, she thought she would have melted into a sizzling little puddle at his feet.

She made a small, hungry sound deep in her throat and pressed as close to him as she could get. His head lifted, and then his mouth was on hers again. He was unmistakably turned-on, hard and hot with wanting her, holding her close and kissing her silly and making her feel things she had almost forgotten she could feel. She was on fire for him, burning deep inside, wanting to get naked and horizontal with him so badly that if he hadn't been bigger than she was, and stronger than she was, and such a really impressive kisser besides, she would have thrown him down on the floor and stripped off her nightgown and had her way with him there and then. But then his hands flattened on her back, slid lower, and she shivered, glad she had waited. They were big and long-fingered and strong, the kind of hands she loved, and she tracked their sensuous glide over the silky nylon with quivering anticipation. They slid over her butt, cupping her cheeks, and she moaned her pleasure into his mouth. She could feel the heat and strength and size of those hands with every nerve ending she possessed, even as he pulled her tight against him and rocked into her.

A quick hard knock on the front door made Maddie jump. McCabe's hands froze, and he lifted his head. They both looked toward the sound.

"McCabe . . ."

The voice, a man's, was muffled but clearly audible nonetheless. Maddie was too dazed and confused to feel so much as the first flicker of fear, and, anyway, a hit man would not be knocking on the front door and calling out to McCabe.

"Shit," McCabe said and looked back down at her. Her eyes met the superheated gleam of his, and held. For a sizzling instant she would have been hard put to remember anything as basic as her name. Then his arms around her loosened and dropped away. He headed for the door.

"Go put your robe on," he said over his shoulder.

Breathing too fast, heart racing, her body tingling in places she'd almost forgotten she had, Maddie took a moment to process what had just happened, while her eyes tracked him to the door. His hand wrapped around the knob. Shrouded in shadows now, he glanced back at her. It was only then that she realized that she was still standing in the bright oblong of light that spilled out of the bathroom, wearing nothing but her thin, white nightgown that, backlit as it was, undoubtedly revealed as much as it concealed.

He was still looking at her with his hand on the knob when the knock sounded again.

"McCabe . . ." The voice was louder now, impatient.

Maddie fled toward her bedroom.

"Don't turn on the light," he said as she reached it. "If he's got any idea about doubling back, we don't want to scare him off."

She stopped, standing stock-still for a moment as she registered the idea that whoever had been on her steps might be coming back. Then she heard the metallic click of the deadbolt unlocking. By the time McCabe had the door open, she was safely in her room.

In order to have any light at all, she had to leave her bedroom door ajar. Maddie crossed to the dresser, put down the can that, ridiculously, she discovered she was still holding, found her robe, and pulled it on. Then she hesitated. She was still shaken, from the dream and the fright and, yes, that impossibly hot kiss. She was alarmed. She was befuddled. What she could do—what she *should* do—was try to thrust her worries out of her head until she could think them through more calmly on the morrow, go back to bed, and trust McCabe to keep watch. But even as she had the thought, she knew that she couldn't do it. Sleep was clearly going to be impossible after what had happened. And the lure of the murmuring voices was too strong. She badly wanted to know what was going on. And there was no way she could just leave things as they were with McCabe.

Tightening the belt on her robe, Maddie padded out into the dark living room. The front door was closed, and McCabe was there in front of it with his back turned to her, standing in the dark with two men that she didn't at first recognize. But the bathroom light was still on, providing just enough illumination to allow her to discern features in the gloom. As she drew closer and they acknowledged her presence with glances and nods, she realized that she was looking at Gomez and Hendricks. All three men fell silent as she stopped beside McCabe.

"So what's happened?" she asked, thrusting her hands deep into the pockets of her robe.

"He got away," Gomez said. There was chagrin on his boyish face.

"He must have seen us," Hendricks added. "We were careful as hell, too."

"It was that damned streetlight. We were right under it when he started leaping back down the stairs." He cast an accusing look at Hendricks. "I told you we should have gone around it."

"If we'd gone around it, he would've had time to get up here and kick down the apartment door and blast the hell out of everybody inside before we got to him."

Maddie felt a cold chill snake down her spine at this graphic description of what might have happened. She had to fight the urge to lean into McCabe.

"Anyway, we're not even sure he saw us," Hendricks said to Sam. "*Something* spooked him."

"Yeah, probably he's afraid of spiders and there was a big one about halfway up the stairs," Gomez said in disgust. Hendricks shot him a dirty look.

"Whatever happened, he's gone," McCabe said. So far he hadn't so much as glanced at Maddie, who had noticed.

"Maybe the locals will pick him up. They're out there cruising around now."

"Maybe," McCabe said. "You guys did good, by the way."

"Thanks," Hendricks replied without enthusiasm. "Come on, Gomez. We better be getting back."

"We'll get him next time," Gomez said. "He's not getting away again. It's uncomfortable as hell in that van."

With that, they left. McCabe locked the door behind them. Looking at his broad back as he closed the door and tried the lock, Maddie felt her heart speed up again.

Wanting him was such a stupid thing to do.

He turned away from the door and their eyes met. Heat surged between them, as sudden and electric as a bolt of lightning. The tension in his stance told her that he felt it, too. But she could see his face clearly enough in the gloom to realize that he didn't look particularly happy about the fact. Not at all the way a man should look if he thought he was about to get lucky. In fact, she registered with a slight knitting of her brows, he was looking downright grim.

"At a guess I'd say that's all the excitement for tonight," he said, skirting around her like she was giving off radioactive cootie rays to head for the kitchen. "Whoever was on the stairs almost certainly won't be back. You should go on to bed."

O-kay. Clearly, sweet nothings weren't in the cards. To say nothing of down-and-dirty, really hot sex.

Damn.

"Where did Gomez and Hendricks come from?" she asked, following him. She'd thought that only he, Wynne, and Gardner were sharing guard duty. Discovering that she had more babysitters even than she'd thought was just a little mind-boggling. Pausing in the doorway, she watched him open her refrigerator door. The faint, frosty light illuminated the front of him from the top of his tousled, black head to the toes of his sneakers. He wasn't looking at her. He was perusing the available food instead. But his eyes were narrowed, his jaw was clenched, and his mouth was tight. Unless he was having an emotional reaction to the leftover salad, that expression was for her.

"They're watching your back door from a van in a parking lot two doors down. I've got two more guys out on the street in a Blazer, watching your front door. We stay in touch." He reached for a quart of milk—she usually drank skim, but this, courtesy of Wynne, was whole milk—and glanced at her. "You mind?"

He was asking if she minded if he drank some of what wasn't even properly her milk.

"Help yourself," she said and declined his offer to pour her some with a shake of her head. He filled his own glass, returned the milk to the refrigerator, shut the door, and drank. *Way to avoid a difficult conversation,* she thought wryly. With the curtains drawn over the windows and the refrigerator shut, the kitchen was almost as dark as the rest of the apartment. But not quite. The streetlight that Gomez had complained of filtered through the thin cotton panels so that she could see McCabe tip his head back to finish the milk, then hear the faint click as he set the glass in the sink.

By then she had made up her mind. It was her life and she could be stupid if she wanted to. And, yeah, she wanted to. A lot. The problem was, he didn't seem inclined to cooperate any longer. Leaning against the door-jamb and folding her arms over her chest, she decided to take the battle into the enemy camp.

"That kiss was a mistake, okay?" she said.

He turned back from the sink to look at her. She could see the shape of his head and the outline of his powerful shoulders silhouetted against the curtains, but his expression was lost in darkness.

"I think that should've been my line." His voice was dry. "I shouldn't have kissed you. I'm sorry."

Great. He was apologizing when all she really wanted him to do was kiss her again.

"Stuff happens." With a delicate, no-big-deal shrug, she turned and padded back into the living room. A wiser woman—or a braver one—would undoubtedly have headed back to her bedroom, jumped into bed, pulled the covers over her head, and thanked God for saving her from her own folly. She sank down on the couch.

"Don't you have to get up and go to work in the morning? It's almost two a.m." He had followed her into the living room and now stood beside the TV, looking at her—was it warily? It was difficult to be sure, given the vagaries of the light, but she thought so.

"Like I'm going to be able to sleep after that. Maybe it's just me, but knowing that there's somebody out there who's trying to kill me kind of gives me insomnia." It was so true she shivered, then firmly thrust the thought of marauding hit men out of her mind. That was a subject to be pondered when her mind was clearer. "Can we turn on the TV, or would that be a violation of the blackout?"

"Go ahead and turn it on. I was watching ESPN when I got the word that someone was headed up your back stairs."

"I hate ESPN," Maddie said, picking up the remote from the coffee table and pressing the power button. The TV flickered to life.

"Watch whatever you want."

The irony of being invited to watch what she wanted on her own TV was not lost on her. Settling into a corner and curling her feet up beside her, Maddie started clicking through the channels. McCabe, meanwhile, crossed to the bathroom and turned off the light. Then he returned to the seating group and lowered himself into the big green chair.

"So, what is this we're watching?" he asked after a moment.

Maddie flicked a look at him. He was slouched in the chair, his long legs thrust out in front of him. He'd kicked his shoes off, and his thick, white athletic socks glowed faintly in the bluish light.

"*Dark Victory,*" she said with relish, naming the 1940s Bette Davis weeper. She'd chosen it deliberately as a kind of subtle revenge for all the hours of sports she'd been forced to listen to since the FBI had barged into her life—and also for his reaction to that aborted kiss.

He gave a grunt of disgust. "Why you women like that kind of stuff . . ."

"The end makes us cry. It's cathartic."

"Well, the middle's going to put me to sleep. Do you think we could possibly watch something else?"

"Like what? Not sports."

"I'm open to compromise."

Since she wasn't really feeling like a weeper, either—if she felt like being depressed, she had plenty of things in her real life at that moment that would more than do the trick—she flipped channels. After a few minutes of negotiation, they settled on a *Seinfeld* rerun.

"I've been meaning to ask," McCabe said as the screen switched to a commercial, "did you get that account you were trying for?"

The memory came complete with its own special little glow. The one great moment in a really crappy week.

"Yeah, we did."

"Good for you."

"It's a really big deal for my company." Despite everything, she was starting to feel sleepy. The couch was huge and comfy and upholstered in chenille, which made it cozy, and, after wrapping her robe closely about her legs to make sure she stayed decent, she scooted down so that her head rested on the big, squishy armrest.

"So how did you come to be the owner of an advertising agency?" McCabe asked as *Seinfeld* reappeared on the screen.

"I worked there. The previous owner wanted to sell it. I wanted to buy it. So I did."

"What, do you have a rich uncle?" There was the faintest note of humor underlying the question.

"I wish." Maddie made a little face and snuggled lower into the cushions. "Since Creative Partners was barely turning a profit, it wasn't all that expensive. I had enough saved up for the initial payment, and Mr. Owens— that's the previous owner—arranged it so that I make monthly payments to him until I own it one hundred percent."

"That new account large enough to help?"

"Oh, yeah," Maddie said, smiling a little at the thought. "It's large enough."

"So what does your family think about you being a big, bad business mogul?"

Her family. Maddie registered that and flicked a look at him. His gaze was focused on the TV.

"I don't really have any family left," she said, and turned the tables. "How does your family feel about you being an FBI agent?"

That won her a glance and a glimmer of a smile. "They're in favor of it, by and large. My grandma gets it confused with the CIA, though. She thinks I'm a spy, and she keeps volunteering to help."

"You have a grandma?" She tried hard not to sound wistful. All her life she'd wanted a grandma—and a mom, and some siblings—but her mother had died when she was two and, since then, all she'd ever had was her dad.

"Oh, yeah."

"Tell me about her. Tell me about your whole family." She'd always loved hearing about families—real families, whole families. To her they were like fairy stories, enchanting tales of never-to-be-visited lands.

He sent her another look. "Well, my grandma is eighty-two, sharp as a tack except for the few things she occasionally gets confused, like the difference between the FBI and the CIA. She says they're all initials so what the hell, and nobody's going to argue with her because if you argue with her, she's liable to crack you over the head with one of her big wooden spoons. My dad's a former cop who retired last year, my mom's a homemaker who secretly rules the roost, and I have two brothers—one a cop, one a lawyer—and a baby sister, who is currently in grad school at the University of South Carolina."

"Wow," Maddie breathed, picturing all those relatives with bedazzlement. "Are you close with them? Do you see them often?"

"When I can." His mouth curled into a smile. "I make it to all the big holidays, anyway."

"Sounds wonderful," she said. She was so cozy and comfortable that she was feeling almost boneless now. With McCabe only an arm's length away, the twin specters of bad dreams and determined killers seemed impossibly distant. "Do you live near each other?"

"Everybody except my lawyer brother and I live in Greenville, South Carolina, where we grew up. He lives in Savannah, and I keep a condo near Quantico."

Her brow contracted, and she tilted her head a little on the armrest so that she could see him better. Kicked back in the chair, with the light from the TV playing over him and his long legs stretched out in front of him, he looked about as relaxed as she felt.

"So what were you doing in New Orleans?" she asked.

His eyes cut to her. His hands tightened on the arms of the chair.

"My job," he said. "Just like you."

His job. For a little while there, she'd almost forgotten what he was. Anxiety twisted her insides, and suddenly she wasn't quite as sleepy anymore.

"McCabe," she said. "What happens when somebody at your job says it's time for you to leave?"

He met her gaze. Alive with the glow of the TV, his eyes gleamed at her.

"What happens to you, you mean?" he asked. Maddie gave a little nod. "I won't leave you until I'm sure you're safe. You don't have to worry."

"I wasn't worried," she said, although she was. "I just wanted to know what to expect."

Although she'd known, of course, from the very beginning. The FBI used people, and when they had no more use for them they discarded them like so much trash.

How stupid was she to let herself forget that?

SIXTEEN

Monday, August 18

When Sam opened the door to Gardner at shortly before eight the next morning, he was not in the best of moods. After Maddie had finally fallen asleep on the couch, he had let her be for a while, trying to concentrate on the TV and his own thoughts instead of noticing the picture she made lying there or her occasional restless movements or the soft sound of her breathing. But ignoring her had proved impossible. Curled on her side with one hand tucked beneath her cheek, she had looked sweet and sexy and vulnerable. Her lashes formed dark crescents on her cheeks; her lips were just barely parted. Her body—no, he wasn't going there; he wasn't even going to *think* about her body. But even when he'd kept his eyes resolutely glued to the screen, he had been unable to push from his mind the knowledge that she was curled up little more than an arm's length away. When he caught himself glancing her way when he should have been watching Shaq mow down Yao Ming, he knew he had to do something. *Out of sight, out of mind,* he'd thought—too optimistically, as it had turned out—and had scooped her up in his arms and carried her to her bed. She

hadn't so much as flickered an eyelid, and, deadweight, she'd been a substantial armful, but as he'd lugged her into the bedroom and deposited her,
still wrapped in her robe, in the middle of her big bed, he'd made a grim
discovery.

His deep, atavistic response to their kiss had not been an aberration.
Holding the soft, curvy warmth of her in his arms, inhaling the sweet, light
scent of her, feeling the satiny smoothness of her skin, he'd gotten hot all
over again. So hot, in fact, that it had taken a large effort of will to stop himself from dropping down beside her and awakening her with a kiss and taking up where they'd left off. She would have welcomed him, he knew. He
wasn't a kid; he'd had his share of women. The look in her eyes as she had
followed him around after Gomez and Hendricks left was unmistakable.
She might as well have been wearing a sign reading *Do me now*. What had
stopped him was the knowledge that he was on the job, dammit, and her last
line of defense besides.

And the little voice inside his head warning that with her, he just might
be heading for trouble.

It don't mean a thing if it ain't got that zing. Damn Grandma anyway for
putting the phrase in his head.

Because with Maddie, he'd recognized it: zing. Zing in spades.

In the very last place he ever would have wanted to find it. His job was
to keep her alive, not get her into bed. Although he seemed to be having a
problem keeping that firmly fixed in the forefront of his mind.

"Hard night?" Gardner looked at him keenly as she walked past him into
the apartment.

Sam replied with a grunt, then asked, "Did you bring it?" as he closed
the door behind her.

"Right here." Gardner jiggled the black vinyl tote she was carrying. Her
hair was brushed close to her head so that it looked sleek rather than spiky,
her eyes were bright, her makeup relatively subdued. She was wearing a
black blazer over a white T-shirt and black pants. Her waist was cinched,
her pants were tight, and her heels were high, but clearly she'd taken the in-

formation that she would be protecting Maddie in a business environment to heart as she dressed.

"I heard about your visitor last night," she added. "Think it was our UNSUB?"

Sam shrugged. "I don't know. Seems kind of amateurish for this guy."

"That's what I thought, too." She looked toward the closed bedroom door and raised her voice. "Morning, Maddie."

"Oh, hi, Cynthia," Maddie called back from the other side of that door, her voice faintly muffled. "I'm almost ready."

"Take your time," Gardner responded. "Nobody's going anywhere without you." She glanced at Sam. "Is that coffee I smell?"

He grunted again, this time as an affirmative. He had, in fact, made a fresh pot—his third since he'd walked away and left Maddie peacefully sleeping in her bed—when he'd heard Maddie get up. Busying himself in the kitchen had meant that he didn't have to watch her emerge all tousle-haired and sleepy-eyed from her bedroom. Which, considering the *zing*, was probably not an image he wanted to burden himself with. Not until he had a handle on how he felt.

"What, are you two bosom buddies now or something?" Sam asked sourly, following Gardner to the kitchen. Last time he'd paid the matter any attention, the two women had seemed to be just about civil and that was it.

"We talked." Gardner dropped the tote on the kitchen table, snagged a cup from the cabinet, and filled it while Sam moved to lean against the counter beneath the window. Outside, he saw at a glance, the world was awash in sparkly sunshine. Birds twittered. Butterflies fluttered. Branches burst with leafy greenery. Inside, he just felt grumpy. "We bonded," Gardner added.

Something about that didn't sound like it boded well for him. "You *bonded*?"

"Yep." Gardner gulped down some coffee and made a face at him. "Over men. Over *you*."

"What?"

"She's your type, isn't she? I recognized it as soon as I saw her."

"What the hell are you talking about?" God deliver him from women. They were all—every single one he'd ever met—screwy as hell.

"Maddie. She's your type." Gardner sounded regretful. "It's one of those things nobody can do anything about. That's why I decided to cut my losses."

"What?" Sam scowled at her for a second, then decided that he really didn't want to go there. Not this morning, not ever. He shook his head. "Never mind. I don't want to know." Time to change the subject. "Any of that stuff we sent off come back yet?"

He was referring to the evidentiary material from both New Orleans crime scenes that had been sent off to the FBI lab for analysis.

Gardner assumed her game face, thank God. "Not yet. They said it would take a few days. They're busy."

"Aren't we all. How about the in-depth backgrounds on our two Miz Fitzgeralds?"

"Stuff's coming in in bits and pieces. The ex-husband's alibi seems to be holding up."

"Yeah. I'd already pretty much crossed him off my list."

Gardner looked at him over her cup. "I take it the UNSUB hasn't called again?"

"Not yet." Along with the *zing* factor, that was one of the things that was making him so antsy. Where *was* the guy? Of course, if he was creeping around Maddie's back stairs, maybe at the moment he had priorities other than picking up the phone.

But Sam didn't think so. Didn't think he was creeping around Maddie's back stairs, and didn't think he had other priorities. The sick bastard enjoyed the chase too much. In fact, Sam got the feeling that the sick bastard enjoyed taunting *him* too much.

It was personal.

Sam suddenly felt as if bells and whistles had just gone off in his brain and somebody inside there had just stood up and shouted, *"Eureka!"*

"What?" Gardner said. Sam didn't know what his expression looked like, but Gardner had lowered her cup to stare at him.

"I know this guy," Sam said, the wheels still turning. "Or he knows me. He's got to be somebody I've busted, or somebody connected with somebody I've busted, or somebody somehow connected with one of the cases I've worked."

"Well, that narrows it down." Grimacing, Gardner resumed drinking her coffee. "To maybe a cast of thousands. How long you been with the Bureau? Ten years? You work on what, maybe a hundred cases a year? Yep, a cast of thousands."

"Not just anyone could pull this off," Sam said slowly. "This guy's a pro. A sick fuck, but a pro."

Maddie appeared in the doorway just then, and Sam shelved the matter as something to be looked into as soon as he got back to their command post in the hotel room where Wynne, hopefully, was holding down the fort.

"I'm ready to go," Maddie addressed Gardner, ignoring Sam completely. So far that morning, she hadn't said a word to him. She hadn't so much as looked at him. As determined as he was to get their relationship back on strictly professional footing, he had to admit that it bugged him to realize that she seemed to have pretty much the same idea.

"Not so fast," Sam said. "Gardner brought you a present."

She looked at him then. Raised her eyebrows inquiringly. Sam felt the impact of those honey-colored eyes in places he didn't even want to think about. God, she was pretty, with her big do-me eyes and waves of shiny, dark hair and her soft, kissable mouth. *Okay, don't go there.* Like Gardner, she was wearing black and white, only her outfit consisted of a sexy little black dress that ended just above her knees beneath a loose white jacket. Unlike Gardner, though, she looked so hot he could practically feel the sizzle from where he stood.

Which wasn't good.

"What kind of present?" she asked suspiciously. They were the first words she'd spoken to him that morning.

Sam straightened, took the few steps necessary to reach the table, picked up the tote, and handed it to her.

"Here you go."

Maddie looked at him, looked at the tote, then pulled out what, if someone didn't know better, could possibly be mistaken for a pale gray, sleeveless windbreaker. For a moment, she simply frowned at it in evident bewilderment.

"It's a bulletproof vest," Gardner said.

Maddie's eyes widened. She unfolded the Kevlar vest and held it up in front of her, looking at it incredulously. Lightweight and thin, the garment was state-of-the-art.

"You've got to be kidding me." Her eyes met his.

"Nope. Ordinarily it goes under your clothes, but since you're only going to be wearing it while you're outside, you can put it on over your dress and under your jacket, if you want."

She looked from the vest to him again. "Do I really need this?"

"Let's see, aren't you the person who got shot a couple of days back?"

Her lips compressed, her eyes flickered, and he could tell that had registered.

"Good point," she said, and, putting the vest down on the table, took off her jacket. Sam couldn't help noticing how slim and shapely she looked in the formfitting dress that somehow managed to be business-appropriate while still hugging every delectable curve. Then she had the vest on and was struggling to zip it up. Still distracted by the view, he reached out to help her automatically, only realizing that this might not be the best idea when his knuckles brushed against cool cloth covering the flatness of her belly and he felt an unexpected spark of heat. Then the scent of her hit him—fresh and clean, with that mysterious hint of strawberries—and he had an instant flashback to how she had felt in his arms. Gritting his teeth, banishing the memory to outer darkness, he pulled the zipper up with cool efficiency and stepped back.

Hoping like hell that he was only imagining the sweat popping out on his brow.

"You wear it from the time you leave your apartment until you're safely inside your office building," he said as she pulled her jacket back on and looked down at the result doubtfully. "When you leave your office building to come home, you wear it. If you leave your office building for anything, you wear it. Anytime you go outside for any reason, you wear it. Got it?"

She nodded. He thought, maybe, that she might have turned a shade paler than before.

"Okay, I have to ask it." She looked up, met his gaze, turned sideways, and gestured at herself. "Does this bulletproof vest make me look fat?"

Then, as Gardner gave a snort of laughter, Maddie grinned at him. And his heart turned over. It was as simple as that.

Because he wasn't imagining it. Despite the brave front she was putting on, there was fear in her eyes. She wasn't alone, either. Now that he was about to send her out where he didn't have total control of the environment and she might really be vulnerable, he was struggling with a whole boatload of second thoughts himself. If he'd been able to think of anything else that might work as well as using her as bait, he would have scrapped the plan right there and then. The problem was, he couldn't.

Lips tightening, he reached out and buttoned her jacket for her, so that as little of the damned vest showed as possible. She had tied a scarf around her neck, he noticed for the first time, a black, gauzy one, and he realized that she was wearing it to hide the bruise where the sick fuck had choked her.

Sam was suddenly so angry he wanted to kill.

"Do you actually think he's going to take another shot at me?" Her grin had faded. She was looking at him steadily. He hadn't been mistaken about the fear: He could see it in everything from the set of her jaw to the tension around her eyes. But she wasn't going to let it show if she could help it, and she was going to go through with the plan regardless.

"I don't know," Sam said, his tone rougher than it needed to be because she was getting to him despite his best efforts to keep it from happening. She was being courageous, gallant even. And he? Hell, face the truth: What he was doing here was using her. Putting her in danger, even while she trusted him to keep her safe. Or, to put the best possible face on it, he was simply doing his job. Which, like now, sometimes sucked. "But there's no point in taking any chances. Wear the damned vest, okay?"

NOW I KNOW *what it feels like to have an entourage,* Maddie thought wryly as the equivalent of the presidential motorcade escorted her to work. It was rush hour, and the expressway was jammed. The urge to put in a call to her good buddy Bob was growing stronger by the minute—*You want to explain what a man was doing sneaking up my back stairs in the middle of the night?*—but there were too many eyes watching and, possibly, ears listening to make that wise. Under the circumstances, her best choice—her *only* choice—was to sit tight, so that's what she did. She sat tight right in the driver's seat of her Camry as she headed east on I-64 toward downtown St. Louis. In front of her was a gray Maxima carrying two agents whose names she didn't know. Behind her, Cynthia was driving McCabe in a black Blazer. She could see them anytime she wanted with a flick of her eyes to her rearview mirror. Behind them came the white van, with Gomez driving and Hendricks beside him. None of the vehicles was too close—apparently, the idea was to make it look as if she were on her own, just in case the hit man might still be harboring some illusions about that—but Maddie was acutely aware of them nonetheless.

The sky was a high, brilliant blue, dotted here and there with cottony clouds. The shimmer of heat that would rise above the city later was not yet in evidence. She drove toward the arch, which gleamed silver in the bright morning sunlight as it curved like a colossus across the horizon. Clustered around it, the angular skyscrapers and Victorian-era domes and needlelike church steeples that filled in the skyline seemed to stretch out endlessly. Maddie got just a glimpse of the mud-brown waters of the Mississippi River rolling lazily by on her right as she turned off onto Market Street. For a moment she marveled as all three vehicles escorting her made the turn with ease despite the crush of traffic, no zooming over from the far lane, no cutting in front of other cars, no squealing brakes or honking horns. Each simply pulled onto the ramp as if, instead of taking their cue from her, they had known exactly where they were going all the time. Which, Maddie realized with an internal *duh* seconds later, of course they did. They were the FBI, after all. Knowing where she worked and how to get there was something straight out of Snooping 101 to them.

Finding herself once again sandwiched in the middle of the procession, Maddie was suddenly all too conscious of the cold weight of the bulletproof vest dragging at her shoulders. Knowing that she was wearing it made her jumpy. Just being back in the car again made her jumpy. McCabe had said that the new glass was all bulletproof, but knowing she was safe and feeling like she was safe were, she was discovering, two entirely different things. The awful moment when that shot had exploded through her windshield had been indelibly etched on her mind, and finding herself back in the catbird's seat, as it were, was nerve-racking. She caught herself glancing around nervously as she drove. Now that she knew how it happened—*fast, bang, out of nowhere, and you're dead*—she didn't think she'd ever be entirely comfortable in any open area again.

By the time she reached the Anheuser-Busch Building, where Creative Partners had offices on the sixth floor, her palms were damp.

The trickiest part, of course, she realized as she parked in the lot behind the building, was getting from her car into the building. Without the shell of the Camry for protection, Maddie felt hideously vulnerable as she got out and headed for the chrome-trimmed glass double doors of the rear entrance. Juggling briefcase and purse, breathing in the tarry smell of the asphalt underfoot and the fishy odor of the Mighty Mississippi with every step, she scrunched up her shoulders protectively and hotfooted it across the pavement while trying to project a business-as-usual air to any and all onlookers. But she was hideously conscious of every passing car, every pedestrian, every metallic glint in a high-up window. Sounds seemed to be magnified—the swoosh of tires on pavement, the rumble of a city bus as it passed, the slamming of car doors near and far. Her minders were fanned out all around her—McCabe and Cynthia in a parking spot a dozen feet or so to her left, the two unknown agents circling the lot near the back, Gomez and Hendricks pulling to the curb on the street near where she'd parked—but for those three hundred or so yards, she felt as alone as she ever had in her life. Even so early in the morning, it was already hot as a steam bath, typical August in St. Louis, with the promise of yet another miserably sultry day to come. But by the time Maddie had made it halfway to the door, she was freezing.

It was chilling to know that the hit man could be anywhere. Even now he could be lifting a rifle, lining up the crosshairs, targeting *her*.

Pushing through the door, Maddie practically fell into the building's air-conditioned gloom. She had to pause for a second in the small rear vestibule, pressing her hands to her face, trying to get her breathing under control. Her fingers felt as cold as ice. Her heart pounded as though she'd just run a marathon. Her mouth was dry.

Get a grip, she told herself. Dropping her hands, she took a deep breath, squared her shoulders, and carried on. The marble-floored lobby that the vestibule opened into was crowded, which was typical at this time on a Monday morning as her fellow tenants headed up to their jobs. Several people greeted her as she joined a group waiting for the elevators. Acutely conscious of the bulletproof vest herself, she was surprised when no one seemed to notice anything unusual about her appearance. Still so on edge that she jumped when someone in the crowd sneezed, Maddie smiled and chatted to a couple of people without even knowing what she was saying or being aware of to whom she was talking. She was, she supposed, operating on autopilot, which might or might not be a good thing. It kept her from attracting the curious attention of her acquaintances, but it might also work against her if she was too out of it to notice something that might give the hit man away before he could strike.

Just as she was stepping into the elevator, her cell phone rang. Maddie jumped before she realized what it was, then glanced nervously around to see if anyone had noticed her reaction. It seemed as though no one had. The blasted thing kept on ringing. It was in her purse, and she had to dig for it. When she finally found it and answered, the elevator was shuddering to a halt on the third floor.

"You're doing great," McCabe said in his patented dark-chocolate drawl as two women squeezed out the door. "There's a short, pudgy bald guy carrying a newspaper on the elevator with you. Do you see him?"

Alarmed, Maddie glanced quickly around as the elevator doors closed and they started up again. Was McCabe describing the hit man, warning that he was near? The elevator was still almost full, but it took just seconds to spot the man standing behind her on the left. Her heart kicked up a notch. As her widened eyes met his, the pudgy guy gave her a slight smile. Heart in throat, Maddie hastily looked forward again.

"Y-es," she said into the phone on a slightly squeaky note.

"Well, pretend you don't. That's Special Agent George Molan. I want you to ignore him, act like he's not even there. He'll see you safely into your office. Gardner's on her way up."

Maddie practically passed out with relief right there in the elevator. "Okay."

"You've got nothing to be afraid of. We've got you covered so tightly that a mosquito won't be able to bite you without us swatting it first."

Good to know, Maddie thought, but before she could say anything, he disconnected.

Sure enough, Molan got off on the sixth floor, trailed behind her as she walked briskly toward the seven-room suite that Creative Partners occupied on the northwest side of the building, then stayed behind to bend over the water fountain as she went inside.

Louise was not at her desk just inside the door. Maddie frowned as she realized that. Her gaze swept the reception area. It was a large room, sleekly modern like the rest of the office, with pearl-gray walls and carpet, and chrome and black furniture. Sunlight streamed through a row of tall windows to cast bright rectangles across the blown-up stills from their most successful advertising campaigns that adorned the walls. Magazines highlighting Creative Partners' campaigns and clients were arranged neatly on various tables. Bold and functional, it was an attractive space, if she did say so herself. Of course, she wasn't exactly an impartial source: She'd designed and decorated it.

Since buying the business, she'd put every spare penny and every spare minute and every spare thought she'd had into making Creative Partners a success. And the look of the place was an important ingredient in impressing clients. Achieving the right look on a piggy-bank budget had been a challenge. She'd scrounged office furniture closeout sales to find new chairs and tables for the reception room, and the modular black leather couch had come from a yard sale. She and the rest of the staff had painted the walls themselves. They'd made the blowups to hang on them. They'd—well, they'd done everything. In the last year and a half or so, they had totally remade Creative Partners in every way to reflect the more dynamic company that they all hoped it would become. Every single change bore Maddie's personal stamp, and she couldn't have been prouder of the result if the company had been her child. In a way, she thought, it *was* her child.

The little advertising agency that could. The hand-painted slogan hung on the wall behind Louise's desk. That was how they thought of themselves, and they'd labored as tirelessly as ants to make it true.

Then, on Friday, they'd won the Brehmer account. And just like that, the world had changed. All the hopes and dreams that each of them had put into the rebuilding of the company now trembled on the brink of coming true.

Or not.

The thought that she might be going to lose it all hung over Maddie's head like a dark cloud as she looked around. She . . .

Someone pushed through the door behind her. Maddie jumped, cutting her eyes nervously toward the newcomer.

"Yo," Cynthia said, then, responding to something she must have seen in Maddie's face, added, "Everything okay?"

Maddie breathed again. "Fine. It's just—Louise—the receptionist—isn't at her desk."

"Is she usually?"

"She usually comes in, sits right down at her desk, and has her breakfast." Maddie shrugged, and started walking. Besides the reception area, there were four offices—one each for Jon, Judy, Herb, and herself—a conference room, and a workroom with office machines, file cabinets, and a desk for Ana. "She's probably in the restroom. Or making coffee."

All right, so having a babysitter was a little irksome, Maddie reflected as she glanced in Jon's, Judy's, and Herb's doors in turn on the way to her own, only to find their offices deserted, too. If Cynthia hadn't been right behind her, her hand moving beneath her jacket to rest on what Maddie hoped was a very large gun as they progressed, she would have been freaked to the point of running out of the office by the time she'd made it to the end of the hall.

"Louise? Jon? Anybody?" she called, sticking her head into the workroom.

Nobody answered, and for a very good reason: Nobody was there.

"Let me open it," Cynthia said, moving in front of her as Maddie reached her office door and started to grasp the knob. "I *know* this place is secure; we had it searched before the building opened and we've had it staked out since, but . . ."

Her voice trailed off as she turned the knob. Maddie knew just what she meant. Finding the office silent and empty was unnerving.

Cynthia threw the door open wide.

"Surprise!" screamed five voices in unison, echoed by a chorus of loud pops that made Maddie jump and Cynthia take a hasty step back. A shower of glittery confetti filled the air. Brightly colored balloons bounced against the ceiling. A big banner stretched across the windows, proclaiming *We got the Brehmer account!* A small sheet cake took center stage in the middle of her desk. Glancing around, Maddie sucked in air.

They were all there—Jon, Louise, Judy, Herb, and Ana. As Maddie looked from one grinning face to the other, they began to clap.

"You *guys,*" she said, her heart swelling, and walked into her office.

SAM SLEPT, only to be startled awake what could have been minutes or hours later by the ringing of a phone. *His* phone. His heart jolted. Lifting his head from the pillow it was buried in, fumbling for his cell phone, which he'd left on the bedside table, he found it and squinted at the message window. The damned thing was impossible to read in the gloom. Blinking at it, still groggy, he realized even as he flipped the thing open that he was in the dark because the curtains were drawn tightly over the windows, and he had been asleep in his room at the Hampton Court Inn.

"McCabe," he growled into the phone.

"What the hell are you doing in St. Louis?" a voice boomed at him. It took him a second to recognize Smolski's bluff tones. "Last I heard, you had the UNSUB pegged to head west from New Orleans."

"There's a woman . . ." Sam began, still trying to collect his wits enough to be coherent, only to be interrupted.

"Isn't there always?" Smolski sounded faintly bitter. "Every damn trouble man has ever gotten himself into in this world seems like it begins and ends with a woman." He sighed. "So how is it that you're in St. Louis because of a woman?"

By that time, Sam was sitting up, and felt slightly more capable of intelligent thought. He filled Smolski in on the state of the investigation.

"I hear you've commandeered about half the St. Louis field office's available agents," Smolski said when Sam had finished. "They called up, griping about how they're shorthanded to begin with. Hell, I hear you've got agents mobilized in three damned states working on this. I've had calls from Virginia to Texas. You want to explain this to me?"

"I'm pretty sure that Walter—the next victim—is going to be hit in Texas. It fits the geographical pattern. The chances that we're going to find out who he or she is before our guy does his thing is remote, I grant you, but I feel like we've got to try. And there are people doing some background work where the previous victims were hit."

"And you feel like your best move right now is sticking to that woman in St. Louis," Smolski said. Something in his voice made Sam think he might disagree.

"Yeah, I do."

That was nonnegotiable, he realized, even as he said it. Sam was surprised to find just how nonnegotiable it was. If Smolski flat-out *ordered* him elsewhere, he wouldn't go. There was no power on earth that was going to get him to leave Maddie before the sick bastard was taken out.

"Your case, your call. They've all got other cases of their own under way. I just ask you to keep that in mind," Smolski said, and Sam guessed that the complaining from certain quarters—Lewis in New Orleans came to mind—was getting fairly loud. Smolski's tone changed. "The woman you're with—would she be that pretty little chickie I saw you hustle into a car when I watched that TV news fiasco?"

"That would be her."

"Tough job we're paying you to do," Smolski observed dryly, and after a few more remarks hung up.

Sam yawned as he set the phone back down on the bedside table, glanced at the clock—it was not quite two p.m.—and got up. Sleep, though necessary for optimum functioning, felt like a waste of urgently needed time, and he had things to do. The fact that the sick bastard hadn't called him for going on three days now was weighing heavily on his mind. This was a change—and as far as this case went, he had the feeling that change was not good. Crossing to the window, he pulled the curtains open and immediately shut his eyes as the dazzling afternoon sunlight blinded him. Opening his eyes again cautiously, he found himself looking down at the parking lot two stories below. It was only about a quarter full—this was the kind of hotel that people checked into at dark then left early in the morning—and he could see the Blazer parked on the opposite side of the lot from where he had left it. From that, he deduced that Wynne had been out and about and was now back again. Even as he had the thought, Wynne himself came into view. Sam watched in slack-jawed disbelief as his partner, clad in a sweat-stained white T-shirt and flimsy blue bike shorts, trotted slowly across the parking lot to the sidewalk, where the overhang hid him from view. It took a few seconds for his mind to accept the truth of what he had seen: Wynne was jogging. *Will wonders never cease?* Sam thought, and grinned. Then, feeling a lot more wide awake than he had five minutes before, he headed for the bathroom to grab a shower.

DESPITE THE PARTY, the morning could not be said to have been an unqualified success. First, Maddie snuck off to the bathroom no fewer than three times to try to reach her pal Bob, but all she got was an automated answering machine announcing that A-One Plastics was unable to answer the phone. Not wanting to leave a number in case her call was returned at an inopportune time—such as any time she wasn't in the bathroom—Maddie was left in limbo to stew. Second, she saw no alternative to introducing Cynthia and explaining to her increasingly wide-eyed staff why an FBI agent was shadowing her every move. They had already heard that her car windows had been shot out—both Louise and Jon had left messages on her answering machine Saturday, which she had returned the next day—but when Maddie confessed that she had been shot, too, and mentioned that the FBI thought that the New Orleans mugger might actually be a hit man who was now trying to kill her, the resulting babble of horrified exclamations and questions had been so loud that she'd clapped her hands to her ears to drown out the cacophony. By the time she'd answered all their questions, listened to their loudly expressed horror, and shown off both her wound and the bulletproof vest, her whole staff had been jumping at unexpected noises. Then Judy and Herb had to hurry off to appointments with clients, Ana had to rush off to class, and she and Jon had to put the final touches on the presentation they'd put together for Happy's Ice Cream Parlors, which was scheduled for one-thirty in the conference room. And, not incidentally, everybody who was left had to pitch in to clean up the mess from the party.

The promised four-star lunch turned out to be takeout deli sandwiches fetched by Louise and augmented by the rest of the cake, which they gobbled down in the workroom. Not that Maddie was particularly sorry. Between the bulletproof vest that she had to wear if she stepped outside the door and Cynthia's ubiquitous presence, lunch out was clearly going to be more of a production than she felt prepared to handle.

Word that Creative Partners had landed the Brehmer account had spread through the small advertising community with jungle-drum speed, and Louise reported happily that she was fielding calls left and right. After the Happy's people left, Maddie started putting together a tentative schedule for implementing Creative Partners' plans for Brehmer's. Her gut feeling, given Mrs. Brehmer's capriciousness, was that the sooner they got going on it, the better. Jon was in his office, and she went over to talk to him about the logistics of getting camera crews and actors and everything else they needed lined up ASAP. Leaving that in his capable hands, she made a quick bathroom trip—still no answer at A-One Plastics—and returned to her office. Unnerved by not being able to get in touch, she suspected that she would have had a total meltdown at her desk had it not been for Cynthia's almost equally disquieting presence—and the panacea of work. The things that she needed to be doing were seemingly endless, and she threw herself into them with something approaching relief. Then Louise started putting calls through, and she spent the next hour and a half on the phone, talking to clients and competitors and giving interviews to reporters for *Business-Monthly* and *Advertising Age*. When she finally stood up, Cynthia, who'd been parked in a chair in a corner leafing through magazines for the past hour, stood up, too, and stretched.

"Now I know why McCabe assigned me to the day shift," Cynthia said, her voice wry. "It's the one where nothing ever happens."

"You say that like that's a bad thing," said a familiar drawling voice from the doorway. Still standing behind her desk, Maddie glanced up in surprise to see McCabe walk into her office with Wynne behind him and Louise, looking a little flustered, behind them. The rush of pleasure she felt at seeing McCabe caught her by surprise, and the smile with which she greeted him was big and spontaneous.

"Guess it's okay for them to come in then," Louise said to no one in particular, apparently in response to Maddie's expression, and retreated. Maddie barely noticed. With the best will in the world for it not to be so, she was focused almost exclusively on McCabe.

"Hey," he said, meeting her gaze and smiling slowly back at her so that his eyes crinkled and his dimples showed. Her heart beat faster and she suffered an instant flashback to that mind-blowing kiss. Feeling her face—and other, more private places—start to heat, she forced the memory from her mind. It therefore took her a few seconds to realize that he was clean-shaven and clad in gray dress slacks, a white shirt, a navy patterned tie, and navy sport coat. Everything was slightly rumpled—Jon's crown as king of the dandies was definitely not in jeopardy—but McCabe actually looked like a bona fide FBI agent for once. With his black hair and swarthy skin and athlete's powerful build, he was always second-glance-worthy, but now that he was all gussied up, he looked so handsome that Maddie was momentarily bedazzled. Wynne, too, was Bureau-worthy in a jacket, tie, and khakis. Although his bedazzlement quotient did not quite equal McCabe's, the look was a big improvement on his usual.

"Whoa, aren't we looking spiffy?" Cynthia looked the pair of them up and down. "What—or rather who—is this for?"

McCabe shot her a quelling look.

"We had to go into the field office here to have a chat with Tom Finster, who's the acting agent-in-charge while Needleman's on vacation," McCabe said. "He was wanting to pull his guys off the case."

"So did you persuade him?" Cynthia asked.

"Finster ended up telling him to get the hell out of his office." Wynne's voice was dry. He was, Maddie noticed, once again chewing gum.

"Chalk up one more victory for those people skills of yours," Cynthia said, grinning at McCabe.

"Hey, I got him to let us keep Gomez and Hendricks, and to agree to provide backup on an as-needed basis, so it wasn't a dead loss," McCabe said. "We're just a little leaner and meaner than I consider optimal, is all." His gaze met Maddie's. "We got you covered, don't worry."

"I'm not worried," she said, truthfully as far as it went. About his ability to keep her safe, she wasn't worried at all. It was the rest of the sorry mess that was concerning her.

"They're out in the parking lot now, sweeping your car. We're here to escort you from the building whenever you're ready to go." He grinned at her. "So, are you ready to go?"

It was only then that Maddie glanced at the clock and realized, to her surprise, that it was five minutes until five. Although five o'clock was the company's official quitting time, Maddie—and the others, too, when necessary—often stayed until six or later.

Before Maddie could answer, Jon appeared in the doorway. An hour before, he'd been looking dapper. Now the jacket to his charcoal suit was missing, his shirt was unbuttoned at the collar, and his tie was askew. His gaze swept the room and it was clear from the flicker in his eyes that he registered the newcomers' presence. It was an indication of the magnitude of the stress he was apparently laboring under that he didn't acknowledge them at all. He spoke directly to Maddie.

"I just got off the phone with Susan Allen," he said. "Houston, we've got a problem."

SEVENTEEN

Maddie felt her stomach tighten as she stared at Jon. "What sort of problem?"

"She's on her way here." Jon walked toward her, making a helpless gesture with his hands, clearly agitated. "Susan. With the dog. I tried to tell her that we didn't have things quite set up yet, but she wouldn't listen. She said that Mrs. Brehmer wanted us to get started right away. Like tomorrow. If we can't, they're going to be taking their business elsewhere."

"You've got to be kidding me." Maddie's heart lurched, and she folded her arms over her chest. Shaking his head, Jon planted both hands on the opposite side of her desk and leaned toward her as they looked at each other in mutual consternation.

"I wish I was," Jon said. "Crap, Maddie, what are we going to do?"

"Oh my goodness," Louise said from the doorway, having apparently followed Jon down the hall and overheard. "I knew us landing a ten-million-dollar account was too good to be true. And I've already sent out the press releases. Oh my goodness."

Maddie looked at Louise, who was standing in the doorway, wringing her hands. Her plump body was clad in polyester pants—today's were pale blue—and a matching floral blouse. An open cardigan, pale blue like the pants, hung from her shoulders. Giant clip-on daisies hugged her ears. Her curls looked iron-gray rather than silver in the unforgiving fluorescent light, and her soft, round face sagged with dismay. Her gentle blue eyes were wide behind her spectacles, and, just like Jon's, they were fastened on *Maddie*. For a moment, Maddie felt like closing her eyes and throwing up her hands and yelling *I give up* at the top of her lungs. Capricious clients, on top of predatory hit men and prowling FBI agents and the balancing act she was having to do just to survive, were almost more than she could deal with at the moment. Then she remembered: She owned the company. If it was Creative Partners' problem, it was her problem. She had to deal with it.

Maddie Fitzgerald, this is your life.

She took a deep breath.

"So, Susan Allen is on her way to St. Louis with Zelda," Maddie said carefully, striving for calm in the face of crisis. *"Now?"*

Jon nodded. "She said they would be leaving for the airport right after she and I finished speaking."

"She surely won't be able to get a flight at such short notice." Maddie was thinking furiously, seeking any loophole to the looming disaster that she could find. "Especially with a dog."

"We're not talking commercial airlines here. You forget, we're playing in a whole new league with them. They're flying in in Mrs. Brehmer's private plane. Susan said they'd be landing in St. Louis about ten tonight. She wanted to know if we could have someone meet them at the airport. Of course I said yes." Jon straightened and tugged compulsively on his tie, which subsequently hung crooked on the left instead of on the right. "What else could I have said?"

"Nothing else. You did the right thing." Maddie moved around behind her chair and gripped its padded back hard. "We knew going in that this wasn't going to be totally smooth sailing. Mrs. Brehmer has a reputation for being difficult, and this is probably just the first manifestation of it. But we can handle it. We *will* handle it. You say Susan's bringing Zelda? Fine. Let's do the easiest thing first. We'll set up a shoot for some photos we can use for their new logo. Zelda in cute outfits, that kind of thing. You go try to line up a photographer, and I'll start contacting stylists." She rolled her eyes. "Do they even have dog stylists? Who the heck knows?"

"Maybe you want a groomer," Louise suggested. "Dogs have groomers. My JoJo goes to the groomer when his hair gets in a tangle."

Maddie remembered Mrs. Brehmer complaining about Zelda's groomer. And JoJo was Louise's elderly shih tzu, so Louise, as a dog owner, would presumably know about such things.

"Okay, groomer," she said. "And costumes. We need doggie costumes. Where do people get those, anyway?"

"If you want, I could start calling costume rental shops," Louise offered. "And I can get you the number of JoJo's groomer."

"Good thought," Maddie said. Pulling the chair out again, she sat down and reached for the phone. "Okay, people, we've got a plan. Let's get it done."

Louise nodded and bustled off.

"I'll meet them at the airport at ten." Jon, looking heartened, smoothed his tie until it hung almost straight again. "I'll call Susan back and let her know."

"Tell her that we can't wait to get started," Maddie instructed with her hand on the phone. "And I'll go with you to the airport."

Nodding, Jon started toward the door, stopped abruptly, and turned back to frown at her.

"Uh, Maddie—what about them?" He looked significantly at the three FBI agents, who had been listening to this exchange with varying degrees of bemusement on their faces.

Maddie looked at them, too. Wynne looked stoic. Cynthia made a face and waggled her fingers at them.

"They'll just have to come with us," she said, her eyes meeting McCabe's to see if this worked for him.

"Whither thou goest . . ." McCabe said with the smallest of smiles.

"Maybe we shouldn't tell Susan they're FBI agents," Jon suggested. "Knowing that they're following you around because they think some wacko wants to kill you is probably not going to give her a real good feeling about being associated with Creative Partners."

"Good point," Maddie said, and looked at McCabe again.

"You won't even see us," McCabe promised. "Unless you need us, that is."

"Great." Refusing to allow the chilling implications of that to even enter her mind, Maddie rolled her eyes. "Is this turning into a three-ring circus or what?"

"It's the Brehmer account," Jon, who was already on his way out the door again, reminded her over his shoulder. "Think ten million dollars a year in advertising."

"There's that," Maddie said, and sat down at her desk again. For an account that size, she could jump through a few hoops.

BY NINE-TWENTY, everything was in place. Limp with exhaustion, Maddie leaned back in her chair and let her hands dangle toward the floor. Cynthia and Wynne had gone, although Wynne was expected to return at any minute. McCabe was sitting in one of the two black-leather-and-chrome chairs in front of her desk. Having walked into her office just minutes before, Jon perched on the edge of her desk, outlining the arrangements he'd made. Louise, who'd followed Jon in, sat in the other leather-and-chrome chair, taking notes. As Jon continued, McCabe rose and crossed to the windows, which took up the whole of the north wall. Maddie's eyes followed him even as she listened to Jon. McCabe had shed his jacket several hours before. For a long time afterward, every time she'd looked at him all she'd been able to see was the very businesslike gun in the shoulder holster slung across the left side of his chest. Now, with his back turned to her, her gaze instinctively shifted lower: His gray slacks hugged a trim waist and an athlete's high, tight butt. Maddie admired both, then let her gaze slide up to watch as he lifted an arm to pull the chain at one side of the windows that closed the vertical blinds. The white dress shirt he was wearing tightened across his broad shoulders. *Sexy,* she thought, then, annoyed at herself, immediately sought a distraction. She glanced past him, out the window, as the blinds slid shut, and saw that it was darker outside than it should have been. Nine-twenty on an August evening in St. Louis was usually a gorgeous, golden time, with long shadows falling across the ground and the sun just beginning to sink beneath the horizon in a burst of oranges and purples. But heavy gray clouds had rolled in during the past few hours to cover the sky, so that now it looked almost like full night outside. It occurred to Maddie then that McCabe had pulled the blinds to keep anyone who might be in a position to do so—from an office inside the skyscraper across the street, say, or on the roof of the smaller building next door to the skyscraper—from seeing in, or worse. In the crush of setting things up for the morrow, she'd almost forgotten the reason McCabe was lounging in her office in the first place. But now, as he turned away from the window and her eyes met his, she remembered, and gave an involuntary little shiver. They were on the sixth floor, true, and the chances that a bullet would come crashing through the window seemed remote. But she didn't think she would ever get over the trauma of knowing that it was possible.

"So it's all set," Jon concluded. Maddie's gaze switched from McCabe back to him, and she nodded. Jon was looking a little less pumped up than when he had entered her office five minutes before, she noticed as she met his gaze, and there was a faint tightness around his mouth and eyes that was new. But his tie was once again firmly in place, his collar was buttoned, and he looked altogether more calm and collected than he had when the news had hit that Susan Allen and Zelda were on their way. In other words, he looked spiffy as usual, which, she concluded, was a sign that all was once again right in his world.

"You done good," she said, smiling at him. Glancing over at Louise, she included her in the smile. "*We* done good." She pushed back from the desk and stood up. "Now, let's go kick some difficult client butt."

Jon slid off the corner of her desk. "You want to ride with me to the airport?"

Maddie's eyes slipped to McCabe, who was still standing over by the windows but was facing her now. He shook his head slightly at her.

She looked back at Jon. "Uh—I think I'll go in my own car, thanks."

"Fine," Jon said, a little shortly. "I'll just go get my jacket."

Was it her imagination, or did his mouth look noticeably thinner as he left the room? Before Maddie had time to decide, Louise spoke up.

"Do you want me to come to the airport, too, Maddie?"

"No thanks, Louise. You can go on home. I appreciate you staying so late."

"Oh, I'm glad to. I'm just so pleased things are going so well for us." Louise beamed at her. "Whoever would have thought where we'd be right now, when you took over from Mr. Owens? It's just a dream come true for all of us." Her smile faltered, and she glanced a little uncertainly at McCabe, then looked back at Maddie again. "You sure you don't need me? I'd be glad to come along with you. I could even come over and spend the night if you want me to. Or you could spend the night at my house."

Her meaning was clear: in case Maddie was afraid. And Maddie was pretty sure that Louise was including McCabe in her mental list of things that Maddie might reasonably fear.

Maddie shook her head. "I'll be fine. Don't worry about me, my babysitter is actually very efficient. See you in the morning."

"Well, if you're sure."

With another doubtful glance at McCabe, who gave her a small ironic smile, Louise left the room.

"Do you have to look quite so menacing?" Maddie asked McCabe as she came around her desk to head for the door. "You're scaring Louise."

"Actually, I thought I was projecting hungry and tired more than menacing." He snagged his jacket from the back of the chair he'd been sitting in, shrugged it on, and said something into the two-way radio he extracted from his pocket as he followed her into the hall. She turned off the light to her office as she went. "If I'd known you were meaning to put in another half-day's work when I got here at five, I would have grabbed something to eat on the way in."

"I'm hungry, too," Maddie admitted, opening the door to the hall closet where everyone's coats were kept and extracting her jacket. "There's salad in the refrigerator at home."

It struck her that it felt good to say "at home" to him, and know that he would be sharing the apartment—and the contents of her refrigerator— with her. She had never realized it before, but maybe, just maybe, she'd been living alone too long. Maybe she'd been lonely.

If so, she reminded herself grimly, McCabe was certainly not the remedy of choice.

"Yippee." McCabe sounded less than enthused. "Forget salad. What I need is a steak."

"Sorry, fresh out."

Louise was walking through the suite, turning off lights, and now only Jon's office and the reception room were lit. Maddie started to put on her jacket.

"Hang on a minute." McCabe came up behind her and reached past her into the closet. "Aren't you forgetting something?"

He pulled out the bulletproof vest, dangling it in front of her. Maddie looked at it, looked at him, and sighed.

"This is a giant pain in my posterior, you know."

He smiled. "Better than a giant pain elsewhere."

"True." He took her jacket from her, and she slipped the vest on. When she had trouble getting the zipper engaged, he watched for a couple tries, made an impatient sound under his breath, brushed her hands aside, and said, "Here, let me."

He engaged the clasp with just a little difficulty, then zipped her up with brisk efficiency. Meanwhile, Maddie found herself studying the flicker of his eyelashes against his bronze cheeks as he looked down to watch his hands at work; the slight twist to his mouth as he struggled to get the clasp into position; and the five o'clock shadow that was back in all its glory, darkening the hard angles of his jaw. When he had the ends of the zipper together at last and glanced up to meet her gaze as he pulled it up, she realized that her heart was beating way faster than it should have been, and her breathing was just a little erratic. He must have seen something of what was going on with her in her eyes, because for a moment after the zipper was fastened, he kept hold of the tab and held her gaze without moving or saying anything at all. The memory of that sizzling kiss suddenly seemed to scorch the air between them.

I want him.

"Ready?" Jon asked, emerging from his office. He paused in the doorway, one hand reaching behind him to grope for his light switch, and frowned at them. His gaze flickered from Maddie's face to McCabe. From where Jon stood, of course, all he could see of the other man was his back. Only Maddie could see the heat in McCabe's eyes.

McCabe let go of the zipper tab and stepped back. For a moment longer, their eyes held. His had darkened, she thought. In the uncertain light, they looked almost black.

"All set," Maddie said. Refusing to feel flustered, or at least to show it if she did, she took her jacket from McCabe with an assumption of nonchalance and slipped it on. As she moved past McCabe toward where Jon, having switched off his light, now stood in the semidarkness, waiting for her, she buttoned it up over the vest. A little bit still showed at the top, but that couldn't be helped. She only hoped that Susan Allen would simply think she was into layering.

"Wynne's secured the elevator," McCabe said behind her. "Gomez and Hendricks are waiting down in the parking lot. They've just finished checking out your car. We're good to go."

"SO, WHAT'S up with you and that guy?" Jon asked Maddie as they waited side by side in the small terminal at the St. Louis airport that serviced private planes. The waiting area was relatively plush, all beige walls and blond wood and brown-leather chairs, with a slick stone floor underfoot. It operated under different security rules than the much larger commercial facility next door, and Maddie and Jon were standing in front of the wall of huge windows, black now except for the halogen glow that lit the wet tarmac outside that looked out over the area where the small planes taxied in. Maddie had already eyed those windows askance, but the chance that a shooter could somehow get out there in the runway area seemed pretty small, and anyway, McCabe didn't seem concerned, so Maddie had made up her mind not to be. The Brehmer's Pet Food plane was already on the ground, a brown-uniformed attendant had just informed them, and they had just risen to their feet and stepped forward in anticipation of greeting Susan Allen as soon as she walked off the plane. Maddie, having swallowed the last of her Diet Coke, was in the process of setting the can down as Jon spoke. Jon, who'd been chomping on peanut M&M's, twisted the small yellow bag closed at the top and stuck it in his jacket pocket.

"What guy?" Maddie asked, straightening to glance at Jon in surprise. Of course, she knew who he was talking about as soon as she said it. But he'd caught her off guard.

"The FBI guy. McClain, or whatever his name is."

"McCabe," Maddie corrected automatically, "and nothing's up."

Even as she spoke, she was having to make a conscious effort not to glance around at the man in question. McCabe and Wynne were both inside the terminal with them. McCabe was seated in a chair on the opposite side of the waiting area, his posture deceptively casual as he gave every appearance of reading the day's newspaper. Wynne was leaning against the wall near the exit, staring reflectively at the ceiling as he chewed his gum. With perhaps another dozen people spread out over the waiting area, they weren't particularly conspicuous. Unless you knew who and what they were, that is.

"Yeah, right. If you seriously expect anybody to believe that, you might want to quit looking at him like jumping his bones is the next item on your agenda."

Maddie stiffened. "I do not—I *do not* look at him like that."

"You do," Jon said, his tone slightly grim. "Look, since it doesn't look like it's going to be me anytime soon, who you sleep with is strictly your business. But that guy—not a good choice. You're letting the gun and the macho FBI agent stuff snow you. You're just going to end up getting hurt, and I'd hate to see that."

He was frowning as he met her gaze. It struck her that, besides being perhaps a little jealous of what he saw as her interest in another man, he was also, at some level, genuinely concerned for her well-being. As a friend.

She smiled at him, a warm and affectionate smile that made his frown deepen. "Just for the record, I'm not sleeping with him. But thanks for worrying about me. That's nice."

Jon looked impatient, and started to say something more, but just then the door they were standing in front of was opened by an attendant, and the sound of a frantically barking dog reached their ears. Immediately, both their heads swiveled toward the sound. Their eyes fixed on the open doorway.

"Zelda," Maddie said, and Jon nodded.

The high-pitched yips grew louder. Then Susan appeared in the doorway, looking tired and harassed and ready to call the whole thing off. She was staggering slightly under the weight of a large garment bag and a medium-size duffel bag, both of which she had slung over one shoulder, and a small plastic animal carrier, which she gripped in one hand. That carrier, Maddie saw at a glance, did indeed contain Zelda. A clearly very unhappy Zelda. A Zelda who was not at all shy about expressing her feelings.

Pinning a bright smile on her face, Maddie stepped forward to shake Susan's one free hand.

"So glad to see you," she said, only to have her greeting drowned out by Zelda's frenzied barking. Susan's answering smile looked more like a grimace, and she replied with something that Maddie couldn't quite hear. Jon stepped forward in turn, doing an excellent job of not wincing at the noise. As they shook hands, Maddie saw with a single comprehensive glance that

Susan's short brown hair was ruffled, her face was pale and tight, and her lipstick was both freshly applied and crooked, as though she had put it on fast, at the last possible minute before she stepped off the plane. Maddie saw, too, that there was a small rip near the button placket in her neat white blouse. Golden brown dog hairs clung to her navy skirt. An enormous run laddered the left leg of her nude hose.

In other words, Susan looked like she had recently been in an accident. Or a fight.

The profusion of brown hairs on her skirt told its own tale: Zelda.

Maddie's gaze shifted to the animal carrier. Zelda's monkey face and shiny black eyes were shoved against the grate at the front, and she was scratching desperately at the unyielding bottom. She was clearly—vocally—displeased, and having a fit to get out of her plastic jail. The carrier shook. The grate rattled.

Jon said something—Maddie thought it was on the order of *good dog*—and tried patting the top of the carrier. It was a mistake. Tiny white teeth snapped together viciously. Jon jerked his hand back. Thwarted, Zelda gave vent to her emotions in the only way that remained to her. She let loose with an ear-splitting howl. Susan gave the carrier a monitory shake. Zelda then seemed to find her inner wolf: She cranked up the volume, and the howl went from deafening to downright hair-raising.

Shades of *The Exorcist,* Maddie thought in horror, resisting the urge to clap her hands over her ears. A roll of her eyes told her that every face in the place was now turned toward them. A gate attendant was hurrying their way. *Forget that thing about necessity being the mother of invention,* she thought. In this case, desperation was. Having looked, listened, and cringed, Maddie had an epiphany: She remembered the cream-filled pastry. Jon was standing right beside her. Thrusting a hand into the pocket of his jacket, she pulled out the bag of M&M's, untwisted it, fished one out—a nice, big, yellow one—and thrust it through the crisscrossed black bars of the grate.

The howls cut off as abruptly as if the dog had a power source and someone had pulled the plug.

"Oh, thank God," Susan gasped as silence reigned, looking ready to collapse. Maddie's own ears were still ringing, so she could just imagine what Susan, who had presumably been enduring the onslaught for a lot longer, was going through. "But—she's on a special diet and she's never allowed to have sweets, and you shouldn't . . . shouldn't . . ."

The crunching sound that had replaced the howls ceased. The monkey face pressed against the grate again. Zelda gave several loud sniffs.

"Give her another one," Susan directed hastily. Maddie did.

Zelda crunched.

"Let's get out of here," Jon said in Maddie's ear. He was clearly getting no more enjoyment out of being the cynosure of all eyes than Maddie was. She gave a barely perceptible nod. The attendant, Maddie was glad to see, was retreating now that peace had been restored. Remembering their manners, a few people were even starting to look away.

Susan had booked a suite at the Hyatt downtown for herself and Zelda. The thing to do was get them into it at all speed.

"So nice of you to come and meet us," Susan said, still breathing hard and giving every indication of being more than glad to relinquish the carrier to Jon as he reached in to take it from her. "I'm sorry not to have given you more notice, but Mrs. B. was very insistent on getting started at once."

"Not a problem." Jon smiled at her, exuding charm as always, and passed the plastic carrier on to Maddie, who accepted it with some trepidation. The thing was surprisingly heavy, and the contents—she would sooner have been responsible for a werewolf. Jon, meanwhile, took the garment bag and the other bag from Susan. In the spirit of warding off trouble, Maddie, hearing a warning *sniff*, poked another M&M through the grate.

Crunch.

"I'm just so embarrassed," Susan said as they all started moving toward the exit. "I can't believe that Zelda made such a fuss. It's all because the airport people insisted that she had to be in a carrier before they would let her inside the terminal. Of course, she hates being in a carrier and she fought me when I tried to put her in it, and when I finally got her in there she just had a *fit* . . ."

"Totally understandable," Jon said.

"We're just so excited that Zelda's going to be the new face of Brehmer's Pet Food," Maddie put in, not entirely insincerely, as she did her best not to list under the weight of the carrier. The plastic handle dug into her hand. The carrier shook slightly as Zelda moved around inside it.

Then Maddie heard that telltale snuffling sound again, and took preventive action: One more peanut M&M was launched through the holes. Realizing then that keeping Zelda happy was going to be an ongoing activity, sort of like keeping a parking meter in the black, Maddie hastily dumped the rest of the M&M's into her pocket. Then, when she heard that warning sniff again, it was easy to fish one out and thrust it at Zelda.

"We're excited, too," Susan replied. If she sounded somewhat less sincere than Maddie, well, Maddie couldn't blame her. From the look of her, Susan had already endured much at the hands—or, rather, paws—of advertising's newest prospective star.

Wynne exited the terminal first. Maddie saw him go. Gomez and Hendricks were in the van, she knew, parked where they could keep an eye on her as she left the building, as well as watch her car while she was inside. McCabe came out last. As she glanced back instinctively to see if he was following—he was—she saw that every head in the terminal had turned to watch them go.

The arrangement was that Jon would drive Susan and Zelda to the hotel, while Maddie, hampered by the trailing FBI agents and the hit man they were hoping would take another crack at killing her, was going to go straight home from the airport.

"Do you want to wait here while I go get the car, or—?" Jon asked Susan as they paused under the overhang. The fluorescent lights set into the concrete ceiling were yellowy and dim. Beyond the overhang the parking lot—this particular terminal had its own—was dark, except for the pools of uncertain light thrown down by tall halogens. The rain had picked up and was now coming down at a steady rate. Little puffs of vapor rose from the pavement. The rain didn't cool things off, as one might have expected. It just made the night muggier. A damp smell hung in the air. Cars drove past, pulling into and out of the parking lot, their tires swishing, their lights glancing off the terminal as they followed the curve of the drive. One paused not far from where they stood, and a man in a lightweight raincoat got out, slammed the door, and hurried inside. The car moved on.

"Go get the car," Maddie said, with an eye to taking care of their guest, although she suddenly felt very exposed. The back side of the airport was protected. This side was not. Anyone could use the parking lot, or be positioned on one of the roads leading to the terminal or somewhere nearby.

McCabe apparently thought so, too. He'd been idling back near the door, not letting on by look or word that he was connected to them in any way, but as Jon turned his collar up against the rain and walked away, McCabe moved—subtly, she had to give him that—until he stood between her and the parking lot. To all outward appearances, he was simply a man who was waiting for a ride.

Maddie did him one better. She took a couple steps to the side and hid behind a giant concrete pillar.

Take that, hit man, she thought.

McCabe glanced around at her and gave a twitch of his lips that was the equivalent of a thumbs-up when he saw where she was.

". . . expect to be here at least a week," Susan was saying when Maddie tuned back into her. She had followed Maddie sideways, apparently subconsciously, and was talking away a mile a minute. "Or even longer, if that's what it takes."

"Wonderful," Maddie said, though she had only the vaguest idea of what they were talking about. The carrier handle was killing her fingers. Maddie set the carrier down on the pavement, sighed with relief, and lobbed another M&M into Zelda. Zelda crunched and snuffled.

Maddie fed the beast.

"You know, that idea you and Jon had of using Zelda as the face of Brehmer's was simply brilliant," Susan said. "Mrs. B. is just thrilled with it."

"I'm so glad." Maddie watched a car coming toward them from the parking lot—was it Jon's? Yes, she thought it was—and dug in her pocket for another M&M.

Unfortunately, she didn't find one. Her fingers probed frantically into every corner of her pocket. Empty. All gone.

"I'm out of M&M's," she said, breaking in on whatever Susan had been saying, her voice tight with horror.

"Oh, no."

They looked at each other in mutual consternation. The huffing sounds coming from the carrier grew ominously loud. In desperation, Maddie crouched and looked in at Zelda. Her furry little face was pressed against the grate; her black eyes gleamed.

"All out," Maddie enunciated the words slowly, as if she were speaking to a hard-of-hearing foreigner with a limited grasp of English, and held out her empty hands, palms up, so that Zelda would get the idea.

Zelda got it, all right. She howled.

"No! No! No!" Susan set up a howl of her own, clapping her hands over her ears and stamping her feet in their sensible blue pumps and basically throwing a tantrum worthy of a two-year-old. Maddie shot upright, so surprised that she was gaping, at a loss as to how to deal with a grown woman— a *client*—who was totally losing it.

"Susan, please . . ." she began, fighting the urge to cover her own ears. A car door slammed. Maddie looked toward the sound to discover that Jon was back at last and striding toward them. Beyond him, McCabe was grinning as he watched bedlam unfold. Beside Maddie, Zelda howled. And Susan, Maddie saw to her horror, now clenched her fists, stomped her feet— and wept.

"I can't take it, I can't, I can't, that dog is a monster . . ." Susan's face was shining with tears. Looking past her, Maddie saw a security guard, who had materialized seemingly from out of nowhere, striding toward them. "She's an *ungrateful, undeserving mutt!*"

Zelda, insulted, kicked it up a notch.

"What the . . . ?" Jon gave Maddie an accusing look and put an arm around Susan. "Susan . . ."

"I hate that dog," Susan wailed, and buried her face in Jon's shoulder.

"What you need is a break," Maddie said desperately, almost shouting to be heard over Zelda's inner wolf. Jon was looking pretty desperate himself while doing that clumsy patting thing men do to weeping women, to little apparent effect. "Listen, how about if I keep her tonight and let you get a good rest without having to worry about her?"

The effect was almost magical. Susan's head lifted from Jon's shoulder. She looked around at Maddie, and gave a shuddering gasp.

"Would you?"

Ten million dollars, Maddie reminded herself.

"I'd be glad to," Maddie lied, trying not to think about how her neighbors were going to react to having a mad dog in the house, to say nothing about how her own nerves would hold out. Then she had an instant vision of McCabe's probable reaction, and that almost—*almost*—made the whole thing worthwhile.

EIGHTEEN

Fifteen minutes later, Maddie pulled into the McDonald's on Clayton.

"Fine," she said to the yodeling dog in the shaking plastic carrier on the front passenger seat. "You want food? Let's get you food."

As she drove around to the drive-through window, her cell phone began to ring. Not that she heard it, exactly. Zelda made hearing anything almost impossible. But it was in her jacket pocket and she felt it vibrate.

Fishing it out just as she reached the plastic speaker where they take your order, she snapped "What?" into the phone as she rolled down the window and yelled "large fry" at the intercom. Not that she exactly heard anyone ask for her order over Zelda, but she assumed.

"What are you *doing*?" McCabe's voice said in her ear.

"Feeding this damned dog," Maddie replied, heard a snort of laughter, and snapped the phone closed. She drove on to the first window and paid for the food.

"Doggy's not very happy," the clerk observed as he handed back her change.

Duh, Maddie thought, but managed not to say it. Moving to the next window, she practically snatched the bag from the girl who handed it over. Fishing out a fry before she even thought about rolling up the window or driving on, she thrust it through the grate.

Zelda's histrionics stopped as abruptly as if Maggie had shut off a valve.

"Thank God," Maddie said devoutly, and drove on, rolling up her window as she went.

Her cell phone rang again.

"What?"

"Stop right there," McCabe said.

She was still in the parking lot just a few yards beyond the pickup window.

"What? Why?" As she automatically hit the brakes, she was looking fearfully all around. The parking lot was well lit and . . .

"We're getting a couple of Big Macs. Want anything?"

Jeez. For a minute there, she'd remembered to be scared.

"No." Maddie glanced in her rearview mirror. Sure enough, there was the Blazer, stopped at the intercom. Apparently, being so close to food that wasn't salad was more temptation than McCabe—and Wynne, who was driving—could stand. Zelda snuffled, and Maddie hastily poked another fry through the grate. The smell of fresh, hot grease wafted to her nostrils. "Okay. Fine. Get me a large fry. And a hamburger. And a chocolate shake. No, wait," she added with a glance at the carrier, "make that about four large fries."

"I like a girl who eats," McCabe said, laughing.

"The fries are for the *dog,*" Maddie growled, then disconnected, pulled into an empty parking space, and spent the next few minutes feeding french fries to Zelda and watching as first McCabe and Wynne in the Blazer and then Gomez and Hendricks in the van went through the drive-through line. It was still raining, not hard but a little, and the swish of the windshield wipers coupled with the sound of the droplets pattering down against the Camry's roof were practically music to her abused ears.

Her phone rang.

"What now?" she said into it, knowing it was McCabe.

"A kid who works here is bringing out your food. I didn't want you to have a heart attack when he tapped on your window."

Nice thought.

"Thank you," she said.

"You know, next time you decide to make a stop we haven't been told about, you might want to give somebody a heads-up before you do it. You lost Gomez back there."

The van had been in front of her as she'd driven past the McDonald's and had her eureka moment about the fries. The Blazer had been behind her.

"It was an emergency," Maddie explained.

"McDonald's is an emergency?"

"You're not up here riding with this *dog*," Maddie said, heard another snort of laughter, and snapped the phone shut.

Sure enough, in a couple minutes a kid in a McDonald's shirt tapped on her window, passed her two big bags of food, and disappeared back toward the restaurant.

"We're set now," she said to Zelda, and took off.

Five more minutes, and she was turning down her street. The blacktop gleamed slickly black and reflected the headlight beams like the surface of a wavery mirror. Inside the car, the faint smell of wet earth and perfumed dog mixed with the stronger scent of fast food. The radio, which she'd turned on as soon as she'd started the car in an effort—futile, as it had turned out—to drown out Zelda, played Britney Spears's latest hit. Zelda, appeased by a continuing infusion of fries, was actually proving to be decent company. Maddie ate too, slurping up her milkshake between bites of hamburger and the occasional fry—she wanted to be sure to save plenty for Zelda—and the two of them munched companionably. Maddie had an uncomfortable déjà-vu moment as she pulled into her parking lot, but, she reminded herself, her windshield was bulletproof now. If the hit man was on the job and tried taking another potshot at her, the bullet would, presumably, bounce off. Or something like that.

No worries, mate.

Just so as not to attract any lingering bad karma, Maddie nosed the Camry into a different spot. Beside her, Zelda gave a delicate little burp. Then a far less delicate sound emerged from the depths of the carrier.

Followed by the most noxious odor Maddie had ever smelled.

"Oh my God," she said, staring in horror at the carrier.

Zelda whined.

M&M's. French fries. Scarfed up with abandon by a dog who'd been on a strictly controlled diet.

Forget that howling fit. *This* was what Maddie called an emergency.

Trying not to gag at the smell, Maddie slammed the transmission into park, turned the car off, slewed around, and reached into the backseat. The halogen shed fuzzy pale light over the motley collection of cars in the lot as well as the tall bushes and scraggly grass at the edge of the pavement, and provided a modicum of illumination inside the car, just enough for her to see that the carrier was ominously still. Equally ominously, its occupant was silent, which, since she hadn't hit Zelda with a fry lately, struck Maddie as possibly being a *bad thing*. Maddie groped frantically around in the backseat. Somewhere back there, along with the duffel bag containing Zelda's belongings that Susan had handed over before escaping, was a leash.

Zelda whined again.

"Hang on," Maddie urged her, trying not to breathe. Her questing fingers touched duffel bag, briefcase, *leash* . . .

"Got it!"

Her phone rang as she turned back around. Cursing under her breath, she fumbled to open it.

"What?" she snapped.

"What are you doing *now*?"

"This dog's got to go."

To Maddie's horror, another one of those long, slow, wet raspberry noises came from the carrier. The smell rose and spread like a mushroom cloud. Talk about your WMDs. . . .

"You shouldn't've offered . . ." McCabe's voice was impatient.

"*Poop*. She's got to go *poop*."

Dropping the phone, Maddie thrust another french fry through the grate, then took advantage of Zelda's momentary distraction to unlatch it. The dog bounded out, but Maddie was too fast for her. Hooking a hand in her collar, praying that the animal was too full of food to feel like biting anything else, Maddie snapped Zelda's leash on her.

Gotcha.

She would have sunk back in relief, except for the smell.

Gagging, she thrust open the door, swung her feet to the shiny, wet pavement, and got out in the rain, sucking in the revivifying smell of wet honeysuckle and steamy asphalt, holding on to the leash with a death grip all the while. Behind her, Zelda got out, too, jumping to the pavement with surprising agility.

And let loose with another of those ominous sounds.

"Come on!"

Maddie slammed the door and half dragged her over to the grass. Zelda immediately hunched and did her thing.

"Thank God," Maddie said. Zelda gave a little grunt, which Maddie took for agreement.

"What the hell do you think you're doing?" The muted roar behind her made Maddie jump and whirl toward the source of the sound: McCabe, of course. She knew who it was in mid-levitation. Backlit by the halogen, he was a menacingly large shape that practically radiated aggravation as he came toward her in quick strides from the Blazer, which was now parked beside her car. Any sensible human being would have been startled half to death by his near bellow—and, apparently, it was enough to startle any sensible dog, too.

Because Zelda jumped at the sound right along with Maddie, and rocketed away into outer darkness.

Maddie stared blankly down at her empty hand. She was no longer holding the leash.

Oh my God. She'd lost Zelda.

"Zelda!" Maddie cried as the full enormity of the catastrophe hit her, then yelled, "Now look what you've done!" at McCabe, and took off in hot pursuit.

Unfortunately, it turned out that hot pursuit and high heels were pretty much mutually exclusive things. Maddie made that discovery as she rounded the end of the honeysuckle hedge, skidded in the wet grass, and nearly went down. Windmilling to regain her balance, she kept on going, kicking off her shoes as she went.

"Maddie! Come back here!"

McCabe was giving chase, too, but she didn't have time to wait for him. She had to get Zelda back. If she didn't, Creative Partners could kiss the Brehmer account good-bye. Panic made her short of breath. More thankful for the halogen light than she had ever dreamed she could be, she peered through the translucent veil of rain, doing a lightning scan of twenty feet of shiny, wet grass crisscrossed with swaying shadows. There! She caught just a glimpse of a golden brown backside disappearing beneath the four-board fence that bordered the house next door.

"Zelda! Here, Zelda!" she called frantically, running toward the spot.

That worked. Damned dog didn't even slow down.

Okay, for her going under the fence was not an option. Hitching up her skirt, Maddie swarmed over it, caught sight of Zelda scrambling around a kiddie pool in the next yard, her leash flapping behind her, and sprinted after her. The rain was hitting the surface of the pool, the sound a quick rat-a-tat that echoed the hurried beat of her heart. She was wet, and getting wetter by the moment. The grass was slick as ice beneath her pantyhose-clad feet. Tree roots and rocks and who knew what else bruised her poor, tender soles as she pounded after Zelda. The yards grew progressively darker as she got farther away from the streetlights. But she could still see, thanks in large measure to the light filtering through the curtained windows of the houses whose backyards she was invading.

"Maddie! *Stop.*"

Running, too, his feet making squelching noises on the soggy ground, McCabe was right behind her as she reached the next fence. Behind him, *way* behind him, she saw with a wild glance over her shoulder, Wynne was heaving himself over a fence. Even as Maddie put one abused foot on the lowest board, McCabe's arm shot forward. Grabbing the back of her jacket, he jerked her back. She fell against him, her back colliding with his chest with a solid thump, her feet slipping out from under her. She would have fallen smack on her butt if he hadn't hooked a hard arm around her waist just as she started to go down.

"Damn it to *hell*," he said, hauling her upright. "Are you *nuts?*"

Both arms were around her now. Except for the fact that they were practically crushing her ribs, she could hardly feel them through the bulletproof vest.

"Let go." She glanced wildly up and back at him as she regained her feet and shoved at those imprisoning arms with both hands. "I have to get Zelda."

"Don't be a . . ." he began furiously, looming over her with a "that's it, I've had it" air that Maddie didn't have to be clairvoyant to realize meant that he was on the verge of losing his temper.

An explosion of ferocious barks split the air, drowning out the rest of what he said. Deep barks. Bass barks. Profundo barks. Mingled with a stream of high-pitched, frantic yips.

"Baron," Maddie whispered weakly, sagging against McCabe as she named the rottweiler mix that was the scourge of the neighborhood cats. Then, in a voice strengthened by horror, she added, "Zelda!"

As the yips turned to yelps and the bass barks went insane, she fought like a tigress to be free.

"Stop it, dammit! You're going to hurt yourself!"

"Let me go! He'll kill her!"

"Shit," McCabe muttered, thrusting her away from him. Maddie found herself colliding with Wynne's huge bulk as McCabe added to Wynne, who'd just come puffing up to join them, "Hang on to her."

Wynne's arms obediently locked around her waist.

"Zelda!" Maddie cried, straining toward the fence.

To her surprise, she saw that McCabe was already vaulting it. He disappeared through the bushes as the sounds of Zelda being devoured reached cosmic proportions and more lights started coming on in the surrounding houses. Maddie could see a little of what was happening now, even through the rain and the screen of bushes that grew profusely on the other side of the fence, and what she saw horrified her. The huge, hulking shape that was Baron had Zelda cornered under something—a child's ATV?—and was barking insanely at her as he tried to get to her. Not that Maddie could see Zelda. What she could do was hear her. Zelda clearly recognized that she had gotten in way over her head. She was letting loose with her trademark howl.

"*Zelda!* Wynne, let me go! I've got to help her!"

Wynne's hold tightened. "No way."

As Maddie struggled to free herself, Baron, still barking, stuck his big head partly under the ATV's frame. Beholding doom, Zelda cranked up the volume. Maddie gasped, knowing that she was about to watch the thing flip. When it did, she was pretty sure Zelda would be sushi.

"Dog!" McCabe yelled over the din, and Maddie saw that he was skirting the edge of the backyard, keeping a wary distance between himself and the action even as he tried to attract Baron's attention. The backyard was dark, shadowy, silvered with rain. McCabe had something in his hand, something he was waving. "Dog! Look over here!"

"His name's Baron!" Maddie shouted.

"Baron! Here, Baron! Look over here!"

That did the trick. Baron quit barking, lifted his head, looked around, saw the man waving something at him and seemed to take a long, hard look. Then he whirled and charged.

"*Shit.*" Throwing whatever it was he was holding, McCabe bolted for the fence. Behind him, with a fearsome volley of barks, the behemoth hit full-throttle.

Maddie's jaw dropped. Her breathing suspended. Her eyes widened as she watched McCabe race toward them like the hounds of hell were on his heels.

Oh, wait, one of them was.

Movement at the rear of the action caught Maddie's attention as she goggled at McCabe's leg-pumping dash for the fence. Zelda, no fool, was taking advantage of the reprieve to dart away.

"Zelda!" she shrieked. "Here, Zelda, this way!"

Zelda seemed to hear, because she tore up the ground, heading in the opposite direction.

"Run!" Wynne yelled encouragement. Maddie realized, with some indignation, that he was shaking with laughter.

Then her indignation lessened as she figured out that, instead of focusing on Zelda, he was cheering on McCabe.

"D'you want me to shoot it? D'you want me to shoot it?" Gomez screamed, practically dancing with agitation beside them as he waved his gun. Until that moment, Maddie hadn't even noticed that he and Hendricks had joined them.

"No!" Maddie cried, horror-stricken at the idea of murdering a neighbor's pet.

"No shooting," McCabe roared. He was only about six feet from the fence and coming on like a freight train. Baron, open-jawed and roaring, was almost close enough to take a huge chomp out of his ass.

NINETEEN

J ump for it! It's gaining on you!" Wynne bellowed.

McCabe glanced behind him.

"*Shit.*" McCabe dived for the fence from about a yard out just as the snarling, slavering beast leaped for him.

And came up short at the end of a chain.

McCabe hurtled through the bushes and crashed to the ground. Baron yelped and crashed to the ground. On opposite sides of the fence.

The men around Maddie let out a collective *whoosh* of breath.

"That thing's a man-killer." Gomez sounded awed.

"Told you," Hendricks said.

Then, with Maddie in tow, they all kind of sidled over to look down at McCabe. Having landed on his stomach, he had now rolled onto his back, where he lay motionless and spread-eagled, eyes closed, chest heaving, with the rain pattering down on his face.

"Now *that*," Wynne said thoughtfully, "I would have paid good money to see."

"Fuck off," McCabe said without opening his eyes.

Having recovered quicker than McCabe, Baron was once again on his feet, straining at his chain and barking hysterically at them from the other side of the fence.

All of a sudden the back door to his house opened and a man stood in the opening, silhouetted against the light.

"Baron! Shut up!" the man yelled, in a tone that sounded like he meant business. The dog kept barking hysterically. The man slammed the door shut again, vanishing from sight.

"Way to control your dog," Wynne said wryly. His hand was locked around Maddie's wrist now. No way was she going anywhere, even if she had wanted to, which, she discovered, she no longer did. Still . . .

"Zelda," Maddie said in a forlorn voice.

McCabe's eyes opened. Lifting a hand to shield them from the rain, he seemed to look her way.

"That was just about the stupidest damned thing I ever saw," McCabe said to her with an unmistakable edge to his voice. Baron was still barking, but his enthusiasm was starting to wane and Maddie heard McCabe's words quite clearly.

Maddie knew what he meant, since that was more or less what she just had been thinking herself: Running into the dark like that after Zelda had been nothing short of dumb. In her panic over the dog's escape, though, she had all but forgotten that *there was somebody out there who wanted to kill her*. And A-One Plastics was still incommunicado. . . .

But thinking she'd probably done something dumb and having McCabe yell at her for doing something dumb were two entirely different things.

She channeled her best Robert De Niro, planted her one free hand on her hip, and glared down at him. "Are *you* talkin' to *me*?"

McCabe sat up. From the way he looked at her, Maddie got the impression that he was spoiling for a fight.

"You think?"

"So, kiddies, how 'bout we head on back to Maddie's apartment before somebody starts taking potshots at us?" Wynne said, making a hasty intervention before things could heat up.

"Good idea." It would have been a perfectly pleasant reply—if McCabe hadn't said it through his teeth.

"I need to look for Zelda," Maddie said mutinously as McCabe got to his feet.

"To hell with Zelda," he said, looming over her.

Maddie bristled.

"Easy for you to say. It's not *your* business that'll go down the tubes if I lose the damned dog."

"To hell with your business, too."

"Time-out." Wynne started to walk back in the direction from which they'd come, pulling Maddie along behind him. From that position, she glared back at McCabe.

"I need that dog."

"What you need is your head examined."

"Cool it, both of you," Wynne ordered. Then, to Maddie in a soothing tone, "After we get you safely back to your apartment, we'll find the dog. Promise."

McCabe was right behind her, close but not close enough so that Maddie could read his expression. She could, however, feel the vibes he was giving off. And the vibes told her that he was in a towering snit. If she'd been less mature, she would have stuck out her tongue at him. If there had been no one to see but McCabe, she would have stuck out her tongue at him. But Gomez and Hendricks were back there, too, so she reluctantly put the impulse on the back burner. Sick with worry over Zelda—all right, over the Brehmer account—as she might be, Maddie nevertheless realized that letting the men look for the dog was only good sense. As vital as recovering Zelda was, it wasn't worth getting herself killed over.

"Well, lookee there," Wynne said softly as they rounded the honeysuckle hedge. He nodded in the direction of the parked cars.

Maddie was bent over, scooping up her abandoned shoes—what with the rain and the mud, they were never going to be the same again—but something about the tone of his voice made her look up instantly. Her eyes widened, and she sucked in a breath of soggy, sweet-smelling air.

There was Zelda by the Camry, scarfing up french fries that must have spilled to the pavement when Maddie had exited the car so vigorously.

Zelda, Maddie almost cried, but, remembering how Zelda had responded to being called by name before, she swallowed the impulse, freezing in place instead so as not to startle her. The men behind Maddie nearly bumped into her before they, too, got with the program and stopped.

"Shit. Here we go again." Maddie could tell by the disgusted tone of McCabe's voice that he, too, was looking at Zelda. His next words were growled in her ear. "Leave it to us this time, okay? We'll get the damned dog for you." Then, slightly louder, he added, "Wynne, you take Maddie on inside."

"Will do."

Wynne's hand tightened around Maddie's wrist, but he needn't have bothered. Being at the edge of her parking lot had made her remember how she had been shot, and remembering how she had been shot made her glance nervously all around and want to run for the hills. If three big, bad FBI men couldn't capture one little dog, the country was in more trouble even than she was, was how Maddie figured it. So as Wynne started moving, she went with him without protest, contenting herself with watching over her shoulder as Gomez and Hendricks, after a hasty consultation with McCabe, crept around behind the Camry. There was no way to be certain, of course, but she guessed that once they were in position somebody would give a signal and the three of them would close in on Zelda, who was still stuffing her face.

Unfortunately, if she was putting money down on the outcome, she'd have to put it on Zelda.

On that happy thought, they reached the door and Wynne ushered her inside. The house was dimly lit and quiet, as it generally tended to be, given the nearly soundproof 1920s construction, plus the work schedules and dispositions of the tenants. The doors on either side of the grand oak stairway that led to the second and third floors were both closed. Maddie trudged upward, her feet in their now-shredded pantyhose slippery on the stairs, her ears keenly attuned to any sounds she might be able to hear from the parking lot. Still in his navy jacket and khakis but now looking a great deal the worse for wear, Wynne huffed behind her, one hand on the banister, leaving a trail of damp footprints in his wake. At the sound of footsteps above them, Maddie glanced up to see June Matthews coming along the second-floor hall toward the stairs. Carrying a folded umbrella and wearing a light-weight black raincoat and heels, she was clearly on her way somewhere. Her face changed as Maddie and then Wynne reached the second-floor landing and she got a good look at them.

"Hey, June," Maddie said.

"Is everything all right?" June asked in a wary tone, pausing with one hand on the newel post to watch as they headed on up toward the third floor.

Maddie glanced back at her, saw her knit brows, and realized in that split second how the situation must appear: herself wet, disheveled, and shoeless, sporting huge runs in her pantyhose and a scowl to boot, with a huge and equally wet and disheveled man right behind her, clearly following her upstairs to her apartment.

"Everything's fine, but thanks for asking," she said, summoning a would-be cheery smile. Wynne, who had looked around when June spoke, smiled too, showing large, even white teeth. Coupled with that cherub thing he had going on, the smile must have done the trick, because June relaxed and continued on her way. Then Maddie and Wynne reached Maggie's apartment, and he followed her inside.

The apartment was dark except for the dim glow of the outside halogen spilling in through the windows. Maddie started automatically for the curtains—closing them before she turned on the lights was what she had in mind—when a series of shrill beeps penetrated her consciousness, stopping her in her tracks just a couple steps into the room. Her eyes widened. Her immediate thought was *bomb*.

"What . . . what . . . ?" she sputtered, even as her eyes flew to Wynne and she realized that he didn't look the least bit perturbed. Either he was deaf, or there was something she was missing here.

"Security system. McCabe had it installed this afternoon. Because we're kind of shorthanded now, you know." He turned to a keypad by her front door that was a new addition to the wall decor and punched in numbers. As Maddie goggled, the beeps stopped. "Your code is the last four digits of your phone number, by the way. Or you can change it if you want."

"Did anybody *ask* me . . ." Maddie began hotly. Then her voice petered out as it occurred to her that under the circumstances a security system was probably an excellent thing to have. She finished in a milder tone. "I'm glad I didn't come home alone."

And proceeded across the room to close the curtains.

"I don't think you're supposed to be alone right now. I think that's the point." Wynne flipped the switch that turned on the lights. "You know, you really shouldn't've took off like that out there. It could have been dangerous."

"Don't you start, too." Having closed the curtains, Maddie turned to scowl at him, realized that he was dripping all over her hardwood floor, and crossed to the bathroom, from which she extracted a towel. "Here." She threw it to him.

"Thanks." He started toweling off. Maddie watched critically. He was such a big man. She tossed him another towel.

"When you disappeared into the dark like that, I gotta tell you, you scared us," Wynne looked up from vigorously rubbing his head to fix her with reproving blue eyes. Wet and woolly now, his hair puffed out like golden dandelion fluff around his head. "McCabe about went ape-shit. He was out the door before I even got the car stopped. He's probably still going to be a little ticked off when he gets up here."

Wynne sounded like he was warning her.

"Good for him," Maddie said, unimpressed. She'd shed her jacket and the bulletproof vest by this time, and was standing just inside the bathroom door and rubbing her hair with a towel, too. The area that had been covered by the vest was relatively dry. The rest of her was pretty much soaked through. It showed just how wet she was that the air-conditioning, for just about the only time in her experience of it, actually felt cold. She could feel the chill as it blew over her skin.

"Especially considering how he got chased by the dog and all," Wynne added in a reminiscent tone. Their eyes met. Wynne grinned.

A vibrating sound made Wynne lose the grin. Reaching under his jacket, he unclipped something from his belt. Maddie saw that it was a two-way radio.

"Yeah," Wynne said into it.

"Damn dog took off again," Maddie could hear McCabe's growling voice clearly. "Looks like we're going to be out here a little while longer."

"Okay." The calm professionalism of his voice in no way reflected Wynne's new and wider grin.

The Brehmer account hung in the balance, and Maddie knew it. But she couldn't help it. She grinned, too.

Chalk one up for Zelda.

"They'll get her," Wynne assured her, clipping the radio back on his belt again, then shedding his jacket, which he carefully draped over the back of the floral chair. Beneath it, he was almost dry.

Maddie could only hope he was right. But since there was nothing she could do about it, she decided to move on to the next thing.

"I'm going to take a shower," she said, and Wynne nodded.

Some twenty minutes later, she had just finished blowing her hair dry when she heard a muffled knock on the front door.

McCabe, Maddie thought, and took a last critical look at herself in the mirror. Stupidly, she'd already applied the merest hint of rosy pink lipgloss and a touch of powder and mascara, because she wasn't planning on going to bed until she knew Zelda was safe, and waiting for Zelda involved seeing McCabe. Which brought her to the stupid part. The makeup had been on account of McCabe.

She wanted to look good for him.

Acknowledging that made her frown, and she was frowning still as she shrugged into her robe and pulled open the bathroom door.

McCabe was standing in a pool of warm lamplight just inside the living room, talking to Wynne. He'd lost his tie and shoulder holster but gained Zelda's duffel bag, which he had slung over one shoulder. Disheveled, with his black hair mussed and his jaw dark with stubble, he once again looked more like a thug than an FBI agent. He was unsmiling, soaking wet, and smeared liberally with mud, and despite all that, he was still so hunky-looking that Maddie's heart gave a little skip. His once-white shirt was plastered to his broad shoulders and brawny arms, and was just transparent enough so that she could see both his sculpted pecs and the wedge of hair that darkened his chest. His gray slacks clung to his narrow hips and the powerful muscles of his thighs, and closely molded what Maddie already knew was a very impressive package.

Remembering how it had felt against her, she felt a quick instinctive tightening in her loins.

Quit looking at him like jumping his bones is the next item on your agenda. . . . She could almost hear Jon saying it.

Realizing that that was exactly what she was doing, Maddie felt a quick flush of both embarrassment and a whole other kind of heat, and hastily shifted her gaze to focus on the squirming navy blue bundle tucked securely under his arm. It took Maddie a moment to realize that the navy blue part of the bundle was McCabe's jacket, and the squirmy part was Zelda. Clearly taking no chances, he'd wrapped the dog in it so that not so much as a furry paw was visible.

Maddie felt a flood of relief.

"Zelda," she said on a thankful note, and went to claim the bundle. As she approached, McCabe's eyes slid over her and his mouth tightened, but he let the duffel slide to the floor. Then he crouched to pull his jacket off Zelda and set her on her feet.

The little dog promptly shook herself, sending muddy droplets flying everywhere. Maddie winced a little as she observed the resultant mess. Floor, wall, McCabe's legs—all were the unlucky recipients of Zelda's largesse. McCabe's expression turned sardonic as he looked down at his legs, which were already so wet and muddy that a few more drops surely couldn't matter. Meanwhile, Zelda took a few tottering steps forward, then sank down on her haunches. Panting, ears alert, she scanned her surroundings. Maddie's eyes widened as she looked at her.

Like McCabe, Zelda was soaked; her coat was muddy and bedraggled; her tail left wet marks on the floor with every twitch. And her topknot had wilted so that it hung limply in front of her left eye, its tiny lavender bow wildly askew.

"Now that's what I call a bad hair day," Wynne observed.

Maddie's lips twitched.

"Oh, dear," Maddie said, and, moving rather warily, picked up the end of the once-elegant lavender leash, which was filthy and limp now. Once she had the end in her hand, she felt more secure. "Come on, let's get you cleaned up."

Zelda looked up at her just as warily, her black eyes gleaming, but made no attempt to run—or worse. Probably, Maddie thought, given all the excitement, she was exhausted.

Which, considering Zelda's propensities, was a good thing.

"You could have been killed," Maddie scolded as she led her toward the kitchen with its linoleum floor and supply of paper towels. A snort pulled her attention from the dog. Her eyes collided with McCabe's.

"Seems like you're not the only one around here with a death wish, doesn't it?" he said, his drawl more pronounced than she had ever heard it.

Her brows twitched together.

"You know what, you probably want to go and take a shower," Wynne said to McCabe in a way-too-hearty tone. "How about I hang around with Maddie while you do that?"

"Yeah." McCabe gave her a long, hard look before glancing at Wynne. "Get Gomez or Hendricks to bring my bag up from the Blazer, would you? I've got some clothes in it."

"Will do."

As McCabe headed off toward the bathroom, Wynne followed Maddie into the kitchen, bringing the duffel bag with him. The curtains were closed and the light was on when she entered, so she surmised Wynne had visited the kitchen while she was in the shower. The smallest of smiles touched her mouth: If he'd been raiding her refrigerator, he'd probably been disappointed; the cold cuts and cheese and potato salad he'd bought the other day were all gone, largely thanks to him. Basically, all he would have found to eat was the salad McCabe had turned his nose up at earlier.

"You need groceries," Wynne said, confirming her surmise. He set the duffel bag on the counter and started rooting around in it.

"There's salad," Maddie replied with a straight face. Wynne made an unenthusiastic sound. Glancing around at him—he still was checking out the contents of the duffle—Maddie grinned. "Is there a bowl in there, by the way? Zelda's probably thirsty."

"Yeah." He produced a bowl and passed it to Maddie. It was silver and heavy, and had Zelda's name engraved on it. Her eyes widened slightly as she turned it over, checked the mark, and realized that she was holding a sterling-silver dog dish.

"This is sterling," she said to Wynne.

He grimaced. "Dog lives better than I do."

"Me, too." She filled it with water and set it down in front of Zelda, who lifted her head. "Water, your highness."

Zelda looked at her, looked at the bowl, then stood up and took a few dainty laps. Maddie took advantage of her distraction to start patting her down rather gingerly with paper towels. Finishing with the water long before Maddie had finished with her, the dog sat and panted but offered no resistance when Maddie gave up on trying to fix the bow on her topknot and instead tugged it from her hair. The look that resulted was kind of an early Beatles mop-top, more sheepdog than Pekingese.

"Cute," Maddie told her. Zelda looked unconvinced.

"Want this?" Wynne reached into the duffel bag and came up with a wire-bristled brush, which he proffered to Maddie. Maddie looked at Zelda, looked at the brush, and shook her head.

"No point in pressing my luck. Anyway, she's going to a groomer first thing in the morning."

Wynne grinned. "Good thought."

"Isn't it?" Having done all she could do to restore Zelda to her former glory and survived to tell the tale, Maddie washed her hands in the sink. From the relative lack of water pressure, she deduced that McCabe was still in the shower.

Knowing how the water supply to her apartment worked, she had to smile. He'd either just been blasted with ice water or scalded.

Zelda was lying flat on the linoleum and Wynne was leaning against the table when she turned around. Zelda, who still gave off a faint wet-dog smell, was doing her fur-rug thing again, only with breathing this time. Wynne chewed gum, gave off noxious grape fumes, and regarded her thoughtfully.

"You know, it's getting late," he said. "You might want to go on to bed now."

Maddie cocked her head at him. A glance at the clock told her that it was getting on toward midnight, but somehow she didn't think that concern over whether or not she got enough sleep had prompted his suggestion.

"Are you trying to keep me from getting yelled at when McCabe gets out of the shower? That's really sweet of you, but I'm not all that thin-skinned."

Wynne's smile was rueful. "The thing is, like I thought, he still seems to be a little ticked off at you. Hey, you scared him. He'll be over it by morning, though. Why not take the easy way out and just stay out of his way until then?"

Maddie's answering smile was noncommittal. The truth was, the thought of quarreling with McCabe had a lot of appeal. "Actually, that's probably a good idea."

Which it was, she realized as she thought about it, but not because of the getting-yelled-at part. Because of the heat. She could feel it blistering the air between herself and McCabe whenever they looked at each other now.

The truth was, she wanted him. And he wanted her, too. She could see it in his eyes, feel it in his touch, read it in his responses to her. His current bad mood was a case in point. He was mad at her because the idea of her getting hurt had scared him.

They were getting emotionally involved.

The thought rocked her back on her heels. There it was, the thing she hadn't wanted to face. She was falling hard for an FBI agent, and he, unless she was very much mistaken, was falling hard for her right back.

Which was stupid. No, worse than stupid: It was dangerous.

Under the circumstances, then, the smart thing to do was exactly what Wynne had suggested: run away to bed while McCabe was in the shower, and stay put until morning. Then keep out of his way as much as she could until this whole thing was over.

However it ended, whether she fell off the tightrope or managed to keep balancing until the end, getting involved with McCabe was the last thing she needed to do.

Maddie made up her mind.

"You're a good guy, Wynne," she said with a wry smile.

"Yeah." He was looking at her steadily. "The thing is, I just don't want to see you get hurt."

Maddie was taken aback. The meaning of that was hard to mistake. Was it so obvious what was happening? She took refuge in denial. "I don't know what you mean."

"Yeah, you do. You and McCabe—anybody can see where that's headed. Don't get me wrong, he's a super guy. In fact, he's my best friend in the world. Wherever we are, whatever we do, he's got my back, and I've got his. But you—you're a real nice girl, and you don't seem like the quickie-love-affair type."

"And that's what this would be." The way Maddie said it, it wasn't a question. It was a statement, because she already knew the answer.

"As soon as we get our guy, we're out of here. You know that." Wynne looked almost apologetic.

"Yeah. But thanks for reminding me." Maddie blew out a little puff of air, then gave him a rueful smile. "By the way, while we're exchanging advice, you should put some moves on Cynthia. She's interested, you know."

Wynne stopped chewing his gum. His eyes widened. A deep puce flush started to crawl up his face.

"Cynthia?" he asked cagily, as if he'd never heard of her before.

Maddie folded her arms, leaned back against the counter, and gave him a don't-give-me-that look. "Come off it, Wynne. You're every bit as transparent as I am, believe me."

A beat passed. Wynne fiddled with the cord on the duffel bag, then looked up.

"So what makes you think she's interested?"

"She told me."

He looked stunned. "Really?"

"Would I make something like that up? Yes, really. And now I think I'll take *your* really good advice and go to bed." Wynne was still looking lost in thought when she bent down to pick up the leash. "Come on, Zelda."

Without lifting her head from the floor, Zelda gave her an assessing look.

"Zelda." Maddie tugged encouragingly at the leash. Zelda sighed and stood up. Wynne seemed to surface again just as they were on their way out of the kitchen.

"Night, Maddie."

"Night, Wynne. And thanks."

"Yeah. You, too."

Maddie could feel Wynne watching her as, with a surprisingly docile Zelda trailing behind her, she headed off toward her bedroom. Fortunately or unfortunately, depending on how you looked at it, McCabe was still nowhere in sight. She closed her bedroom door all but a few inches, got Zelda settled on a folded blanket, climbed into bed, and turned off the light.

Zelda jumped up on the bed.

"Hey," Maddie said.

Zelda turned around a few times at the foot and plopped down with a sigh.

Maddie considered. Zelda wasn't howling, she wasn't biting, and she wasn't lost. As far as Zelda was concerned, this was probably about as good as it was going to get. This was, in fact, a battle she didn't really want to fight. There were far worse things than letting a doggy diva sleep at the foot of her bed.

"Night, Zelda," Maddie said.

A rattling little snore was her only reply.

Maddie lay on her back with her head propped up on a pair of pillows and her arms crossed over her chest, listening to Zelda blissout and thinking about sleeping. With the bedroom door ajar, the room wasn't particularly dark and, in addition, she could hear everything going on in the apartment. She listened to McCabe emerge from the bathroom, to him and Wynne talking, and, finally, to Wynne leaving. This was followed by a series of tiny beeps that had Maddie frowning for a moment until she figured out that it must be McCabe setting the new alarm.

Good to know that one day, when her resident FBI agent went bye-bye, she wouldn't be left entirely unprotected. There was more hair spray in the bathroom, too.

The light in the living room went out. The TV came on, flipping from channel to channel. In a matter of minutes she was treated to the sounds of about four dozen different programs, maybe more. It didn't require genius to deduce that McCabe was once again parked on her couch with her remote in one hand. To her disgust, the very thought made her heart beat faster.

Every iota of common sense she possessed told her to close her eyes, block out the sounds, and try to sleep. Every scrap of self-preservation that remained told her to at least stay put and stare at the flickering shadows on the ceiling if sleep just wasn't in the cards. The very last thing in the world she needed to do under the circumstances was get out of bed and walk into the living room and pick a fight with McCabe.

Unless she wanted to end up in bed with him, that is.

She lay there a moment longer, then abruptly sat up and swung her legs out of bed, carefully so as not to disturb Zelda. McCabe was a temporary fixture in her life, here today and gone tomorrow. Nobody anybody with any sense would allow herself to get attached to. Wynne had warned her. Not that he needed to; she knew it perfectly well herself. At best, a quickie love affair was all that was in the cards. But then, life was uncertain at best. Her life was more uncertain than most. The hard truth was, it could come crashing down around her ears at any moment. The only thing she had for sure was tonight.

And tonight she wanted McCabe.

So call her stupid.

TWENTY

Tuesday, August 19

Except for the flickering TV, the living room was dark when Maddie walked through the bedroom door. That was no surprise, of course. She'd known that all the lights in the apartment were out, and that she would find McCabe sprawled on the couch, watching something mind-deadening like ESPN. Except, he wasn't there. The couch was empty. The TV had no audience. A sweeping glance around confirmed it: McCabe was nowhere to be seen.

Maddie frowned. Every bit of good sense she possessed combined forces with the last flicker of her self-preservation instinct to urge her to thank her lucky stars for the reprieve and head straight back to bed.

But she didn't do it. Instead, she zeroed in on the faintest of whitish glows that seemed to be coming from the kitchen, and headed that way.

I'M A SICK MAN, Sam concluded glumly as he studied the meager contents of Maddie's refrigerator. He was turning himself on. Or, at least, the strawberry smell he couldn't seem to lose was turning him on. He breathed in, and he pictured Maddie. The mental images were so vivid that they had driven him from the couch to the kitchen in search of distraction. Unfortunately, the distractions in her refrigerator were minimal: Besides milk and orange juice, the only marginally edible thing was a Saran Wrap–covered bowl of salad.

Yech.

Grimacing, he picked up the half-gallon of milk, tried to check the expiration date, couldn't read it with only the dim light from the refrigerator for illumination, and opened the carton to sniff at the contents suspiciously.

And he got a big whiff of strawberry-scented shampoo for his pains.

Damn it to hell and back anyway. If he'd known, when he'd used her shampoo in the shower, that he was going to be tortured like this for the rest of the night, he would have stayed dirty. He'd figured it out about halfway through scrubbing his head, when he'd inhaled the scent of strawberries and thought, for a sudden, heart-stopping second that Maddie had stepped into the shower with him. His eyes had popped open—damned shampoo had burned the hell out of them, too—and he'd immediately figured the whole thing out: He was alone, and the smell was the shampoo.

So far, his damned stupid dick hadn't caught on.

He'd taken the longest shower he just about ever had in his life, trying to rinse off the smell, to no avail. It still clung to him like skunk scent, driving him out of his mind with its erotic associations every time he inhaled. With each breath, he had brief, tantalizing visions of Maddie's big, honey-colored eyes looking all dazed with desire as he'd lifted his head up from kissing her, her mouth all soft and sweet and seductive as her lips parted for him, her body—*God, that body*—all hot and willing.

Willing. That was the thing that made it so torturous. She was his for the taking, and he knew it. She wanted him. She would welcome him. All he had to do was walk into her bedroom and . . .

No. Hell, no. He wasn't going there. He'd already made a decision about that. He wasn't going to do it. She was his job, damn it, not his girlfriend. He was there for one purpose: to catch a killer.

Bedding his bait was not in the program.

Okay, so maybe she was more than bait. Maybe she was more than just a body to be bedded, too. Maybe she'd gotten to him, just as he'd feared she was going to. Maybe her feistiness, and her courage, and the sweetness with which she'd rocketed to Wynne's defense, and the surprising way she'd won Gardner over, and the intelligence and passion and plain old hard work she brought to running her business had clicked with something inside him. Maybe . . .

Hell, maybe he was breathing in too damned much strawberry shampoo.

With that thought, Sam decided to throw caution to the wind. Tilting the carton to his mouth, he took a big gulp of milk.

"Are you drinking out of the carton?" an outraged voice demanded out of the darkness.

Sam jumped and almost spit the milk back out again.

Lowering the carton, he looked around, choking a little as he swallowed. Maddie stood in the doorway. She was wearing her big white bathrobe over what he was pretty sure would be a slinky little nightgown, and her fists were planted on her hips in a way that told him he was in the doghouse big-time. The robe ended at her knees, and below it, her killer legs and feet were bare. Her hair waved in a loose, dark cloud around her face. Her skin was pale and smooth. Her mouth, even pursed disapprovingly as it currently was, made him hot just looking at it. And her eyes were big and luminous—and fixed accusingly on him.

Except for the accusing part, he thought, taking her in with one sweeping glance, she looked like the embodiment of every erotic dream he'd ever had.

And trouble. Standing there in the doorway, glaring at him, she definitely looked like trouble. Trouble with a capital T.

"It was the last little bit," he defended himself in a mild tone, closing the refrigerator door and setting the empty carton down on the counter, knowing even as he turned back to face her that he was playing with fire here. If he wasn't way careful, he was going to end up getting burned.

———

"DIDN'T ANYONE EVER tell you that drinking milk out of the carton is not only disgusting, it's unsanitary?" Maddie shook a monitory finger at him. He'd jumped guiltily when she'd caught him with the milk, which had actually been kind of cute, she thought. He was facing her now, leaning back against the counter with his hands propped on either side of his hips. With the refrigerator closed and the window behind him, she couldn't make out his expression at all. He was a tall, broad-shouldered shape in the dark, and if she hadn't known him, she would have described him as formidable-looking. But since she did, the description that came to mind was *sexy as hell*.

Her heart gave a little lurch.

"Like I said, it was the last little bit." If he was still mad at her, she couldn't tell it from his tone. "Why are you up?"

"Maybe because listening to you flip channels lacks something as a sleep aid."

She crossed the kitchen toward him and thought he tensed, although it was hard to tell in the gloom. But her ostensible target was the milk carton, which she removed from the counter and tossed in the trash can near the back door. That brought her to within three feet of him. Close, but not— quite—close—enough.

"So, the TV bothers you?" he asked, folding his arms over his chest. "Fine. I'll turn it off."

Maddie frowned, leaned a hip against the table, and considered him. This was not going the way she had hoped. He was being way too accommodating. Too cool. What she wanted to do here was spark some heat.

"And do what?" Her tone was deliberately provocative. "Sit there in the dark and twiddle your thumbs?"

"I've done it before."

Her eyes narrowed. "All part of the job, huh?"

"Yep."

"Just like I'm part of the job?"

He hesitated a second, as if mentally testing that. "Yeah."

This wasn't working. He was getting cooler by the second; she was the one who was starting to get ticked off.

"So why did you get so mad at me for chasing off after Zelda?"

"Because that was one damned dumb thing to do."

Yes. She couldn't see his expression, but she could hear the hardening of his voice.

"I could have been killed," she said, with a deliberate touch of mockery.

"Yeah, you could've been." His tone was positively flinty. " 'Course, if you're bound and determined to give that guy out there another chance to get in some target practice, there's only so much I can do."

A beat passed.

Her voice went soft. "So what's it to you?"

McCabe didn't reply right away. Their eyes met, but the enveloping shadows made it impossible to read anything in his expression. Silence stretched out between them, vibrating with a tension that was almost tangible.

"Darlin', believe me, I'm not in favor of anybody being killed," he said finally. Cool again. And casual. Too cool and casual.

To hell with it. Subtlety had never been her strong suit anyway. Tightening the belt on her robe with the air of a fighter getting ready to step into the ring, Maddie took the three steps necessary to put her directly in front of him. He still leaned against the counter, but he stiffened a little and almost seemed to brace himself. This close, she could see the black, restless gleam of his eyes, the high, hard cheekbones, the long, mobile mouth, the lean stubbled jaw. He looked big, dark, and dangerous.

Her heart turned over.

"McCabe . . ."

"Hmm?" He sounded slightly wary.

"Did it ever occur to you that maybe we're developing a relationship here?"

"A relationship?" There was no slightly about the wary this time. His eyes narrowed. His jaw hardened. His fingers tightened around the edge of the counter. He was suddenly as still as if he'd been carved out of stone.

Not that he had to say anything. Electricity leaped between them, so strong it practically ignited the air.

"Yeah," she said. "A relationship. As in, I'm crazy about you, you're crazy about me. . . ."

His eyes flared at her. Holding his gaze, she reached out and ran a semi-teasing finger down the center of his chest. As she had thought, he was wearing a T-shirt. It felt old and soft, and the muscular contours beneath felt masculine and hard.

She'd wanted heat. Now she was feeling it in spades.

He sucked in air through his teeth. His hand came up to catch hers. She felt that big, warm hand wrapping around her slender one clear down to her toes. He kept her hand trapped, a willing prisoner flattened against his chest, and her pulse rate skyrocketed.

"Maddie . . ."

"Hmm?" His eyes were suddenly as black and shiny as jet.

"For all kinds of reasons, a relationship between us right now would be a really bad idea."

With her hand pressed to his chest, she could feel the rhythm of his heart. It was beating hard and fast—way too hard and fast for a man who was basically telling her to take a hike. He wanted her. There was no mistaking that.

"Too late," she said softly, almost whimsically, and took a step nearer. She was so close now that the hem of her robe brushed his jeans.

"What do you mean, too late?" His voice was low and a little rough around the edges. She could feel the pounding of his heart beneath her hand.

"I told you: I'm crazy about you. I'm sorry if it's a problem for you, but it's too late to do anything about it."

She smiled up into his eyes, and he straightened away from the counter fast, releasing her hand in favor of catching her by the elbows and holding her as if he couldn't decide whether to pull her close or push her away. Her hands flattened against his chest, fingers pressing into the warm, resilient muscles there, and his grip on her elbows tightened. She was tingling all over, tingling in places she didn't know she had, and filled with a spreading warmth that had its center somewhere deep inside her body. Whatever came of this, she was going into it with no regrets. Once again, she was proving herself to be her father's daughter: She was taking a gamble, going for it, making a play for what she wanted.

And what she wanted—so badly that her heart was pounding and her blood was racing and her throat was dry—was him.

"Maddie . . ." There was strain in his voice, and a sense of deliberately exercised control. "This isn't something we need to be doing right now."

She could feel the tension emanating from him, and the heat. She could feel the slamming of his heart beneath her hands.

"Are you saying you're not crazy about me?"

A beat passed.

"No," he said at last. "I'm not saying that."

And for that piece of honesty, she went up on her tiptoes and kissed him.

For just a second his lips were warm and soft beneath hers, but as she deepened the kiss they hardened and parted.

"McCabe," she whispered, licking into his mouth.

He made an inarticulate sound, and his hands released her elbows to slide around her waist. Suddenly he was kissing her, pulling her close and slanting his mouth across hers as she wrapped her arms around his neck and kissed him back. His lips were warm and dry, and the inside of his mouth was hot and wet and tasted, very faintly, of milk. His tongue slid against hers, claimed her mouth, and her stomach clenched and her knees went weak. His arms around her were taut with muscle, and his body was taut with muscle, too, and taller than hers and broader than hers and harder than hers. Excitingly harder than hers. She could feel the unmistakable evidence of his desire pressing against her abdomen even through her robe, and sucked in her breath.

He deepened the kiss, leaning back against the counter again, pulling her against him. Her heart pounded and her legs trembled and her stomach tied itself in knots. She could feel the urgency in him, feel the tension in the arms around her, in the rigidity of his shoulders and back and neck beneath her hands. Letting him take her weight, she pressed herself against him, sliding her tongue deep into his mouth, sliding her fingers through the short, crisp strands of hair at the back of his head.

She was melting for him. Hungry for him. Her body was on fire. . . .

His mouth left hers to feather kisses along the line of her jaw.

"You're beautiful," he whispered against her skin. "Gorgeous. Sexy. Edible."

He nibbled at her earlobe.

Maddie's breath caught. Her knees gave. If his arms hadn't been around her, she would have dissolved into a little puddle of desire at his feet.

"And you're crazy about me." She was surprised she could talk at all.

He raised his head to look down at her. The diamond-hard glint in his eyes was enough to make her racing heart skip a beat.

"Yeah," he said. "There's that."

"Thought so," Maddie breathed, and he smiled and she got all gooey inside over his dimples, and while she was still distracted he kissed her again, with a hungry urgency that made her dizzier than she already was. She clung to him, kissing him back as if she'd die if she didn't, while her head spun and desire coiled tightly inside her body and delicious little shivers of anticipation raced over her skin.

"McCabe," she whispered, trembling a little at the hot, wet slide of his mouth along the exquisitely sensitive chord at the side of her neck.

He lifted his head and looked at her. The gleam in his eyes was almost tender. "Don't you think it's about time you started calling me Sam?" His voice was low and husky, but with a touch of humor mixed in there, too.

Maddie gave a shaky little laugh.

"Sam," she said obediently. Then, *"Sam,"* because his hands were parting the edges of her robe and sliding beneath it, pushing it from her shoulders so that it crumpled to the linoleum with the faintest whisper of sound. Big, warm, long-fingered hands that were moving over the satiny pistachio slip that she'd chosen to sleep in just because it was the sexiest nightgown she owned, and she wanted to be sexy for him. Strong and capable hands that stroked over her breasts and teased her nipples and molded her waist and slid down over her butt to pull her tight against him. Expert masculine hands that slid under the edge of her slip . . .

"Sam," she moaned as his hands closed on her bare cheeks. Her slip had ridden up around her navel now so that there was no longer any barrier at all between her body and the hard, urgent mound beneath the cool abrasion of his jeans. Rocking her against him, he kissed her mouth, her neck, her ear, while her heart pounded and her breathing came short and fast and her body quaked and burned and throbbed.

"This is such a bad idea," he said in a thick voice, pulling her closer yet and sliding a thigh between her legs and moving it against her in a way that felt so incredibly good that all she could do was gasp and shiver and wrap her arms around his neck and hang on for the ride.

"I don't care," she replied, barely able to think, let alone speak. His thigh between her legs was a revelation, a pleasure-giving machine of awesome proportions, and she pressed back against it instinctively. The resulting undulating waves of desire made her moan with dazzled surprise.

"Hell, me neither." His voice was hoarse and thick, scarcely louder than a growl.

His mouth found hers again, and she kissed him back with the kind of abandon that came from being totally, completely, toe-curlingly turned-on.

She wanted him. God, she wanted him. She wanted him naked and inside her and . . .

First things first.

Her hands measured the breadth of his shoulders, slipped down the front of his chest, found the edge of his T-shirt. Then they moved beneath it, flattening against his lean middle, loving the firmness of the muscles there, loving the satin-over-steel quality of his skin. She could feel him breathing, feel his chest heaving as if he'd been running for miles, feel the pounding of his heart as she slid her hands up over his rib cage. Her own heart was pounding, too, and her breathing came fast and erratic as she stroked the thicket of hair that covered the center of his chest, flattened her palms over the wide, firm curves of his pecs, then touched his flat male nipples.

He lifted his head at that and inhaled.

"You're killing me here," he said in a low, shaken voice. For a moment he simply breathed and looked at her, his eyes heavy-lidded and so hot that they made her dizzy, and then with a quick, sweeping movement he pulled his T-shirt over his head. She could see the heavily muscled contours of his wide shoulders silhouetted against the curtains. She could feel the damp heat of his skin all around her, beneath her hands and against her arms and burning through the thin nylon of her gown. She could smell something vaguely sweet—her brow wrinkled; was it strawberries?—and beneath it his own special brand of *eau de man*.

Her loins clenched. Her heart gave a great, shuddering leap. Leaning into him, she pressed her open mouth to the salt-tinged column of his neck and slid her hand over the tensile, hair-roughened six-pack of his belly. Encountering his waistband, she slipped her hand beneath it.

He was there, right there, burning hot, damp, and so huge and hard that he was all but bursting out of his jeans. She touched him, wrapped her hand around . . .

"Damn." He said it through clenched teeth. Lifting her head, she saw that his face was hard and fierce and his eyes blazed down at her. Wanting him so much that she was dizzy with it, she withdrew her hand and began to fumble with the button on his jeans. For a moment he stayed perfectly still. Then his hands tightened on the round curves of her cheeks and he lifted her up off her feet. Squeaking with surprise, she clutched at his shoulders as he took two steps with her and put her down. Barebottomed. On the cool, smooth oak surface of her kitchen table. And pulled her nightgown over her head.

Before Maddie had quite grasped that she was now sitting on her kitchen table *naked,* he was kissing her again and shucking his jeans and spreading her legs and moving between them. It was dark, but not so dark that she couldn't see that he was huge and hung and ready for action. Her heart pounded, her body burned and clenched, and she trembled with anticipation. She reached for him, but he caught her hands before she could make contact and guided them to his shoulders.

"Sam . . ."

"Sit tight."

Perched almost on the edge of the table, she clung, breathing hard as that huge, hot part of him just brushed her while he slid slow, thrilling hands up the insides of her thighs.

At the exquisite sensation, she gritted her teeth and curled her toes and almost forgot to breathe.

"Do me *now*," she said, shocked at herself, but wanting him so much that she didn't *care*, loving the way he felt between her thighs, so turned-on that she was woozy with it, so ready for him to come inside her that she could scream—but he didn't.

"Soon," he promised, his voice guttural now. He bent his head and put his hot, wet mouth on her breast, and slid one of those big, warm, long-fingered hands down between her legs.

"Sam," she whispered. Then, as his mouth tightened and pulled on her breast and his hand started working its magic, she said in a very different tone, *"Oh, Sam."*

He kissed her breasts and delved into the velvety delta between her thighs, finding that part of her that ached and yearned and burned for his touch, then leaned her back against the table and kissed her there, too, keeping at it until she was mindless, until she had no inhibitions left, until she was arching her back and reaching for him and begging. When she was almost there, when she shivered and quaked and dug her nails into the oak and thrashed and moaned, he stood up and gripped her hipbones and pushed into her, filling her to capacity, so big and hard and hot that she cried out and twined her legs around his waist and surged to meet him. Then he took her, hard and fast, plunging into her with a series of fierce, deep thrusts until she lost all sense of time and place, until she was crying out at the wonder of it, until finally she came with a shattering intensity that caused the night to explode against her closed eyelids in a burst of thousands of glittering stars.

"Maddie," he groaned then, thrusting himself deep inside her shaking body and holding himself there as, at last, he found his own release.

———

THE SEX had been great. Mind-blowing. Earth-shattering. The aftermath was—awkward.

When a woman had just been thoroughly done on top of her very own kitchen table, there was just no romantic, dignified, or even moderately unembarrassing way to bridge the transition from hot sex to cold reality, Maddie decided.

However, continuing to lie naked in the center of said table like a turkey on a platter was probably the most humiliating of the available choices.

She sat up, and slid off.

Sam was watching her. He was a few feet away, he was naked, and even with the bloom off the rose, so to speak, he was looking hot.

Unfortunately, she was feeling cold. And embarrassed. And very, very grateful that the kitchen was dark.

A lesser woman would have wrapped her arms around herself and scuttled from the room at that point. A more poised one would have come up with something witty and charming to say to ease the situation.

But with his eyes on her and her mind still semiblown and the memory of really hot sex simmering in the air between them, the best she could manage was a weak, drawn-out, "So . . ."

"Want your robe?" he asked, holding it out to her. She hadn't realized he'd been holding it in one hand until then. He sounded like himself again, like McCabe rather than Sam, and the familiar, drawling cadence had the unexpected effect of making her tingle, just a little.

"Thanks." She took her robe, pulled it on, and immediately felt a little less vulnerable. Okay, no point in pussyfooting around. Might as well get the thing right out in the open and have done with it. With what she considered a very creditable assumption of ease, she tightened her belt and said, "Tell me we did not just do it on the kitchen table."

"Yeah," he said, folding his arms over his chest and leaning a hip against the counter and looking her over. His eyes gleamed at her. "We did."

So much for ease. Her heartbeat quickened under the silent perusal of those heavy-lidded black eyes. What was he thinking? Was he sorry? She couldn't tell. She couldn't see him well enough to read his expression at that distance—and it was impossible to divine anything from his tone. But he might well be sorry. If she was going to look the truth squarely in the eye, she had to admit it: *She* had seduced *him*.

I'm crazy about you. . . .

She could almost hear herself saying it. The thing was, he'd never actually said it back.

"Well—I think I'll just go take a quick shower." As far as graceful exit lines went, that left something to be desired, she knew. But under the circumstances, it was absolutely, positively the best she could do. What she needed was time alone to regroup. And a little personal grooming wouldn't go amiss, either, in case he should at some point decide to turn on a light. Her mouth felt swollen, and her hair was a bush. . . . When she'd recovered her equilibrium and was feeling more like herself, she could pursue this thing between them—maybe.

Or maybe not.

Maybe she'd just leave it at a single session of really mind-blowing sex.

"Sounds like a plan," he said, and started picking up his clothes.

Swallowing, feeling as ridiculously uncomfortable as a teenager on a first date, she headed out of the kitchen.

"Maddie." His voice stopped her just as she reached the doorway. She turned back to glance at him inquiringly. "Forgot something."

He tossed her nightgown to her. Even as she caught it, even as she felt the slide of the silky nylon through her fingers and breathed in the scent of sex that seemed to cling to it, she had an instant flashback to the moment when he'd pulled it over her head.

Just like that her loins clenched, her breasts tightened and swelled, and she felt a sudden, unmistakable upsurge of heat.

Her eyes met his, and her breath caught, and she knew: For her, this was already more than a quickie love affair.

Turning on her heel, clutching her nightgown in suddenly nerveless fingers, she headed for the bathroom and sanctuary. But even as she closed the door and turned on the taps, she could not escape the refrain that beat endlessly in her brain. It was one word, repeated over and over again: *Stupid.*

IT WAS the scent of strawberries that was to blame. Sam came to that conclusion as he walked into the bathroom five minutes later and inhaled it along with a lungful of steam. The security system was on, the bathroom door was unlocked, and his firm intention not to fuck his bait was blown all to hell. He was nuts, and he knew it, and that was the only explanation he could find: The faint, insidious smell that had been haunting him since he had first met Maddie had finally driven him totally insane.

That being the case, he was going to go with it.

She was still in the shower, and he was still naked. Seemed like destiny to him.

Pulling the curtain aside—she jumped and squeaked, and he had to grab her arm to steady her—he stepped into the tub and moved under the warm spray with her. Crowded, she backed up and looked up at him, wide-eyed, the shampoo bottle clutched in her hand. Her face was shiny wet and suds were in her hair and water sluiced over her drop-dead body and dripped from her delectable rosy-tipped breasts. His gaze touched on creamy shoulders and those perfect round breasts, then slid over the slender curve of her waist and the satiny flatness of her belly to the soft, sable triangle of curls between her truly gorgeous legs.

She was so damned beautiful that his stomach clenched. Along with several other notable body parts.

"What are you *doing*?" she demanded.

So far, he realized, he hadn't said a word, and she was looking at him like he was crazy. Not a surprise, since he clearly was.

"I forgot to tell you something." He took the shampoo bottle from her hand and reached around her to set it back in the white wire rack that hung from the shower nozzle. That brought him so close to her that he could feel the jiggle of her soft, warm breasts against his chest.

He looked down at the strawberry-tipped, creamy pale globes nudging into his chest hair and felt himself getting the mother of all hard-ons.

"What?"

"I'm crazy as hell about you," he said, and wrapped his arms around her and pulled her against him and kissed her. Then he proceeded to do what he could to prove it.

LATER, MUCH LATER, they were in her bed. All three of them. Sam lay on his back with one arm curled beneath his head and Maddie draped across his chest. That damned nuisance of a dog sprawled at their feet. He and Maddie were naked, and she and the dog, whom he'd given up trying to kick off the bed, were asleep. One of them was snoring, delicate rattling gasps that were as rhythmic as the tick of the bedside clock. He was pretty sure it was the dog, but he was too tired to look and see.

The pretty little strawberry-scented thing on top of him had just about worn him out, Sam reflected, and he would have grinned if he could have mustered the energy. He wouldn't have believed such a thing was possible if he hadn't just experienced it.

She'd been surprising him since they'd met, and she had surprised him between the sheets, too.

Just as he had foreseen, he'd played with fire and had gotten burned. Or, rather, gone up in flames. Not that, with the wisdom of hindsight, he was thinking that was such a bad thing.

She'd made him hot. She'd made him crazy. He'd made her his.

Seemed like a pretty fair trade to him.

Sam was just thinking that, except for a few minor problems like a killer on the loose, all was nearer to being right in his world than it had been for a long time, when his cell phone started to ring.

It was on the bedside table, along with his gun. Tensing, he reached for it. Maddie lifted her head. The dog looked up.

"Sam?" Maddie said on a questioning note, even as he picked the thing up and it continued to ring.

"It's my phone." He fumbled with the bedside lamp. Turning it on, he looked at the ID window.

Error, it said.

"Shit." He was suddenly as juiced as if he'd just taken a hit of speed.

"What?" she asked, scooting off to lie beside him, her eyes wide on his face.

"Don't make a sound," he warned her, and, sitting up, flipped open his phone. "McCabe."

"Hey, asshole," the familiar voice said. "Miss me?"

"Like a bad case of the clap." It hit him that he was talking to the sick bastard who had tried—was trying—to kill Maddie, and he felt a murderous spurt of rage. She was staring at him, propped up on her elbows beside him, flushed with sex and naked, and he felt a fierce, hard rush of protectiveness and possession. "Where you been?"

I'm gonna take you down, he promised the guy silently. He listened hard, heard something in the background. He couldn't quite make out what it was. The computers would automatically pick up the call, he knew. Later they could get the background sounds enhanced. . . .

"Busy. I've been busy." The son of a bitch sounded almost affable. The sounds in the background—Sam still couldn't quite place them. But he was getting a bad feeling about this. Something was wrong. "You quit playing the game, McCabe."

"What are you talking about?"

Time. He had to play for time. One of these days, the sick bastard was going to talk too long and they'd have him. Just one second too long, and it would be all over. The computers would be busy now, trying to locate him. Gardner would have heard the call come in. She would be up and listening. . . .

"Our game. The game we've been playing. You quit on me. So I've decided to up the ante."

"We're not playing any game." Sam hoped the alarm he was beginning to feel wasn't audible in his voice. *Cool. Stay cool.*

"Say hello to Carol Walter, asshole."

The sounds in the background were getting louder, like they were coming closer to the phone, or the phone was coming closer to them. It sounded like—*sobs.* Someone sobbing.

Someone who was now weeping into the phone. He could hear gasping sounds, sniffles. . . .

"Help. Please help me. Please. Please." A woman's voice, terrified, shaking, the words interspersed with sobs.

Jesus. Sam's gut clenched. He knew. He already knew. . . .

"I'm going to kill her now. And you're going to listen."

"No!" Sam yelled, catapulting out of bed, but he was helpless, he couldn't stop it, he could only stand there beside the bed and listen as the woman wept and begged, at a slight distance from the phone now, "Please don't, please don . . ."

Bang.

The first shot echoed through the phone, through his head, through his soul.

"No!" Sam yelled again, and then, his voice shaking, "You sick fuck, we're going to get you. We're going to . . ."

Bang.

The second shot rang out, stopping Sam in full spiel. Insurance, of course. The woman was already dead. He knew it, but he still felt that shot like a body blow. His heart slammed against his rib cage. Sweat streamed out of his pores.

"Now you're playing again." The bastard was back on the line, sounding delighted. "That's good. I'm in Dallas, by the way. 4214 Holmsby Court. And once again, you're too late."

Keep him talking. The computers—and Gardner—were hearing this, too, and the cops would be on the way.

"I didn't know we were playing a game," Sam said, trying to clamp down on every emotion except the need to catch a killer. It required the effort of a lifetime to sound cool, sound dispassionate.

"Now you do. And now that I'm having so much fun, I'm going to up the ante even more. Next time, I might even let you watch."

"Next time . . ." Sam began. He was interrupted.

"Here's your first clue. Where in the world is—Kerry?"

Sam thought he could hear, very distantly, the sound of sirens coming over the phone. *Keep him talking.*

"I don't . . ."

Definitely sirens. The cavalry was on the way. Just keep him talking. . . .

"Better hurry, asshole."

There was a click, and suddenly Sam found himself talking to air.

"Shit," Sam said, feeling as if he was bleeding inside. "Shit, shit, *shit*."

He looked up and saw that Maddie was staring at him. She was sitting up now in the middle of the bed, her eyes wide as saucers, her mouth open, her skin paper-white. The covers were clamped under her armpits, and the dog was huddled against her legs. She'd heard everything, it was clear. Probably she'd been traumatized for life.

But he couldn't worry about that now.

"Sam . . ." she said in a thin, high voice. "Who . . . ?"

"Wait." He was already punching numbers into the phone. "One minute."

Gardner answered, sounding wide-awake despite the fact—he glanced at the clock—that it was 3:28 a.m. Probably she'd been goosed by adrenaline, too.

"Did you get that?" he asked.

"Yeah," she said, rock-steady as always. "The cops should be pulling into the driveway of 4214 Holmsby Court any minute now."

Too late, Sam thought. *Too fucking late.* Snapping the phone shut, he nearly crushed it in his fist.

Then he looked at Maddie and thought, *That could have been you.* At the image that thought conjured up, he felt as if all the air had suddenly been sucked out of the room. It required real physical effort on his part to force himself to breathe.

TWENTY-ONE

I'm in mourning, Maddie thought.

That was the only way to describe how she felt as she basically sleep-walked through the following day. Listening to that poor woman being murdered last night had been a horror almost past bearing. She'd been up the rest of the night, unable to sleep, unable to get the sounds and the terrible images they had conjured up out of her mind. It was almost as if she'd been there and seen what had happened—and she knew why. She *had* been there, once upon a time. She had seen what had happened. Seven years ago . . .

Then it had occurred to her with a rush of icy fear that she had almost shared Carol Walter's fate in that hotel room in New Orleans. *That* was the death her attacker had planned for her.

Still had planned for her.

At that realization, Maddie had broken into a cold sweat.

Seeing her fear, Sam had pulled her into his arms and buried his face in her hair and sworn to her that whatever happened, he would keep her safe.

And then he'd kissed her, a deep, fierce kiss, before putting her away from him and getting to work.

Curled in a corner of the couch, she'd watched him pacing restlessly through her small apartment, tracking the progress of the investigation over the phone. She'd been forcibly reminded that he was an FBI agent, and it hadn't mattered. He was, simply, Sam to her now. He had assumed a veneer of hard professionalism. She had seen through it, though. Seen his guilt. Seen his pain.

Just like he had seen her fear.

It had been then, as they waited for Wynne, who had immediately rushed over to babysit her while Sam headed for their hotel to take long-distance charge of the frenzied hunt for the killer, that Sam had told her the whole thing, in quick bits and pieces interspersed between phone calls. Maddie had listened, appalled, to the story of how he had chased the killer across the country, of the phoned-in clues and the rising body count and the constant race to save yet another life. And by the time he had finished, she had realized something: She was going to have to tell Sam the truth.

She didn't know who the killer was, but she knew where to start looking. With seven people already dead and another life on the line, the price of keeping her secret had suddenly grown too high.

She'd almost told him last night. The words had trembled on the tip of her tongue as they had waited for Wynne. But then she'd looked at Sam, and the truth had stuck in her throat. She was crazy about him—no, face it, she was crazy in love with him—and what she was going to tell him would blow this shiny, new, wonderful thing between them sky-high.

Imagining how Sam would look at her once he knew made her feel like she was shriveling up and dying inside.

And there was Creative Partners, too. And Jon and Louise and Judy and Herb and Ana. The Brehmer account. Her apartment. Her *life*.

If she told the truth, it was gone, all of it. The clock would strike midnight. Her fancy coach would turn back into a pumpkin. Her glittering gown would revert to rags. As for her handsome prince—well, he would stay a handsome prince.

She was the one who would be turning into a frog.

"WHAT THE HELL are you still doing in St. Louis?" Smolski bellowed over the phone. "You're supposed to be in charge of this investigation, so get your ass down to Dallas and take charge of it."

"I'm staying put," Sam said. It was shortly after three p.m. He and Gardner were in the hotel room that served as their base of operations. The curtains were open, and they had a prime view of brilliant blue sky, busy interstate, and the nearly empty parking lot two floors below. The air conditioner hummed, working hard. The files he'd been reviewing when the phone rang—the most recent of the cases he'd been working on—were spread out across the bed. Gardner was seated at the desk, working at her laptop. A printer attached to another laptop across the room was spewing out pages of composite photos based on witness descriptions of suspicious persons observed in the vicinity of last night's crime scene. Unfortunately, the witness descriptions were all over the map, and so far none of the resulting photos matched composites from the previous crime scenes, making it unlikely that anyone who'd been interviewed so far had seen the actual killer.

"What do you mean, you're staying put? You got any dead bodies in St. Louis? Hell, no. The dead body's in Dallas. What you got in St. Louis is a piece of ass."

"He's going to come for her. I mean to be here when he does."

Smolski grunted and said, "You don't know that."

"I'm as sure of it as it's possible to be."

"What about this new target, huh? Whosit—what'd you say the name was?"

"Kerry."

"What about Kerry, huh?"

"We're working on it here, and we've got people out doing legwork in every likely city, trying to come up with an ID. Just like we got people doing legwork in Dallas on last night's homicide."

"But you think the best thing you and your team can do is stick with that hot little St. Louis gal." There was no mistaking the sarcasm in Smolski's tone.

Sam kept his voice steady. "Yeah, that's what I think."

"What if I ordered you to get your ass down to Dallas?"

Sam grimaced. Knowing Smolski as he did, he had been expecting this. "Then I'd have to decline. Respectfully."

Smolski grunted. "Respectfully, my ass." A beat passed. "Like I said before, your case, your call. But McCabe—"

"Yeah?"

"If we don't get the UNSUB pretty shortly, it's your ass."

With that, he hung up.

"Shit," Sam said, and turned back to see what Gardner was doing. Her fingers had stopped moving over the keyboard. She was staring at her computer screen, seemingly transfixed.

"Something up?" he asked, his attention caught, and moved over to stand behind her. Looking at the images glowing up at him from her screen, he realized she'd just come up with a fingerprint match.

"You are not going to believe this," she said in a strangled voice. And she pointed at a way too familiar picture on the screen.

"COME ON, ZELDA," Maddie said dispiritedly, trying to hurry Zelda across the parking lot and inside the Brehmer's Pet Food factory. The QuikStop where she had gotten gas was just visible to her left through the tall chain-link fence. To her right, the interstate overpass blocked her view of the corner where she'd seen the hooker at work. The drone of traffic rushing past on the expressway provided background noise to the nearer sound of cars cruising through the lot, looking for a place to park. The white gate at the entrance gave a dull thud each time it was raised or lowered to allow a vehicle to pass through. It was getting on toward five, and she was supposed to meet Susan and Jon, who'd been checking out various interior locations in the plant as possible spots for the soon-to-be-filmed commercials featuring Zelda, in the manager's office at five, at which time she would hand over the poky pooch to her rightful guardian. Thank goodness. Not that Zelda wasn't being reasonably well behaved, because she was. At the groomers, at the photo shoot, at lunch, at the office—everywhere they'd been that day, Zelda had been as little trouble as anyone could expect an animal she'd had to take everywhere with her and pamper like a doggy diva-to-be. Of course, some of Zelda's good behavior could be thanks to the supply of snacks Maddie had armed herself with. Right now, the pocket of her aqua linen jacket was half-full of goldfish crackers, which she'd been dispensing judiciously throughout the car ride from her office to the plant. Unfortunately, since Zelda had already consumed a large quantity of pretzels, bagel bits, and french fries (Maddie had decided against giving her any more candy after Louise had told her that chocolate was bad for dogs), she'd had some gastric issues over the course of the afternoon.

All in all, though, Maddie considered noxious gas and near-hourly dumps a small price to pay for relative peace.

And as far as she was concerned, the problem would soon be resolved, because it would soon be Susan's.

Meanwhile, the air smelled of car exhaust and melting asphalt, the heat was tropical and intense, and the sun blazed in the endless blue sky, although just at that moment the shadow of the building in front of her sheltered her from the worst of its rays. The parking lot was filled to overflowing with cars, as another shift arrived to replace the workers who would soon be going home. As soon as she handed Zelda over to Susan, she would be heading home, too. According to Wynne, who was trailing at a more or less discreet distance behind her, Sam would meet them at her apartment to take over for him.

The prospect made Maddie nauseous.

The moment of truth was speeding toward her on winged feet.

The sad thing was, for one brief shining moment last night, she'd taken a look around her bedroom and realized that she finally had everything she'd ever wanted: an unbelievably sexy man, a cute little dog, and a successful, respectable life.

Too bad none of it was hers to keep.

"You can't stop and sniff everything," Maddie told Zelda with exasperation, tugging on the leash as the little dog, trailing behind, stopped in her tracks yet again, then took a detour beneath the bumper of a small red pickup. She emerged moments later, looking pleased with herself as she chomped on what looked like the remains of a burrito.

"Zelda, no!"

But it was too late. The burrito was gone. Zelda licked her lips, looked at Maddie with shining black eyes, and wagged her tail. Then she gave an unmistakable belch.

"Oh, Zelda."

"Dog must be part goat," Wynne said, coming up behind her.

She glanced around at him. He was wearing a bright blue Hawaiian shirt, khaki shorts, and a baseball cap in what she assumed was an effort to look like something other than the FBI agent he was. He succeeded in that, but he did not succeed in being inconspicuous. In St. Louis, giant blond cherubs were pretty thin on the ground.

"She's been kept on a strict diet," Maddie said excusingly, and dredged up a smile. The thing was, just looking at Wynne made her stomach twist. Soon he was going to know the truth. Ridiculous as it seemed, over the course of the last few days she had come to consider him a friend. She'd be losing that, too.

The list of losses she was getting ready to suffer was growing so long that she could hardly bear to think about it.

"Think you two could move it along here?" Wynne asked as he walked past her. "Remember, the objective is to get inside the building as fast as you can."

He stopped about three cars up from her, propped his sneaker on a bumper, and made a business out of tying his shoe. He was trying to pretend that he wasn't with her, that they were strangers exchanging casual conversation in a parking lot, Maddie knew. Gomez and Hendricks were present, too, watching from the van, which they had parked not far from her car. The entire exercise seemed pretty pointless, however. Unless the hit man did his thing within the next half-hour or so, he was out of luck. She was going to be sounding the death knell on this little travesty herself.

"Come *on*, Zelda."

Sniffing around the truck for a second course, Zelda ignored her. Maddie tugged at the leash, sighed, and faced the truth: Unless she was prepared to drag Zelda across the parking lot, they were basically going nowhere fast. It was too hot to be covered in dog hair, especially given the fact that she was zipped up from neck to hips in a bulletproof vest, and her jacket and matching tank and white linen pants had just come back from the cleaners, but there was no help for it if she wanted to get inside the factory anytime soon. She bent to scoop the animal up. So far today, Zelda had shown no inclination to bite the hand that fed her, and with that in mind, Maddie held another goldfish cracker in front of the dog's flat little face as she headed toward the plant.

Zelda gobbled it up, and rewarded her with a lick on the wrist.

"I know the way to *your* heart," Maddie said sourly. She had almost reached the gray metal door set into the side of the building marked *Office* when she heard Wynne, who was once again some small distance behind her, speak.

"Yo, what are you two doing here?" he said, sounding surprised.

"Gardner'll fill you in." It was Sam's voice, and its tone was grim.

Maddie turned so fast that her jacket swirled. Despite everything, a smile trembled on her lips.

Sure enough, it was Sam. He was wearing jeans, sneakers, and a white polo shirt that hugged his broad shoulders and wide chest and made his hair look as black as the melting asphalt and his skin mouthwateringly tan.

He was in his dark-and-dangerous mode, with a hint of stubble, no trace of a smile, and a pair of Ray-Bans wrapped around his eyes to shield them from the sun. He was closing the distance between them fast, his tall, powerful body cutting like a knife through the shimmering veil of heat that rose from the pavement. Her eyes flicked beyond him to Cynthia, who was dressed in a black T-shirt and slacks and had a hand on Wynne's arm. She was saying something to Wynne, and he was frowning down at her.

Then she looked at Sam again, and her heart lurched. There was something about the way he moved. . . .

Her smile died.

"Sam?" As he reached her, she looked up at him uncertainly. His jaw was hard and set. His mouth was a thin, straight line. His head tilted toward her, and she thought he was looking at her, though it was impossible to be sure with the sunglasses hiding his eyes.

"We need to talk," he said. Taking hold of her arm, he turned her about and took her with him into the building. There was nothing remotely gentle in his grip. Where before she had been almost suffocatingly hot, now she felt suddenly very cold. It was possible that this was because she'd just stepped out of the sun and into an air-conditioned building, but she didn't think so.

"What—what is it?" Her heart was beating very fast. His fingers holding her were like iron. She glanced up at him as he hustled her down the hall past the manager's office, where Jon and Susan were probably already waiting. The harsh fluorescent lighting in the narrow hall hid nothing. She could see the whiteness at the corners of his mouth, see the tension in his face, see the muscles bunched in his jaw.

This was bad.

Her breathing quickened. Little curls of panic twisted in her stomach. She could feel a hard knot of dread tightening beneath her breastbone.

"Sam . . ." She tried again, fighting for a measure of calm, looking up at him almost pleadingly.

"Wait till we get somewhere private." The words were clipped, the tone harsh.

Maddie despaired. He knew. She knew he did. There was no other explanation for his behavior. She'd just found him, just fallen in love with him, and now he knew and was lost to her forever.

She said nothing more as he pushed open one door after another and marched her along a series of hallways. She wasn't even surprised that he seemed to know exactly where he was going. Of course he knew the layout of the plant, knew where to find privacy in a factory teeming with people. He would have checked. He would have found out before coming. He was an FBI agent, after all.

It was the FBI agent whose hand was wrapped around her arm.

Maddie realized that she was shivering as he pushed open one last door and she stepped through it to discover that they were at the very back of the building, in a high-ceilinged, metal-walled, cement-floored space that she guessed, from the tractor-trailer-sized garage doors, was the loading dock. It was the size of a small warehouse, and sunlight filtered in through grimy little windows set high up in the walls. The huge overhead doors were closed, but a smaller, ordinary-size door was propped open in the corner to her right. Dust motes hung in the air, and the place smelled, vaguely, of beef.

He shut the door through which they had just entered behind him, and let go of her arm. Maddie stepped a few paces away, then turned to face him. She was hugging Zelda close, too close for the little dog's liking, in a reflexive attempt to find what comfort she could. Only when Zelda squirmed did she realize that she had the dog in her arms at all. Taking a good grip on the leash, she set Zelda on her feet and straightened, looking at Sam apprehensively.

He took off his sunglasses. His eyes were as cold and hard as chips of black ice as they met hers. His jaw was unyielding. His face could have been carved from granite.

She wet her lips.

"Sam," she said. To her dismay, she realized that her voice sounded all croaky.

His eyes flashed at her.

"A funny thing happened this afternoon," he began almost conversationally, hooking the sunglasses in the neck of his shirt and folding his arms over his chest. There was a terrible burning anger at the backs of his eyes that stopped her breath. "We ran all the fingerprints that came out of your hotel room in New Orleans through the Automated Fingerprint Identification System a couple of days ago, and the results came back today. There was only one set of flagged prints. They came complete with a picture. The picture was of you. The name that went with it was Leslie Dolan. That ring any bells?"

She'd known it, of course. Known it from the moment she got a look at his face. Still, his words hit her like a blow to the solar plexus. She hugged her stomach, shivering, feeling bile rising in her throat, as corrosive as acid.

"Sam," she said. Her voice was piteous now. She would have been ashamed of the poor, pitiful begging sound of it if she hadn't been so busy listening to her world shattering into a million tiny pieces around her like a dropped globe of delicate handblown glass.

"Just to jog your memory, Leslie Dolan was arrested in Baltimore eight years ago and charged with being an accessory after the fact to first-degree murder as well as with money laundering, racketeering, and a whole bunch of other, slightly less impressive charges. She was looking at a sentence of maybe twenty, twenty-five years of hard time. But she never came to trial. Somebody sprung her on bail. Then, a little over a year after she was arrested, Leslie Dolan died."

Something about the flatness of his tone coupled with the hard, black glitter of his eyes made her physically ill. If he didn't stop, she feared she might vomit. She shook her head, took a step back.

"Are you saying you deny it?" His voice was suddenly sharp, as cutting as his eyes. "Before you do, maybe I should tell you that I didn't believe it at first. I thought there had to be some mistake, identity theft, something. So I checked into the background of Maddie Fitzgerald. Madeline Elaine Fitzgerald. You, right? And you know what? Nothing checks out. Western Illinois University has no record that a student by that name ever attended. Holloman High School in Winnipeg, Illinois—Maddie Fitzgerald's high school—has no record that a student by that name ever attended. Parents, John Fitzgerald, dentist, and Elaine Fitzgerald, homemaker, don't turn up on any records anywhere. Credit agencies, Social Security, the IRS—everywhere we checked came up empty. For the parents always, and for Maddie Fitzgerald, until just about seven years ago. You know what that means?" A deep, high flush had crept up to stain his cheekbones. His voice cracked like a whip at her. "Until seven years ago, Madeline Elaine Fitzgerald— you—didn't exist."

The words echoed around the four walls, bounced off the ceiling. Maddie felt faint. Her head spun. Tears blurred her eyes as she looked at him.

"I was going to tell you."

"You were going to tell me." The words were heavy as stones.

"Tonight. I was going to tell you tonight."

"You are Leslie Dolan." It was a statement, not a question.

She shuddered and nodded.

He was looking at her as if he wanted to kill her. "No wonder you didn't want to talk to me. No wonder you didn't want us protecting you. You were hostile from the beginning—and that's *fucking why.*"

"Last night . . ." she began, meaning to explain to him how hearing Carol Walter's murder had tipped the scales for her, made her see that she couldn't keep the secret any longer. Meaning to beg him to listen, to try to understand.

"Last night," he interrupted, his eyes blazing at her. He took two hasty steps toward her, grabbed her by the arms and hauled her up against him. Her heart hammered. His face was hard with anger. His voice was harsh with it. "*Last night.* Yeah, let's talk about last night. What, did you decide to fuck me to soften me up for when I found out?"

Maddie recoiled as if from a blow.

"That's a terrible thing to say," she whispered, shaking.

"*A terrible thing to say?* You've got to be kidding me. *A terrible thing to say?* Darlin', as far as I'm concerned, skipping out on your old life to beat an accessory-to-murder charge, creating a whole new identity, living a lie for seven years, and then, when you had to realize you were about to be found out, fucking the fed who was in line to bring you in is a *terrible thing to do.*"

"No." Maddie had to fight for air. "That's not how it was."

"So how was it?" His hands tightened on her arms. His fingers dug into her skin, and for a moment she thought he was going to shake her. "I'm listening. Go on, Leslie Dolan. Tell me how it was."

Hearing herself addressed by the name she hadn't used for seven years tore something inside her. It was as if a lid had been ripped off her emotions, and suddenly everything she'd been bottling up inside for all those years flooded through her: the shame, the fear, the anger, the hatred.

He was an FBI agent.

She hated them most of all.

"You," she said, glaring up into his eyes, loathing him at that moment. "*You.* With your badge and your gun and your power. *You,* with your grandma and your family and your whole white-bread world. *What can you possibly know about me?*"

Ripping herself from his hold, she took a step back, stumbled, and nearly fell. He caught her arm, kept her from hitting the floor, pulled her upright again.

"Let go of me." Jerking her arm from his grasp, she took a deep breath and stood up, proud and tall. If she was shaking to pieces inside, if part of her was dying inside, she was too wild with anger and fear—and, yes, grief—for what she was losing now and for the girl she had once been to notice. "All right, yes, my name was—*is*—Leslie Dolan. So now you know. What are you going to do about it? You want to arrest me? Well, I'm right here. You got your woman, Mr. Special Agent. Go ahead and take me in."

Fury blazed at her from his eyes as she thrust both hands out at him, close together as if waiting to be handcuffed.

"You want to cuff me? You can cuff me. You can march me right out of this building and turn me over to whoever the hell it is that arrogant jack-asses like you turn people over to, and then you can go on back to your nice, safe life, knowing that you've taken a dangerous criminal off the streets."

She didn't realize that the tears that had been stinging her eyes had spilled over until she felt them, wet and hot, running down her cheeks.

God, she was crying. She hated that she was crying. *How pathetic; how weak . . .*

Dropping her hands, she turned her back on him and started walking away. She might not be able to stop herself from crying, but she could stop him from watching. He wasn't Sam any longer, not to her. Sam was gone. In his place was this hard-eyed federal agent who was not ever again going to be able to see past who she had been.

And now, she realized with a dreadful clarity, who she was once again.

"Goddamn it to hell and back," he said, his voice low and harsh.

He had seen her tears. She could tell it from his tone. A glance over her shoulder showed her that he was standing stock-still where she had left him, staring after her, his face dark with anger, his hands curled into hard fists at his sides. He made an abortive movement, and for a moment she thought he was going to come after her. But he didn't. Muttering something under his breath, he swung around and started walking very fast in the opposite direction.

At least, if she was now a frog, so was her handsome prince.

She found herself by the open door and leaned against it for a moment, welcoming the heat now as an antidote to the terrible shivering cold that seemed to be creeping through her bones. She felt broken, shattered, raw. Impossible to believe that the world still smelled prosaically of melting asphalt and ozone. Impossible to believe that it was the same bright blazing afternoon that she had left behind when Sam had dragged her into the building. Impossible to believe that there were still lazy tendrils of white clouds floating across the brilliant blue sky and that heat still rose from the macadam and that people still went about their daily lives. For the garbage men, for instance, who were backing their rumbling green truck up to one of the three huge metal Dumpsters that lined this end of the lot, nothing had changed. The factory worker, apparently late to his job, who was hurrying across the pavement, was still going about his business as usual. The driver

of the white pickup she could see heading for the exit had no idea that behind him, a life had just ended.

Her life.

Tears streamed down her face at the thought.

Okay, get a grip, she told herself savagely, and scrubbed at her streaming eyes with both hands. As she had already learned many times over in
her life, tears didn't do anything except give you a stuffy nose. The truth
was out, and the happy, healthy, hopeful world that she had created as Maddie Fitzgerald had crashed and burned. Those were the facts. She was just
going to have to deal with them.

I could run.

The thought of her secret garage, of her car and her emergency kit, popped
into her head like a shiny, tempting bauble. No one knew about those. . . .

She was standing in an open doorway at the top of a quartet of narrow concrete steps that led down to the parking lot. If she could get to
her car . . .

Glancing over her shoulder, she saw that Sam was clear on the other side
of the loading dock. He had stopped pacing, and was standing with his back
to her, his head down, his hands locked behind his neck, thinking or cursing or getting a grip on his anger, she had no idea which. He looked tall and
dark and handsome, all of those clichés, and for a moment, just a moment
more, she let herself grieve the loss.

Then she looked determinedly toward the future.

And saw Zelda darting under the wheels of the garbage truck.

Until that moment, she had forgotten all about her. Now she realized that
the leash, which was trailing after Zelda, had also just disappeared beneath
the truck. She had no idea when it had dropped from her hand.

"Zelda!" Maddie cried, horror-stricken, and swarmed down the steps as
everything flew out of her head except the need to protect the little dog from
her gluttonous self.

The truck was rumbling as it backed up, the sound loud enough to block
out almost everything else. But it was moving very slowly, inch by terrifying inch.

"Stop!" Maddie raced toward it, waving at the driver, who was looking over his shoulder and didn't see her. "Zelda!"

Darting around the cab—she wasn't quite stupid enough to run behind the thing when it was backing up—she found herself in the narrow, shady space between the truck and the chain-link fence, with its thin line of weedy trees.

And she saw Zelda. The little dog was trotting out from beneath the huge truck, not inches away from a wheel big enough to turn her into puppy pizza, as if she didn't have a worry in the world.

A red McDonald's fry container was clutched between her teeth.

"Zelda!" Laughing, crying, almost nauseous with relief and reaction and God knew what else, she swooped down on the runaway, gathering her up in her arms. She was still hugging the dog when, with her peripheral vision, she became aware of a tall, shadowy figure looming behind her.

"Hello, Leslie," a man's voice said in her ear, and in that instant she realized that the unthinkable had happened. Her past had just caught up with her again. And this time it might very well prove fatal.

She started to whirl, opened her mouth to scream, filled with a mindless, soul-shattering terror.

She didn't want to die....

Something slammed hard into the side of her head, and everything went black.

TWENTY-TWO

Maddie—for Maddie, she discovered, was how she still thought of herself—came back to awareness slowly, reluctantly, resisting consciousness with every fiber of her being. Consciousness hurt. No, she hurt. Her head felt as though it had been split in two, her hip ached, and her hands and feet felt swollen and numb.

They felt that way because they were bound, with some kind of thin, smooth rope that had been pulled so tightly that it was cutting into her skin. The realization that she was tied—shades of her dream—made her stomach contract with fear. She was out of the sun, indoors, lying on her side on a hard, cool surface—concrete. A concrete floor. She could smell oil and a musty odor that made her think of damp earth. And . . . and some kind of food. Something greasy. The smell of it made her want to heave. If she looked, she would know exactly what it was. But looking struck her as a really bad idea.

If there was food, there were probably people. And, though she didn't hear any sounds that would confirm it, she got the sense that she wasn't alone.

The good news was that she wasn't dead. The bad news was that that fact could change at any second.

For the moment, she preferred to concentrate on the good news.

She remembered then. Remembered that a man had said her name—her old name—just before something had exploded into the side of her head.

Oh, God. Have I been shot? Had the hit man . . .

No. If the hit man had found her, she wouldn't be alive.

Something cold and wet touched her face. She jerked, unable to control the reaction in time. It was all she could do not to scream.

Zelda. She knew it even before she heard the telltale snuffling sound, even before she gave in to overwhelming temptation and opened her eyes a slit to find the small, monkeyish face not three inches away from hers. It was Zelda all right, complete with a mustache of goldfish-cracker crumbs, munching away. Maddie realized that she was no longer wearing her jacket—or her bulletproof vest, for that matter—and surmised that Zelda had discovered the jacket somewhere nearby. Except for those items, she was fully dressed in her aqua tank and white pants. She only hoped that whoever had taken off her jacket and vest had done so in some kind of search for, say, a gun.

The thought of anything else happening while she was unconscious made her skin crawl.

Zelda was regarding her from behind unblinking black eyes. Her leash still hung from her collar, and her tiny satin bow—pink again, freshly styled by the groomer that morning—was askew. Maddie took what she realized was a ridiculous amount of comfort from the little dog's presence.

It was possible that the hit man might be keeping her alive for some nefarious purpose of his own. But would that somehow include Zelda? She didn't think so.

The sound of a door opening made Zelda look off to the left. Maddie would have looked, too, except she couldn't. She was too busy playing unconscious. But she had a funny feeling that the door opening was not a good thing.

"DiMatteo says we should get her to tell us where the stuff is." The speaker was male, about medium height, she thought, although it was hard to judge from her position on the floor, heavyset, fortyish, with thinning black hair swept back from his face, small eyes and mouth, big nose, jowls. He was wearing pale gray Sansabelt slacks with a cheap-looking black rayon shirt tucked into it. The shirt was unbuttoned far enough that a thick silver necklace, a deep V of pale skin, and a meager quantity of black chest hair were on view. In other words, too far.

The hit man? She didn't know. But her heart was beating very fast.

She watched through her lashes as he walked across the garage—now that Zelda had moved on, she could see that she was inside a multicar garage, though only a blue Ford F-150 pickup truck was currently parked in it— toward another man, who was sitting at one end of what looked like a work-bench built into the far wall of the garage.

"So, how do we do that?" the other man asked, chewing. This guy was thin, wiry even, too thin to be the man who had attacked her in New Or-leans. He was maybe in his early thirties, with thick black hair and big, loose lips and a receding chin, and he wore a short-sleeved blue shirt. She could only see him from the chest up, because he was seated at the table, so the rest of him remained a mystery.

The heavy man shrugged. "Torture her, I guess."

"You torture her. I'm eating."

The heavy man looked around at her. Horrified, she just managed to re-member to breathe.

"Hell's bells, Fish, why me? I had to carry her in here. She's no feather, that's for sure."

Maddie would have felt insulted at that if she hadn't been so scared.

"Because I'm eating, lunkhead. Can't you see? Me—eat." He took a huge bite out of what looked like a fast-food burger.

"What about me? I'm hungry, too."

"Torture her, then eat."

"My food'll be cold."

"You can put it in the microwave."

"Shit." Lunkhead sighed. Then he came toward her, and she felt her blood run cold. "If I have to torture her, then you have to shoot the dog. I don't do nothin' to dogs."

"I don't know why you brought the damned thing anyway."

"Because it was there. Because it was barking. Another couple of minutes, and everybody in the damned factory would have been coming out to see what was going on. Lucky I was able to grab hold of its leash. It would have given us away." Lunkhead was standing over her now, and Maddie concentrated on emptying her mind of everything, imagined being in a calm, serene place, concentrated on her breathing. *In out, in out*. Like in her dream.

She shuddered.

"I saw that," Lunkhead said triumphantly. He reached down, grabbed her under her arm, and hauled her roughly upright, his fingers digging painfully into her flesh. "Come on, I know you're awake. Don't make me hit you."

That was said so casually that she knew it wasn't an idle threat. Her eyes flew open, and she sucked in a deep breath as she tried to find her balance. But with her ankles bound and her feet numb, she couldn't. Her shoes were gone, she realized, as her bare feet made contact with the cold floor. She couldn't get her feet squarely beneath her, and she had a feeling that, even if she could, they wouldn't support her weight. Unable to help herself, she sagged heavily against him. He was soft with flab and smelled of cologne. He didn't feel like her attacker, either.

Unless her senses were deceiving her, the hit man wasn't in the room.

Not that that meant she was in the clear. It just meant that multiple people seemed to want to do her harm.

"Over to the table." Lunkhead gripped her tighter and started dragging her in the direction he wanted her to go.

She gave a little hop, then, overbalanced, fell heavily forward onto her knees. Her kneecaps banged into the concrete. It hurt, and she cried out.

"Get up." Lunkhead loomed over her.

"I—I can't."

He kicked her, his shiny black loafer making brutal contact with her thigh. Pain exploded up and down her leg. She yelped, crumpled.

"Now try." He reached down to drag her upright again.

"My feet . . . ?"

The disorientation she'd experienced on first regaining consciousness was totally gone now. In its place was pain and a hard cold fear. This guy's casual brutality told its own tale—he had no qualms about hurting her. He would have no qualms about killing her.

"Oh, jeez, untie her feet. She's not going anywhere," the man at the table said.

"Yeah."

The fingers digging into her arm let go. Maddie hit her knees again, then toppled forward, barely managing to twist enough to smack the concrete with her shoulder rather than her face. She cried out again as pain shot through her knees, her hip, her arm. Then, as she lay, panting, on her side on the concrete, she saw something that made her temporarily forget both pain and fear.

Sam was sprawled on his back on the concrete floor not far from where she lay. His eyes were closed, blood trickled sluggishly from a corner of his mouth and smeared his white shirt, and his arms were stretched over his head. Eyes widening with horror, she saw that he was handcuffed to the truck's bumper.

"Get up," Lunkhead said again, and hauled her upright. The rope around her ankles had been cut—she caught a glint of silver as he refolded a serviceable switchblade and stowed it in his pocket—but she had been so focused on Sam that she hadn't even realized that he was doing it.

Was he badly hurt? That was her first, instinctive thought. Then, as she was forced to walk on her tingling, throbbing feet, she remembered that she hated him.

But not enough for this.

"Sit down," Fish said when Lunkhead had dragged her, hobbling, to the workbench. It was table-height, made of unfinished planks, with an open toolbox and various tools jumbled together and shoved toward the wall. Fish's lunch was spread out in front of him on a sandwich wrapper: a half-eaten fish sandwich, a couple of unopened packs of tartar sauce, fries, and a large soft drink with a straw and a lid. Moby Dick's, Maddie saw from the other small, white bag that waited near the edge of the table with its top rolled shut. This, clearly, was Lunkhead's meal, which he had not yet had time to eat. Three cheap plastic chairs had been pulled up to the workbench, one at each end and one in the middle. Lunkhead pulled out the chair in the middle and shoved Maddie into it. Fish was to her left, Lunkhead behind her chair. If she glanced sideways, she could see Sam.

She was terrified, she realized—and not just for herself.

A door opened at the rear of the garage, and Zelda, lucky dog, disappeared beneath the truck. A man stood in the opening, scowling at them. He was stocky, bald, and dressed in dark suit pants, a striped dress shirt, and tie. The hit man? She didn't know. There was no way to tell. But the build was right. Her heart started slamming against her ribs in quick, panicked strokes. Her breathing suspended. Would he come in now and kill her? If he did, there was nothing she could do. No escape . . .

Be calm, she told herself. *Focus.* Behind the new arrival, she could see the outdoors: a strip of concrete and, beyond it, grass and the crowded trunks of a stand of skinny pines. Where were they? Impossible to tell.

Zelda, we're not in Kansas anymore.

"You know what we just heard on the police scanner, shit-for-brains?" the guy in the door demanded. "An APB for the fed. What the hell did you have to dick around with him for?"

"I told you, we didn't have any choice," Lunkhead said. "He came around the side of the truck just as I was throwing the dog in. He saw me. He was going for his gun."

"If I hadn't been right there to clobber him with that tire iron, he would've had us. I didn't even have time to pull out my stun gun," Fish chimed in.

"Yeah, we weren't expecting him. Had her, had the dog—then here he came. What are you gonna do?" Lunkhead shook his head and shrugged.

"Well, idiots, you just escalated our problems, big-time. They wouldn't have looked that hard for her. They'll look like hell for him, and now we got no choice but to kill him. Just make sure, when you do it, that you get rid of the body someplace where it's not gonna be found. Chop it up or something and bury the parts separately. Got it?"

Maddie went all light-headed.

"Yeah," Fish said.

The man in the doorway turned his head sharply, as if he heard something. Then he disappeared from view, leaving the door ajar. The light outside had the mellow, golden quality common to a summer evening. The trees cast long shadows toward the east, which told her that sundown was nearing. The meal Fish was eating and Lunkhead wasn't must be supper.

The terrible thing was, freedom was less than twenty feet away. It might as well have been a thousand miles. Two men inside, undoubtedly armed and clearly ready, willing, and able to kill her. At least one man outside, and probably more.

And handcuffed to a truck, one man whom, Maddie realized, she wasn't willing to leave behind even if she should somehow get the opportunity to run.

"He's pissed," Lunkhead said to Fish, sounding glum.

"Yeah. Well, we better be getting them what they need, then." Fish looked at Maddie. His eyes were cold now, and hard. Fear tightened her stomach, dried her mouth. He could kill her, she realized, and go right back to eating his fish sandwich. "This is all your damned fault," he said to her. "Why the hell didn't you just stay off TV?"

Maddie was so surprised by his comment that she forgot, for a moment, to be afraid. "What?"

"TV. What kind of stupid person who's on the run goes on TV? You got us all in trouble here." He looked at Lunkhead. "Cut her hands free."

Maddie felt her stomach clench. *Why does this not sound like good news?*

"What? What?" she said, as much to keep them talking as for any other reason. Lunkhead was using his knife on the rope that bound her wrists. She could hear the sawing sound it made, feel a painful increase in pressure as the rope dug tighter into her skin. "What are you talking about? I never went on TV."

Fish looked at her with disgust. "You got some big business award. Velasco saw it on the news. He's one of our guys now, but he used to live in Baltimore and he recognized you. Said he remembered you because you were such hot stuff. Only you had some trouble, and you were supposed to be dead. He kept wondering about it, and finally he gave the guys in Baltimore a buzz. Then all hell broke loose."

Her hands were free now. The blood flowing back into them made her fingers tingle and throb painfully. She scarcely noticed. All this—*all this*—because they'd run a clip of her receiving the Chamber of Commerce award on the evening news?

Talk about your butterfly effect. She would've had to laugh if she hadn't felt so much like crying.

Fish grabbed hold of her wrist and put her hand down on the table. Maddie was still looking at her outstretched fingers in surprise when he picked up a hammer and brought it down hard on her pinkie.

She screamed, snatching her hand away. Smirking, he let it go. The pain was blinding, intense, made even more horrible because it was so unexpected. Her stomach turned inside out. She went all woozy. If Lunkhead hadn't been behind her, holding on to her shoulders, she would have fallen sideways out of the chair.

"That's just a sample of what's going to happen if you give us any problems," Fish said. He'd already put down the hammer, Maddie saw, as her vision cleared enough for her to be able to see again, and was taking another hungry bite out of his sandwich. The pain, coupled with the smell, made her want to vomit. "That stuff you said you had—I want to know where it is."

"What stuff?" Maddie cradled her injured hand close to her chest. She was nauseated, dizzy. The end of her pinkie was purplish and already starting to swell, and blood welled into a small cut beside the nail. Maggie realized it was where her skin had split, and felt cold sweat begin to ooze from her pores.

"Don't play dumb." Fish was eating his sandwich as though this was the most ordinary of conversations. "The stuff you told Mikey you had. When you called him."

"When I called . . ." Mikey being Bob Johnson, of course. It wasn't so much that Maddie was slow on the uptake, although pain and fear certainly were having some mind-clouding effects. It was that she could see where this was going all too clearly. If she didn't tell them what they wanted to know, they'd continue causing her pain until she did. If she did tell them, she would die.

Fish put down his sandwich and reached for her hand again.

"No," she gasped, cold sweat drenching her in waves. She cradled her hand tighter against her chest while Lunkhead, behind her, bore down harder on her shoulders. "It—I'm just not thinking so clearly because—because you hurt my hand. I know what call you mean. A-One Plastics. When I called them, right?"

"That's right," Lunkhead said behind her. "You shouldn't go around threatening people, you know. Nobody likes that."

"Shut up, would you?" Fish growled, shooting Lunkhead a look. Then, to Maddie, "I'm gonna ask you one more time, nice, then I'm gonna smash another finger. Where's all that evidence you said your dad took?"

Maddie's stomach cramped. Ice-cold terror shot through her veins. But terror wouldn't help her. Calm, clear thinking probably wouldn't, either. But it was all she had, so she fought back the terror and went with the calm-and-clear thing. They were in a garage, which was obviously attached to a house. The door the man had left open led to a parking area. Beyond it was—someplace better than here. If she wanted to survive, what she had to do was make it to the door and run.

They were armed, she was almost positive. They'd shoot her in the back if she was able to outrun them. But she'd rather die trying to escape than be tortured until they killed her.

Sam. She couldn't leave Sam. Glancing sideways, she discovered to her surprise that his posture had changed. His body was in the same position as before, but his muscles seemed to have tensed. And she couldn't be sure—

BAIT 305

his lashes still fanned his cheeks—but she was almost positive that he was looking at her.

"What, do you think we've got all night here? Time's up." Fish grabbed her wrist with one hand and the hammer with the other. Maddie screamed, resisting his attempts to lay her hand on the table.

"No, no, I was just thinking . . ." she babbled. "I'll tell you, okay? I'll tell you."

She drew a deep, sobbing breath, thinking furiously all the while. He let go of her wrist and put the hammer back down. Sam was watching her, she was almost sure of it now. She was positive he'd stiffened when she screamed. But there was nothing he could do. He was as helpless as she. Zelda, equally useless, was close, too. Maddie could feel the little dog snuffling around her ankles.

Probably she was smelling food, and hoping for a handout from the table.

"You're stalling." Fish grabbed for her hand again.

"The evidence is in a strongbox near where we used to live in Baltimore," Maddie gasped, jerking her hand back and, in the course of the small struggle that ensued, managing to knock the bag containing Lunkhead's food on the floor.

"Yo, that's my . . ." Lunkhead began, letting go of her shoulders to retrieve it.

Then, just as Maddie had prayed she might, Zelda popped out from under the workbench, grabbed the bag in her teeth, and trotted away.

"Hey, that's my dinner," Lunkhead said, sounding more surprised than anything as he lunged after her. Zelda saw him coming and, bless her gluttonous little soul, put the pedal to the metal, scuttling across the floor with a really impressive burst of speed and racing out the door, bag and all.

"Goddamn dog! Come back here with that!" Lunkhead roared, giving chase.

She, Fish, and, she thought, Sam, too, were all so surprised that all they could do was stare after Lunkhead as he pelted through the door. But, since it was more or less what she'd kind of planned, Maddie recovered fastest.

Hammer-time.

Lunging across the table, she snatched up the hammer. Even as Fish re-acted, milliseconds too late to do any good, she slammed it down on his head with every last bit of strength she had left. The resulting *thunk* was almost as satisfying as watching his eyes roll back in his head before he collapsed sideways onto the floor.

Take that, you creep, Maddie thought exultantly, and gave herself a mental high-five as she sprang away from the table and her gaze swung around to Sam. His eyes were open. He was struggling to sit up.

"In his left front pants pocket. The keys to the handcuffs are in his left front pants pocket," Sam said urgently, as her gaze locked with his.

Jesus, God, and every other heavenly being, let Lunkhead not come back.

Heart pounding, operating on adrenaline now, Maddie stuck her hand into Fish's pocket and, since it was the only thing in it, came up with the key at once. Then, with one wary eye on the door, she darted to Sam.

"Hurry," he said.

No shit, Sherlock, was the rejoinder that popped into her head, but she was too busy sweating bullets and trying to fit the teeny, tiny key into the teeny, tiny lock to answer. Shaking, panting, one eye on the door, she finally got it in there and turned it.

That was all it took. Jerking free of the bumper as the cuffs dropped to the floor with a metallic clatter, Sam scrambled to his feet and headed for Fish, who was beginning to stir.

"What are you *doing*?" Maddie was already racing for the door.

"If he's got a gun, I want it," Sam said, leaning over Fish. Maddie was treated to the gratifying sight of him slamming his fist hard into Fish's jaw. As Fish went limp again, Sam patted him down.

"Shit."

Maddie took that to mean no gun.

"Come *on*." As far as she could tell, the coast was clear, but it was un-likely to stay that way for long. There were two cars in the paved area be-yond the garage—and a garbage truck.

Maddie had an instant epiphany: The bad guys had been in the garbage truck.

Then she saw something that completely erased everything else from her mind. Like a boomerang, Zelda was returning. Leash flapping behind her, she raced back toward the open garage door with the bag still in her mouth and Lunkhead in hot pursuit.

"Oh, no!" Heart pounding, panic clutching at her stomach, Maddie jumped back from the door and looked at Sam, who was straightening away from a now limp and supine Fish. "He's coming back. Lunkhead's coming back."

"Get in the truck."

As he said it, Sam was already leaping for the garage door directly behind it. The door was metal, and looked to be heavy-duty. Not the kind of garage door even a Ford F-150 could just burst through.

"Sam . . ."

"Here. They were in the slimeball's other pocket. If we run out of time, if something happens, you *go*." He tossed her the keys. She caught them instinctively.

"But . . ."

Leave him if necessary, he meant, which wasn't happening. But she wasn't going to argue about it at the moment. She scrambled behind the wheel. He turned the lock with a sound so loud it made her jump, and bent down to drag up the garage door.

Fish was moving again.

Then three things happened simultaneously.

Handicapped by her throbbing finger, Maddie fumbled with the keys, found the right one, thrust it into the ignition, and turned the engine over.

The garage door went rattling up.

And Zelda, with panic in her eyes, burst through the open door.

She'd saved them, so saving her back was nothing short of quid pro quo. And she was cute, kind of, when she wasn't being a pain in the ass. And there was the Brehmer account. Not that Maggie was probably ever going to have to worry about it again, but . . .

"Zelda," Maddie cried, opening the truck door and wrenching at the gearshift at the same time. Seeing Maddie, Zelda scrambled toward the truck and took a flying leap that landed her almost on Maddie's lap. Maddie grabbed her collar and hauled her the rest of the way on board.

"Hit it." Sam dove into the passenger seat beside her. The transmission locked into reverse . . .

"Now," Sam yelled, slamming his door, and Maddie hit it, slamming her door and elbowing Zelda to the middle at the same time as she stomped on the gas.

"What the—?" Lunkhead burst through the door just as the truck shot backward out of the garage. He ran into the space they'd just vacated, fumbling behind his back for what Maddie assumed was a gun.

Maddie caught just a glimpse of Fish shaking his head groggily and sitting up as she steered in a wide reverse doughnut that barely missed the garbage truck.

"Forward! Go forward!" Sam screamed in her ear. She had the impression that if he hadn't been afraid of making them wreck, he would have shifted for her. *No duh,* she thought, but this was definitely not the time for conversation. With her heart pounding so hard that it felt as though it was going to beat clear out of her chest, she slammed on the brakes, throwing all three of them forward, then shoved the transmission into drive.

The rear window exploded. Maddie screamed, ducked, and stepped on the gas so hard that the truck catapulted forward like a rock out of a slingshot.

TWENTY-THREE

Keep your head down!" Sam yelled, hanging on to the dashboard as another bullet whistled past Maddie's ear, shattering the windshield. Glass blew out over the front of the pickup, rattling like hail. More glass from the rear window littered the seat like spilled popcorn, bouncing and sliding onto the floor as the truck shot away from the house. Zelda, bag and all, had been thrown down into the passenger's footwell when Maddie hit the brakes, and she stayed down there, clearly smart enough to recognize that she had found the safest place in the vehicle. A place where she could devour her booty undisturbed.

"I'm trying!" Crouched as low as she could get and still see where they were going, Maddie hung grimly onto the steering wheel and kept her foot mashed down on the gas.

The road was a winding gravel track with thick piney woods on one side and a brush-covered ravine ending in more thick piney woods on the other. A hunted glance into the rearview mirror showed her a one-story lodge-looking house in a clearing behind them. Hills covered with more piney woods rose behind it, and the sun in all its orange and purple and pink glory was just getting ready to sink behind the hills. The garage they'd just exited was to the side of the house. Lunkhead stood in two-handed firing stance on the paved area in front of the garage, while Fish and two other men ran for the cars.

"Keep your eyes on the road!"

Maddie looked forward again just in time to see that they were coming up on a curve. She swung the wheel hard, and gravel spurted up around them, hitting the side of the truck. In seconds they were around the curve, out of sight of the house—and still on the road.

His face grim, Sam reached around her, grabbed her seat belt, pulled it across her body, and clicked it into place. Maddie barely noticed.

"They were in the garbage truck." She was still having trouble getting her mind around that. Something about the garbage truck bothered her . . .

"I figured that out about the time I woke up in the back of it and that fat dude hit me with a stun gun. Just be glad there wasn't any garbage in it." Sam's voice was wry. He was fastening his own seat belt as he spoke.

"There was a garbage truck near my apartment the morning I got shot," Maddie gasped as her mind hit on the elusive memory. She glanced back reflexively to see if the bad guys had rounded the curve yet.

"Shit. We got trouble," Sam said. At first Maddie thought he was talking about something she was missing behind them. Then she looked forward.

A small yellow car had just rounded the next bend, and was hurtling up the track toward them. It was smack-dab in the middle of the road. Clearly it wasn't intending to let them get by.

Maddie did some quick mental calculations. Big truck, little car—could anyone say "Let's play chicken"?

"Yee-haw," she said grimly, and charged toward it without giving an inch. Beside her, Sam sucked in air. His eyes widened as they stayed glued to the oncoming car.

"Maybe you want to . . . *swerve right!*"

Maddie did, at the last possible second, just as the car, in the same desperate attempt to avoid a head-on collision, swerved the other way. They zoomed past each other with inches to spare.

"Jesus." Sam looked sideways at her. "And I thought Wynne was a scary-ass driver."

Maddie laughed.

And then something hit the back of the truck with all the force of an exploding grenade. The truck's rear end slewed sideways as if in an insane attempt to pass the front. And the truck slid off the road and plunged down the ravine.

Maddie screamed and stomped the brake. Sam yelled and held on. The truck hurtled downward, bouncing over the ground like a kid on a trampoline. Bushes and scrub trees flashed past. As the bottom rushed up at them, Maddie could clearly see what looked like a solid wall of trees . . .

She was steering hard to the left when they hit with a *bang*.

She must have blacked out, because the next thing she was aware of was that she was being dragged out from behind the wheel. Hard hands under her armpits. Her left ankle thumping down painfully on the running board. Someone locking an arm around her waist, dragging her upright.

"What?" She tried to resist. Her eyes blinked open.

"It's okay; it's me," Sam said. Blood ran from his nose. Before Maddie could register more than that, he said, "Hold on," and heaved her over his shoulder.

Then he took off at what felt like a dead run.

Maddie clutched the back of his shirt and hung on. His shoulder dug into her stomach, making breathing an effort. With her head bouncing against his back like a basketball being dribbled, it was hard to think, let alone see. But she knew that they were in the woods because she could see the brown carpet of fallen needles and the thin, gray trunks with their stubby, denuded branches like small arms as they flashed past. It was already a deep purple twilight there, where the last rays of the sun couldn't reach. The air was cooler and smelled strongly of pine. The high-pitched chorus of insects was almost drowned out by the thud of Sam's feet on the ground and the harsh rasp of his breathing.

Zelda was with them: Maddie could see her bounding along behind, her leash slithering like a lavender snake over the pine needles.

Whatever else she was, Zelda was no fool. She clearly knew the bad guys from the good.

As she gradually became aware enough to take inventory, Maddie realized that she had the mother of all headaches; her stomach was being pounded to smithereens; and the little finger of her left hand throbbed horribly.

She also realized that Sam was tiring. His breathing was growing more labored, and his steps were slowing. His shirt felt damp, and she realized that he was sweating.

As Lunkhead had said, she wasn't any feather.

"Sam." She tugged on his shirt, then poked his ribs to get his attention. When he flinched, she knew she'd succeeded.

"Sam." She poked him again.

He slowed, then stopped as she poked him once more, and leaned forward so that she spilled off his shoulder. To her surprise, her knees refused to support her. They buckled, and, with his hands on her waist to keep her from collapsing completely, she maneuvered into a sitting position on the ground. The scent of pine rose all around her. The needles were as thick as good carpet, and felt smooth beneath her. Zelda came limping over and collapsed beside her, panting. Her top-knot hung down over her left eye again, and Maddie, performing an act of mercy, pulled the bow off.

"What?" Sam was leaning over as he looked at her, his hands on his thighs, gasping for breath.

Okay, so maybe she wasn't any feather. But she wasn't all *that* heavy.

"Are you all right?"

"Just . . . winded."

"You don't have to carry me any farther. I can walk."

His eyes slid over her skeptically. "Looks like it."

"I can. Just give me a minute."

"That's about all we have: a minute." His nose was still bleeding, but only a trickle now, and he must have felt it because he dashed it away with the back of his hand. His face was liberally smeared with blood. His shirt was splotched with it, ugly dark flowers against a white background.

"They're chasing us, right?" Maddie felt a clutch of fear. Not a really strong clutch, because she was now so battered and sore and shell-shocked that her sensory processing center was about out of room. But a clutch nonetheless.

"By now? Oh, yeah. But I don't think they saw us go off the road. At least, I saw their cars shoot past as I was dragging you out of the truck. But it wouldn't take them long to figure out we weren't ahead of them, and then they'll backtrack. We have to assume that by now they've found the truck." His voice was grim.

Fear elbowed everything else out of the way and made itself some room.

"So what happened? It felt like we got rear-ended, but when I glanced back, there wasn't anything there."

"I think they shot out a tire. Whoever was in the yellow car. That's what it felt like, anyway." He straightened, took a deep breath, and leaned against a tree.

Maddie grimaced. The reality of the situation was starting to set in again. They were, it seemed clear, still somewhere in Missouri—at a guess, not that far from St. Louis. But from the quick look around that she'd gotten as they'd driven away from the house, they were on one of the many small mountains that ridged the countryside west of the city. It was a sparsely settled area, and she hadn't seen any other houses or buildings. Though, admittedly, she'd had only a brief glimpse.

On a positive note—the only time in her life that she had ever considered this a positive note, come to think of it—she was with an FBI agent. A highly trained, highly skilled, highly competent law-enforcement professional who would certainly know what to do in a situation like this.

"Okay, Mr. Special Agent, so what's the plan?"

He laughed. The sound was short, unamused. "We walk. We hide. We try to stay alive."

"Well, shoot, *I* could've come up with that," she said, disappointed.

"They took my gun, they took my cell phone. We got no wheels. Sorry, darlin', but that kind of leaves us fresh out of options."

That drawled *darlin'* did something to her insides. Her stomach went all fluttery and her heart skipped a beat. For the briefest of moments, she simply looked at him and remembered that this time last night, they'd been falling in love.

"Maddie . . ." He must have seen something of what she was feeling in her eyes, or felt something of the same himself, because his voice was suddenly low and deep, achingly intimate. Then his face hardened abruptly, and his voice went flat. "Leslie, I mean. I take it that you know what that was all about back there?"

Suddenly her past and the rift it had created between them hung in the air, as tangible as the scent of pine.

Her heart ached, and the taste of regret for what they'd had and lost was bitter on her tongue. But there was no changing what was, and now that the truth was out in the open, she was not going to shrink from it. She'd lost everything else. Pride was just about all she had left.

"Maddie works. I left Leslie behind a long time ago."

"Maddie, then." It was dark under the trees now, she realized, because she could no longer read what was in his eyes. "So?"

She realized that he was prompting her to answer his question.

"They're mob," she said. "The guy who's been trying to kill me, who killed Carol Walter and all those other people—I'm pretty sure he's a professional hit man."

"Yeah." Sam didn't sound as though that was some big news flash. "Either of those guys back there, you think?"

Maddie shook her head. "I don't know. I don't think so. The man who was in my hotel room—they didn't seem to fit with what I remembered. But the guy in the doorway—the third guy—maybe. He looked about the right size and everything but, like I told you before, I didn't see the guy who attacked me."

"Okay. I heard you say something about some plastics company—and a strongbox full of evidence?"

Maddie sighed. "A-One Plastics is one of the names they use as a front in Baltimore. When I realized that they'd found me—that would be when I was attacked in New Orleans—I called them up and made some threats about some stuff my dad, who used to do some jobs for them, kept in case he ever had to use it as leverage. The thing is, I left the strongbox behind when I left Baltimore, but they don't know that. I thought maybe I could get them to back off."

"You called them up?" There was a curious note in his voice. He was watching her closely, but she couldn't read anything in his expression.

Her chin came up. "Yeah. If you want their number, I'll give it to you when—if—we get home."

"I definitely want their number." She could see him frowning. "You *made threats* to the mob?"

"I didn't know what else to do. I thought about running, but I figured if they found me once, they could do it again. Especially now that they know I'm alive."

A beat passed.

"You ever think about telling *me*? I was right there. Convenient."

The hint of sarcasm in his voice stung.

"I thought you'd probably react just exactly the way you're reacting."

"How the hell else am I supposed to react? You . . ."

But she'd stopped listening. Zelda's head had come up. The little dog was looking at something back in the direction from which they'd come, and Maddie, following her gaze, caught her breath. At first glance she'd thought the bobbing yellow spheres in the distance were lightning bugs, so tiny were they. But then they'd grown a little larger, and she'd recognized them for what they were: flashlights. Distant, but headed their way.

She felt an icy thrust of pure terror.

"Sam . . ." she breathed, pointing.

He looked, stiffened, turned back to her. "Shit. Let's go."

Then he reached down to grab her elbows, and she let him pull her up.

"Give me the damned leash. Why the hell you didn't leave her—too late now. If they find her, they'll know which way we came."

Maddie had been holding on to Zelda's leash for dear life since she'd seen the flashlights—Zelda was a dog, after all; counting on her continued good sense could be a bad thing—but she handed it over without protest. She felt shaky, weak, ill. Her head hurt, her finger throbbed. Her thigh ached where Lunkhead had kicked her.

Her heart hurt, too. It felt bruised and battered and sore just like the rest of her. Because despite everything, she'd discovered, to her dismay, she was still in love with Sam.

And, considering who he was and who she was, that was a bad thing.

"No," she said, shaking her head when he made a move to swing her back over his shoulder again. "I can make it on my own."

"Fine." There was a clipped quality to his voice. "Come on, then."

Grabbing her uninjured hand, Sam took off through the trees at a steady jog. Gritting her teeth and calling on reserves of determination she'd forgotten she had, Maddie managed to stay with him. Zelda scuttled along silently beside them, seeming to realize their danger. They ran at a right angle to the path the flashlights seemed to be taking, and after a while they couldn't see them anymore. The woods were so dark now that the trees were no more than grayish blurs as they flashed by. The insect chorus grew louder. An owl hooted. Here and there the eyes of a nocturnal animal glowed at them. Ordinarily, Maddie would have shivered at the thought of the creatures that might be roaming the woods, but tonight she was just too darned tired, and, anyway, nothing was as scary as the two-legged predators on their trail. The pine needles were cool and slippery underfoot, and would have made a decent running surface if it hadn't been for the things hidden beneath them. Having lost her shoes, Maddie had no protection from the roots and rocks and pinecones and other mushy things she preferred not to even think about, with which the ground was littered. They found a creek and ran parallel to it, turning downhill. Head pounding, stomach churning, her knees feeling like they might give out at any second, Maddie concentrated on putting one foot in front of the other. And ran. And ran. And ran.

Until, finally, she stopped.

"That's it," she said, wheezing and bending double, brought low by a stitch in her side. Sam had stopped, too—she'd pulled her hand from his—and loomed over her, Zelda now tucked like a football beneath his arm.

"Okay, I think we can walk now."

At least he had the decency to be breathing hard. She would have felt better about that, except she could scarcely breathe at all.

"No. No walk."

"Just a little farther."

"No."

"So I'll carry you."

"*No.*"

"Just as far as the rocks up there. See them?"

Maddie looked up. Maybe it was just her, because her head was pounding so hard that it was making her eyes all blurry, but all she saw was a whole lot of dark.

"I don't want to scare you, but they may be looking for us with night-vision goggles by now. I was getting ready to stop because of that anyway, but we need to find some shelter so they can't see us if they scan this patch of trees."

Crap.

She straightened, both hands on her hips as she sucked in air, and narrowed her eyes at him. He was no more than a big charcoal-gray silhouette in the dark.

"Fine," she said.

She thought he grinned, but her eyes were too blurry and it was too dark to be sure. Anyway, she didn't care. All she wanted to do was rest.

Which she eventually got to do, after scrambling over a lot of big rocks and edging around what felt like a wall of solid stone cliffs that rose straight up from the creek bed and, finally, collapsing in the squishy depression carved out of the bottom of yet another cliff that he deemed safe.

TWENTY-FOUR

Wednesday, August 20

The ground was covered with pine needles. Whatever was beneath the needles was spongy, soft. Maddie preferred to think that it was grass. Or moss. Yes, moss. Velvety green moss as thick as a mattress.

And if it wasn't moss, she didn't want to know.

She flopped down on her back, closed her eyes, and breathed. The scent of pine combined with a tinge of earthy dampness from the *moss* filled her nostrils. The pine needles slithered beneath her outstretched arms. After a moment, she opened her eyes, inhaled, and found herself looking up into a whole heaven's worth of stars. They were sprinkled like glitter across the satin midnight sky, twinkling down at her. The moon wasn't visible— what she was seeing was basically a cutout circle of sky framed by jagged-edged cliffs—but it wasn't needed. The universe wheeled above her, perfect and whole.

"Sam," she breathed, forgetting that they had issues in her eagerness to share the vision overhead.

No answer. She cut her eyes around their little hideaway, which basically looked like a giant had taken a bite out of the base of a rocky cliff. No Sam. Groaning, she sat up and took a better look around. The space wasn't that big, a semicircle maybe ten feet deep by eight feet wide at its widest point. Certainly not big enough to conceal a full-grown man, even in the dark.

Maddie looked carefully around at the rock walls one more time, and reached the inescapable conclusion: Sam was not there. Neither, now that she thought about it, was Zelda.

Panic was starting to feel like her natural state.

Clambering to her feet, she took a couple steps forward and stopped. What was she going to do? Hunting around a dark forest populated by night-vision-goggle–wearing mobsters who wanted to do her harm was clearly not a good idea. Likewise, yelling was out.

Sam came around the edge of the opening just then, making Maddie jump. He was carrying a small bundle under one arm, and Zelda trailed him wearily.

"You scared the life out of me," she said through her teeth. The fact that she was whispering did not in any way take away from the vehemence of her tone. "Where did you go?"

"I backtracked a little. I thought that was an old campsite we passed back there, and sure enough, it was. Look, we hit the mother lode. A blanket"— he held up a tattered scrap of cloth about the size of a beach towel—"and a jacket"—it looked like a man's long-abandoned windbreaker, and Maddie thought that she'd have to be naked in Siberia before she wore it—"and a can. I even filled it at the creek and brought you back some water. You've got blood on your face, and I thought you might want to wash it off before you start attracting bears. They're drawn to the smell of blood, you know."

Maddie's eyes widened as she took what looked and felt like a battered tin can out of his hand. "You're kidding."

With the sky open above them, there was just enough light to see him smile.

"Maybe about the bears. Not about the blood on your face. You've got a tiny little cut just . . . here." He reached out a forefinger to feather a touch across her cheekbone just below her eye, almost exactly as he'd done once before.

And her heart skipped a beat.

Stupid.

"Thank you," she almost growled at him, backing away with the can. "And you've got blood on your face, too, by the way."

"Not anymore. I washed it off in the creek."

"Oh. Well. It's too dark to tell."

Maddie retreated with the can to the edge of the enclosure so that she wouldn't get their mossy carpet wet, then rinsed her face, her neck, her hands. The cool water felt so good to her poor, abused finger that she let it soak inside the can for several long moments. When she pulled it out at last, though, it throbbed even worse than it had before, as if somehow she'd woken sleeping nerve endings. Grimacing, she dried it on the hem of her shirt, and then used what was left of the water in the can on her feet. Her poor bruised and tender feet that, wet, picked up dozens of pine needles when, having finished her impromptu bath and abandoning the can, she tromped back toward Sam. He was sitting at the very back of their little dugout with his back leaning against the wall, one knee bent and Zelda in fur-rug mode at his side.

"Feel better?" he asked as she sat down, not too close, on his other side.

"A little." She leaned her head back against the rock and looked up at the stars. Squinting, she thought she could just make out part of the Little Dipper.

"Sam?"

"Hmm?"

She looked sideways at him. His head was turned her way, and he met her gaze. Glinting black eyes in the dark . . .

At the memories that image conjured up, her body tightened somewhere deep inside.

"Do you think we're safe here?"

He made a face. "As safe as it's possible to be under the circumstances.

Unless they stumble across us by accident, they're not going to find us. Night-vision goggles can't see through rock. And if they should try using heat-seeking devices, the rocks will block those, too."

"Heat-seeking devices? Do you think they have those?" Maddie never would have thought of that. It was scary to think that on her own, she would still be stumbling around through the woods, vulnerable to detection by devices that had never even crossed her mind.

"Hey, the world's gone high-tech."

There was a pause in which Maddie stared up at the stars and contemplated that.

"I think you saved my life a couple of times today. Thank you."

"Just doing my job," he said with no inflection at all.

There it was, then. Her answer. For him, there was no going back to what they'd had. She might as well face it: As she had known it would, the truth had changed everything.

"Yes, I know," she said, looking back up at the stars while her throat ached with what felt uncomfortably like unshed tears. "But thanks."

Out of the corner of her eye, she saw his head turn toward her again.

"Anyway, I owe you, too. You could have left me cuffed to the bumper of that truck," he said.

A quick smile trembled around the edges of her mouth. "Not if I wanted to drive it."

"There's that."

He was smiling, too, faintly. Maddie felt another sharp pang in the region of her heart. The truth had changed everything—except the connection they still seemed to have. There was an easiness, a comfortableness, a *friendship* between them. That was going to be almost harder to lose than the rest.

"Sam . . ." She didn't know what she meant to say. Something, anything, to make it all better. Even knowing that there was nothing that could make it all better. Nothing that could take her past away.

He cut her off. "Look, why don't you try to sleep a little? As soon as the sun's up, we've got to get moving. Here, take the blanket, take the jacket, make a bed."

She accepted the items he produced from the shadows behind Zelda and held out to her, then hesitated. "What about you?"

"Darlin', I'm an FBI agent. Going without sleep is what us agents do."

The *darlin'* got her, and the joking tone got her. Her throat closed up. She wanted to laugh. She wanted to cry. She wanted to turn back time. She wanted to scoot over next to him and wrap her arms around his neck and rest her head on his chest and have him hold her. She wanted . . .

. . . what she couldn't have.

So she shook the blanket and spread it out not far from him, then shook the jacket, too, and rolled it into a pillow. Trying not to think about how filthy the items probably were and what they might have been used for in the past, she lay down on her makeshift bed, then turned onto her side so that her back was toward him, closed her eyes, and tried to sleep. It was almost certainly after midnight, she calculated, although it was hard to judge precisely how long it had been since the truck had run off the road. Her body ached from head to toe. If she had to pick the thing that pained her most, though, it would have to be her poor pinkie. Having been awakened by the water, it didn't seem to want to return to its former seminumb state. Cradling her injured hand close to her chest, she had an instant mental picture of Fish slamming the hammer down onto it and shivered.

Don't think about it, she told herself. Then her thoughts skittered to Sam, and that wasn't sleep-inducing, either, so she deliberately tried to empty her mind. Immediately, the sounds of the night seemed to increase tenfold. She could hear every whir, squeak, and hoot. She could hear the whisper of a breeze blowing over the top of the cliffs, although she couldn't feel it down in her cozy nest. She could hear the rumble of the nearby creek. She could hear the soft rattle of Zelda's snores.

She was counting them when she fell asleep.

Sometime later, the dream came.

Once again she was lying on that small, narrow bed in that house that wasn't hers, bound hands and feet, shaking with terror. The dark silhouette of a man watched her from the doorway.

He was going to kill her . . .

"Maddie! Jesus, Maddie!"

She came awake to the sound of Sam's voice, to the feel of his hand pressing down over her mouth, to the sight of his face looming over hers. Her eyes opened wide, but it was a moment before she registered more than just those facts. Then she saw the starry sky high above his head, and smelled the scent of pine, and felt the coarse blanket beneath her aching body. And she remembered where she was, and what had happened.

No wonder she'd had the dream.

"Maddie? Jesus, what was that?"

Sam removed his hand from her mouth cautiously, and she saw that his face was hard and anxious, and his eyes were worried. She was flat on her back now, and he was lying on his side beside her, propped on an elbow, his hand still hovering above her mouth.

"Did I . . . yell?" Maddie couldn't help it. Her voice quavered.

"Screamed is more like it."

"Oh, God." She closed her eyes. She was shaking all over, she realized, still terrified, as she always was in the aftermath of the dream—and terrified, too, that she might have given them away. "Do you think anybody heard?"

He shook his head. "Not unless they're so close they're about to find us anyway. Not much can get past these rocks."

Thank God for the rocks. Maddie closed her eyes and tried to stop shaking. Tried to push the nightmare images from her mind.

"Bad dream?"

She nodded. His hand slid down her arm, paused halfway.

"You're trembling."

"It's a *really* bad dream." She got the words out with an effort. But she couldn't make the trembling go away.

"About what happened today?"

"N-no. I get it—sometimes. It's about—my—about something that happened in the past."

She could feel tears leaking out past her eyelids. She could no more stop
them than she could stop the trembling.

"Shit." He must have seen, because his arms came around her, and he
pulled her against him, stretching out at full length on the blanket beside her
and settling her so that her head rested on his shoulder and her hand with
its poor, injured pinkie lay atop his chest. He sounded almost resigned. "All
right, darlin'. Talk to me."

"Sam . . ." His tone registered. He was talking to Maddie-with-a-past, and
the knowledge hurt so much that she could hardly bear it. Her eyes opened,
and she took a deep, shaking breath. Tears were sliding down her cheeks
without her being able to do anything about it, and she blinked and
sniffed, and wiped her eyes. "It's a bad dream, okay? I get it sometimes. No
big deal."

"Looks like it." His tone was skeptical. Then he sighed. "We were going
to have this conversation in a few days, when we were safe out of this mess
and emotions had had time to cool down. But you're having nightmares and
crying, and I've got nothing but time. So talk to me. You don't want to tell
me about your dream, fine. Tell me about your past. You said your father
was in the mob."

Maddie shook her head and sniffed again. "I said he used to do jobs for
the mob."

"There's a difference?"

She nodded. The tears had slowed to a trickle now. Soon, she knew,
they'd stop entirely. "My dad hated the mob. He hated what they made him
do. He just . . . couldn't help himself."

"What do you mean, he couldn't help himself?"

Maddie glanced up at him, slightly surprised to find his face so close. He
smelled of creek water, a little, and of fresh air and himself, and he felt
warm and solid and very male against her. The starlight touched on his
eyes, making them gleam. Her eyes slid over his lean, bronzed cheeks, his

banged-up nose, his square, unshaven chin. His wide shoulder seemed made to pillow her head, and she could feel the gentle rise and fall of his chest beneath her hand. Being held like this in his arms felt so good, so right, that she didn't even want to move away although she knew, in the interest of salvaging what she could of her poor, battered heart, that she should. Instead, she gave a little sigh of surrender. For better or worse, she was going to bare her soul to him. It was up to him to make of the truth what he would.

"My dad—Charles, his name was Charles Dolan—was a gambler." The faintest of smiles touched her mouth. "A very bad gambler. He always lost. Way more than he—*we*—had."

"He's dead?"

She nodded. Her throat threatened to close up.

"What about your mother?"

That was easier. "She died when I was two. I don't even really remember her. My dad kept a few pictures, and when I think about her, one of those pictures is what I see."

"Brothers and sisters?"

Maddie shook her head. "Just me and my dad. It was always just me and my dad."

"So, tell me about him. You said he was a gambler."

"When I was a little girl, he had a job. He worked for a car lot in Baltimore. He didn't make a lot, but we had a nice apartment and groceries and the whole bit. But he gambled, all the time. On everything. I found out later that when he lost, he'd do something to get the money. Skim parts from the dealership he worked for, or break into a bunch of cars and steal stuff out of them and sell it, or something. Eventually he lost his job, of course, and that's when we started moving around, from apartment to apartment, mostly in Baltimore, sometimes in D.C. He'd work at whatever he could find, and I'd go to school wherever we were. When I was fourteen, I lied about my age and got a job as a checkout clerk in a Walgreens after school. It didn't pay much, but we were living in a cheap little apartment, and what I made each month would just about barely cover the rent. I usually managed to catch my dad whenever he got paid to get enough for groceries and the utility bill, so we didn't go hungry or anything. I thought we were doing all right. Not fantastic, not even real good, but all right. But he was gambling. I didn't know how much he was gambling."

"It's a sickness with some people," Sam murmured. His arm was sliding up and down her arm, just barely, offering wordless comfort, she thought.

"It was a sickness with him," Maddie confirmed. "He was a great guy except for that one thing."

"So how did he start doing jobs for the mob?"

Maddie drew a breath. "It was the gambling. He made a big bet and he lost. He borrowed money from a loan shark to cover it, and then he couldn't pay. I didn't know anything about it until one night these two guys beat my dad up in the parking lot of our apartment building. It was summer. I had just graduated from high school, and I was working full-time. I got home from work and saw my dad on the ground and these two guys just pounding on him and kicking him. He was a big guy, strong, and he just lay there and covered up his head and let them do it. I started screaming and ran over there to help him, and they just stopped and got into a car and drove off. And . . . and one of them yelled out his window that I should tell my dad that he ought to pay his debts or next time he was going to wind up dead."

"Shit," Sam said, and the hand that had been moving on her arm stilled. Glancing up at him, she could see that his eyes had narrowed and his jaw was hard. "You give any thought to going to the police?"

"That's your answer for everything, isn't it? The police," Maddie said with gentle scorn. "Actually, at the time, I wanted to call the police, but Dad wouldn't let me. He said if I did, they'd kill him. So I didn't. But he was hurt and shaken up, and he told me about the loan shark. It was so much money. I knew it would take us years to pay it off, if we ever could. So the next day I went to the loan shark—it was this one guy, John Silva, who had a business called Paycheck Loans—to see if we couldn't set up a payment plan or something."

"Why am I not surprised at that?" Sam asked into the air, closing his eyes. Then he looked back down at her. "So what did the loan shark say?"

"He wasn't a bad guy," Maddie said defensively. "At least, I didn't think so then. He laughed. He said he didn't do payment plans, but if I wanted to work for his company and try to pay it off, that would be okay. And he said he'd give my dad some jobs that he could do to pay it off, too."

She felt him take a breath.

"Let me guess: You and your dad both started working for the loan shark, and your dad kept gambling and getting in deeper."

"Yeah." Maddie's tone was rueful. "Dad just couldn't get out from under it, and Mr. Silva started loaning him to other people, mob people, to do things—bad things, I found out later . . . and then . . . and then . . ."

"And then what?" Sam prompted when Maddie's voice trailed off.

"Then these two FBI agents started sniffing around Paycheck Loans." Her voice was flat. " 'Course, I didn't know what they were at first. They were undercover."

"Ahh." The drawn-out syllable signified that light had dawned. "Go on."

"But one day one of them came by the apartment when I was there by myself and told me that he was an FBI agent. He told me my dad was involved in illegal activities, and if I didn't want to see him arrested and put away for a long time, I had to get some information from Mr. Silva's files for them."

"Shit," Sam said, and the arms around her tightened. A beat passed, in which he seemed to be thinking about something. "You wouldn't have happened to have caught their names, would you?"

"One went by Ken Welsh and the other by Richard Shelton, but I'm almost positive those weren't their real names."

"Probably not, if they were running an undercover operation," Sam conceded. "So then you were on a slippery slope, *hmm?*"

Maddie nodded. "They kept wanting me to do more for them. They kept coming back for more, threatening me as well as my dad with going to jail if I didn't do what they wanted. Then . . . then my dad got into something way over his head. He . . . he went out on a collection job that turned into a murder. He came home and broke down, just cried all over me and told me everything. The guy was someone he knew, a man named Ted Cicero, and he said he just had to stand there and watch the guy he was with whack him."

"So, what did you do?" Sam asked.

"I was scared. I was scared for me, and I was scared for my dad. So I did what I thought was the one thing that might get us out of the whole thing for good. I went to Ken Welsh and Richard Shelton and told them everything." She sucked in air. "Instead of helping me, though, they used what I told them for leverage. They wanted my dad to start wearing a wire for them. He wouldn't do it. So they arrested me and charged me with all that stuff, and told my dad the charges would be dropped if he cooperated. So he did. He wore a wire on a couple of jobs. And they found it on him."

"Oh, Jesus." Sam closed his eyes, then opened them again and looked down at her. "Was it bad?"

Maddie nodded. There was a constriction in her chest now that made it hard to breathe. This was the part that hurt to remember. This was the stuff of the nightmare that had haunted her for seven years.

"They grabbed me in the parking lot, and tied me up and took me to this little shotgun house not that far from our apartment. Mr. Silva was there, and three men I didn't know, and my dad. They had my dad tied to a kitchen chair. He was beaten up real bad. They took me over to stand in front of him and told him they were going to kill me in front of him and make him watch and then kill him. And my dad started crying."

Maddie's voice broke.

"Then they took me into a bedroom, and threw me on a bed, and tied me there. And . . . and I had to listen while they beat up my dad some more. I could hear them talking, and one guy—this one guy with this really oily black hair and a big, swoopy mustache—kept coming to the bedroom door and l-looking at me. Oh, God, I was so scared he was going to come in and get me, because I knew when he did it would be because he was going to kill me, and then kill my dad. I kept praying he wouldn't come in, but finally he did." She paused, took a deep, shuddering breath, and continued, almost oblivious now to the tension in Sam's body, or the hard arms around her, or his hand stroking her arm. "They untied my feet and took me into the living room. Ken Welsh was there. I was really surprised to see him. I was just so thankful, though, I thought we were saved, I thought it was all over, so I didn't really think it through. But he just looked at me and kind of smirked as this guy dragged me on past him, and then I saw that Mr. Silva was showing him some money, a briefcase filled with money. Then Ken Welsh took the money and left. He just left us there, my dad and I. To die."

"They paid him off," Sam said softly, his hand stilled, his arms like steel bands around her now. "They paid him off to leave them alone."

Maddie nodded. That was the conclusion she'd come to, too, over the years. God, she hated to remember. Her heart was racing. Her stomach was in knots. She was starting to tremble. Maybe she should just stop there. Maybe that was enough . . .

"Okay." Sam's mouth was grim. "I know this is hard for you, but I need to hear it. What happened to you and your dad?"

Maddie took a deep breath. He wanted to know. She wanted him to know. She wanted him to hear the full, complete truth. So she gathered up every last scrap of inner strength she had, and went ahead.

"They stood me in front of him and the guy with the mustache put a gun to my head." She spoke rapidly, trying to get it all out as quickly as she could. "I thought I was going to die right that minute. But this other guy said—I can still hear him saying it—'Wait a minute. Why just shoot her? Hell, let's have some fun with her first.' And he dragged me back off toward the bedroom. I looked back over my shoulder and saw them put a gun to my dad's head. Then I couldn't see anymore because I was inside the bedroom, but I heard a shot. And a . . . a kind of . . . gurgle."

Her eyes closed, and more tears leaked out. Sam cursed and turned onto his side, wrapping both arms around her. Her head was pillowed on his arm, and she clutched the front of his shirt and hung on for dear life.

"Tell me the rest, baby." His voice was impossibly gentle.

She wanted to, but she could hardly speak. Her voice was a poor broken thing, but she managed to force the words out.

"I knew they shot him. I knew it. I just . . . went crazy. The guy was try-ing to k-kiss me and I bit his tongue. Savagely. Just as hard as I could. He screamed and threw me away from him so hard that I crashed partway through the window. Then he started coming toward me and blood was pouring out of his mouth and I just kind of threw myself at the broken win-dow, trying to smash through it, trying to get out. And the house blew up. Just like that. And somehow I was thrown out through the window, thrown clear. And . . . and I lay there in that overgrown backyard, bleeding and cry-ing and w-watching as that little one-story house turned into a blowtorch in about the blink of an eye. There was no way anyone who was in there lived. My dad—even if they didn't shoot him, he was gone."

Even after all these years, the scene was as vivid in her mind as if it were happening in front of her. Tears poured from her eyes.

"I'm sorry. So sorry, baby," Sam whispered, rocking her against him.

The pain was so intense that she couldn't speak. She closed her eyes, shaking, holding on to him as if he were the only solid thing in an insane world. She felt his mouth against her temple, then against her cheeks, which were wet with tears. Then he lifted her poor, injured hand and pressed first the palm and then, very gently, the injured pinkie to his mouth.

"Sam," she whispered, opening her eyes to watch this touch of his mouth on her hand through a veil of tears. He put her hand back gently against his chest, then bent his head to kiss her mouth.

TWENTY-FIVE

His arms around her were warm and hard; his body was firm and muscular; his mouth was wet and hot. And he was Sam.

Sam. Sam. Sam. Sam.

She discovered that she was saying it aloud, that she was whispering his name against his skin as he lifted his mouth from hers to press comforting little kisses against her cheeks, against her ear, along the line of her jaw. His bristly cheek brushed over the softness of her skin, and she loved the prickly abrasion of it; his hands stroked her shoulders, her arms, her back, and she loved the size and warmth of them; she pressed her mouth to his neck, and loved the salt-tinged flavor of his skin.

"Don't cry, baby; it's all over. It was a long time ago. Everything's going to be all right now." He was murmuring to her between kisses—soft, disjointed phrases that she only partly heard—offering what comfort he could.

"Sam," she whispered against his neck, because it seemed to be the only thing she could say.

"I've got you safe," she heard, and that almost made her smile despite the tears that were still sliding down her face because they were so very far from safe, and she knew it, and he knew it, and still, with him holding her, she *felt* safe, which was stupid.

Stupid.

"I love you, Sam," she said clearly, because she did and there was just no doing anything about it. He lifted his head and looked down at her, the dark, hard lines of his face faintly silvered, his eyes gleaming black and hot in the starlight, and her heart swelled and throbbed and ached, and she knew that what she'd just said was true, that she loved him, that somehow, amidst terror and danger and heartbreak, she'd found the man who was supposed to be hers.

And she didn't care if it was stupid.

"I love you, too, whoever you are," he whispered against her mouth, and because it was just exactly what she wanted to hear yet sounded so absurd, she was smiling a little when his lips slanted over hers. She noticed that he was smiling, too, with those dimples just visible for an instant, and realized that he'd said it that way precisely to make her smile, before she closed her eyes and forgot everything except that he was kissing her.

Her hands slid up under his shirt and flattened on the warmth of his skin. She felt the softness of his chest hair, the wide firmness of the muscles beneath, the quick, hard beating of his heart. And she wanted him. Wanted him with a desperateness that was quite outside her experience, with a deep, primal need that tightened her loins and made her breasts swell against his chest, with a life-affirming urge that had her reaching for him, stroking over the hard bulge at the front of his jeans as his hand flattened hard over her breast. She needed this, she needed Sam. She needed to feel warm again. She needed to block out the memories. She needed to feel *alive*.

"Sam," she breathed, her blood heating to scalding as she pressed close against that big, warm hand.

"Maddie," he answered in a deep, guttural voice, and ran his lips down her neck. His hands went beneath her tank top, pushing it up out of his way, and his mouth was on her breast, burning her through the thin white lace of her bra, and she gasped at the goodness of it, the rightness of it, the wonder of it. Then he released the clasp of her bra and pushed the flimsy thing out of his way and opened his mouth over her nipple, stroking his tongue over it, making it quiver and tighten and ache.

"Make love to me," she whispered, her fingers curling around his waistband and then quite forgetting their mission as his lips slid across her body. His tongue branded her, leaving a trail of fire as it licked its way up the slope of her other breast. Then she arched up into the heat of his mouth as it claimed her nipple, and cried out.

"You are so beautiful you take my breath away." He lifted his head, pulled her tank top and bra off, and then, as she lay bared to the waist with the starlight playing over her, just looked down at her for a moment, devouring her with his eyes. "Let's get you naked."

"And you," she said, her heart pounding, her body tightening and aching and burning. Then she remembered what she had been doing before and reached for his zipper again. "I want you naked, too."

"Oh, yeah," he said. "That was the plan."

But she was naked first, because he peeled her pants and underwear off before she could even get a good grip on that damned hard-to-manipulate button that always seemed to fasten jeans. But that was okay, because he took care of the problem himself, stripping off his clothes like a man in a hurry to get down to business until, for an instant, he stood naked in the starlight.

His hair shone blacker than the night, and his face was hidden in shadow. But she could see the muscled breadth of his shoulders, the classic V of his torso, the lean hips, the long, powerful legs.

And what was between them.

She stared, and felt the urgent tightening in her loins pulse hotter and faster. She wanted him. God, she wanted him.

But first . . .

She sat up, then curled up onto her knees and took him in her mouth, her hands sliding around to caress the tight, round curves of his butt. He froze for, perhaps, the space of a heartbeat. Then he groaned and buried his fingers in her hair, and said "Maddie" in a voice that sounded like it was killing him to talk at all.

Finally he said "damn" and pulled away. Before Maddie had time to do more than open her eyes, he was pushing her back and coming down on top of her and thrusting inside her and taking her so hard and fast and urgently that she could do nothing but wrap her arms and legs around him and hold on for the ride. He made love to her until the air around them turned to steam, until she was mindless with passion, writhing with it, needing . . .

"Oh, God, *Sam*," she gasped, unable to bear it any longer, her body peaking and breaking and going into hard, tight convulsions that he must have felt, because his arms clenched around her and he came into her with deep, fierce thrusts that carried her right over the edge, that carried her to some blissful nirvana that she had never before even imagined existed, that caused the starry night sky to burst in all its glorious profusion around her even though her eyes were firmly closed.

"Maddie," he groaned, and held himself inside her, and came.

"I UNDERSTAND I'm your type," Maddie said a long time later. Sam was lying flat on his back, listening to the dog snore and the creek run and the insects canoodle, and she was sprawled naked on top of him, playing with his chest hair.

"What type is that?" Sam asked, glancing down at her. He had been staring up at the star-sprinkled night sky, not really seeing it because there was too much else on his mind, from the firm, warm curves of the woman on top of him, to the possible whereabouts of the hunting party that was almost certainly still combing the woods for them, to the tantalizing knowledge that, thanks to Maddie's story, he now had the key to the identity of the sick bastard he'd been chasing for the past month.

The problem was, he just didn't know which door the key unlocked yet.

"Slim, pretty brunettes. Sweet little wholesome girls." She sounded like she was quoting from memory. She also didn't sound really happy about it.

Sam considered that for a moment. She had her chin resting on her hand now, looking at him seriously. As dark as it was, he couldn't see the things that made his gut clench, like the small cut on her cheek or the red, swollen tip of her little finger. All he could see was the dark cloud of hair around her lovely, luminous face, and her eyes—those big, honey-colored eyes— gleaming at him.

"You're kidding me, right?" he asked. Then, realizing where she must have heard it, he added in a resigned tone, "You've been talking to Gardner, haven't you?"

Her eyes narrowed a little. "Maybe." A beat. "So, am I your type?"

This, Sam felt, was a loaded question. One of those damned-if-you-do, damned-if-you-don't conundrums beloved by women worldwide that, fortunately, he didn't have to think his way out of on this occasion, because the truth was so irrefutably obvious.

"I hate to break this to you, but if that's my type, you must be shit out of luck."

"What's that supposed to mean?" She sounded all huffy now. For some kind of masochistic reason that he'd have to puzzle out at some other time, he loved it when she got huffy. Besides the obvious, of course, that's what had attracted him to her from the very beginning, he realized. Forget "lie down and die." When backed into a corner, this babe was full of fight.

"Okay, you're a slim, pretty brunette, I'll grant you that. A sweet little wholesome girl? You may be stretching it there, but that's nothing I'd want to claim anyway. You leave it at that, and half the female population of the country's probably my type. But you—you're something special. You're gorgeous and sexy and smart—and no matter how hairy things get, you never say die. You got balls, babe. You're one of a kind."

A beat passed.

"That's a compliment, right?" Maddie asked, eyeing him with a trace of suspicion.

"Yeah," Sam said. "It is."

"Sort of a clumsy, masculine way of saying you love me, right?"

"Absolutely." Sam grinned, and rolled with her so that she was on her back and he was looming over her. "Darlin', in case you haven't realized it yet, you pretty much had me the first time you scowled at me."

"Oh, yeah?"

"Yeah."

She was smiling up at him, and her cool, smooth hands were sliding up his arms, and he remembered, suddenly, fiercely, the explosive spurt of murderous rage he'd felt when that thug had brought the hammer down on her delicate little finger. That's when he'd first begun to suspect that, no matter how furious and betrayed and suspicious of her motives he'd felt, the feelings he had for her were not just going to go away. He'd known then that he was in love—for better, worse, good solid citizen or criminal—even if he didn't much like it. He'd still been hooked, even when he'd thought the worst. When he heard her story, though, heard the hell she'd suffered through, and the abuse and the pain, only to emerge triumphant on the other side, even if she might not quite be legally in the right, he'd been hit by a combination of tenderness and protectiveness and pride and fury on her behalf that had been like a lightning bolt striking deep into his soul.

His grandma had always told him that he would know it when it happened, and, as annoying as it was, she was once again proved absolutely right: He had recognized it right then. What he felt for Maddie was a forever kind of thing.

He wasn't quite sappy enough to put all that into words, but the way he chose to express himself was more fun anyway.

He kissed her. Then he showed her.

MADDIE ONLY realized that she had fallen asleep when someone shook her awake. For a moment she was disoriented, not quite understanding who it could be or where she was.

"Maddie," a voice said from somewhere not too far above her ear.

"Go away." It couldn't be time to get up yet, she didn't have to be at work until eight, or, actually, since it was her company, whenever she wanted to get there, and . . .

"Maddie." The hand on her shoulder shook her again. Her eyes opened.

Sam was leaning over her, looking more disreputable than ever as he hunkered down, fully dressed, beside her. There was a swollen bump on the bridge of his nose that hadn't been there before, he needed a shave badly, and he looked tired as hell. She blinked sleepily up at him, felt her heart swell with joy—and then saw the purplish-gray sky behind him, dotted with only a few stars now, and remembered with a flash of dismay where they were and what had happened. Dawn was at hand. In this case, that was definitely not good news.

"Oh, God," she groaned, lifting a throbbing hand to her aching head, and sat up.

Sam grinned at her, or maybe smirked was a better word, in an annoying, masculine way that let her know that she was naked and he was enjoying the view. Beside him sat Zelda, looking just about as disheveled and full of get-up-and-go as Maddie felt.

"We need to be making tracks, beautiful."

That earned him a scowl. She didn't feel beautiful. Heck, she didn't even feel human. And she had certain personal needs that absolutely did not require his presence.

"Don't you have somewhere else you need to be for a few minutes?" She was careful to add "for a few minutes" to that, because the thought of him disappearing for any longer was enough to give her palpitations.

"I brought you more water. It's right there." He nodded at the can before giving her another of those all-seeing looks and then leaving her to her own devices.

Zelda tottered over to the can and started lapping.

"Great," Maddie said, watching dispiritedly. When Zelda had drunk her fill, she turned and looked at Maddie and whined.

"No food. Sorry." Maddie held out her empty hands to demonstrate, and Zelda looked disappointed. She flopped down on her belly again, and watched with a moody expression as Maddie washed and dressed in the water the dog left and did what she needed to do.

Sam came back just as she was starting to worry about him. He was carrying a stout stick a little longer than and about the thickness of a baseball bat. It was, Maddie realized with dismay, their only weapon.

"Here," he said, handing her something. It took her a minute, but she realized that they were his socks.

"You can't go running around barefoot," he said impatiently as she looked at the big, semiwhite things with mild revulsion. "Your feet are already all scratched up. I'd give you my shoes, but they'd fall off your feet."

A glance down at what looked like his size-twelves confirmed that. With a sigh, Maddie surrendered the last of her hygiene standards.

"Did you see anything?" she asked as she pulled the socks on. Now that they were about to leave their little hidey-hole, she felt scared all over again.

He shook his head.

"You don't think we should just stay here, do you?" she asked in a small voice as she finished pulling on the socks and stood up. "They haven't found us yet."

"They will eventually."

That was so chilling that Maddie shivered. Sam saw, dropped a quick, hard kiss on her mouth and another, gentler, one on her injured hand, then headed out around the edge of the enclosure. With Zelda trailing forlornly behind her, Maddie hurried to keep up with him.

"Tell me we've got some kind of plan," she said as they skirted the base of the cliffs. It was still dark, but dawn was definitely coming. The birds were starting to call to one another. The creek tinkled merrily alongside them. Zelda munched on trash she'd found along the creek bed. There was happiness in the world, Maddie reflected. At the moment, however, she just wasn't feeling it.

Sam grinned at her, but he must have realized that she was too scared and tired and achy for humor, because he gave her a straight answer.

"The house they took us to yesterday was on the east side of the mountain. The driveway led downhill. We're still on the east side of the same mountain, so I'm guessing that if we go far enough downhill, we'll find a road. We can follow it out, or hitchhike, which is a little dicey because we don't know who'll stop. Our best bet, probably, is to find a phone. If there was one house up here, there are bound to be more. And there's always the chance that the cavalry will show up. Believe me, they're busting their asses right now to find us."

What he didn't add, but Maddie knew, was that finding them would be like looking for a needle in a haystack. No matter how optimistically she tried to look at it, she didn't think waiting to be rescued was going to work.

They followed the creek downstream as the sky lightened gradually above them, walking until the cliffs were a distant memory and they were once again in the heart of the piney woods. It was still dark under the trees, but more of a thick gray now than a pitch black. The air smelled of pine and dampness. The humidity was tangible. It was almost as if the ground itself was sweating. Mist hung beneath the trees like fog, making it impossible to see farther than a few feet in every direction. The footing was slippery and treacherous, especially for Maddie in her socks. The sounds of the forest were all around them, but if there were any other humans within shouting distance, Maddie couldn't tell it. Conversely, this made her jittery. Goose bumps crept over her skin. She kept glancing nervously all around, and every crack of a twig or unexpected sound made her jump.

It was eerie being there among the trees in the foggy gray hush of dawn. Especially knowing as well as she did that a shot could come out of nowhere at any time, or that behind any given bush, or hidden within any shadowy clump of trees, someone could be waiting . . .

When Sam stopped, it was so unexpected that she nearly bumped into him.

"What?" she whispered, her heart pounding as she peered around him.

"Bingo," he said, his voice low, too. "If we're lucky, we'll be back at your place in time for breakfast."

Then she saw it. A small log cabin stood on a slight rise in front of them, its shingled roof rising above the mist. The trees had been cleared around it, and a narrow dirt track led up past it to a shed or barn or garage. Maddie's heart gave a great, hopeful leap . . .

But what if they weren't lucky? Maddie had a sudden vision of Hansel and Gretel, and the witch's gingerbread house.

"What if whoever lives there is a bad guy?" Maddie asked, still surveying the house doubtfully from the shelter of Sam's back.

"Then we've got trouble," Sam said, way more cheerfully than the situation called for. "See the lines leading to the house? There's a phone in there. You wait here, and I'll go summon the cavalry."

"Not in this life." Maddie grabbed his arm, alarm in every syllable. "No way am I staying here alone. If you go, I go."

He looked around at her. What he saw in her face must have persuaded him that she meant what she said, because he sighed.

"Will you at least promise me that if there's trouble, you'll run for it and leave me to handle it?"

"Sure," Maddie said. "I promise."

Meaning she'd wait and evaluate the situation when and if it happened. But right at that moment, the chance of her abandoning him was looking like it was somewhere between slim and none.

Sam looked at Zelda, who was drooping like a wilted flower.

"Could we at least leave the dog tied to a tree?" Sam asked.

"She'll bark. Anyway, if they find her, they'll kill her. You heard what they said."

"I feel like I'm leading a parade," Sam said. "All right, come on."

They had just started walking again when a sharp *craaak* pierced the charcoal-gray dawn. And something smacked hard into the trunk of a pine not six inches from Maddie's head.

TWENTY-SIX

S*hit!*" Sam yelled, grabbing her hand. "*Run!*"

Maddie didn't need him to tell her a second time. She bolted like a deer from hunters, head low, feet slipping and sliding on the pine needles underfoot. Head spinning, heart pounding, sure she was going to die at any second, she ran as though the hit man was on her heels.

Oh, wait, he was.

Craaak. Another bullet smacked a nearby tree, so close that she felt a blowback of splinters spray her cheek. Maddie almost screamed, but she choked the sound back just in time. It would only help the hit man take better aim. Having lost his stick, Sam pounded along beside her, head down, dodging and weaving among the trees, and somewhere, poor Zelda was lost in the gloom. Maddie had dropped the leash when she started running.

She said a heartfelt little prayer for Zelda—and for herself and Sam.

"Marino, they're to your left," a man's voice yelled. Maddie had just registered that his voice sounded fairly distant and that he was somewhere behind them and to the right when there was another sharp *craaak.*

A shower of pine needles rained over them. Maddie realized that once again their bullet had been heart-stoppingly close.

"Jesus," Sam said, and there was something in his voice that scared Maddie almost more than the bullets.

The charcoal silhouette of a man stepped out of the mist not thirty feet in front of them, a rifle at his shoulder pointed straight at them.

"Freeze!" he yelled.

"Keep going." Sam let go of her hand and pushed her hard to her right so that there was a little stand of trees between her and the shooter. Then, to her horror, he ran straight for the man, crouching low, barreling headlong through the trees. He'd made the choice for her. She could only go for it. Heart slamming, stomach churning, gasping for air and trying to watch Sam at the same time, she ran for her life.

"Over here, they're over here!" someone cried. That voice came from the right, too, and sounded closer than the first.

Craaak. The mouth of the rifle Sam was running toward blazed yellow through the fog. To her horror, Maddie realized that she could no longer see Sam.

Oh, God, is he hit? Maddie's heart gave a terrified lurch and her stomach dropped clear to her toes. There was no way to know, and nothing she could do. Except run. And pray.

Please, God, please . . .

Pulse pounding, sobbing for breath, running for her life, she heard what sounded like thudding footsteps nearby, but she couldn't be sure; it might have been the beating of her pulse against her eardrums, and the mist was so dense she couldn't see—and then another man stepped out of the trees directly ahead of her, so close that she almost smacked into him.

He lunged toward Maddie, and she screamed.

"Got her," he yelled as he grabbed her, catching her by her hair as she tried to dodge and yanking her back against him. With a single terrified glance she saw that it was Fish and that he had a rifle in his other hand. It was pointed toward the ground as he struggled with her. Heart hammering, breath rattling in her throat as though she was dying, she realized that this was her chance, maybe her only chance, to escape. Fueled by a burst of adrenaline, she whirled in his grip and slugged him in the nose as hard as she could.

She felt the impact all the way up her arm to her shoulder. The sound made her think of a melon hitting the floor and splitting open.

Fish howled and she tore free, leaving strands of hair behind in his fist. Almost falling to her knees, she recovered and scrambled away.

"Where? Where are they?" The cry, from multiple voices, echoed through the trees. As panicked as she was, Maddie thought that they came from all around her, everywhere. All she could see was mist and trees. All she could hear, besides the dying echo of the voices, was the frantic thudding of her own heart.

A flying tackle brought her down. It hit her in the small of the back, knocked the breath out of her, knocked her off her feet. She slammed to the ground, then skidded face-forward through the mulch on the forest floor. With a burst of stomach-twisting terror, she realized that it was Fish who was on top of her. She struggled wildly, her nails digging into the ground as she tried to fight her way free.

"You're dead now, bitch," Fish howled, straddling her, and slammed his fist hard into the back of her head. Maddie gasped and saw stars.

"Don't you fucking move," Sam said, in a deadly voice unlike anything Maddie had ever heard come out of his mouth. "Go on, give me an excuse to blow your head off. I want to."

For a moment she thought that she must be hallucinating, that the blow was causing her mind to play tricks on her, but Fish, though he still straddled her, went as still as if he'd been turned to stone.

"Get your hands in the air," Sam ordered, and Maddie felt Fish move and guessed that he had obeyed.

Shaking, breathing like she had been running for miles, she dared a glance around then and saw that her mind hadn't been playing tricks on her, that it was Sam who was standing not six feet away, mist swirling waist-deep around him, stalking closer with a rifle against his shoulder that was pointed at Fish's head. She felt a wave of thankfulness stronger than anything she had ever known because he was still alive, and a fresh wave of terror, too. Just because he was alive this minute didn't mean that in the next he might not be dead.

He'd come back for her. He'd saved her life by pushing her away from the shooter, then gone after him and wrested a rifle away from him and come back to save her again. . . .

And then she heard it, echoing through the forest like multiple blasts from a chorus of synchronized bugles.

"Federal Agents! Drop your weapons! Don't anybody move!"

The cavalry had arrived. They were saved.

She went limp with relief, letting her head fall back down to rest against the cool, damp mulch, breathing hard, heart still pounding as her body tried to absorb the news that the danger had passed.

"Get off her," Sam said to Fish, still in that deadly voice. "Maddie, are you okay?"

"Fine," she said, which was the truth because "fine" meant that she was alive and he was alive and it was all over and they would both live to see another day. Fish got off her, moving slowly and carefully, and she rolled onto her side, watching as Sam spread-eagled Fish against a tree and started patting him down. The rifle that Fish had apparently dropped when he dived after her now rested against a tree near Sam's side.

"McCabe! Maddie!" It was Wynne's voice, echoing out of the mist.

"Over here," Sam yelled while Maddie slowly, carefully sat up.

"You okay?" she asked.

"Fine." He grinned at her over his shoulder, faintly breathless, and Maddie felt her chest slowly expand, as if she could breathe again. It was over.

"Thank God," she said. "We're alive. We made it."

"You sound like you had doubts."

"Maybe just a few."

Sam grinned at her again. "Just for the record, me, too." He took something from Fish and stepped back, then, as Fish made a restive movement, Sam said to him in an entirely different tone, "You want to live, you don't move unless I tell you to move."

It was growing lighter under the trees now, and she could see that he was looking cheerful and pleased with himself and more lighthearted than she had ever seen him. Her heart gave a little lurch. It was over and they were both alive and she loved him. That was what was important. Actually, that was all that mattered.

But now the truth was out. She was going to have to deal with that.

There was general commotion in the surrounding area, voices and thuds and the clink of metal, the sound of many people moving through the trees.

Then Wynne materialized out of the mist.

"What took you?" Sam said to him, his eyes and the rifle still on Fish.

"Think finding this place was easy?" Wynne's eyes moved over Fish, then slid down to Maddie before returning to Sam. "You can thank Cynthia that we got here at all."

"Cynthia?" McCabe cast Wynne a sideways glance and then shouted for somebody to come and take Fish away. "What did *Cynthia* do?"

"I saved your ass, McCabe, that's what I did," Cynthia said, appearing through the mist along with another man whom Maddie didn't know but who was apparently another law-enforcement type, because he slapped cuffs on Fish and hustled him off.

Sam reached a hand down to Maddie, and she let him pull her to her feet. Wynne, meanwhile, was looking at Cynthia like a proud parent might look at a precocious child.

"Cynthia checked Maddie's . . . I mean, uh, Leslie Dolan's"—this was accompanied by a quick, almost covert glance at Maddie, who was by then leaning against Sam's side—"cell-phone records, and found that she'd placed a whole bunch of calls to a plastics company in Baltimore over the last few days. Turned out it was a front for a mob operation, and our guys at that end had been investigating them anyway. With what we told them, they had enough to run 'em in, and then they leaned on them until they gave

up Evergreen Waste and Disposal right back here in St. Louis. Seems the
Baltimore group had asked the Saint Louis group for a favor, and the Saint
Louis group had agreed to do it."

"What kind of favor?" Sam growled. They were walking by that time,
slowly, the four of them, moving through the mist toward the voices of the
other law-enforcement agents and the sounds that accompanied a gang of
thugs being rounded up and placed under arrest. Sam was holding the rifle
in one hand and had the other arm wrapped around Maddie's waist. Weak-
kneed and a little shaky as reaction set in, she had an arm around him, too,
and was leaning against him as they moved. Wynne and Gardner walked together on her other side, and kept shooting her little sideways glances. Maddie was too drained to care.

"Well, first they wanted, uh, *her* killed—best we can figure it, that's
when she got shot in her car—and then they changed that to kidnapped and
forced to hand over some evidence she's apparently been trying to black-
mail them with and *then* killed. The guy sneaking up her back stairs and
yesterday's snatch by the garbage truck were apparently part of the kid-
napping plan."

"What about the Carol Walter murder? And the others? We got a handle on the guy who did that, the one who attacked Maddie in her hotel
room?" Sam's tone was urgent. Maddie remembered that another victim had
already been designated, and shivered.

Gardner shook her head. "Nobody's jumped out at us in regards to that
yet," she said regretfully. "But then, we haven't been talking to them long."

"Okay." Sam's tone was absent, as if he was thinking about something.
"We need to keep after it. So what happened when you zeroed in on our
friendly neighborhood garbage company?"

"They folded." Wynne grinned reminiscently. "Once they knew we
were on to them, nobody at Evergreen wanted anything to do with the
murder of a federal agent. They couldn't tell us where they'd taken you fast
enough. Then, of course, we got out to that house where you'd been held—
that was about an hour ago—and nobody was there. But we found Maddie's—*uh, er* . . ."

"Maddie works," Sam said as Wynne hesitated over the name again. "I'll tell you the whole story later. But she's not a criminal."

"Good to know." Wynne shot Maddie a slightly less uneasy look.

"Yeah," Cynthia said, giving Maddie a little smile. "We like her. And looks like McCabe *looves* her."

"Shut up, Gardner," Sam said good-naturedly, and the arm around Maddie tightened fractionally.

"I like you, too," Maddie said to Gardner and Wynne.

Sam made an impatient sound. "Go on, Wynne. You found Maddie's . . . ?"

"Her jacket. And her vest. Kind of scared us, to tell you the truth. She'd been there—and we were pretty sure you were with her—but when we got there, she wasn't. That kind of thing is enough to give you cold chills."

"He was picturing you guys buried out in a field somewhere," Gardner said. "But then we found the wrecked truck, and that gave us something to go on. After that it was easy. A couple of helicopters, a few dozen heat-seeking devices"—Sam smirked at Maddie here—"half the law-enforcement officers in Missouri, and the thing was done."

"Of course, it helped a lot that they were shooting at you there at the end," Wynne added. "Made you kind of hard to miss."

"Yeah." Sam grinned. "I bet it did."

The mist was starting to thin now, and Maddie could see the man walking toward them quite clearly. It was Gomez. And at his feet trailed Zelda.

"Lose something?" Gomez called as he got closer.

"Zelda," Maddie said thankfully, accepting the proffered leash. She was ashamed to realize that she had forgotten about the little dog in the last few hectic minutes.

"You can have french fries when we get home," she told Zelda, who gave a feeble wag of her tail as if in acknowledgment.

"You guys didn't walk all the way here from the truck, did you?" Sam asked as Gomez fell in beside them.

"If you'd kept on going the way you were going, you would have hit a road in about another quarter-mile," Wynne said. "That's where we're parked. You almost ran right into us."

"Way to conduct an investigation," Sam said and grinned.

Sure enough, in another few minutes they emerged from the piney woods onto the narrow blacktop road that curled around the mountain. The sun was rising directly ahead of them now, painting the horizon in bold shapes of purple and red and gold. A fleet of marked police cruisers, unmarked cars, paddy wagons, and an ambulance were parked partly off the road, strobe lights flashing. Uniformed cops and plainclothes law-enforcement officers of various stripes herded miscreants into the backs of various vehicles. It looked like a cast of hundreds. Probably, Maddie thought, it was a little less.

Given the number of head blows she'd suffered, Sam insisted that she go to the hospital to be checked out, and Maddie didn't feel like arguing, so she agreed. She had half feared being arrested by him or someone else as soon as they were out of danger, but it didn't happen, and she started to relax a little. With Wynne driving, Gardner riding shotgun, and Zelda, pacified by a pit stop through a McDonald's drive-through, on her lap, Sam rode with her back to St. Louis, which was about half an hour away. On the way, he gave Wynne and Gardner the abbreviated version of Maddie's story, and told her that he was fairly certain that, given the circumstances, he could talk to the district attorney's office in Baltimore and get the charges dismissed. That left Maddie feeling a whole lot better than she had in a long time.

By the time Sam left her in the emergency room in favor of the urgent press of work, Maddie felt as though her life was moving in a more positive direction than it had for some time. Of course, the fact that Sam insisted that Gardner stay with her, and his warning that until they had positively identified the hit man, they couldn't be sure they had him, was a little daunting.

But still, Maddie realized, she was happier than she had been in years.

The whole staff of Creative Partners, agog, converged on her at the hospital. Maddie was relieved to discover that they knew no more of what had happened than that the man who'd been trying to kill her had made another failed attempt, and that he now seemed to be under arrest. The truth about her identity, the secret she'd kept for so long, was personal, and she didn't want to reveal it, even to these trusted friends, unless she had to. If it was possible, she wanted to remain the woman she had made herself into. Leslie Dolan was her past. Maddie Fitzgerald was her present, and her future.

With that in mind, she handed Zelda off to Louise with instructions to rush her right off to the groomer. And she sent Jon, who with true presence of mind had kept Susan Allen from learning anything at all about Maddie and Zelda going missing by hurrying her away from the factory as soon as he'd realized something was amiss, to babysit Susan for another day. And then she'd hugged the others, promised them that she was fine and would be back on the job without fail the next day, and sent them off to work. Finally, when the hospital had finished with her, she had headed home with Cynthia, taken a shower, eaten a meal, and fallen into her own clean, comfortable bed.

And slept like a log. No dreams at all.

Until she woke up to a dark apartment, and the feeling that something wasn't right.

TWENTY-SEVEN

Maddie sat up. It was ten-forty p.m., she saw with a glance at the bedside clock, and the apartment was dark because night had fallen while she'd slept. The flickering blue light from the living room told her that the TV was on. It was, apparently, the only light in the apartment. Now that she was fully awake, she could hear it. It wasn't quite as loud as she was accustomed to, because Cynthia was watching it rather than Sam. The thought made her smile a little. Sam would be there soon enough.

Swinging her legs out of bed, she got up and padded barefoot to the doorway. Since it had been the middle of the afternoon when she'd fallen asleep, she was wearing loose, gray sweatpants and a white T-shirt. No bra, but otherwise, she was fully dressed. Cynthia was sitting on the couch with her legs curled up beside her, watching something on TV. Unlike Sam or Wynne, she wasn't flipping channels. She, like most sane people, actually watched a program all the way through.

A glance around the room confirmed it: Everything was fine. That uneasy feeling that had awakened her was probably the result of the adventures she'd been having lately. Her mind, like her body, had clearly not yet fully recovered from the trauma.

She went into the bathroom, came back out, and stood for a moment beside the couch. Cynthia was watching QVC. Why that seemed funny, Maddie couldn't have said. She had already learned that Cynthia was far more feminine than she looked.

"How you feeling?" Cynthia asked.

"Hungry, but otherwise okay," Maddie said, although the list of her aches and pains was long. The pain pill she'd taken before falling into bed was supposed to be operational for another two hours. Maddie shuddered to think what she would feel like when it wore off.

"McCabe'll be here soon." Cynthia gave her a little smirking smile.

"I know."

"You guys make a cute couple."

Maddie paused en route to the kitchen to look Cynthia over searchingly. She was wearing stretchy black pants and a soft pink T-shirt, and her hair was softer looking than when Maddie had first met her.

"Do you mind?" Maddie asked.

"About you and McCabe?" Cynthia grimaced. "Nah. I decided that sexy hunks of burning love aren't my type."

"Really?" The description made Maddie grin. Sam would love it—*not*.

"Yeah. But you go for it, honey. I can see he really likes you. I've never seen him that lovey-dovey with anybody."

This thing she had with Sam—it was too new and too precious for her to easily talk about. It had to sink in for her first.

"I'm going to get something to eat. You want anything from the kitchen?" she asked.

Cynthia shook her head.

Maddie walked into the kitchen, which was dark except for the filtered glow of the streetlight behind the curtain. The sounds of a woman hawking a pantsuit for $29.95 followed her. She was thirsty rather than hungry, she decided, and opened the refrigerator to get some orange juice. She would've preferred milk, but she was fresh out. Sam had seen to that.

The thought made her smile, and she was still smiling and reaching for the juice when a hand clamped down hard over her mouth, yanking her backward while the mouth of a gun jammed painfully into her temple.

She jumped, instinctively started to struggle, to scream, while her heart went from zero to sixty in under a second and every tiny hair on her body stood upright.

"Make a sound, and I'll put a bullet in your head where you stand," a man's harsh voice whispered in her ear. The hand over her mouth had her in what was basically a headlock, clamping her close to the burly body behind her. He was wearing gloves, Maddie realized, and her blood went cold. This was the man from her hotel room—the hit man. Gun or no gun, she was going to have to scream, to fight, to get Cynthia in here, because no matter what she did, he was going to kill her.

"We can do this one of two ways," that terrifying voice whispered. "You and I can walk out this back door and down these steps together quietly, and settle our differences between ourselves. Or you can make a commotion that gets your friend in here, and I can kill you first and be ready to kill her when she walks through the door. Your call."

Maddie went very still as she thought about Cynthia in the next room, watching TV all unsuspecting. She remembered the night in her hotel room in a burst of terrifying detail. His gun had a silencer—he could put a bullet in her brain that second and Cynthia wouldn't even hear the shot.

She nodded once, jerkily, then went very still while her heart slammed against her rib cage like a wild animal trying to escape and cold sweat broke out over her body in waves.

"Smart girl." He was already shoving her toward the door. Maddie thought about the security system with a wild burst of hope. It was on, she was sure it was on, she was almost positive she'd seen its little blinking red light on the living-room wall when she'd been talking to Cynthia. But then she realized that he was inside; if it was on, how had he gotten inside?

"Open the door," he said. She turned the lock, turned the knob, opened the door—and nothing happened. No tinny little beeping. No sound at all.

Except the pounding of her heart as he shoved her through the door onto the little platform at the top of the stairs.

"Close it," he said, and she did, her hand slippery with sweat as she pulled the door closed behind her, very softly, no point in getting Cynthia killed, too. "Now walk very carefully down the stairs."

Then as he shoved her forward, Maddie caught a glimpse of his face, and terror rose like bile in her throat. He had changed a lot, and if she hadn't seen him up close, she might not even have recognized him. But there was no mistaking the shape of his nose and mouth, or those cruel eyes.

It was Ken Welsh.

LIKE THE TRUTH, the killer was out there. Sam knew he was close, felt it in his gut, could almost taste it. But he couldn't quite find him. The problem with the number of mob goons they'd arrested last night and that morning was that there were a lot of them, both in Saint Louis and Baltimore. A lot of goons meant a lot of processing, a lot of background checks, a lot of interviews. Just a lot of crap to wade through, with no guarantee that the kernel of truth he was seeking was anywhere in that particular dung heap.

His gut told him that it wasn't.

Not that he didn't trust the new owner of his heart, but Sam had checked—skepticism was a trait highly prized by the FBI—and every verifiable detail of Maddie's story had proved to be true. He'd traced Leslie Dolan from birth to the moment she had "died." Records showed that a small shotgun house in a rundown section of Baltimore had indeed been blown apart by a bomb seven years ago, killing everyone inside. The inferno had been such that only minute amounts of human remains had been found. IDs had been based on certain personal effects that had been recovered from the periphery of the blast site—in Leslie Dolan's case, it had been part of a burned jacket and a shoe—and the identities of people known to be inside. A neighbor had seen her going in. No one had seen her leave.

The general feeling was that it was a hit, but not much of an investigation had been done. It was a poor neighborhood, and the victims were known to have ties to the mob. The sad truth of the matter was that no one had much cared about their fate.

Sam was waiting for a records check to come back with the names of the agents who had been working in the Baltimore field office at that time. He was really interested in learning the true identities of Ken Welsh and Richard Shelton.

Wynne came up behind him. Sam knew who it was without even having to look around. The smell of grape bubblegum was a dead giveaway.

"Anything?" Wynne asked.

They were in the St. Louis field office, the better to process the reams of information that had come in over the course of the day. It was late, getting on toward eleven p.m., but the office was still bustling. Like he'd said earlier, when that many crooks went down, it made a lot of work for everyone involved. But Sam, personally, was dead beat—he'd had no sleep the night before—and he was ready to call it a day.

The thought of going home to Maddie—because that's what his upcoming stint of night duty felt like—made him smile.

"Not yet." Sam pushed back from the desk. What he'd been doing was cross-checking, comparing material from the hit man's victims with material from Maddie's past with material from cases he'd worked on, seeing if he could find a common thread. So far, nothing jumped out at him. He had a feeling that it was there, though. He just wasn't seeing it. Maybe tomorrow, when he wasn't so tired.

"You ready to go?" Wynne asked, and Sam nodded and stood up. It was a big room, beige and nondescript, divided into small cubicles with walls that didn't reach all the way to the ceiling. People were coming in and out, and a few had gathered in a conference room to the rear. Computers glowed in a number of cubicles around the room. Gomez was seated in front of one of them, typing away. He and Hendricks were supposed to be on duty, staking out Maddie's apartment starting at dark, and the sight of him sitting there made Sam frown.

"Yeah," Sam said, and walked over to Gomez. "I thought you were supposed to be on surveillance."

Gomez threw him a distracted look over his shoulder. "I'm coming. Just let me finish this and get Hendricks, and we'll be there. God, did you ever see so much paperwork in your life?"

"The paperwork can wait. You need to get your asses over there."

"We're coming, we're coming."

"You don't think we've got our boy yet?" Wynne asked as Sam rejoined him and they headed for the door.

"Who the hell knows? But I'm not willing to chance it." Not when Maddie's life was at stake.

Wynne had just come back for him after being gone for about an hour, and Sam got his first good look at him since his return as they rode down in the elevator together. Sam's brows twitched. He was so tired he was almost punch-drunk, he had a lot on his mind, and his nose was giving him some pain. But he didn't think Wynne had been wearing a jacket and tie, to say nothing of a white shirt and pressed khakis, the last time he'd set eyes on him.

"You change clothes?" he asked, slightly amazed, as the elevator delivered them to the ground floor.

"Yeah." Wynne looked almost embarrassed.

"Why?"

"I got a date, okay?"

They were out in the parking lot by that time. It was a postage stamp–sized square of asphalt next to a large silver rectangle of a skyscraper. Halogens glowed yellow overhead, holding back the night.

"A date?" Sam's mind boggled. Wynne all dressed up for a late date in St. Louis? Who . . . A lightbulb clicked on in his mind. "Gardner."

Puce was starting to creep into Wynne's cheeks. "Yeah. We're going to

Morton's. We were going to go last night—it would have been our first date—but, ahem, *circumstances* intervened."

Circumstances meaning the frantic search for him and Maddie, Sam knew. They had reached the car by that time. Opening the driver's door—he'd had enough of scary-ass drivers now to last a lifetime—Sam grinned at Wynne over the roof. "Way to go, dude."

"Yeah." Wynne grinned back, and they got in the car.

Sam's cell phone started to ring just as they were pulling out of the lot.

He tensed reflexively, fished it out of his pocket, looked at the ID window, and relaxed.

"McCabe," he answered, turning right into a steady stream of traffic. It was late for so much traffic downtown, and he guessed a ball game or a concert or something must have just let out.

"She's gone," Gardner yelled in his ear. She sounded distraught, frantic even. "She's gone. She's not here. McCabe, are you hearing me? Maddie's disappeared from the apartment."

MADDIE'S STOMACH was cramping, and she was so frightened that she was light-headed. They were in his car, something big and black. She was pinned in the front passenger seat, her hands cuffed behind her back, the seat belt pulled tightly across her body to hold her in place. Behind them, her apartment building was fast receding into the distance. She had kept expecting the cavalry to show up—Gomez and Hendricks, or whoever was supposed to be staking out her building; Cynthia, having realized that she was gone; Sam, who was due back at the apartment any minute—*somebody. Anybody.* But nobody had come, and he'd taken her down the stairs and cuffed her and put her into the car and *she hadn't even resisted.* And the chance of rescue was growing more remote with every yard of pavement that passed beneath the wheels. He hung a left on Big Bend, and she went into shock as she faced the truth: She was on her own with a killer.

"What do you want with me?" she asked. The light from the streetlights flickered in and out of the car as it passed beneath them, and she was able to see him clearly. She hated to look—the terrible familiarity of his profile was enough to make her break out in a cold sweat—but she couldn't help herself. There was a horrible fascination to seeing this face out of her nightmare in the flesh again.

"I want that strongbox of Charlie's. And you're going to tell me where it is."

Oh, God, nobody had ever called her dad Charlie but him. . . . It had been a way of cutting Charles Dolan down to size, of letting him know who was in charge. The lights and passing trees and buildings blurred as tears sprang to her eyes.

"I don't know."

"We're going to find out, aren't we? Believe me, dollface, if you know, you'll end up telling me." He sent her a mean little smile that sent an icy finger of fear sliding down her spine. "Actually, you're lucky I want it. You get to live a little longer. I would have whacked you right there in your kitchen if I hadn't. Last time we met, in your hotel room—'member that, baby? You fucking stabbed me in the leg, didn't you?—I didn't know about it. Nice of you to start calling up all your old friends and warning them about what you had."

He sent her a look that made the hairs prickle to life on the back of her neck. He was going to make her pay for that pencil in the leg. He was going to hurt her—and then he was going to kill her. Maddie wanted to scream. She wanted to bang her head against the window in a futile attempt to attract attention, to smash it, to try to escape. She looked out the windows, hoping desperately to see a passing cop car. If she did she would—what? She couldn't reach the horn, the lights, the accelerator. She couldn't even roll down the window. And . . .

"Oh, look," Welsh said. "There goes your boyfriend's car. Want to talk to him, baby? How about we give him a call?"

Maddie looked, and sure enough, there went the Blazer, speeding in the opposite direction with Sam at the wheel. There was no mistaking Wynne's blond Brillo-pad curls shining in the glow of the streetlights.

"HE JIMMIED the security system." Sam's blood raced. His heart pounded like a trip-hammer. He had just run up to the apartment, taking the stairs two at a time, ascertained that Maddie was not there and that the security system was still armed, and run down the back stairs to check the box outside the building. The system was designed so that if anyone tried to tamper with it, an alarm immediately sounded and a call was routed to the police. But it had been rigged with a double loop of wires that tricked the system into thinking it was still armed, even though it wasn't. Sam looked at it and felt bells go off in his head.

Not many people knew how to circumvent a system like that. He did, though. It was exactly the kind of rerouting legerdemain that he might have used himself if he wanted to break into a secure building.

He'd learned it from the FBI.

"He's a fed," Sam said, trying to stay calm, trying not to think of what might be happening to Maddie at that very instant as he turned to look at Wynne and Gardner, who were behind him. Gardner was ashen with guilt, her usually confident demeanor shattered. Wynne was protective and grim at the same time. Sam spoke to Gardner. "Get on the computer, get on the phone, I don't care how you do it, but get me the names of the agents who worked in the Baltimore office seven years ago *now*." Gardner nodded and started running toward her car. Sam looked at Wynne. "You stay here and take charge of things."

The alert had already gone out to the St. Louis field office, to the local cops, to everybody Gardner could think of to call. Sam could already hear the sirens in the distance.

Sam had one foot on the stairs when his cell phone started to ring.

He froze, then dug in his pocket and pulled out the phone. He knew, he already knew, before he saw the ID window: *Error*, it said.

"McCabe," he said, trying to keep his voice steady as icy terror flooded his veins. His gut clenched. He already knew what he was going to hear.

"Hey, asshole," the digitally altered voice said. "Welcome back to the game."

"THERE IS no game." Maddie could hear Sam's voice clearly. It was strong and steady, and she yearned toward it, aching, willing him to feel her through the phone, to be able to somehow divine where she was.

"Sure there's a game," Welsh said. His expression was gloating, triumphant, and Maddie hated him so much that she shook with it. He used to look at her like that, at her father like that. When he thought he had them under his thumb. "I took your little girlfriend. The tables are turned, my friend. You thought you were going to use her to trap me?" He gave a brutal little laugh. "Now I've got her. You come find her. You better hurry, though."

"We can work something out," Sam said, and Maddie thought his voice sounded hoarse. "If you don't kill her. A plea bargain for the others. Take the death penalty off the table, maybe."

"*Oh-ho.*" Welsh sounded delighted. He cast a glance at Maddie, clearly eager for her reaction and enjoying the fact that she was there to see him gloat. "Now you *are* playing. Just one problem, asshole. Why should I worry about a plea bargain when you're not going to catch me?"

"Oh, yeah," Sam said. "I am going to catch you. I'm close. Closer than you think. Right on your tail."

This made Welsh frown and cast a quick, furtive look in the rearview mirror. For a moment, Maddie felt a wild rush of hope. But then Welsh's face cleared and his smirk returned.

"You're blowing smoke out your ass, dickhead. You're nowhere near catching me."

"You're a fed," Sam said.

Welsh stiffened. "Not even close."

"Yeah, it's close. And I can get even closer. I got two names for you. Want to hear them?"

"More smoke."

"Richard Shelton. Ken Welsh. Those ring a bell?"

Welsh cast Maddie a glance that made her shiver. He looked positively evil, driving through the night with his teeth clenched and his eyes hard and his cheeks flushed with growing rage.

"Remember, last time we talked, how I told you I was going to up the ante? Remember how I told you that next time I whacked someone, I was going to let you watch? Well, here's what your threats got you, asshole. I'm going to take your girlfriend here somewhere and shoot her. And I'm going to get it on videotape. Then I'm going to send it to you and let you watch."

"Wait," Sam said sharply, but Welsh wasn't listening. He held the phone in front of Maddie's face. She stared at it, heart racing, falling apart inside, wanting to scream, to cry, to beg. . . .

"Say bye," Welsh said to her.

"Sam," Maddie said instead. And couldn't help it if her voice shook.

She heard a sound as though he inhaled.

Then Welsh disconnected.

"DID YOU get it? Did you get it?" Sam was sweating bullets. His heart was pounding as hard as if he'd just run for a hundred miles. For a moment, Maddie had been there, on the other end of the phone, and he'd wanted to reach down in there and pull her through it, to grab her, to save her—and he couldn't. The bastard had disconnected.

He was going to kill her. Sam had talked to him enough that he recognized the rising excitement in the sick bastard's voice, the escalating violence, the anticipation of causing pain, of causing fear.

He was getting all psyched up, like a predator toying with its prey before the kill.

Gardner was sitting beside him, in the front seat of her car in Maddie's parking lot, with the laptop she always kept in her car open on her lap. The screen glowed up at him, all digital lines and images.

Please, he thought. *Please.*

Gardner looked up at him, her face white.

"Not enough time," she said.

"YOU," WELSH SAID, looking at her with loathing. "You told him, didn't you? You gave him my name."

"Yes," Maddie said, hating him, not seeing any point in lying because he knew, and he was going to kill her anyway.

Welsh swore, his face dark and ugly now, his eyes cutting toward her with a viciousness that made her cringe. Then he backhanded her across the face, snapping her head back against the whiplash guard. The blow hurt, and she cried out.

"If I had killed you, that night in your hotel room, none of this would have happened. But I made a mistake, one damned lousy little mistake—who would have thought that there'd be two damned women staying there under the name Madeline Fitzgerald? What are the chances of that?—and look what happened. The whole thing. The whole thing's going to hell because of you."

He backhanded her again. Maddie whimpered and cringed against the door.

Then, as her eyes watered and her vision blurred in reaction, she saw that the phone, which he'd dropped onto the console, had been knocked into her seat.

It rested between her butt and the seat back, and if she moved forward a little, just a little, it might drop behind her back.

She couldn't let him realize . . .

"Why didn't you just leave me alone in the first place?" she asked, to cover what she was doing. "I wasn't bothering you. Leslie Dolan was in the past. I made a whole new life."

Blinking to clear her vision, she tried wriggling forward just a little, and the phone did just what she had hoped: It slid behind her back. If she could just manage to pick it up . . .

"Because I made a whole new life, too. I'm going places now, big places, and I can't have little pissant nobodies popping up out of the woodwork everytime I turn around. One day you might have seen me, recognized me, said something—and there it would all go. Same thing for the others, too. You are all part of my past that I want to keep in the past. Skeletons in my closet, and I'm cleaning the closet out."

"I wouldn't have told on you," she said, easing her cuffed hands sideways, touching the phone, fumbling with it. "I still won't, if you let me go."

That was bullshit and she knew it, and knew he knew it too, but she wanted to keep him occupied so that he wouldn't realize what she was trying to do.

"Give it up." He was breathing hard now, and she got the feeling that he was growing more agitated. Heart pounding, stomach churning, terrified that he might notice the phone was missing at any moment, she finally managed to pick up the phone. "I already got a plan for you. I think McCabe was bluffing. I think he just picked those names out of some little sob story you told him and used them to rattle me. There's no way he can find out who I am. Not if I get rid of you, and Thomas Kerry. Then it's all done. Except for McCabe, I mean. I meant to save him for last. But I don't think I will."

His voice turned thoughtful, and he glanced at her. Maddie froze, feeling the blood pumping through her veins. Did he know what she was up to? Did he guess? She had one shot at this, and one shot only.

But he looked back out at the road again. "I'm going to kill you, then call him and tell him where you are. When he comes to find you, I'm going to kill him. He was going to use you as bait to catch me? Watch this: I'll use you as bait to kill him."

Welsh had held the phone up to her face when he'd told her to say goodbye to Sam. She had stared at it, imagining Sam on the other end, trying to conjure him up through the phone—and that might stand her in good stead now. Clutching the phone, she concentrated, trying to visualize the arrangement of the buttons.

Her fingers slid over the buttons. She said a little prayer, then hit what she hoped was the redial button.

SAM WAS in the car with Gardner, driving her toward the hotel that they were using as a command post, when the phone rang again. He snatched it from the console where he'd placed it and looked at the ID window.

Error, it said.

His heart stopped, the world receded, and when he flipped the phone open, he realized his fingers were shaking.

There was only one reason why the sick bastard would be calling him back, he feared.

He'd never considered himself a particularly religious man. But as he lifted the phone to his ear he found himself praying like he'd never prayed in his life.

Please, God, don't let him kill her. Please, please, please . . .

"McCabe," he said.

"YOU HATE HIM, don't you?" Maddie said, continuing the conversation. She had to keep him talking, had to keep talking to him, because it had occurred to her that if she'd been able to hear Sam's voice, Welsh would probably be able to hear it, too, and Sam would surely answer with his customary *McCabe* even if he said nothing else.

"McCabe?" Welsh glanced at her. "Hell, yeah, I hate the bastard, damned workaholic Boy Scout. He's *incorruptible*." Welsh's tone made this a bitter sneer. "He never lets up, never quits, never fucking goes home. You know what he did? He started looking into some old cases. Years old. Closed. Gone. And he started trying to solve them in his free time. You remember how it was back in the day. Shit happened, and one of these cases was about some of my shit that happened. He was digging into it, too. I had to distract him, to get his fucking mind off it, before he dug deep enough to find out I was the one who whacked Leroy Bowman."

"Leroy Bowman?" Maddie said faintly. She hadn't heard a thing from the phone, but then again, Welsh's voice was growing louder the longer he talked. All she could do was pray she'd pressed the right button.

"Another fucking incorruptible special agent," Welsh said with disgust. "You deal with guys like that, they don't see reason, they don't look at the big picture, what are you gonna do? He was easier than McCabe, though. Just *boom,* one night, and that was it. I was afraid that if I whacked McCabe while he was digging into the Bowman case, which everybody knew he was doing, somebody else would pick it up, thinking that maybe that was the reason. So I had to get him out on the road, provide a distraction, another reason why he'd get hit. And I needed to clean up some previous messes, too, like I told you. So I decided to combine it all, take care of the people I needed to take care of, lure McCabe out onto the road until I could whack him, and put a tidy little end to the whole problem at once so I could move on with my life."

"Just like you put an end to your problems when you blew up that house my father was in?" Maddie could feel sweat running down her spine. They'd been driving on back roads that had grown progressively darker and less busy, and she had completely lost all sense of direction some time back. Now he seemed to be peering out through the windshield, like he was looking for something, a landmark or something, that he was afraid he might miss in the dark.

Maddie had a feeling that this was not a good sign.

"You're smart, aren't you?" Welsh sent her a glance filled with venom rather than admiration as the car topped a rise and came down the other side. "Yeah, I did that. And it *almost* put an end to my problems. Except for you. Again. Always you."

They were at the bottom of the hill now. He pulled off the side of the road. Glancing around with widening eyes, realizing that this might be it, Maddie saw that they were in a bowl-like depression with hills rising all around. The area was rural, with no lights visible at all. To her left, across a field of scraggly, knee-high weeds, she saw the gleam of water. It was a small pond, a farm pond, peaceful under the sky, which was vast and black and covered with endless stars. On the other side of the pond was a dilapidated-looking barn. Beyond that, the land rose up into rolling hills covered with scrub pine.

The tires bounced over grass and gravel. And then he stopped the car.

"I found this place yesterday," he said, looking at her with a terrifying smile. Just having him smile at her like that made her blood run cold. "Just for you."

He turned off the engine and the lights and got out.

Oh, God, this was it.

I don't want to die. Please, please don't let me die.

He was coming around the front of the car toward her. She was suddenly so frightened that she seemed to be disassociating from her body. She felt weird, light-headed, queasy. Her palms were sweaty, her fingers like ice. Was there nothing she could do? She struggled against the seat belt, but it held her fast. Could she somehow manage to twist her arms around and unlatch it? She tried—he was almost at her door—she couldn't do it. She couldn't do it.

He reached for the door handle. The starlight gleamed off something metallic in his other hand—*a gun*.

All of a sudden, with hideous clarity, she remembered the sounds of Carol Walter being murdered. Now she was getting ready to find out what it felt like to die that way. Would she beg, too? Would she cry?

The door opened. The sweet smell of summer grass reached her nostrils. The chorus of insects was suddenly loud.

"C'mon, dollface, time to get out."

Maddie's stomach twisted itself into a knot. Her heart threatened to pound its way out of her chest. Cold sweat poured over her in waves.

No.

He reached in around her and unfastened the seat belt. Then he grabbed a handful of her hair and pulled her from the car.

And saw the cell phone on her seat.

"What the hell?" He looked back at her, his face ugly, scary. Maddie's legs went all rubbery.

Then a helicopter topped the rise and plunged toward them. A bright searchlight caught them in its beam.

"FBI! Freeze! Drop your weapon!"

The order boomed through the air. Glancing up as the chopper hovered over them, Maddie saw a sharpshooter armed with a rifle. His weapon was pointed at Welsh. Then, over the rise, she saw a whole convoy of headlights speeding toward them, and heard the distant sound of sirens.

"Drop your weapon! *Now!*"

Welsh did. With a single deadly glance at her, he let go of her hair and raised his hands. Then the ground troops were there, and it was over. Maddie's knees gave out, and she collapsed in a little shivering heap on the ground.

LEAPING FROM the first car as it screeched to a stop, Sam saw her collapse and thought, for one heart-stopping moment, that the bastard had shot her. Icy terror ricocheted through his veins. His life passed before his eyes. He raced toward her, crouching beside her as the rest of the cavalry rushed to take control of the suspect.

Who, he was surprised and yet not surprised to see, was Leonard Smolski. He and Gardner had listened to every word the bastard had said from the time the cell phone had been activated. They hadn't recognized his voice—the technology he'd used to disguise it had held up—but some of the things he'd said, plus the information that Smolski had worked in the Baltimore field office during the time in question, which had come in over Cynthia's cell phone as they had driven in hot pursuit of their suspect, had made the discovery much less of a shock than it would have been.

"Sam," Maddie said in a voice like a sob when she saw that he was there, and wrapped her arms around him. He did a quick check to make sure that she was in one piece, then gathered her up in his arms and buried his face in her hair and held her until they both stopped shaking.

EPILOGUE

Friday, August 22

Maddie hurried into the small private terminal at St. Louis airport at shortly before five p.m. Jon had called her an hour before to tell her that Susan Allen had gotten an urgent call and was returning to New Orleans.

As Creative Partners' owner, she wanted to see Susan—and Zelda—off.

The last day and a half had been hectic. Sam had had to fly back to Virginia to wrap things up, although he was scheduled to return today. She would be picking him up after seeing Susan off. He'd called last night to tell her that, among other things, the strongbox had been found. The key to locating it was an address her father had scrawled on the back of a business card and told her to keep. She'd snatched it, Fudgie, and a few necessities from their apartment before running, then sewn it, along with a last few relics of her life as Leslie Dolan—the watch her father had given her, her senior-class ring—into Fudgie's stuffing. The strongbox had been just where Charles Dolan had left it, and in it had been enough evidence to put all kinds of bad guys away for a long time—and to completely clear her name. Charles Dolan had recorded Ken Welsh—Smolski—talking about the charges that had been filed against his daughter, and had asked him point-blank if it bothered him that they were bogus. And Smolski had laughed and said not at all.

Maddie spotted Jon and Susan and Zelda across the plush beige waiting room before she was anywhere near them. Not that they were hard to spot. Zelda, confined to her carrier, was once again giving vent to her inner wolf.

Everyone in the terminal was staring. The gate attendants were hovering around helplessly. Jon was trying to comfort Susan, who looked on the verge of an apoplexy.

And no one was feeding Zelda.

Maddie rolled her eyes.

"Does anyone have any food?" she asked over the din.

Jon fished in his pocket and produced a mint. Maddie snatched it, unwrapped it, and popped it through the grate. The howling stopped instantly, and Maddie heard the familiar snuffle.

Her heart gave a little pang. She was actually going to miss Zelda.

"You like her, don't you?" Susan asked, looking at Maddie intently. The gate attendant was opening the door that led out to Brehmer's plane.

"I *adore* her," Maddie said, and realized that she wasn't being insincere at all.

"Then keep her."

"Keep *Zelda*?" Maddie asked, wondering if Susan had lost her mind.

"That isn't Zelda," Susan said with a sniff, and Maddie's jaw dropped. "That is a dog I picked up from a Pekingese rescue organization in New Orleans. She's had three different families and nobody's ever kept her and *I can see why*."

She shot a venomous look at the crate, from which ominous snuffling sounds were emerging.

"Do you have another mint?" Maddie asked Jon urgently. Jon obliged, and Maddie pacified Zelda.

"What happened to the real Zelda?" Jon asked, looking as floored as she felt.

"She got away from the groomers," Susan said. "They're friends of mine, and we've all been searching frantically for her for the past three weeks. We even hired pet detectives. I didn't dare tell Mrs. B., of course." Susan shuddered. "But I got a call this morning: They found her. Thank God. So I can go home."

"You can go home?" Maddie asked.

"I only brought Zelda—no, not Zelda, *that dog*—here on such short notice because I was afraid Mrs. B. was starting to suspect. And don't worry, it won't affect your having our advertising account at all. Just consider this a dry run."

Maddie knew her mouth must be hanging open, because Jon's was.

"Miss," the gate attendant said, "are you ready to go?"

"Yes," Susan said. "I'm leaving." She looked at Maddie. "Do you want her or not? I can always take her back to the rescue society if you don't. Although I hate to fly with her again."

She gave a shudder.

Zelda was snuffling.

"Mint," Maddie said urgently to Jon, who complied. She popped one in to Zelda, and suddenly knew that there was nothing in the whole world she would like better than to keep her.

"I'd love to have Zelda," Maddie said.

"*That* is not Zelda." Susan turned to go. "I'll be back in a couple of weeks with the real Zelda."

"Are you *nuts?*" Jon said when Susan had gone and they were exiting the terminal. Since he was now out of mints, Zelda had once again started to howl. "That dog is a monster."

"No she isn't." Maddie set the carrier on the pavement and carefully opened the grate. The dog bounded out, silenced by the prospect of freedom, and Maddie grabbed the end of her leash just in time. Then she reeled her in, picked her up, and looked her in her bulbous black eyes.

"You're mine," she said. "And just for the record, you'll always be Zelda to me."

Then, walking across the pavement toward her, she saw Sam. He was dressed in a jacket and tie, and looked so handsome that she caught her breath. He looked up and smiled when he saw her, and Maddie felt her heart skip a beat.

Then it occurred to her: She finally had everything she'd always wanted. A man. A dog. And her life back.

For keeps.